Twice as Perfect

Twice as Perfect

Louisa Onomé

FEIWEL AND FRIENDS

New York

A FEIWEL AND FRIENDS BOOK
An imprint of Macmillan Publishing Group, LLC
120 Broadway, New York, NY 10271 • fiercereads.com

Our books may be purchased in bulk for promotional, educational, or
business use. Please contact your local bookseller or the Macmillan Corporate
and Premium Sales Department at (800) 221-7945 ext. 5442 or by email at
MacmillanSpecialMarkets@macmillan.com.

Library of Congress Cataloging-in-Publication Data
Names: Onomé, Louisa, author.
Title: Twice as perfect / Louisa Onomé.
Description: First edition. | New York : Feiwel & Friends, 2022. |
Audience: Ages 14–18. | Audience: Grades 10–12. | Summary:
Seventeen-year-old Nigerian Canadian Adanna Nkwachi must deal
with an estranged older brother, uncertainty about her future,
and helping her cousin plan a big Nigerian wedding.
Identifiers: LCCN 2021051174 | ISBN 9781250823502 (hardcover)
Subjects: CYAC: Brothers and sisters—Fiction. | Family—Fiction. |
Nigerians—Canada—Fiction. | LCGFT: Fiction.
Classification: LCC PZ7.1.O656 Tw 2022 | DDC [Fic]—dc23
LC record available at https://lccn.loc.gov/2021051174

First edition, 2022

Book design by Angela Jun

Feiwel and Friends logo designed by Filomena Tuosto

Printed in the United States of America

ISBN 978-1-250-82350-2 (hardcover)

1 3 5 7 9 10 8 6 4 2

Maka umuaka di ka m.

The problem with trying to one-up yourself
is not that you might die by your own hands
but that you'll be able to justify why
without feeling anything.

—Shazia Hafiz Ramji

"Conspiracy of Love," in *Port of Being*

CHAPTER ONE

AUNTIE FUNMI PULLS ON THE measuring tape held tight around my waist. I hold my breath, suck in my stomach a little, because I want the dress to *fit*, like really fit. But Auntie Funmi is the best seamstress my mom knows, so she taps my arm—smacks, more like—and hisses at me in her strong, Yoruba accent, "Ah-ah! Adanna! So you want to be doing like this at the wedding the whole time?" And she holds her breath and shifts side to side like she can't walk or bend her knees. "You will just look uncomfortable."

Chioma snickers from where she's sitting at the dining table. She has a swath of bright ankara fabric over one knee while she flips through a catalog of old-school dress styles. We lock eyes and she snickers again, none too remorseful for the situation I'm in. Auntie Funmi is pissed she has to redo all these bridesmaids' dresses only two months before Chioma's sister's wedding, and she's taking it out on me just because I'm the last girl to be fitted. How is it my fault, though? Does she know how difficult it is to be me right now? I'm in my last year of high school—debate team, staying on honor roll, plotting my law school track—I have so many other things I have to do aside from plan what I'm going to wear for Genny's wedding.

Auntie Funmi wraps the measuring tape around my arm and tightens it, peering down her nose at the small black numbers that overlap. Her eyes flick over to mine. "Are you still losing weight?"

"I wasn't to begin with...," I murmur. Auntie moves on quickly. My eyes dart to the book she's scribbling in where she keeps our measurements. Auntie Funmi has been doing clothes for my family since I was very young, but I don't think I've changed that much from last year. Chioma's aunt and uncle had a dedication ceremony for their newborn, and the two-piece dress I had made still fits me just fine. Auntie Funmi is just being a busybody.

Chioma flips a large page in the catalog and scrunches up her nose like she's smelled something bad. Her thick Senegalese twists fall over her shoulder and she has to shimmy and shrug to push them back over. "Auntie," she calls, "are you sure the style Genny picked for the dresses is in here?"

Auntie doesn't bother looking up as she runs the tape from my shoulder to my knees. "Yes."

"But they're all so tacky," Chioma whispers. Auntie doesn't act like she heard her, but I chuckle a little. "She couldn't find something on Pinterest? Why does she want us to look ugly at her wedding?"

"*Tch*, as if you don't know your own sister," I sneer playfully, jutting out my bottom lip in arrogance. Genevieve, Chioma's older sister, who used to get both Chioma and I to braid, unbraid, and wash her hair while we were growing up because she just got shellac done and do we know how much shellac costs? Genevieve, Chioma's older sister, who used to crop family members out of pictures where she was the only one who looked good. Genevieve, Chioma's older sister, who went viral for a hot second as "Jesus girl at Riley's" last summer and leveraged it to the max.

Where do I even begin with that story? Riley's is a vegan joint that sells pastas and things in Toronto's east end. Genny isn't vegan, but she was going on a date with this guy, I think his name was Jacob. He wasn't bad looking, but one time he posted a pic of him and Genny on his socials, and she told him to take it down because she knew it wasn't that serious for her. He was trying to become an influencer or something, so he was always filming things. Jacob gets this bright idea to take Genny to Riley's even though neither of them are vegan (we later found out it was for a "First Time Trying Vegan Food" video he was working on). Genny gets to the counter and asks what the cheese is made out of, since it couldn't have been dairy. The lady says "cashews" and Genny gets this blank look on her face like she's transcended time and space. Her mouth cracks open a smidge and she pouts, unsure, before she narrows her eyes and utters, "Je-*sus*..." with the most contempt I've ever heard. It's hilarious and you couldn't go anywhere online for a month without seeing her face.

Cut to last Christmas when she and her girls were vacationing in Nigeria. They were in a club in Abuja when someone in VIP recognized her as the Jesus girl and invited her and her friends to their booth. Neither of us were surprised hearing this when Genny first told us because she's always had that kind of effortless charm. She just gets things when other people have to struggle. But wow our mouths dropped when she recounted how she spotted the one and only Skeleboy sitting there. Yes, *that* Skeleboy, Mr. Obafemi Oluwadurotimi Balogun, arguably the best Afrobeats artist-producer-turned-philanthropist-artist-producer of our time. Skeleboy me, Skeleboy this money, everything na Skeleboy—*that Skeleboy!* Genny came back home after her vacation and they did the long-distance thing in secret with her slipping off to Nigeria here and there. Fast forward to one day when she comes back with a real diamond ring from Skeleboy—and plane tickets

(tickets!) for Genny and her immediate family to fly to his Lekki mansion in Nigeria to meet his parents. Unreal!

I'll never forget the look in Chioma's eyes when she barged into my house the day after she got back on Canadian soil, skin tired and blotchy, looking like a whole haggard wreck from the long flight. With manic eyes and a lofty, ghostlike twinge to her voice, she recited, "Adanna... Skeleboy me, Skeleboy this money... everything na Skeleboy o!" And we cried for an hour.

I can't believe I'm about to be related to Skeleboy.

Well, not actually related. Chioma and I aren't real cousins—our parents met each other when they immigrated here and wanted to hang with other Nigerian Igbo families. No, the only real family I have are my parents, and Sam. Obinna Samuel, my brother. He's older than me, but younger than Genny. He's not around anymore.

And we're not allowed to talk about him.

Chioma's ringtone goes off and it's a Skeleboy song, his most popular one, "Yanga." I laugh. "You're going to have to change that, bro. Imagine if your future brother-in-law hears that. So embarrassing."

She closes her eyes and begins to hum the song, dancing side to side, while she sings: "Do me, do me, do me yanga!" She sounds horrible.

"*Gpek-gpek-gpek*," Auntie Funmi teases, dropping her

measuring tape from my back and folding it into her hands. "Sounding like common fowl."

Chioma laughs so hard the fabric on her leg slides down and she has to bend to pick it up. She folds it neatly and sets it back on the table. The gold and blue fabric will look so nice once all our clothes are made. I can imagine all us cousins lined up in our uniforms, posed super extra for the family photo—the family photo with Ske-le-bo-yeee. Oh god, how close will I be allowed to stand to him? Will his entourage circle him and Genny or will he want to hug us, suddenly enamored with our hybrid Igbo-Yoruba-some-Ika-some-Isoko-cousin family dynamic? Tribal conflict where?

Auntie Funmi closes her book of measurements and turns to lean against her table, arms folded. She says something in Igbo, and I know it's in Igbo because suddenly she sounds more like my mom and less like the Yoruba of a Skeleboy song. When neither Chioma nor I move, Auntie Funmi begins to cackle. "What is it? You no know say I sabi Igbo?"

"Well, we don't, so...," I say. The wave of shame is not lost on me, and it's like saying it aloud brings about a layer of guilt I don't need right now.

Auntie Funmi's cackle is almost sinister. "I know, o! You oyinbo children. I said, 'Okay, that's it, you can go.' You don't even know that one?"

Those magic words have me slipping away from Auntie

as fast as I can and darting straight for my sweater and bag in the corner. "When do we pick up the clothes?" I ask over my shoulder.

"Give me, hmm, one month," she says, chewing her bottom lip in contemplation. "I will call your mom and tell her."

Chioma gets to her feet and we both thank Auntie Funmi, even though it was only me getting measured. Chioma came because I need her to drive me to Williams after. It's four thirty on a Thursday and I promised to be at Williams Café before five to go over debate plans with Justin. He thinks Mr. Patel may have slipped him our topic for the next competition, and Justin can be dramatic and ugly competitive sometimes, so I'm not surprised at all that he wants to practice so early. Too bad this was the only time I could come and get measured. I'm just lucky Chioma can drive and her dad agreed to give her his old rusty-ass sedan.

I settle into the passenger's side and tap the dashboard like we're in some movie and someone is chasing us. "Okay, fast fast, hurry," I say, bobbing impatiently in my seat.

I'm half kidding but Chioma is whole-annoyed. "Don't fast fast me, Ada," she hisses as she turns the key in the ignition. The old car roars to life, but just barely. Its engine is loud and it's taking seventeen years to back out of its parking spot. "If you were in such a hurry, you should've asked Tayo to drive you."

I feel my heart thump in my chest at the mention of his

name, and at the thought of me being alone with him in a car. It's not like I haven't been alone with him before—we're friends and, most of the time, we do everything together. We're just close like that. Still, I stumble over my words, "Wh-what? No?"

"Why not?"

"He *just* got his license! He'd kill us. That boy can't even parallel park."

"No one actually can, though."

"And he's busy anyway."

She grins, glancing at me. "So you did ask him?"

I button up quickly, unsure if my next words will be my last. Chioma is always teasing me about Tayo, probably because he's a boy and I'm a girl and we're both the only Nigerian kids in our grade. Plus, like I said, he's my friend. We're *friendly*. God, why am I even getting into this with her? Chioma graduated high school already, but she's so interested in my life. Doesn't she have university things to care about or something?

"He said no?" she presses again. "Huh?"

"I didn't ask him," I tell her. "I just *know* he's busy because I saw him at school earlier. Whatever. Turn right here. It's a shortcut." I quickly point down another road and Chioma does as she's told.

At a stoplight, Chioma quickly plugs her phone into the aux cord and turns on "Yanga." I snicker as she rolls her shoulders, bobs her head, and gets ready to launch into full car dancing mode. "Get it out of your system now, o!" I tease in pidgin, in my acquired Nigerian Igbo accent. It doesn't sound quite as authentic as Mom's or Dad's, but it works for us cousins. We talk like this sometimes when we're all together. Our vernacular and sentence patterns change like we're enjoying malt and chicken somewhere outside a restaurant in Ikeja—or, whatever it is that Lagos youth do, anyway. "You can't be behaving like this in front of your in-law."

"I know, I know," she says, still giddy. "Sing with me."

The beat tricks us and Chioma starts to sing a whole five seconds before the first verse, which has us laughing even more. By the time Skeleboy launches into his first "do me," we're clawing over each other trying to match up to his rhymes. "D-do me—do me! Do me yanga, o!"

The song goes into its last verse while Chioma pulls into the Williams parking lot. There are a few cars littered around, but it doesn't look like it's too full. This place gets packed on the weekends with university kids who need that perfect blend of coffee-shop ambience and two-for-one espresso to ace a test. It also gets packed during the evenings, but I wouldn't know anything about that. I'm usually at home by the time the sun goes down, studying in my room while my Spotify playlists rotate through the night. Mom and Dad don't like me going anywhere in the evening these days, that is, unless Chioma is with me. Can't believe they trust her so much, honestly.

I turn down the music in Chioma's car really fast. It's quiet out here and I don't want to disturb the peace. Plus, we can't be that car blasting Afrobeats after hours in this neighborhood. There aren't a lot of passersby on the street, but I can still feel phantom eyes on us. People are probably looking through the windows at Williams to see whose car is making all that noise, you know, who's disturbing their second two-for-one espresso deal.

Chioma recoils at the sudden emptiness in the air. "What's wrong with you? Let me finish my song," she says.

"This is a public place," I say, sounding a lot like my dad, and quickly gather up my things before she can spike the volume again. "Thanks for the ride. Tell your parents I say hey."

She manages a wave even though she's frowning, still mad about the volume. She's acting like she isn't about to turn it up the second I leave. If there's one person who doesn't know that her sister is about to be married to a top star, well, they'll definitely figure it out by the time she's done belting the next song.

CHAPTER TWO

MY NAME AT SCHOOL IS Sophie. My name at home is Adanna. Everyone at school calls me Sophie, my middle name, and whenever I hear it, it's my trigger to put away the Skeleboy and brazen Afrobeats playlists, to stop slipping in and out of pidgin English, and turn on my white voice. Chioma laughs and says I shouldn't call it that, but I can't even lie, that's what it is. My voice boosts half an octave, my words are fuller, and I start saying things like, "if I remember correctly" with the same sharpness as someone who has just been given the wrong drink at Starbucks.

In kindergarten, everyone still called me Ada. But when my parents were called in once for teacher-parent interviews, they cringed at how badly my teacher butchered my name—their words, not mine. Instead of the short *a*, they pronounced Ada like "ay-da," and my parents snapped. The next day, my teacher was calling me Sophie and I adapted to who a Sophie was: smart, vocal, tenacious. At home, I was still Ada, also smart, also vocal, also tenacious. It may not sound like there's a difference, but there is. It's just a feeling. Sophie and Ada cannot mix.

That's why when I hear "Sophie!" called out in the poorly lit café, my ears perk up, my demeanor changes, and suddenly I am Sophie Nkwachi who spends her time thinking less about Genny's wedding to a Nigerian mogul and more time thinking about how to streamline her way into law school.

Justin is sitting in the middle of the café. We lock eyes and he waves me over once, twice, before diverting to a video on his phone. His hair is getting so long in the front that when he leans over, his phone practically disappears underneath it. From far away, he looks more like his white Canadian dad, but when he pushes his hair back and I can see more of his soft cheekbones and high brow, I am reminded how much he looks like his Chinese mom from up close. Celia Lam John's face is plastered all over the city, especially now that her home renovation show just got syndicated on cable. Justin's mom is legit like a celebrity. He hates it, but he also drives a Mercedes, so really, he probably doesn't hate it that much.

"What are you doing?" I ask, shuffling into the seat opposite. We're seated at a table for two, and beside us in another table for two are Joshua and Arjun, the other members of our debate team. I wave at them and they return the gesture fast before diving back into their case notes. Sometimes we all prep together, even though our region does British parliamentary style, so it's not always necessary. Josh and Arjun are partners like Justin and I are partners, but if they score high at a competition, it doesn't mean we score high too. So yeah, we're all teammates, but we really have to look out for ourselves.

From where I'm sitting, I have a clear view of the counter: fresh cakes behind a display, LED menu blinking overhead, harried baristas running back and forth with piping hot mugs. This place makes me hungry even if I'm not.

"Look," Justin says and turns his phone around to show me. I frown instantly. "A debate video."

"Not just *any* debate video," he presses on, already sensing my annoyance. How many of these is he going to show me before he realizes I never want to see another one again? Mr. Patel is always showing us these at the club and I'm tired. If I have to sit through one more dry-ass point of inquiry ... "These kids won college nationals in 2007."

"Ancient. That's why I can't see anything with this quality," I utter, trying to zoom in just enough that I can make out something other than this janky frame rate. "Why are we watching college kids, anyway? That's not even at our level."

He furrows his brows, confused. "What? We're in the top percentile of our grade, we always get chosen for opening team, *and* we won Mr. Patel's debate tournament trophy. Of *course* that's our level."

Josh clears his throat from beside us and gives a roll of his eyes. Josh thinks Justin is full of himself, but I bet that's because he's not on Justin's level, which means he's barely on my level. No offense, of course.

It's hard to forget that Justin and I have practically been top of the class together since middle school. It's either him or me. One of us is a one, the other is a two, but there hasn't been a one or two that wasn't him or me in ages. I should hate him for it, for all this heavy academic competition, but I don't. We get along okay. We're real friends. And if I'm being honest, maybe I wish we were more than just real friends. Maybe when I picture myself with someone else, half of the time the person I'm picturing is Justin. But every time my mind starts to wander, I gotta reel it back in for my own sake, and my family's too. If only his last name was Okoh or my family knew his family or something, then it could work. Then it'd be easier.

The video ends and I'm jogged back to attention. I am no longer thinking about Justin and how we'd make a really good power couple, both of us ultra-smart and ultra-ambitious lawyers or angel investors or something. Instead, I let my mind fill up with nothing but the sounds of the café, the rich smell of cold brew coffee, and the *scratch-scratch-scratch* of Arjun's pencil across his notebook. "Okay, so?" I say. "What does this video have to do with us?"

"Everything." He clears his throat and sits up straighter, adjusting the sleeves of his sweatshirt. Josh and Arjun glance over. "We have a new motion now. Mr. Patel is sure this is the right one this time," he tells me. It takes all my willpower not to roll my eyes at the idea of Mr. Patel being sure about something. He thought our last two motions were legit too before he switched them out on us. He gets new tips each week, it seems. It's mad unethical, but he's best friends with one of the chief adjudicators and he keeps feeding us motions that he thinks we may get for the competition. If anyone finds out, we're dead. This is technically cheating, but Mr. Patel has that "they have to catch me first!" attitude and it's started to rub off on us. He's a good talker. I guess that's why he's spearheading the debate club. "He talked to his adjudicator friend and he's absolutely one hundred percent sure our motion will be related to…" Justin spins the phone back around and resets the video before turning to me again. This time, I notice the title. It's real obvious and I wonder how I didn't see it before. My eyes scan over the words at the same time Justin's voice pierces my ears: "Cultural appropriation."

I cringe immediately and flip the phone around so it's

facing him again. I lean back, so far back that I feel cool air in the space between where I was leaning against the table. Justin isn't fazed by my reaction. Fact: We're friends, but do we ever see eye to eye? No. Number 102 why we'd never work as a couple and I should let that dream die. So I groan, "No way. It can't be," and press my knuckles into my cheeks.

He chuckles. I've heard him laugh so many times before, but somehow knowing it's because of me makes my face warm with a hidden shyness I normally don't show. I push my hair over my shoulder and channel Genny: fierce, strict, firm. Genny is not shy. She is a mogul's future wife. "I'm not doing it," I tell him.

He raises an eyebrow. "We literally have to switch the topic, though."

"No, no way," I push on. "Mr. Patel is sure he knows what our motion is going to be every week. He has us switching motions like mad out here. We did *too* much research on economics in South Africa."

"Yeah," Arjun cuts in with an apologetic smile. "I actually never want to say the words 'I believe that South Africa would abandon the African Union's plan for a single currency' again."

"Exactly!" I grunt. "We did way too much research to scrap everything now and just assume our official motion will be related to cultural appropriation. There's no way they'd give that to us. You think they were like, '*Oh, this* school has all the ethnic kids. Black kid, half-Chinese kid, Filipino kid, Sri Lankan kid. Let's go with cultural appropriation'?"

"Come on, you know that's exactly what they said," Justin jokes. "But think of it this way: We have a higher statistical advantage at winning if we're given a topic like this. The past college winners? Racialized topics, ahead by varying points."

"It's true," Josh says, turning so he can face us. We really should've just gotten one table of four. "Check the stats for the latest regional competition."

"Okay, but…" I reach for Justin's phone and skim through the related videos. Just as I thought. "Here, look. All the kids are black," I say, gesturing loosely to the phone. "Look at us. We're clearly down a black kid here—down *three* if you count both our teams."

That makes Justin laugh, like really laugh. The lines of his face stretch with warmth. He throws his head back and rubs his hands tiredly down his face while he sighs, "Oh my godddd." It makes me chuckle too but I purse my lips tightly to keep the giggles out. I like that I make him laugh. His smile makes me think about what our future could be like even though I—should concentrate on work. I need to concentrate on debate. "What do you expect me to do about that, huh?" he teases, and I want to reach forward and pinch his face and I don't know why.

"I don't know," I chuckle. "Find me a new debate partner, damn."

"Wooooow—"

"Someone tall, though, with a nice fade so at least if he's not smart and he tanks my chances, I can stare at him while my future crumbles."

"Just, *wow*."

Josh and Arjun share a look before Josh pipes up, "L-let's focus, guys."

Justin is still smiling when he says, "We *are* focused. This will be fine, don't worry. I got an idea already."

I snort. "Of course you do."

He knows that isn't a compliment, but he grins anyway. "Most of the judging panels in our district are pretty white," he goes on. "I know white people. My dad is one."

"*Please* stop talking."

"Cultural appropriation is a notoriously white issue."

"Yeah, and it will make people uncomfortable," I say, letting my eyes land on the phone screen before I look at Justin. "You want to make a room full of white people uncomfortable? We're never going to win that way."

"Sophie's right," Arjun grumbles. He's put away his notebook and is facing our table too. "And, like, we obviously want a bench sweep, so don't do anything stupid."

"Of course not. So let's say we flip the topic," Justin tells us, and I sigh loud enough that I'm sure the others can hear it over the whirring of coffee grinders at the counter. "According to Mr. Patel, we could either be hit with 'the house believes that cultural appropriation is wrong' or 'the house believes that cultural appropriation and appreciation are byproducts of a capitalist society'—"

I snort. "Sorry?"

"Yeah, exactly." He rolls his eyes. "But if we completely divert from popular theories related to the white gaze—like, just sidestep anything that assumes our audience is white or all appropriators are white—we could probably get away with it. We just gotta distract the judges with points on, for example, third-culture kids or cross-cultural kids."

Josh raises his eyebrow. "Meaning?"

"Well—"

"And, to clarify, I meant what is *your* point, not that I don't know what a cross-cultural kid is." Wow, he really brought the "just to clarify..." all the way to Williams? Now I know he's pressed.

"I'll answer," I say, shooting up my hand like we're in debate. I'm being corny on purpose and Josh rolls his eyes because he can tell. "The point is that by directing the judges' attention away from assuming that *all* appropriation is done by white people, we can create room for points on how third culture and cross-cultural kids—that would be, kids who have grown up and/or created a meaningful relationship in two separate cultures, one of which may be different from their parents' culture—are handled within the larger discussion of cultural appropriation. Like, is it okay for someone who comes from a marginalized culture to take on identities or aspects of another marginalized culture, even if they actually belong to it? Stuff like that."

Josh doesn't look impressed, but he rarely is. Justin has stars in his eyes and it makes my face warm to think he's even a little bit in awe of me. "Now," I begin, a mischievous smile on my lips. "I'll tell you why that won't work."

Justin and Josh switch reactions. "Ha!" Josh breaks into a grin at the same time Justin raises an eyebrow and says, "Are you serious?"

"It's pretty much impossible for many reasons, but the main one being this." I clear my throat. "I think cultural appropriation needs the white gaze. Without a dominant white culture hanging over, siphoning, and stealing from racialized cultures, I mean, then how could you have appropriation? That's how it works, right?"

"Not necessarily," Justin goes on. "Cultural appropriation just needs a dominant culture. If we focus it that way, then we could get away with it."

I lower my eyes at him. "Isn't that a technicality? What if their definition doesn't work with what we're planning?"

"What do you mean? For sure it will," he says simply.

I dream of the debate competition and what it'll be like when we're standing on the stage in front of those harsh, beaming lights. We will be dressed similarly, of course. I think of how married Nigerian couples dress in the same fabric at events, but I have to squash that thought because we are not married and we—*he* is not Nigerian. I imagine the stage, how it creaks under my polished dress shoes, and how I'm going to try my hardest to focus on just one judge so I don't get nervous. And if that one judge opens his mouth and says something like, "Sorry, our definition is actually a bit different…," well, not even God could save Justin from how loud I'd scream.

My eyes wander as easily as my mind does and suddenly, I'm imagining—Sam.

Wait. Sam?

I can see Sam. In real life. I'm not imagining it. This tall black boy at the register with his back turned to me, pointing out which cake he wants to buy. He has to crouch a little to get a better look at the display case, to take it all in. My breath shuts itself in my throat and refuses to come out. Memories flood my brain, knocking around, trying to win the others out. Memories of us frying chicken—why is that the one memory that comes out on top? Mom brought chicken out of the freezer one time when I was seven, and she told Sam and I to fry it before she got home. "Protect your arm," Sam had warned, gesturing to my exposed wrist. "The oil will splash and you'll get burned. So flip, and then dip." He flipped over a piece of chicken, and then backed away before the oil popped. I followed suit, but got burned, two thin splashes just above my wrist. Sam pressed sea salt on the burn while I held my breath, sighing through the pain. He tried to smile for me. "At least it'll be a sick temporary tattoo, eh?" And he laughed.

Why does my mind still hold so much space for someone who *left* me?

Still, I push my chair back from the table, wide-eyed and staring, willing him to turn around.

And then he does.

And it is not him.

Justin watches me the entire time, casting uneasy glances over his shoulder to get a better look at whatever it is I'm seeing. He frowns, confused. "Are you good ...?"

"Yeah," I answer, my voice suddenly small.

"You know that guy?"

"N-no. I thought I did, but no."

Justin and I stare at each other: him, unsure of what to say next, and me, breathing heavily through this weird twist of shame and guilt and resentment. All resentment. Of course that isn't Sam. How could I think it was? How could I, when he probably looks so different now? He probably doesn't have the locs in. Or maybe he does. Our parents always hated them, so if he's smart, he would've shaved them off. Or maybe he kept them because he can do whatever he wants now. If he's even alive. And if he's still around, why not call? Why not tell me what he's done to his hair? Why not talk to me about his aesthetic choices while I gripe about... about how hard I've had to work to fill the void he left in our family? How I've had to study, never get anything below an 80 because I am afraid of disappointing the parents he abandoned. Disappointing the *family* he abandoned. Like me. I am the family. Me.

I hate him.

Mom and Dad won't even speak his name, and for a long time, I was curious as to what must've happened, but I don't even care anymore. If someone can just walk out and leave their family like this, then they don't deserve my curiosity. He doesn't deserve anything.

I fucking hate him.

But then, but then I remember him coming into my room that day before he left, smiling at me. Who's to say I'm not making up his face, his voice, in my memory? I can't even hear the way he pronounces my name anymore: Ada. A-da. In my head, everything is beginning to just sound like Sophie.

CHAPTER THREE

DAD IS HEATING UP EGUSI soup this early morning and the more the scent of burnt melon seed creeps up the stairwell, the more annoyed I become. I have this really nice floral perfume and the thing I like the most about it is that it's long-lasting but very light. Our school is pretty strict on perfumes because some kids have allergies, but I can usually get away with wearing this one because it's hard to detect unless you're right up against me. But now I'm going to smell like fading flowers and harsh, spicy Nigerian soup. This is one conversation I don't want to have with a teacher, so I shut my door, pop open my window, and rush to get ready as fast as I can.

My pressed hair is thickened by layers of clip-ins and my

face is clear, save for an earthy lip cream that complements my brown skin well. Genny always says it's important for a girl to have nice skin when she doesn't wear makeup. I don't know why that's considered an important thing, but she gets a lot of her advice from YouTube beauty gurus and wayward Nollywood films where all the women look impeccable, so, on some level, I want to believe she knows what she's talking about. Plus, she's marrying Skeleboy soon, so her opinion is highly regarded these days. I once heard Auntie Yvette ask her something that wasn't age-appropriate at all, and it was the talk of our cousin group chat for days.

When I come downstairs, Dad is eating boiled yam with his egusi soup. I snicker at the heavy meal as I dance around the kitchen for a glass of water and oatmeal cookies. "That's not breakfast," I say, teasing.

Sometimes Dad isn't in a joking mood, especially when it comes to my grades, but he laughs so easily now, his shoulders shaking under the weight of his throaty chuckle. He flashes a cheesy-ass grin at me, and says, "Nwa m." My child in Igbo. It's one of maybe five Igbo words I know. It makes me happy when he calls me that, like I'm his one and only. I'm the one who stayed. "Didn't I ever tell you about six-to-six?" he asks.

I snort. "No. What's that?"

He gestures down to his plate. "Six-to-six. Yam. A meal so heavy that you eat it at six and don't get hungry until six that very evening." He laughs again. I take a full bite of an oatmeal cookie, and he tsks at me, shaking his head. "So I'm eating yam and you're eating cookies to school. Ada. *A-da*."

"I'm not that hungry."

"Eh heh."

"I'm not, though."

He cuts another piece of the dry yam, swirls it in the soup, and shoves it in his mouth without breaking eye contact. It's true, Dad doesn't usually take lunch because he's always so busy at the office. He's the engineer, Mom's the doctor. There's always at least one in every Nigerian family, or so I'd been told growing up. I thought they were just kidding, trying to get me to pick one of the very narrow, acceptable career paths for a first-generation kid, but then I met Auntie Suzanna, Auntie Judith, Uncle Edafe—all doctors, nurses, or medical surgeons. And then I met Uncle Mike, Uncle Dele, Auntie Florence—all engineers in some way. The only other acceptable career? A lawyer, the one I'm choosing. Law is considerably less math than becoming a doctor or engineer. It's more logic and speaking, which I'm good at. For me, it's an easy choice. A safe one.

Mom gets back by the time I leave for school because she's on night shifts this week. I hug her as she dances past me into the kitchen, her hair tied into a messy ponytail at the back of her head. She reaches for a glass of cold water and chugs it quickly, cringing and grimacing through what

I assume is the worst brain-freeze ever. After she sets down the glass and breathes her way back to a functioning state, she tells me, "Adetayo is outside."

My signature face-warm, chest-thump reaction shows up right on time. "What? How come?"

"I don't know, o," she sings back. I can hear the fatigue in her voice from her ten-hour shift at the hospital. "Don't you have to go to school today?"

"What..." I grab my bag off the floor and head toward the front door to put my shoes on. I peek out through the window and see Tayo's car, definitely a car Tayo currently has but may not actually own, sitting in my driveway. "Bye Mom, bye Dad," I call over my shoulder and push my way outside.

The air is colder than expected for March in Toronto. I pull my thick sweater tighter around my shoulders just as I catch sight of Tayo in the driver's seat, dancing obnoxiously to some song on his sound system. I stop and try to mirror his dance moves from outside, and I can hear him shout, "He-ey!" while he continues, grinning. Tayo is too damn much. His vibe is infectious, even this early in the morning. But if I'm being honest, that's probably why my heart beats so fast when I see him and why I get insta-warm when I hear his name, or his voice. That's probably why I like him.

When I pull open the door, the music blares out, way

louder than it sounded a second ago. I settle in and shut the door with a loud bang. Tayo doesn't stop miming and dancing for a whole minute while I sit in the car and watch him. "Ah-beg-ee," I chuckle, letting pidgin English roll freely from my lips. "Can we go? Is this how you want to be dancing all the way to school? Oya, let me drive—"

"You can't even drive," he cackles, and then puts his hand on the gear stick like he's prepared to move. But the chorus of the song kicks in and he's mouthing over lyrics again like someone asked for an encore. He's singing to me, "*I love you, I love you, o,*" like this is some music video where I left him for another guy and took all his money. I have to look away because he sounds a bit too sincere. While he's mid-croon, I lunge for the gear stick and he swats my hand away. "Okay fine, fine!"

"We're going to be late, you know."

"No way, we'll be good."

"Huh."

He finally pulls out of the driveway and onto the road, driving way too fast in this residential area. So bold for someone who pretty much just got their license.

"Congrats, by the way," I say, turning to him. His hands are gripping the steering wheel so hard that I can see beads of sweat forming at his temples and his hairline. "Ooh, new haircut?" I ask.

"Yeah, Dad took me," he says. "After I passed my test. It's been a week. How'd you not notice?"

I did notice, but would I give him the satisfaction of knowing that? No way. "I don't stare at your head all day, Tayo."

"But this line-up is so fresh."

"Please."

"Where'd you go yesterday after school?"

"Oh…" I purse my lips and get real quiet trying to remember. "Dress fitting with Auntie Funmi," I count off. "Then I had to meet up with Justin and the debate squad." And then I thought I saw Sam. Even though Tayo knows what went down, how Sam left unceremoniously one day, I still can't bring it up in front of him. Our cousin gang is cool, but we're still so influenced by our parents, so heavy under their thumbs. Who knows what his parents said about Sam. Who knows what they've said to Tayo. I don't want to put him in a position to defend his parents, so I keep quiet and let it go. What's the point in bringing up Sam, anyway? He abandoned Mom and Dad. Simple.

Tayo shrugs his shoulders and juts his lip out the way my parents do when they're trying to understand something. "So you met up with your oyinbo friend."

"Ha," I snort, feeling my face get all hot, though I can't pin down the reason why. "He has a name."

"You guys are both nerds," he chortles. "You talk about it like you met up to do normal people things, but I know you've been studying the dictionary—"

"Because I'm in debate, you goat!" I snicker. "I need to know how to communicate, obviously."

"Who's a goat?" he laughs back. "You, eh? You realize Igbo girls have the highest bride price, right? You fine sha, but too much wahala. Your parents will never marry you off."

I kiss my teeth real extra, drawing it out like there's something stuck between my molars that I need to suck out. "Whatever. Yoruba demon. As if you've seen anybody who wants to marry you when you're like this." As I say it, I wave a hand up and down from the crown of his close-shaven head to his feet outfitted in new kicks.

"He-ey!" he cries in mock shock, clutching his chest like an OG Nigerian movie actor.

"Use-less Yo-ru-ba de-mon," I say again with a playful sneer. It sounds like I'm carving the words out of thick wood with the dullest knife, but it's not that deep. This is how we play-fight all the time. Me and Tayo, or me and Chioma, or Genny and Chioma. It's times like these where it's just me and any snippy insults I've picked up from hours and hours of listening to our parents talk. It's when I feel the most at ease, when Ada can chill and be herself without any repercussions.

"Wow, okay, get out of my car, then." Tayo steps on the

brakes and pretends to pull over, but we're both laughing so hard by then that nothing else matters. All I'm thinking of now is what other Nigerian pidgin insult I can come up with, what else I can say that would be a good verbal slap. But then Tayo glances at the clock and straightens up. "Snap, we're actually going to be late, though." He speeds the rest of the way to school. I'm still trying to think of a good comeback by the time we pull into the parking lot.

Tayo parks carefully in the far corner of the senior lot. I wrestle with my bag as he watches, and I think for a second that he's trying to come up with something mean to say to me. But then he says, "So when is your debate competition?" and my defenses come down.

Ugh. I don't want to think about debate right now because when I think about debate, I think about Justin. And I can't think about Justin when I'm with Tayo because—because when I'm with Tayo, the power couple is no longer me and Justin as successful immigration lawyers and investment bankers; the power couple is me and Tayo, hanging out, feeding each other fried plantain, just being together. He is my 50-percent-of-the-time dream. Maybe there's something to Chioma constantly teasing me about him. Maybe it's because I kinda sorta like him . . . *a lot.*

We hang out all the time and we just laugh, and that's when I can be my truest self. Our families are tight so they never bat an eyelash when he's teaching me a new dance move, standing dangerously close as he tries to nudge my hips a certain way. They barely shout when the two of us are in my room sprawled across my bed, trying to watch something full screen on my laptop and squinting at the small subtitles. They don't say, "No boys in your room!" because Tayo is already like family. We're already so . . .

Man, the movies never tell you how shitty it is liking two people at once. For someone who's an ace at logic and pleading my case, you'd think I'd be able to figure out what to do here, but no. Instead, I just blush and stammer and sidestep from Tayo's car as I say, "Uh, the competition is sometime in April. I have to double-check with Mr. Patel. I'm kinda nervous about the whole thing."

"Why would you be nervous? You're Nigerian," Tayo snorts, rolling his eyes with that same bravado my dad would have if I doubted myself for even a second. He shuts the car door and falls in line with me on the way into the building. "I can't say much for your friends, though."

"Please."

He chuckles. "Genny's wedding is after the competition, right?"

"Yeah," I say, letting the excitement and anxiety of the impending event rush back to me. It's even enough for me to forget about Auntie Funmi and the way she pulled the measuring tape around my arm like she wanted to graft it into my skin. "Bro, I still can't believe she's marrying Skeleboy. Like, *the* Skeleboy!"

"Yeah, and that he's letting you plebs attend," he snickers. "Yo, he's rich enough to do a wedding in Dubai with elephants and giraffes he flies in from Nairobi. How nice of him to choose our gentrified Toronto suburb for his wedding."

"Exactly!" I think of Skeleboy coming downtown to Queen Street in the summer for ice cream with us; picture him sitting outside while we struggle to eat chocolate dipped cones that are melting in obscenely humid weather. I've been told the weather in Nigeria is dry heat, scorching and angry. He'd have to get used to the smogginess here. It makes me laugh but only because it could really come true. Skeleboy, a local. A *local*!

"Sucks my invitation got lost in the mail, though." He eyes me, lips buttoned together, waiting for my response. Tayo is taller than me by a head, so I can feel the strength of his gaze hit my right temple like a bullet. It's practically burning a hole into my skull.

"You know I can't just invite you," I tell him softly. "It's Genny's wedding. Her wedding planner—you remember her friend Blessing? Well, she has a guest list, and I mean a real one, not just 'so-and-so and his five children.'"

"Yeah, but don't you need a plus one?"

"I don't know…" He watches me, my face heating up with

each second his eyes are on me. Do I need a plus one? Genny is making me a bridesmaid and there was already a long discussion about that. My parents thought I'd be an automatic shoo-in, and for the record, so did her parents. But it turns out Genny needed to evaluate my bone structure before she eventually said yes. Her exact words were: "You're in. You have the cheekbones and red undertones for the kind of makeup look I want my bridesmaids to have. Also, you fit my Fenty 430 perfectly."

"I can get you an autograph?" I offer, trying to lighten the mood. "Hey, I know the only reason you want to go is because you want to see Skeleboy, anyway. Your twin." We joke that Tayo and Skeleboy look a lot alike: the same sharp jaw, the same full lips, the same soft brown eyes.

Tayo gives one last, lingering chuckle, and suddenly, that glow I like about him begins to fade. He flashes me a forced, stiff smile and mutters, "Ha, yeah."

Awkwardness creeps over me like a blanket. This isn't the first time Tayo asked me about going to the wedding and it definitely won't be the last. Genny's friend Blessing is high off planning Uncle Shola's second wedding (she secured a video shoutout from Tiwa Savage during the speeches, it was actually amazing), so I doubt she'd be okay with me wanting to mess with her guest list. I convinced myself that I don't need to invite someone, but if I'm being honest, Sophie would love to have a plus one—and if he's Nigerian? Even better. That makes things so much easier. I wouldn't have to be Sophie *and* Ada. I could just be Ada. Adanna Nkwachi. But this isn't any case; this is Tayo we're talking about. Our parents know each other because of the Nigerian Network, aka WhatsApp and cultural associations, and we practically grew up together. If he shows up as my plus one, what's everyone going to think? That we're dating, obviously. And as much as I love that idea in my head, I don't know how I feel about that in real life right now.

"Let's get burgers," I blurt out amid the chaos storm of Nigerianness in my head. Tayo's ears perk up at the sound of food and he turns to me, a bit more intrigued, a bit less sour. "After school. The Burger Joint has half-off suicide burgers today, right?"

"It does, it does," he replies, stroking an invisible mous-tache. "I'll drive."

"Obviously you will."

"You buy the burgers." He laughs when my mouth opens and shuts with force as the reality behind his words hits me. "Snake!" he cackles at my shocked face. "So you expected me to drive *and* buy food?"

"Listen, I know your parents only gave you a twenty to spend for this whole week, so really, it's my mistake for assuming."

"Woooow."

We reach the crossing where he heads left to his homeroom, biology, and I head right to my homeroom, media arts. Usually we just wave at each other and split, but today I am compelled to give him a hug. He says, "So bye," and turns to leave, but I reach forward and squeeze my arms around him like I'm being forced to. He doesn't see it coming and sticks out his elbows to shove his hands into his pockets before my arms get around them comfortably. The hug is quick and sloppy and weird and I don't know why it's happening. Maybe it's an apology for me not being able to invite him as my plus one, but even then, it hardly stacks up.

Ms. Kay runs my homeroom class like we're on a yoga retreat. After morning announcements, she tells us all to take a deep breath and stretch forward onto our desks. Sometimes Annie Prasant doesn't want to do it because she spends a lot of time on her makeup in the morning and Ms. Kay expects that we all lay our faces flat on the tables. "It's unhygienic," she complains as she does it anyway. When she comes back up, you can see the places on her desk where her eyeshadow and brown foundation has rubbed off a little.

Ms. Kay usually does the exercise with us. Her large, flouncy afro covers her entire head to the point that when she puts her face down, we can barely see a trace of her eyes or nose. She pops back up after five minutes with a huge smile. It's such a contrast to all of our tired expressions. "Morning, class," she says with a grin, shaking out her shoulders. Ms. Kay used to do modern dance, so she's always very limber, rocking back and forth, swaying to no music. She's a bit spacey but means well, and she is probably the only interesting thing about this class. Media arts is an elective and not one I actually wanted to pick. Art has nothing to do with law school, but at least it'll make it look like I have hobbies. Universities love that stuff.

Annie Prasant grumbles from behind me, uttering her daily string of curses. "So out of pocket, fucking who the fuck, eyelashes cost more than her fake-ass crochet braids..." She's so petty. Ms. Kay's hair is obviously not crochet.

"Today..." Ms. Kay gets up and wanders to the front of the class, her long skirt flowing behind her. "We're going to get into your final projects a bit more. I know we talked about them briefly last week, remember? Who remembers?" She puts up her hand and maybe two other students do the same. A knowing smile catches her lips, and she nods, slow. "All right. Quick refresher: We're exploring how compound media works and the effects of dual level storytelling. So, for example, how a painting can be enhanced by music, or how a dance performance is aided by visuals. How two media components can tell one story. I know I said you could get started, but I was thinking about the *compound*-ness of it all, and I had, um, a revelation this past Monday." Ms. Kay is always having revelations. "How about partners?"

"Aww, Miss, no!" Carter Jones cries out almost instantly from the back corner. He does double time with his wave brush, brushing out his hair back to front as he speaks. "We have group work for every other project. We should just do solo work."

"Tch, okay, and?" another student pipes up in the opposite corner.

"Right, right," Ms. Kay cuts in, smiling. "Art is collaborative. It gains meaning from its interaction with the outside world—you can't have one without the other."

"But I don't want to work with anyone."

"These will be, um, what I want to call a more intuitive pairing," she goes on, closing her eyes for a moment to feel out her answer. One girl tries to make eye contact with me in a moment of solidarity, like, "*wow, Ms. Kay is weeeeird as fuck,*" but I avert my eyes quickly. I don't know anyone in this class like that and I want to keep it that way. Most of these kids have been taking the arts since our first year, so they're all friends. Meanwhile, I've been avoiding art ever since that first mandatory class. I'm just here to keep my head down, literally and figuratively, and fulfill high school requirements.

"So," Ms. Kay says, clasping her hands together. "I'm going to call out names in twos. Those will be the partnerships. You'll find that this may be a person you haven't worked with before, but still, you know, *connect* with." Someone behind me snorts when she says "connect." "Okay, so. John and Tyrell. Kandi and Jared." Chairs start to shift around as people turn to find their partners. Waves from across the room, screams in excitement, and wild hand gestures fill the air. Then she calls, "Sophie and Patricia."

I look around the classroom trying to place the name to a face. Patricia? Can't say I've heard that name before. I turn around, trying to lock eyes with anyone who is looking for me, but there's no one. To my left? Grudging pairs of students who may know each other but don't necessarily want to work together. To my right? Groups of boys who are already planning their final project—a movie, an action movie, with real fake explosions and, I don't know, like a homage to a video game. It appears as if everyone is paired off already. So weird. Who's Patricia?

"So . . . phie? Right?"

I whip back around and face the desk in front of me to see another brown-skinned girl watching me hesitantly. She waits, almost for some sort of acknowledgment, before she fully turns around to face me. She's wearing so many brace- lets that the sound seems to cling and clang every time she moves her arms. She also has a nose piercing, and that's how I know she's probably not African. One time Chioma wanted to get a cartilage piercing and even that required intervention. Her parents accused her of being in a gang for a year, saying things like "*So you want to be following oyinbo palava?*" all the time. "You're Sophie, yeah?" she asks again, her voice a bit stronger.

"Yeah, I am," I answer.

She smiles, forced and stiff. I'm getting a lot of these today. "I'm Patricia. We're partners, I guess."

"I guess, yeah." I didn't mean that to come out so harsh, so I force a smile too, to try and make her feel at ease. She returns it, and soon we're just force smiling at each other for a good minute. I wonder if she's looking forward to this. I wonder if she can tell I'm not.

CHAPTER FOUR

CHIOMA TEXTS ME WHILE I wait for Tayo by his car after school. I lean against the passenger side door and scroll through my phone. Usually, she tries to text me about covering for her. Chioma is always getting into something she shouldn't be, like that time she gambled away the money her parents gave her for tuition, or the time she caught a bus to Montreal and made me tell her parents she was chaperoning my debate club trip. But nowadays, with the wedding of the century impending, her texts are all about Genny and how she might murder her. "*come over and be the buffer pls,*" she writes. "*this girl wants me to kill her, o!! is this how she'll DIE before her wedding?*"

I chuckle at the mental image of Chioma and Genny

having the ultimate battle on her wedding day. Chioma can be gracious but if she snaps, everyone will know Genny drove her to it. Everyone knows what Genny is like these days, anyway. It's like what Mom always says when she's about to talk smack about Auntie Celine: "If I go mad, they will say I am mad."

"*just think,*" I text back. "*soon, you can call skeleboy brother-in-law!*"

"*brother-in-law ke! let's wait until after the wedding for this kind of talk, ah-beg.*"

Footsteps approach in the distance and I turn to see Tayo shuffling up to the driver's side. He smirks, cool and casual, when he gets my attention. "What's wrong with you today?" His smirk turns into a laugh so easily, and I'm lulled by the sound of his voice even though it's me he's laughing at. He unlocks the door and we both clamber into the car. "Huh?" he asks again while he fumbles with his keys. "You look like someone beat you. Like someone did something wrong to you today."

I laugh too. "What? No, no. Chioma texted me, uh..." I trail off, suddenly unsure if now is the best time to bring up the wedding again. It's only been a morning and I still don't have any answers for Tayo about if he can be my plus one or not.

He snickers through the soft burr of the engine, but I ignore him and reach for my phone and the aux cord instead. Instantly, my music player blasts Skeleboy. God is playing tricks for real.

Tayo hears the first beat of "Yanga" and I can feel him tense up from where I'm sitting. Without another word, I switch the song. "Have you, uh, heard this one?" Another Afrobeats song begins to play.

He shakes his head. "Nope. New artist?"

"Every Naija artist is a new artist," I snort. That makes him smile at least.

The drums and electric, silky beats push through the speakers as Tayo drives. I check my phone again, thinking I should shoot Chioma another text, but I don't know what about. Instead, Justin texts me. Says he's thinking about debate stuff, fleshing out information about cross-cultural kids and whatnot. My fingers fumble over a response, and in the end, I reply with a simple: "*k.*"

Suddenly, Tayo pipes up. "The Burger Joint, right?"

"Yeah."

"Half-off suicide burgers."

I nod. "I'm ready."

Suicide burgers at The Burger Joint are double patty, hot sauce, and jalapeño pepper burgers. So many people our age hate them, but Tayo and I crave their richness. After growing up drinking Nigerian pepper soup at every family gathering, we're practically immune to spice. Being six and being forced to sit at the kids' table with a steaming hot bowl of soup is a memory ingrained in my pores with sweat. My nose would run and my throat would be dry and hoarse from all the crying and protest, but still, neither my parents nor my aunts and uncles would let us escape. We had to drink it, they said. It's good for us, they said. They would polish off their bowls and begin dancing to old highlife songs in the living room while us kids sat at the table and schemed our way out of finishing our respective soups. Genny always drank hers after a bit of cajoling. She wasn't like the rest of us; she was born in Nigeria and spent six years there, so she always acted tougher than us kids, whether she actually was or not. She'd slurp it down and then point a stern finger at each of us, her fading accent inspiring a level of fear usually reserved for our parents. "You people better finish this soup! Otherwise, thunder fire you!" And with that, she'd disappear to go dance with the adults. I would try and catch my parents' attention, because surely they'd vouch for me, but they always seemed to be preoccupied. Sam took the diplomatic approach and tried to reason with the adults, but they would just laugh, call him Mr. Man, and tell us all to be quiet and finish our food. Eventually, Chioma and I would take spoonfuls of each other's soup, as if that would somehow make the task easier. Years of this strategic struggle not only made us wilier kids but increased our tolerance for pepper tenfold without us realizing it. This is why Tayo and I walk into The Burger

Joint, the door swinging wildly behind us, and boldly ask for two suicide burgers without batting an eyelash.

The young, pimply girl at the register chuckles as she punches in our order. "That's our spiciest burger. I just have to warn you, otherwise it's a liability."

Tayo turns to me and whispers, "Oyinbo pepper," and I stifle a laugh.

"It's fine," I say.

"Together or separate?" she asks.

"Separate," I say at the same time Tayo says, "Together." We glance at each other sheepishly. "Can we do separate?" I ask him. "I know I said I'd buy you one, but I legit have, like, ten dollars to last me the week."

"No, no, I'll pay," he says.

"What?" My cheeks burn hot with the sudden gesture. "Why would you buy me food?"

He shies away from my gaze with nervous laughter. Before I can say anything, he hands the cashier a twenty and waits for change. "It's okay," he says finally. "Just think of me when you ask Genny about your plus one, okay?"

I narrow my eyes at him. "So this is a bribe?"

"No, no," he says. "Just trying to be nice."

"Hmm."

"But also, yeah, don't forget to ask her."

Tayo and I settle by the window at a table for four with

our burgers. He is barely seated before he takes his first bite. "Mmm," he hums, dancing around in his chair. He's legit always dancing. "It never disappoints. Never."

I take a bite too and relish in its spiciness. The burger isn't too dry; it works so well with the ketchup, hot sauce, and jalapeños. Whoever invented the suicide burger knew just what I needed in this very moment: a reasonably spicy burger to take my mind off school and life and this stupid media arts final assignment.

I groan a little just thinking about it. I can't believe Ms. Kay thought our final projects would be better if we did them as partners. Everyone knows group work is a waste of time because the smartest kid ends up picking up the slack—which would be me. No offense to Patricia, but we both know how this will go.

Tayo takes another bite of his burger just as I nudge him with my foot under the table. He looks up. "What?"

"Ms. Kay, right," I begin, taking another bite too. "She's making us do group work for our final media arts project. We have to use at least two different media art forms to tell one story by looking at dual level storytelling or, or whatever. It's like a painting and music, or a movie and photography, or something like that. Using two elements to tell one narrative."

He grimaces, cringing like I ran a cold finger down his spine. "Group work is so dumb. We both know how that'll go."

"Exactly!" I whine. "The smartest kid always does all the work—"

"So you, pretty much."

"Yeah—*yes*," I moan. "And I don't have time to babysit someone else. I have real work to do, you know. Also, I need to prep so many things for debate with Justin and the guys."

Like clockwork, my phone rings. It's front facing on the table so Tayo sees Justin's name stream across my screen before I do. He stops chewing and locks eyes with me, raising an eyebrow in concern, confusion, whatever else. "Is that your oyinbo debate friend?" he asks, pointing to my phone with his lips.

"He has a name," I say, setting down my burger and ignoring the sudden judgment arching from his eyes. Wiping my hands haphazardly on my napkin, I swipe for my phone and bring it to my ear. "Hello?"

"Yeah, hey." Justin always sounds so cool on the phone, the raspiness in his voice amplified by the fuzzy transmission. I wouldn't actually say this to him, but I do like when he calls me. "Where are you? I *just* came up with solid arguments for and against cultural appropriation by cross-cultural kids. You're not busy, right?"

I glance up at Tayo who takes a ridiculously huge bite of his burger the second we lock eyes. He's being mad shady so I shift away to face the window, looking onto the bleak parking lot. "Okay, but what if I was?" I reply.

He laughs. "It'll only take an hour or two."

"An *hour*?"

"I can come to you, if it's easier?" he adds. "I already have all the notes with me."

"Of course you do."

"Are you home?"

"Ha," I snort. "No way would I let some random guy into my house. My parents would murder you."

He laughs too. "*Random* guy? I've known you since, like, middle school."

Tayo straightens right away, eyebrow raised and then narrowed while he watches me, as if he's straining to hear or trying to crack some kind of code. I avoid his gaze again, but he's staring at me so hard that it's like being blinded by headlights in the dead of night. Can he chill? "I'm at The Burger Joint with a friend right now, though," I say into the phone, loud enough for Tayo to hear and hopefully back off. If he hears, he definitely doesn't act like it.

"Cool," Justin says. "I'm maybe five minutes away from that place."

I shake my head. "That wasn't an invitation."

"It's cool. It'll just be—"

"An hour?"

"I can knock it down to thirty minutes," he says.

We both hang up. I take another bite of my burger, letting my eyes find their way back to Tayo. He's watching me intently as if he has something to say to me, or like I have something to say to him. I swallow and take another bite. "So," I begin, "Justin's dropping by for a hot second to talk about school stuff."

He gives an exaggerated groan, but I'm used to him acting this way whenever I mention Justin. The soft curve of his eyes turns harsh. The pout in his lip straightens. It's like he's a different person. "Cool. Should we get him a burger too?" he asks before taking an unnecessarily large bite of his food.

"No," I tell him. "He's not staying too long."

"Just him? What about your other debate friends?"

"They're not coming. I mean, all of us *could* prep together, but Josh and Arjun are a team on their own, just like how Justin and I are a team, so it's not always necessary..." I've explained the way debate works to Tayo a million times. At this point, I know he's just asking so I can reiterate, again, in layman's terms, that it'd be just me and Justin hanging out together. Like always.

Tayo grunts in response and chews faster like he's got somewhere else to be. I know it's because he doesn't want to run into Justin, but I bet he doesn't realize how much I don't want to be in the same room with the both of them either. Him and Justin are pretty different, but more than that, I'm pretty different when I'm around them. Ada would be a bit too crass for Justin, and Sophie, too tame for Tayo.

Not to mention how confusing my two separate fantasies are—Tayo and I aren't high-profile lawyer types, and Justin and I aren't feeding each other fried plantain! No, if anyone should be annoyed at how this entire meeting will go down, it's me.

Tayo polishes off his burger and gulps down his water. I watch him, a nervous chuckle escaping my lips as I ask, "Are you running away or something? Why'd you eat that so fast? Don't look but the lady at the counter is staring, wondering if you're okay."

He snickers and pushes his chair back. "She's worried for nothing. She should know fire can't kill a dragon."

I bite my lip to stop from smiling. "You're dumb. Leave *Game of Thrones* alone. We don't talk about that ending."

"Yo, I know!"

After a few minutes, I spot Justin appear in the doorway carrying nothing but a large notebook. He has a pen stuffed casually behind his ear like the nerd he is. It wasn't cool when we were twelve and it's not cool now. The cashier at the counter calls to him but he ignores her once he spots my table. I wave him over, which is mistake number one. Tayo catches my wave and turns just as Justin settles into the seat beside me. Tayo's normally soft, welcoming gaze hardens and he fixes his stare on Justin. And me, stuck in the middle, smothered by my own feelings. This is literally the most unnecessary thing I've had to deal with since learning about that art project.

"Hey," Justin says. He nods to Tayo, who nods back in that way guys do. The two of them take each other in for a moment, both trying to evaluate the situation. Justin glances at the empty burger wrapper in front of Tayo, and Tayo eyes the notebook with vitriol as if it's witchcraft.

"Hey," Tayo says eventually. "You two are studying?" He nods again to the notebook.

"Oh, uh, yeah," Justin tells him, glancing at the notebook too. "It's just debate stuff."

"Debate stuff, again," I add. Tayo's distrust of Justin is so tangible. His face? Straight up Nigerian face of disapproval. The subtle bend of his lip, the flatness behind his eyes—it's easy to miss if you don't know what to look for. But I've seen this face my entire life. I've seen it from my dad when I failed to finish all my rice and stew before bed. I've seen it from my mom when I forgot to wear earrings to a baby's church dedication. I saw it—I saw it that day before Sam left, too.

I shut my eyes tight, trying to shake the memory of Mom's classic disapproving face as she waltzed down the hall from Sam's room. She left and Dad stormed in, crossing paths with her for a second before a roar erupted like nothing I'd ever heard before. Dad and Sam arguing. Yelling.

Something being thrown. I tried to leave my room, but Mom rushed to my door, hissing, "Where are you going?" and told me to stay put. So I did.

This memory won't die.

"Oh, so you guys are *actually* busy." Tayo's voice cuts through my thoughts and I'm brought back to the sobering reality that I'm here in this burger shop and not at home, not with that horrible memory. My eyes refocus as Tayo gets to his feet and assembles his things. I watch him, halfway between shock and offense. He's leaving? How am I supposed to get home? "I'll see you later, Ada." He doesn't say anything to Justin, but they both nod to each other again, and he's out the door.

Justin quickly takes his spot across from me and flips open his notebook. He doesn't seem at all fazed by the exchange, but I'm still unsettled. He goes through notes, doing double takes at his handwriting like he can't read it. I peer down at the page too, and yeah, it's a bit hard to place. "I think it's this...," he mumbles, shifting the book toward me. "I was thinking we could start off with base definitions and build our understanding that way. Then, we can brainstorm some main argument points."

"Yeah," I echo. "Brainstorm."

He looks at me and I nod again, like, yeah, I heard you. My phone beeps and for a moment I think it's Tayo texting about how he's stupid for just up and leaving like that, but it's not him. It's Patricia. Confusion replaces apathy as I skim over the message: "*hey, it's patricia. wanna get together next week to start brainstorming ideas?*"

Wow, *everyone* needs a brainstorm session with me? Is there something in the air? I snatch my phone up and text back, my fingers punching the word "*sure*" as if it owes me something.

Justin watches me slide my phone back to the table. He looks halfway between concern and indifference, a dimple forming above his eyebrow as he stares between me and the device. It kinda makes me want to laugh. "Is . . . everything okay?" he asks.

"Yeah," I say. "Speaking of brainstorming, though, do you want to help me with something?"

"Is it schoolwork?"

I snort. "What, are you excited?"

"N-no."

"Tch, yeah, you are." I reach for my phone again, letting the rubber-cased device slide between my fingers. I turn it over and over in my hands. Eventually, I say, "I have this project. It's for this media arts class I have to take."

"That's your arts elective?"

"Yeah," I grumble. "It's dumb."

"It's whatever." He shrugs.

Justin knows it's not just whatever; he knows what I'm about with school and being serious about law. He just always has to disagree with me—me, wanting to do pro bono law work, and him, so capitalist that the idea haunts him at night, but somehow, we are still a "we," in my head. "Yeah, well…" I shrug too. "We have to do group work and I got paired with this girl. Apparently, we have like two months or something to come up with a mixed media project. I can't remember."

"Sounds cool."

"It isn't."

"So you're just not going to do it?"

"I mean, I will," I tell him. "I just don't have any ideas. I have zero idea what a…a mixed art project is. And, honestly and truly, I don't care."

Justin snickers, saying, "I got an idea. Naturally," all smug. My distaste is palpable, but mostly because I enjoy his smugness more than I should. He reaches for his phone and swipes it open, poking and prodding different apps and keys for a minute. "I got a cousin who's part of this arts collective. I don't know. Really hippie stuff. She plays guitar with these guys and they have this online forum where they post all their weird art projects and stuff." He pauses and turns his phone around to show me. The forum is called SEA. The collective's name? SEA Creatures. It takes all my willpower to not roll my eyes. "I can add you to the group and you can creep them for ideas. Honestly, the weirdest shit gets posted on there, but you should be good to find inspiration for this mixed media thing."

"You think?" I sigh. Justin sends me the sign-up link and I click on it, effectively adding myself to the group. The entire main page is filled with tweet-style posts of people hashtagging their events and whereabouts. Members put up posters and start discussions around art shows they're producing, trying to get people to come. Some are free, some are paid. Some are *local* local, some are international.

I see a poster for an animated movie premiere featuring a group of high school kids who apparently learned all their skills from YouTube videos. Hard pass. Then I see an ad for banjo lessons. *Banjo* lessons? In this economy? I can't believe people actually care about this stuff. Right now, I'm looking into a parallel universe where people apparently play music all day and still live decent lives. They don't have the watchful eye of their immigrant parents hovering just an inch above their heads. Maybe these people don't have immigrant parents. Maybe that's what it is.

I scroll a bit more, preparing myself for the next banjo lesson ad, when I see it.

"Poetry Slam, The Ballroom at 2020 Brick Avenue. Come see classic MCs, new and old, throw down on Wednesday at 7. Featuring Jace, Miss Stacey B, and Obi."

And then I see him.

Him.

No.

He's…

No.

It's—he's on the right side of the poster. Shaved sides, high cheekbones, cool brown eyes. My heart burns, beating like a frantic drum in my chest, pounding and pounding until I can barely hear anything else but the blood rushing to my brain. There's a lull, a buzz. I drop my phone, hearing it clang against the table, before I scramble to pick it up again. My eyes trace the hoodie pulled over the top half of his head, and my mind fills in the blanks immediately. Black and white becomes color. I can see this hoodie in my mind. I can feel its softness as I pull it out of the dryer, march it down the hall, toss it into his room, yell, *"Your stuff is always mixed in with mine!"* before stalking away. I know this hoodie because I know who's wearing it.

It's him. I know it is.

It's…it's my brother.

CHAPTER FIVE

I SAVE THE POSTER TO my phone and stare at it every day for what feels like forever, but truly, it's only been about a week. I've studied the poster's color scheme, its typeface, its information so hard that I could reproduce it with my eyes closed if I had to. I know the way the artists are positioned on the poster. I know the font size ratio from "Poetry Slam" to the address. I know the size of Sam's head, his massive, massive head, in relation to the other pictures.

I know *Sam*.

My eyes work super hard taking in what I can see of his facial features and how much of it fits with my memories. There are no pictures of him in the house anymore. Mom and Dad made sure of that. For a moment, I had wondered what happened—why he left, why he left *us*, all of it—but Mom and Dad never did. They didn't give me the option to, either. *"Don't mind him,"* they had said with the strangest aggression. From then on, I stayed clear (he left, it's fine), tried to be obedient (keep your head down, it's fine), tried to be good (keep going, it's fine). Didn't want to anger my parents because what was the point? The pool of hurt in their eyes was enough for me.

And yet, what I remember of his face is what I see in my parents. Dad's forehead, Mom's eyes. I can barely recall it on my own anymore, but seeing this picture now is like confirmation. In a weird way, it reminds me that he did exist once. And he's alive.

Alive—and a poet.

A whole poet performing at a poetry event.

Sam would be twenty-five by now, and the last time I saw him, he was one exam away from finishing his second year as an engineering major. He was like me: all good grades and high scores and nothing more. In our house, we didn't have time for things like this. Mom and Dad are down with the Afrobeats because it's our music, but anything else is counterproductive, and that includes a poetry slam.

As my eyes glaze over the poster again, I wonder if this is why he left. I wonder if he wanted so badly to do poetry and break free from our parents that he decided leaving, running away like this, was his only option. My hands are clammy clasping my phone. The thought that he could just...just *leave* our parents because of *this*?

Poetry? Is he mad? How—*how* is this even worth it?

Damn, if this is real, I need to go. If this is really Sam, then I want to see him with my own eyes and see what's so good about poetry that he had to fucking abandon our family. I punch the information fast and hard into my phone's calendar: "Poetry, The Ballroom at 2020 Brick Ave, Sam."

A soft pillow hits my head and I'm brought back down to earth, back to Chioma's room on a Sunday night, where she, Tayo, and I are watching the latest episode of *Tuppervengers*. When I look up, blinking at the fallen pillow, I hear Tayo tsk from the corner. "What's so good about your phone right now? We're in the middle of an auction," he says, gesturing wildly at the TV.

I hide my phone and sit up straighter, more intent on getting back into this episode. There's no point to bring up Sam with them right now. They know as much as I do about Sam and his abandonment, and who knows what their parents talk about when I'm not there. It's not worth it.

Chioma stuffs a handful of extra buttery popcorn into her mouth. She's lying on her bed while Tayo spins slowly in her desk chair. I snatch the pillow that hit my head and hug it to my chest as I zone back in on the negotiation.

"Okay, so, Rainbow Steve, this Chicago man, is trying to bargain for this stylish BPA-free Tupperware container.

He's not going to get it, by the way," Chioma utters while she chews. "Not with that lowballing."

"Yeah, eh?" Tayo kisses his teeth. "Hasn't he ever watched this show? BPA-free containers *always* go for higher."

I nod in agreement while I reach awkwardly up toward the bed to snatch a handful of popcorn. Chioma smacks my hand and I recoil with only a few kernels. "What? You can't eat the entire thing by yourself," I say.

"Shh, shh!" She puts a finger to her mouth. And we wait. Rainbow Steve's face is small and red with a single bead of sweat coursing down the bridge of his nose. Numbers come up on the screen showing his bid and the highest bid, and it wasn't him. He got outbid by Jack Sutherland, some ex-stockbroker who got into avocado farming in California. Chioma gasps. "I knew it! Yo, Jack was looking like he was going to snake him. You could see it in his eyes."

Tayo snickers. "Yeah! He was mad sketch. Did you see when he was eyeing the other contestants like he was already planning who to outbid?"

Chioma cackles, pushing herself up to a seated position. Her long twists fall around her shoulders, making her look more like Genny than ever. "Yes! He knew already."

"Maybe he's just a really good player," I interject to boos and hisses and "*shut up!*" from the two of them. "What's wrong with you people? He might be! Maybe he just knows what he's after. That's why he always wins. What's wrong with that?"

"Ah-beg-ee!" Tayo chuckles, waving away my words. "It's Sunday. We're watching a show about people trading Tupperware. Can you relax?"

"You, Yoruba boy," I taunt, pointing a menacing finger at him. He places a hand across his chest like I punched him. "You're lucky we even let you into this my cousin's house, eh? You're just lucky."

Tayo laughs, piercing but warm like always, but it's cut short by the swish and swoosh of the front door opening downstairs. The three of us jump in place, startled by the overwhelming loudness. We hear footsteps, then keys hitting a table. Genny's voice bursts out from the landing. "Who's home, who's home? I'm in *crisis!*"

The three of us freeze and look at each other. Quickly, Chioma snatches the remote and puts the volume all the way down so the sound of *Tuppervengers* won't carry to the ground floor. Chioma is egging me on with her eyes, looking at me and then looking at the door. I shake my head. "Are you mad? You go. She's *your* sister," I whisper.

"No—Tayo, you go," she says.

"Ah-ah!" Tayo scoffs. "Me? Am I even going to her wedding?"

We don't even hear the footsteps; Genny just appears in

the doorway like the crash of thunder that she is. The three of us jump again, stumbling over our legs and feet as she looms by the door, eyeing us carefully. Genny never used to elicit this kind of reaction from us—we swear she used to be cool—but when her and Blessing link up these days, it's madness. Genny has turned from Nollywood ingenue, like a fresh Mercy Johnson Okojie, to Nollywood villain, like OG Patience Ozokwor. I want to blame Blessing, the original tafia queen, whose sharp eyes and sharp mouth are always looking for her next bit of gossip, but that wouldn't be fair. We know Genny has always been this intense.

I hide my phone extra hard as if Genny can see through it, as if she knows what I've been looking at. Her bold, dark eye makeup is even more intimidating when she glares at us like this. Her lips are puckered like there's a sour taste in her mouth. So we wait. And wait. And she says, "So…"

None of us breathe.

She takes a step into the room. Chioma averts her eyes. "So…I was downstairs calling and none of you people could answer?" she asks, taking her time to look at each of us. Her voice is so slow, so rich, so thickened with her disappointment that it's hard not to feel like we're being yelled at by a parent. She slips in and out of her fading Igbo accent sometimes, but we've been hearing it full force lately. At this point, Genny has spent more time in Canada than she has in Nigeria, but it feels like she maintains it just for times like these, when she wants to crush someone under her heel. "Instead, you're just up here watching Netflix. While I'm *dy-ing*."

"Genny, honestly," Chioma sighs. I'm not sure if it's bravery or stupidity at this point. "We just... We were about to come downstairs—"

"Chioma, ah, please!" Genny cuts her off, pressing her thumb and index finger together. She might as well have slapped her. "I can't believe the level of disloyalty in this house."

A perfect Nollywood villain. Normal Genny would actually find it funny that she's basically become a Nollywood trope personified. But Wedding Genny? She's the closest thing to an actual nightmare in heels.

She pushes her long hair over her shoulder in one dramatic swoop. "Anyway," she goes on. "When I tell you people I'm *stressed*. Can you believe Blessing called the caterer and he won't do ofada stew for me? Hmph." She crosses her arms and rolls her head back. "I specifically requested it for Femi's mother and now he's pretending as if he doesn't remember when Blessing called him two months ago. As if I'm asking him to give me jara. Bush man. I'm beginning to think he only agreed to see us because of that meme nonsense." Truthfully, Genny being a somewhat recognizable face hasn't really changed her life too much. I mean, yeah, she *did* get into VIP at that club and meet Skeleboy, but

Genny is the kind of girl who people will pay attention to anyway.

Tayo utters, "Yeah, yep," and Chioma just nods. I squeeze my phone tighter and tighter.

Genny won't stop sighing. She runs a hand through her hair again and says, "Okay, come downstairs and help us pick color swatches," and disappears just as fast as she showed up.

Blessing is already downstairs by the time we get there. She's wearing leggings and an oversize T-shirt that still manages to show a good amount of her bra strap while she flips through a booklet on the sofa. She forces a smile when she sees us, not because she's mean or anything, but because we're basically kids and she thinks speaking to Tiwa Savage over the phone puts her in a different league. "Where's Genny?" she asks us. "Did she tell you about the situation?"

"She did," I say just as Chioma gasps and bounds over to her.

I didn't notice before, but there's a patch covered in cling wrap around Blessing's wrist. Chioma points at it, suddenly giddy. "What'd you get?"

Blessing smiles humorlessly as she covers her wrist with her other hand. "It's just, like, a rose. Nothing special."

"I can't wait to get one." Chioma swoons, holding her midriff. She's been going on about getting a tattoo for a while but I doubt she'll go through with it. No way her parents would let her stay in the house if they found out. "I'm thinking either my initials or my favorite quote of all time—"

"'Talk shit, get hit'?" Tayo interrupts and begins to snicker.

Chioma bites her lip to stop from smiling, and when she turns, she points a menacing finger at Tayo. "You're looking like you want me to slap you."

He lets out a crass chuckle before shuffling over to a vacant sofa.

Blessing keeps flipping over the same few pages, a knot forming between her brows as she focuses harder and harder on the color swatches. Chioma disappears to pop another bag of popcorn in the kitchen, so for a while, all Tayo and I hear is the sound of paper flipping. Meanwhile, my phone is still pressed facedown into my palm. Fear won't let me flip it around.

Tayo notices me fiddling with the phone and he snorts, nodding to it. "What's wrong with your phone?"

"W-what?" I clasp the phone tighter, pressing it into my thigh. "Nothing's wrong with it."

His eyes leer at the device and for a split second, I am afraid he's going to lunge and try to steal it from me. But then he slowly leans over toward the coffee table where he grabs another color booklet from Blessing. She eyes him carefully, and the moment he cracks it open, she says, "I've earmarked all the ones we're choosing from, so just pick from there. You too." She nods to me.

"S-sure," I say and reach for a stray booklet. I don't bother flipping it open. My hand tightens around the phone. All my unease mounts in the tips of my fingers and it takes everything in me to not flip the phone back around, stare at the poster, and make sure, make *real* sure, that it's Sam in that picture.

"Yo, can I ask you a question?" Tayo pipes up.

I startle, prepared to launch into some kind of an answer, when I notice his gaze is on Blessing, not me. It takes her a while to recognize too. She glances at me, as if to say, "*Why am I in the middle of this?*" before she turns to Tayo. "Sure?"

"I know I missed the extremely narrow window of opportunity when you added my parents to the guest list and they didn't bother telling you I, too, wanted to come," he explains. It's hard to miss the annoyance in his voice. "I get it. How could you have known to call back when my mom wasn't distracted by wrestling to reconfirm that, actually, her son would like an invite too—"

"Get to the point, please," Blessing cuts in.

Tayo takes a deep breath. "Can I finesse my way onto the guest list? I'll do anything—call the caterers for you, choreograph the first dance, anything. I could even, uh, be your driver."

Blessing chuckles, warm but matronly, as she sits back

against the sofa. "Why would you waste your time? If you want to be on the guest list, I can just add you."

Tayo's face lights up. It's actually so cute to see how his eyes pop and his mouth hangs open in complete disbelief. "Don't play with me."

"Does it look like I have time for games?" Blessing says as she tosses her hair over her shoulder. "Just text me your first and last name as you want it on the name card in twenty-four hours so I don't forget. Also, dietary restrictions and if you require additional assistance getting into the venue."

"Yessss!" Tayo starts dancing in his seat. He's all hand gestures and smooth shoulder moves. I bite back a chuckle, looking away. But when he says, "I tried to get, ahem, a friend of mine to add me as her plus one, but she was being sketch." I know his eyes are on me.

Blessing catches on immediately. As the reigning gossip queen, she knows gist when she sees it. Her eyes sparkle at the thought of there being something she doesn't know about someone. A thin smile stretches across her lips as she asks me, bluntly, "So why didn't you want to go together?"

Oh my god.

"She was probably holding out for her debate friend," Tayo says, smug and pointed. It feels like a jab to the chest—even though it's not true.

I hear the microwave beeping in the kitchen corner and for a moment, its beeping is the only noise downstairs.

Then, I say, frazzled, "He has a name. And no, I wasn't." My mind is consumed by this poster and Sam being a real, tangible person again, but Tayo talking about Justin is enough to make me lose it. Can he relax? I'm literally in the middle of a crisis and he's saying all this stuff in front of Blessing, who he knows will spread it on WhatsApp like a virus. The thought itself is making me want to curl up and scream. "Listen, you guys, I'm not dumb," I hiss, a bit too tersely. "Me, taking a boy to Genny's wedding? My parents, *your* parents, would literally kill me."

Blessing grimaces. "I don't envy you kids at all. You can't even date in private without someone turning it public." Yeah, someone like you!

"W-we're not..." I gulp. My nerves are making my throat dry. Tayo and I glance over, each one cautiously regarding the other. He doesn't say anything in protest, but he doesn't hold my gaze either. I have no idea what he could be thinking.

Ugh, this is too much right now. My mind can't take all this wedding talk and Tayo talk and—and Sam. Does Tayo know my brother is a poet? This is what I want to say: Sam is a poet and I'm like 99 percent sure that's why he abandoned my family, because he thought pursuing some flippant art form was more important than sticking together. And now I might see him in person. In real life. Life!

"You're not...?" Blessing prods. Man, she's really not letting this go.

I sit on my phone. Out of sight, out of mind, theoretically, and I force myself to zero in on Tayo. It's not that I didn't want to ask him to be my plus one. I want him there—he's so fun to dance with and we always have so much fun tasting all the different malts at a party—but a plus one is so final. Whether it's intentional or not, that kind of thing says we're a *we*. In my mind, we are already a "we," but bringing it into the present isn't something I need to think about right now.

—because my brother is a poet and he really thought—he *really* thought!

"Ugh, damn, you're right," I grunt, pressing my hands into my eyes.

Blessing won't stop smiling, her mind probably working a mile a minute.

Tayo raises an eyebrow. "I'm already on the guest list, bro, so we can just drop it."

"No, sorry—no, I'm just...thinking about something else."

He blanks, his eyes scanning my face for any sort of hint on what, but I just shake my head. My mouth struggles against my mind's sudden need to bring up the poster. "It's really fine. I'm just distracted. I, um...school." Excellent word choice, there. "We can...go together," I say through a shaky sigh. For a moment, I let the words hang in the air between us, so desperate to course-correct and "well, actually . . ." into oblivion. I'll let Blessing assume whatever she wants. I'll let Tayo assume whatever he wants too.

"True," he agrees, tapping his chin. "I'll think about it."

"Think about what?"

"Being your plus one."

I gasp. "Are you mad? So, after you harassed me into taking pity on you—"

"My people will text your people," he presses on, smug. He makes a big show of reaching for his phone and typing wildly, his thumbs flying over the screen. My phone buzzes and I reluctantly dig it out from under my thigh, navigating over to my inbox for Tayo's message. It says: *"Yes, i'll go with you to skeleboy x genny. geleboy. skelenny."*

"Geleboy," I snort. "That one's worse."

"Let's not lie: They're both trash."

"You're right."

CHAPTER SIX

MONDAY MORNING COMES IN LIKE a soft blur. Aside from agreeing to go to Genny's wedding with Tayo and maybe googling one definition of "cross-cultural kids," I've done nothing but analyze this Poetry Slam poster and search up the address online. This morning, I spent a total of ten minutes zooming in on the street through my map app. This venue looks like one of those that are bigger on the inside, because according to what I found online, there are two meeting rooms, a community center–like multipurpose room, and a space called The Ballroom where artists can showcase work or perform. It's located along a row of what looks like historic buildings that have been renovated to house new shops. A place that sells nothing but french fries, a small café, and a boutique clothes outfit surround the eponymous 2020 Brick Avenue. The area looks a bit hipstery. Artsy, too. Apparently, this new Sam is into this kind of scene.

For so long, I hadn't thought of him. The morning after he left, as I was getting ready for school, I had stopped by the kitchen where Mom was bringing dishes out for breakfast. Innocently, and maybe a bit naively, I asked where Sam went, if we should leave rice for him, stuff like that. Mom didn't answer. I asked again, this time louder because I was convinced she would reply if she could hear me, but she still kept quiet. The clanking of plates against the hardwood table filled the kitchen and emptied my mind. Dad came in just as I'd asked a third time, and I heard the sharp hiss of his voice before I felt his hand clench around my arm, spinning me around. "Shut up! Don't you *ever* ask such questions again," he harped. He was so strict, his eyes so steely and dark. Dad has moods. He can be mean and stern, his voice always echoing a warning that we traveled to this country and we can't afford to get out of line. Still, something about the way he snapped at me was so unlike him. It *is* so unlike him, but he got his wish: I didn't ask any more questions about Sam.

Sam's leaving left a rift in my family and scarred Mom and Dad more than I care to know. It didn't matter to me how good Sam was, or how smart; his disappearance, this betrayal, ended up being the most glaring, heavy thing. A part of me doesn't want to see him again, but another part of me needs that closure. I need to see for myself the life that he thought was better than ours.

Mr. Patel finds me before I manage to get to homeroom. He has his own homeroom class, but in the mornings, he tends to wander the halls with a cup of vanilla-scented coffee, making sure students get to class on time. The irony is he's always late.

"Sophie, talk to me." He waves me over, taking a quick sip of his drink. I watch him recoil as the liquid stings his lip. He brings a many-ringed hand to touch his mouth. "I thought this cooled down enough."

"Guess not," I say with a shrug.

He frowns, tapping his lip to stop it from stinging. "Well, anyway. Did you talk to the guys?"

"I did."

"Aaaanddd?" He steps closer, his voice lowering to a whisper. Another teacher passes by and we both give stiff nothing-to-see-here smiles in his direction before he utters, "My buddy at the office definitely thinks this is the one. I can see it now: the most diverse group of kids this region has ever seen, winning off a cultural appropriation smackdown."

"That's *if* we get the right side," I say, crossing my arms. At the debate, if the house decides that, for example, cultural appropriation is wrong, then I'd prefer we're on the side proposition so we can agree. If we're on side opposition, we'd have to argue that the house's position is wrong and I don't think my soul can take that.

Mr. Patel winks, or tries to, anyway. After a few attempts, he says, "Oh, we'll get the right side. Trust me."

"Sir—"

"Or, as the youths say: Trust."

I choke on a laugh. He's so chaotic.

"Okay, get to class. Try to bring those grades up, eh?" He smirks before turning to take another sip of his drink. I race down the opposite hall to media arts class.

Without Mr. Patel and our upcoming debate to distract me, I think of Sam and 2020 Brick Avenue again all through homeroom. It isn't until Patricia's textbook smacks the hollow of her desk that I finally refocus on the classroom in front of me. That's right, this project; this weird project about a subject I don't care about. I flip my phone over just as she settles into her desk, turning to face me. And she says, "You can't ignore me forever, you know."

Her face is stoic, poised, and I don't know her well enough to know if she's joking or not. She doesn't break once, so I stutter out, "S-sorry, what?"

A small, nervous smile breaches her lips. So she was teasing, then. "I texted you about the project..." She gestures to the phone clutched tightly in my grasp. I move it away as if she can see through the case. "I guess you didn't get it?"

"No, I didn't," I say. Patricia recoils at the unexpected harshness in my voice. Two, three seconds pass and it's too late for me to say sorry, so I keep quiet and wait. She watches me hesitantly as she opens her notebook across my desk, but quickly retrieves it the longer I stare at her. I probably don't look too friendly right now. My thoughts are still somewhere in my memories. "You can... you can keep the book there," I stammer, trying to soften my voice.

She purses her lips. "You sure?"

"Uh, yeah?" I choke out a nervous laugh. "Why not?"

"I mean, you just—never mind." She sighs and flips another page, carefully moving her book around to show me. I push my phone to the side and focus solely on the page so I don't have to deal with another awkward exchange, but the moment my phone is out of my grasp, I feel the need to hold it again. To look at the poster. What's wrong with me? "Here." Patricia's voice grounds me in the classroom. "I came up with some ideas for our final project. We don't have to do these, but, you know, it's better we start somewhere. Try and get a feel for what each other is good at."

"Why does that matter?" The words are out of my mouth before I can temper my tone—Ada's tone, not Sophie's. Sophie would never be this sharp.

Patricia's eyebrow twitches and her lips button together with all the things she probably wants to tell me. "I didn't mean it that way," I add, hurriedly. "I meant we should just pick whatever. We just have to get through the assignment, anyway."

"Get through it?" she repeats, shock oozing from every word. She gawks at me like I have two heads.

"Yeah," I say, bluntly. "Get through it. Were we not planning on getting a good grade or...?"

"Obviously, but then we should pick something we like so it'll be easier."

"I mean, but then why not pick something we're good at instead?"

She rolls her eyes at me—rolls her eyes! "Just so we can 'get through it,' right?"

She asks it sarcastically, but I nod anyway because, yeah, what's wrong with that? School is a simple input-output system. The best way to get ahead, to get a good output, is to learn how to study and how to produce good work. Whether I *like* what I'm doing or not doesn't directly relate to how good of a grade I get. At least that's been my experience, anyway. There's nothing wrong with working on something only because you're good at it.

"Okay." She shrugs, pushing her chair back an inch so she can fold her arms across her chest. "So. Okay. Let me tell you my idea, and then you tell me yours. After, we can just pick based on which one we both think we can get a good grade with."

I shrug too. "Fine with me."

She wrinkles her nose, peering over its roundness to her notes on the table. When her eyes catch sight of the words, she frowns as if she can't wrap her head around what she wrote. Then, it clicks. "Oh! Yeah, this would be good," she says, suddenly lighter. "Okay, so, we need two different media, right? How about we do, like, an animated video and a song? It's essentially a music video, but I think Ms. Kay will allow it depending on the subject matter."

"What's the subject matter?"

"I was thinking the history of the school. Didn't people get lobotomized here?"

"Oh ... Did they?"

She taps her chin as she thinks. "It's a rumor because obviously they'd never say, but it used to be part of a women's hospital in the 1940s. You know where the gym is? They say that area was part of a larger building that's since been torn down. That's fucked up, huh?" She cringes. "But it might be something cool to look into. Like, we could do a performance piece where, um, we paint our faces with different size holes." And she touches her forehead. "It'll be kinda nasty, but whatever. It'll get us a good grade because we'll be different. Guaranteed no one else will do a project as creative."

"Different" isn't the word I would use, but I keep quiet, absorbing all Patricia said and all she is. She waits for a reaction, but the only thing I can think is, full offense, is she serious? This would never work—it's *too*...too ridiculous. It's exactly what I'd expect from someone who wears so many damn bangles. There's no way I'm going to be swindled into making this some passion project instead of something we can actually do well on.

"I don't know...," I say eventually, trying to sound polite. "But I'm down. It's whatever. Let's just go with it."

She frowns, clearly unimpressed. Why's she so mad? Shouldn't she be happy I'm going along with her idea?

Suddenly, I feel something on the desk vibrate and, like a reflex, my hand reaches for my phone. I swipe for it, but my finger rushes it over the edge of the desk before I can grab it. The phone clanks against the classroom tile but doesn't get scratched as it slides to the corner of my shoe.

I dip down and snatch it, dusting it off against my sweatshirt. My finger brushes the sensor and for a split second, the screen lights up and all I can see is the poster. It's all Patricia can see, too. She tilts her head, trying to read the words from her side of the desk. "A poetry slam?" she asks, and then stifles a laugh. A laugh! Who does this girl think she is? "*You're* into poetry?"

I shouldn't even be mad that she's saying it like it's the most incredulous thing in the world, because, yeah, the idea of me liking poetry is ridiculous. Actually, the idea of anyone liking poetry is ridiculous when you take into account how inconsequential it all is. Like, what is anyone going to do with poetry? It might look good on the hobbies and extracurriculars part of a résumé, but that's about it. And let's be honest: No one even reads those sections.

Patricia smirks like she's figured me out and suddenly all my behavior makes sense to her—as if this is the reason I didn't automatically agree to her lobotomy music video, and not that it's genuinely a baseless idea. "We can do a poetry thing if you want," she offers.

"I don't want to do a poetry thing," I bite back. "We'll just stick with your idea. The lobotomy song."

She snorts. "Lobotomy song."

"Um, unless you have another idea?"

"Why're you trying to come for me like you actually helped me with this brainstorm session, though?" she says pointedly, and then nods to my phone. "If you're not interested in poetry, then why are you looking at a poster for a poetry slam?"

"I'm—ugh." I glance at the poster one last time before turning my phone back over on the desk. Patricia still has her arms folded as she watches, judges, more like. As if I'm the irrational one. She should know I'm the sensible one in my family—I'm the one who stayed and didn't dash my hopes, my parents' hopes, out the door because of iambic pentameter or whatever.

"My brother...," I start saying, but the words sound so awkward on my tongue. I haven't said "my brother" out loud in ages. It almost sounds like it echoes, like it reverbs around the room and into the street, like it can reach my parents wherever they are. And I'm too scared to say any more. I'm too angry.

When I don't elaborate, she prods, "Does your brother... do poetry?"

"Yeah, he does," I say with misplaced bravado. There's nothing to be proud of here.

Patricia gestures to my phone again. "So what, then? Are you going to his show, or... When is it? This week?"

My hand tenses on my phone as I pull it back, away from Patricia's gaze. Of course I'm going to go, just to see if this is really Sam and ask him if all this was worth it, but when I picture myself walking into the venue, staring up at the stage—no, I can't do it. Can I? My parents will find out somehow—Mom will have a dream or a premonition or some shit—and I'll get in trouble. They'll think things; things like, I'm supposed to be the good one now and how could I? Things like, I'm the only one they have left and how could I?

Patricia doesn't understand that. She's not in my family and she wasn't there, so how could she know? That's why she pries.

"Can't" is all I say. "Anyway—"

"Why not? He's your brother. I'm sure—"

"It's not a big deal. Anyway, if we—"

"But, like, he's your *brother*."

"Okay, but is he *your* brother?" I nearly snap. "Don't you know how to mind your own business?" My voice is louder than I intend it to be. A few boys nearby hiss, holding their fists to their mouths as they croon "oooh!" and "shiiiit!" at my sudden outburst. Ms. Kay even looks over from her desk, concerned and ready to tell me to take a deep breath. But I don't want to *breathe*. I want to sigh and scream and cry and rub my face until this itchy, prickly, heavy feeling goes away. The frustration creeps up my spine and heats up my cheeks, burning my eyes until I can't take it anymore. I get up and rush out of the classroom.

My feet are slow at first and then fast while I race down the hallway. I've never left class like this before, and every straight-and-narrow bone is telling me to just suck it up and go back. Now that I'm out and away from the classroom, I realize I don't want to cry at all. The hotness in my face and dryness in my throat doesn't feel like it's beckoning tears. It just burns and burns, and it makes me mad. Mad at myself, mad at my parents, mad that I have to keep it together. Mad that the reason I have to keep it together is for fucking Sam and his—his everything.

I make it to the hallway outside the girls' washroom before my good sense kicks in and I stop. My feet slow and stick to the tile underneath them. My mind clears. "What the hell...," I utter to myself once the realization I skipped class sets in. This is so unlike Sophie. It's so unlike Ada, too.

And all because Patricia asked if I would go to the Poetry Slam? I'm going anyway, so what's my problem?

The hallway is quiet save for the sounds of seniors in the cafeteria around the corner. I drag myself to the café and slip into the tail end of a bench full of boys playing dominoes. They yell and laugh and throw things at each other, not realizing I've settled into the corner. One boy slams down his double three so hard the entire table shakes and the boys erupt in a new wave of crowing and cheering. I've only played dominoes once and I sucked.

Actually... Sam let me play with him and his friends, but they were already so good at strategically counting the tiles, predicting each other's next move, that there's no way I stood a chance. The boy who slammed his double three looks a bit like one of Sam's old friends. I think his name was Kofi. He soaks up the attention from the other boys around him as they crow and holler in awe of his skill. Maybe this boy is as good as Kofi, counting tiles and calling, *"Why don't you drop that three-blank now, fam?"* before their fingers touch the tile.

My phone screen lights up again with the Poetry Slam poster. God, I really can't stop looking at it. This is too much. I have so many things to do, so many things to think about, and here I am staring at this poetry thing. Looking at the address like I'm going to do something about it.

I hear Patricia's voice in my head: *"Are you going to his show?"*

But then I hear Dad's voice: "*Don't you* dare."

I shut my eyes for a second. Two seconds. The sounds of the cafeteria amplify around me, like roars or cheers in a crowd. In my mind, I'm at the entranceway of 2020 Brick Avenue. The lights will be low and the only thing that guides me forward will be the dull, static burn of the stage. A large man will stop me and, amid the venue buzz, hold out his wrist like he wants to check my wristband. I'll have one and I'll show it to him. He'll be distrusting because I look so young, but he'll step aside and wave me in. The smell of alcohol and secret smoke will hit me. People will be lined up around the walls, crammed into booths, crowded by the bar, all waiting for the show to start. There'll be nowhere to sit, of course, so I'll try to hide somewhere in the middle, but someone will see me and coax me forward. There's more room at the front, they'll say, and even though I'll protest, they'll urge me through the crowd. Every single person I'll try to hide behind will push me forward until there I am, right at the front of the stage.

The lights will come on then. The host will come out, this gangly-looking girl whose shoulders and knees jut out in all directions. She'll grin and wave, hyping the crowd, and they'll holler and shout back. Everyone will be so excited about this poetry thing. Anxiety will build in my chest as she introduces the first act. It'll be him; I know it will. I won't be able to hear when she says his name, but I'll know when the hazy blue lights that take over the stage disappear, he and I will be standing in front of one another. For the first time in years, we'll be standing face-to-face.

But when the lights come up, it's someone else. It's just another imposter, like always.

My eyes shoot open. I'm still in the cafeteria at school. The sounds of 2020 Brick Avenue melt into the laughs of the boys beside me as they whip dominoes back and forth at each other. One of them gets decked in the forehead, but he laughs the loudest.

CHAPTER SEVEN

I TALK; JUSTIN WRITES. HE doesn't look at me while he scribbles notes, instead focusing on the page, brows pulled together in a quiet frustration that is more distracting than he realizes. In fact, everything about him is disarming. Words are spilling out of my mouth about cross-cultural kids and how they navigate and identify with their first and second cultures, but in reality, I'm way too focused on the intensity in his face and how jarring it is against the backdrop of my kitchen. Because that's where we are: my house.

Somehow, by some act of God, Justin is in my house while we prep pros and cons for debate. Mom and Dad were already pissed about me skipping yesterday, so I asked them about having a friend over to study with. They were almost peak mad anyway, so when Justin showed up, daring to be both a boy and not Nigerian, they were past the point of cussing me. It was too late. All my dad could do was give a resigned sigh, ask Justin what his parents do for a living after spotting the Mercedes, and begrudgingly let him in.

"Time," Justin says. He's not even looking at a clock so I don't know how he knows it's already been five minutes.

I reach for his notes but he pulls them away from me across the dining room table. The one condition of him being here is that he can't go upstairs and we have to sit in the open-concept dining room. Behind Justin, I can see Dad's head bobbing in the distance as he watches TV in the family room. Every now and then, he glances over just to make sure we're still sitting on opposite ends of the table. And not touching.

"That was good," he says. When I reach for the book again, he moves it away from me. "Want me to read it back to you?"

"I could just read it myself."

He tsks, as if I can't read or something, and brings the book up to his face just as I fling my pencil at him. It ricochets off the back of the notebook and falls back to the table. Dad's ears perk up at the sound and he cranes his neck to look at me.

"I only took down main points that I think could be

useful for bigger arguments," he says from behind the book. "So far you said no, cross-cultural kids can't be appropriators, and also can the definition of cross-culture include a mash-up of the two, etcetera—"

"No one says etcetera in real life—"

"My mom does."

"Yeah, but she's a TV celebrity," I say, and he nods because yeah, true. "You know, my dad was hardcore watching her show the other day, so I'm actually surprised he didn't see the resemblance when you walked in."

Justin moves the book away from his face, frowning. "What resemblance?"

"You and your mom, obviously."

Confusion bores into his eyes. He considers my words like I told him something weird. "Oh, I guess" is all he says. It's so unlike him; I half expected him to say he actually looks more like his aunt and if I'd met her, I'd know. Instead, he dives back into his notes. "You mentioned something really cool about, um, cultural appropriation that I think we should keep. Um, 'If a child is born from two parents of a certain culture, but they happen to be living in another country, they are immediately immune from these pre-conceptions because there is no dominant adoption—this is the crux of what cultural appropriation is. There is no appropriating what you really are.' Yeah." We lock eyes over the book and I am startled, looking away like I'd just been caught staring. Suddenly, my heart is beating so fast and so loud that I'm sure my dad can hear it from where he is.

Justin nods coolly, setting the book down. "Yeah, it's good. I think you have a lot of cool situational references. Like, the Anglicized names thing is pretty legit."

"I need to work on it more," I tell him with a sigh. "It's so hard to articulate what I want to say . . ." I have wild ideas about explaining what it means to be one person operating with two different names in different spaces—a Nigerian name in Nigerian spaces, an English name in English spaces—but it feels weak to me. I don't know what I want to say, and what's worse is I don't know how to say what I feel.

I sigh again and lean forward on my elbows. I must have shifted too far out of my dad's peripheral because he sits up straighter immediately. He calls to me in Igbo and I hate when he does this because he knows I don't understand. Like, he *knows* that, right? All it sounds like to me is "something something studying something abi?" Luckily, something loud happens on the TV and his attention is diverted for a hot second. He's being so embarrassing. This is why I never have friends over!

Justin glances over his shoulder before turning back to me. "What'd he say?" he whispers.

"Uh," I clear my throat and get ready to lie. "Um . . . he . . . he hates you, so. He just said he hopes we're actually studying."

He snickers. "He hates me because he doesn't think we're studying?"

"No, he hates you because you're a boy and he thinks you're disturbing my studies."

"But we're debate partners."

I snicker too. "And so?"

The doorbell rings and just like that, the smile on my face wipes clean. "Who is that?" I hiss, looking over my shoulder. Unexpected house visits are another reason I tend not to invite anyone over. Extended family come by whenever they feel like it, which is cool sometimes and uncool other times. This—when I'm boldly seated in the middle of the dining room with Justin—is the latter.

Dad walks by me to the door. He says something else in Igbo and I go on pretending to understand. I don't know if I do it to save face in front of Justin or what—it's not like he knows or cares whether I can understand it. The whole thing has me feeling pitiful, but all that self-pity is rammed back in its place when I hear Tayo's voice loudly greet my dad at the door. Now all I feel is panic, panic, panic.

"Tayo, Tayo," Dad laughs heartily as he smacks him on the shoulder. My dad's meaty hand is no match for Tayo's broad but skinny stature. It weighs him down like a sack. "How are you? How are your parents?"

Tayo laughs while he wiggles his way out from Dad's

grasp. "They're good. I came to pick up meat for my mom, actually."

"Shaki," Dad says and Tayo nods. "I know, I know," Dad goes on, wiggling his eyebrows at Tayo. "Your mom is making that her famous shaki stew. I know."

Tayo laughs again, this time boisterously, at how ridiculous Dad is being. Tayo's mom's assorted meat stew is bomb. It's a well-known fact in the community among the kids, but we don't ever mention it to our parents. The second one of our mothers knows that we like another auntie's stew, it's over. They'll try to out-stew each other and only the kids will suffer.

"Are they preparing for Genevieve's wedding?" Dad asks him. "Come to think of it, are *you* preparing for Genevieve's wedding?"

Tayo pops an invisible collar and I'm so embarrassed I have to turn back around. I snatch Justin's notebook from under his nose and bury my face in it, pretending to be fully engulfed in his notes. It doesn't help. I still hear when Tayo puts on his accent and says, "Uncle, na Genny dey marry so, but that party na for me."

Oh my godddd. My forehead meets the table with incredible force. Incredible.

Dad cackles his infamous cackle. "Ezi-okwu, nwa m! Yes, o, who else will teach us how to azonto?" I don't even need to look up to know Dad is trying the dance move right now. My secondhand embarrassment becomes firsthand. It transmutes through the air.

"Oh my god," I groan, lifting my head from the table. I call over my shoulder into the foyer, "Dad, azonto is so old now. No one does that anymore."

"Ah-beg, what do you know?" Dad teases. "Even when your mates were doing azonto, could you?"

Tayo laughs especially hard at that. They approach from down the hall and I can hear Tayo's heavy shuffle slow to an uneasy stop when he sees Justin. Panic and pure anxiety creep up my spine so much that I have to roll my shoulders to shake some of it out. I don't need to see Tayo's face to know he's confused and shocked. I'm surprised to hear him speak up as he rounds the table. "Hey, Justin, right?" There is no suspicion in his voice. The lack of suspicion makes me suspicious, but that may be because I've watched too many Nigerian movies. "You guys are studying?" he asks.

Dad looks at Justin for confirmation so he nods right away. "Y-yeah, just studying. For debate."

Tayo nods too like he's content with the answer. Then, he turns to me. "Ada, did Chioma text you? Did she tell you?"

"No, tell me what?"

He frowns. "Yo, check the group chat sometimes. Read it when you can and then we can talk." The way he says *talk* sounds like he's air quoting it. He gives me a sly smile even though he knows I'm not in on whatever it is he's referring to. "Uncle," he says to my dad, "which freezer is the meat in?"

"Eh heh, come, let me show you." Dad waves Tayo over and they disappear around the corner to the kitchen.

There's a beat of silence where I don't know what to say to Justin. He is staring at his notebook extra hard, his eyebrows twisting with all his thoughts. Nervously, I open and close my mouth a few times before I finally settle on: "Sorry about my dad. A-and I didn't know Tayo was coming."

Justin cracks a small smile. "It's all good. It's, uh, yeah."

"People drop by all the time sometimes," I go on, the words spilling out of my mouth like water. "It's—like, I normally don't have people visit because, you know, at any time ... family."

He raises an eyebrow. "You and Tayo are related?"

"Oh, no, no," I say. "He's *like* family. Our parents all know each other. He's like a cousin friend. But, like, not blood related."

He nods at once and says, "Got it." I want to launch into another string of explanations fueled only by my anxiety and mad desperation. I can't tell what Justin's thinking. Did I lose him the second my dad and Tayo started speaking in pidgin? Or did I lose him when my dad started dancing? "Can I ask you a question?" he says and my heart stops for a split second. I nod, bracing myself for the absolute worst. But then he asks, "Who's Ada?" and I just stop.

"Who's Ada?" I repeat right away, doing little to hide the incredulousness in my voice. He waits while I wrap my head around the question. It takes me a second to realize no one's called me that before in front of him. No one calls me that at school. As far as he's concerned, I'm just Sophie. I've known Justin since middle school and he's only ever known me as Sophie—Sophie who excels at whatever she does, Sophie who is unwavering all the time. Not Sophie who transforms into Ada the second she gets within an inch of another Nigerian person. Not this Sophie.

"That's—that's me," I tell him finally. "That's my name."

He glances away, contemplating what I said. "I've known you forever and I had no idea you had two names."

"Don't take it any kind of way. My family calls me that. It's my native name," I say. "Ada. Adanna."

"Say it again."

"Ada."

"Ada?"

"Hmm, no. Ah-*da*. Stronger on the 'd' sound, less on the 'ah.'"

"Ada?"

"Close enough," I concede.

"Cool. It's pretty," he says, and my face fucking ignites. This is the stuff my successful lawyer and executive team future is made of. I bite back a smile and nod repeatedly because I don't know what else to say besides "thank you."

Then he says, "You probably get this a lot from, I don't know, people like my dad, but does it mean anything?"

I choke on a laugh. "Why are you throwing your dad under the bus like this?"

"When I tell you we went to Mexico and he embarrassed me so much I still have nightmares, though."

"I bet he just gave you another Mercedes to make up for it," I tease.

He glances away, raking his hands one after the other through his hair, and I entertain the extremely depressing thought that I might be right. "So, what does it mean?" he asks again.

"It means 'father's daughter'...," I say. Father's daughter, father's heart. That was me and Sam. Obinna. The memory of Mom explaining it to us comes out of nowhere, like a rush from the depths of my mind. She says we are named after her father and her mother, but I secretly believe we are named this way because Dad loves us more than anything in the world. He wanted to make sure everyone knew how much he loves his daughter and how much he loves his son.

His son.

God, like, I wonder if they still think about Sam. This entire time, they've warned me not to, but do they sometimes wonder where he went? Why he left? Honestly, I bet they'd be surprised to learn the son who was always all business all the time, always studying to become an engineer, chose to run away because he wanted to be a poet. Something so impractical, something so unlike the Sam of our memory. Or maybe just my memory. Maybe they don't think about Sam at all. Maybe we're all better off for it.

Justin notices my smile fade and concern replaces whatever curiosity he had. "I can still call you Sophie if you want," he tells me hurriedly. My mind tries to pull away from Sam, but I can't completely and I hate it. He's infiltrated my memories so much and all because of this stupid Poetry Slam.

"It's fine. Either is okay," I mutter. "I was just thinking about something else."

He frowns. "About what?"

"About, um..." I hate how close the words are and how badly I cannot say them. I wouldn't *dare*. Dad is in the kitchen with Tayo. I can hear their footsteps, their casual conversation, their light laughter. The second my mind even goes back to Sam, I'm paralyzed with a prickly hot fear that rattles my heart. He betrayed us—he betrayed our parents. Why should I want to talk about him? What's the point?

Still, I reach for my phone and pull up the poster. I slide the device across the table for him to take a look. "I found this on that page you sent me," I say, my voice dropping to a whisper. "It's for this event, this Poetry Slam."

He looks at it without picking up the phone. "Cool."

I shake my head. "No, not cool."

"Not cool, got it."

"My—ugh." I clear my throat and lean in a bit closer. "My brother…he's going to be at this event, but I haven't…we haven't seen him…I mean." I swallow, nervously, anger rising, and push back from the table. My eyes stay trained on the phone. The screen dims and I tap it again before the image disappears. "It might not even be him, you know?" I mumble, thinking of the times I thought I saw him in the past.

"Backtrack," he says. His voice is softer now and I'm thankful he caught on that this is a touchy subject. He leans toward me across the table. I inch forward too. "You haven't seen him in how long?"

"Almost six years," I whisper. "He just left the day before I started middle school. No one really knows why, but—" I stop talking immediately at the sound of rustling around the corner. No footsteps follow, so after a moment, I continue even quieter, "But suddenly, he's, like, a poet or something. He probably ran away because he wanted to do poetry, or, I don't know. My parents, my family, no one talks about him anymore."

"Weird."

"It's like he's a ghost."

Justin says, "But he's not," and nods to my phone on the table. The screen nearly dims but I tap it again. Maybe it's my imagination, but Sam's figure on the poster stands out more than before. I hate it and I hate him and I hate this.

I flip the phone over so it's facedown. "I have to go and see if it's really him, but I'm so, *so*, s-so mad." Saying it out loud makes my hands tremble. I hate how Sam left, I hate how he didn't even look back, I hate that I don't even know the real story—but I hate most of all how he left me to fill a two-person-size void. How he broke the path for me before I could even take my first step. How I will be in law school carrying both our weights while he gets to write fucking po-e-try.

Anger bubbles up through my arms and I'm tempted to grab my phone and throw it. I swallow once, twice, to try and push it away, but there it is, knocking its way back. Justin notices. I almost expect him to reach for my arm and give it a comforting squeeze, so I stay perfectly still. I am paralyzed by the fear that Dad might walk back here any second and see Justin staring so intently at me—and I'm paralyzed at the thought of Tayo seeing too.

I am fearful of everything: seeing Sam, hearing his voice, finding out the real reason he left, learning that it might have something to do with us. Or me. Maybe the worst part isn't that he thought he was good enough to leave us; maybe it's that he left and he never looked back. Didn't even care about the sister he was leaving behind.

Justin looks away for a second. He's at a loss for words and I'm afraid if I say anything else, I may start to cry in front of him. So I say the only thing I can think of, the only thing that grounds me amid my confusion: "Come with me."

Justin raises his eyebrows, intrigued. "Actually?"

I wish I could grab him by the arms and plead properly. "Please? I can't ask anyone else because they're—it's ... it's complicated."

"I get it," he says, even though I'm not sure he does. "I'm down to go. If you're scared."

"Understatement." I try to joke, crack a smile, but it feels flat and disingenuous. *If* I'm scared? I'm terrified. "It's tomorrow evening," I say.

"Okay," Justin answers right away. "So I'll pick you up, then."

I open my mouth, a "yes, okay" at the tip of my tongue, but then I see Tayo standing in the doorway and I swallow the words. He purses his lips together and nods a bit as he ducks by the table to the doorway with two hefty bags of frozen meat. He doesn't make eye contact with me as he goes and that's how I know he must have heard everything.

CHAPTER EIGHT

HIS NAME IS AYODELE MICHAELS, but in our cousin-only group chat, Chioma says Genny says we can call him Ayo. From pictures, he looks like he's been an extra in a Skeleboy music video before. Actually, I swear I've seen him in "House Party 2," that fifteen-minute extended music video Skeleboy and his entourage filmed a few years ago, unless there's some other sunglass-wearing, close-shaven, tight-clothes-wearing assistant somewhere. To be honest, there probably is. Everything about Ayo's pictures screams Lagos chic.

He is flying in today after a week in London finalizing the groomsmen's native clothes, so after school Tayo and I wait at Genny and Chioma's place. Blessing is there too.

Their living room, usually ripe with the sound of Nigerian news blaring from some inconsistent cable channel, is silent now, save for the sound of Chioma's nails clicking and swiping through any pictures of Ayodele Michaels she finds on a Google image search. There are a few pictures of him tagging behind Skeleboy and a slew of pretty Nigerian women, and Chioma squeals and giggles because this guy—this guy who's so close to Skeleboy—is about to be in. Her. House.

Blessing is the first to break the silence as she raises her phone, turning the screen around, though none of us can see from where we're all seated around the room. "Gossip sites are saying the wedding will be huge," she tells us. "They know Skeleboy's assistant is coming *and* a few sites mention me. See? 'Blessing Chukwudi, responsible for several high-end weddings, set to blow the roof off Skeleboy and Genevieve's Toronto nuptials.'" She touches her forehead, carefully padding her skin in distress. "Ah-ah. I don't know how they're finding all this out."

Chioma snorts, her gaze fixed on Blessing. "You really don't know?" I hear the words Chioma isn't saying: "*As if your big mouth had nothing to do with it.*"

Blessing plays coy and, with a shrug, she says, "How would I? Genny's socials have gained a lot of followers, and besides, we know the I-Just-Got-Back crowd loves her."

"Mmhmm."

Despite all the banter and excitement about Skeleboy's

assistant, my mind is at 2020 Brick Avenue. In two hours, I'll be down there for the Poetry Slam, and I will see Sam, the real Sam, for the first time since he left. My emotions are high and low, deep and shallow, all over the place. I'm mad but also scared and a little excited. I'm anxious, apprehensive, skeptical. Bitter. I am nervous because I have never been in a club before.

Tayo lets out a plain laugh from beside me. I turn just as Chioma shows him a picture on her phone, but the moment he catches me looking, he falls back into his seat and avoids my gaze. I haven't felt the same vibe from him since he left my house yesterday. He keeps turning on his phone screen and swiping through a multitude of apps. I watch his hunched-over profile, his eyes focused on the screen. He doesn't say anything to me, and I kind of hate it because I'm freaking out inside and I miss the calmness of his voice. I should be able to tell him about the club, but he's acting so sketchy that it makes me not want to talk to him at all.

Genny enters the room, her lush silk robe flowing behind her. Her native name, Isioma, is embroidered on the back in cursive red lettering. She crosses the room to the window that faces the street. Guaranteed she only does that so the robe will sweep dramatically in front of our faces. I can't even be mad because the robe is a gift from Skeleboy, and if my rich boyfriend bought me a silk robe with my name in fine stitching, nothing could stop me from wearing it at home, to the store, to school, everywhere. "He's not here yet?" she asks, poking her head past the blinds.

Tayo and Chioma are engrossed with their phones—although I'm sure Chioma is pretending at this point so she doesn't have to talk to Genny—so I pipe up, "Nope."

Her eyes are marred with uncertainty. "These people and their Naija time," she utters. Her voice is shaky and lacks its usual confidence.

"He'll be here," Blessing cuts in, getting to her feet. She joins Genny at the window. "He knows how important all this is to you and your reputation."

I watch Genny pull her robe tighter around her shoulders as she turns back to the window. "He better. Does he think this is his Lagos or something? If he thinks he's going to derail my wedding—"

"Ooooh my god," Chioma cuts in, groaning. This time she looks at Genny, rolling her eyes. "You said he said he'd be here at four forty-five. It's four forty-two. Please relax."

Genny turns on her heel, an accusatory long, manicured finger pointed at her own chest. She scowls. "You're telling *me* to relax? Chioma?"

Chioma sits up straighter, her long twists falling over her shoulder. I can hear her pent-up frustration from how she takes a deep breath. Tayo raises a hand and stretches. "Let's all shut up, let's all relax," he calls out. "Genny, if he doesn't show up by five, then we can just tell him to come some other time."

Blessing lets out a huff and crosses her arms. "Which other time? We have a schedule to stick to. Please, these boys better not be coming up in here to ruin everything I've worked hard to build. Does he think I got Tiwa Savage to do a video shoutout for Uncle Shola's second wedding by being this lax?"

"Oh, whoa, damn," Tayo chortles. "I thought this was about Genny."

"It is, it *is* about Genny," Genny cuts in, staring between the two of them. "Listen, Adetayo, you may have time because all you have is high school, but I have a *life*—I don't have time to work around his schedule. Ah-beg, is it not my wedding?" And she kisses her teeth so loud that I am less offended and more in awe of her tenacity.

Tayo chuckles. When I look at him, his smile disappears so fast that it makes me question if it was there in the first place. Damn, he's being petty. What does he think he knows that has him so mad?

The sound of a car horn vibrates through the living room and Genny presses her face against the polished glass to look outside. "Finally," she gasps, and sweeps back across the room. That can only mean one thing: Ayo is here. Skeleboy's assistant is going to be inside this room in a second. We get to our feet, teetering back on our heels or fidgeting with our fingers, waiting impatiently for the doorbell to ring. Chioma adjusts her bra. Blessing runs her hands through her hair. But when Tayo smooths a hand down his face, over his cheekbones and freshly shaved chin, I want to laugh so bad because he's radiating such nervous energy. I chuckle, my voice low, "This isn't your marriage meeting."

He gives a faint smile. And that's it.

I frown. "What is it?"

"What's what?"

"Why are you being so weird? Did I say something to you?" I ask.

He scoffs, glancing away. "Not everything is about you," he says. I feel that one in my chest.

"I never said—"

"Yes, o, he's right!" Genny cuts in, clapping her hands together loudly. Whatever nervousness I thought she was feeling has subsided. Wedding Genny is back. "Don't bring your personal problems into this house right now." She takes a deep breath and touches the edges of her hair tenderly, making sure it's still slicked down and perfect. "Please, nobody embarrass me. Especially you, Chioma."

Chioma's aura crackles like a live wire. I can practically feel the sparks fly off her. She says nothing; instead, she turns to face me almost mechanically, eyes flaring with muted shock, and she just stares. I want to laugh again, but the last thing I need is the wrath of Genny and Blessing to rain down on me in this living room. And definitely not right when we're about to meet Skeleboy's assistant, too.

The doorbell finally rings and Genny stares at Chioma until she gives in and goes to answer it. As soon as Chioma pulls it open, Ayodele Michaels walks in looking just like how he looks in all his pictures: sunglasses even though we're indoors, red Gucci blazer, black Gucci pants, polished Louis Vuitton shoes, and a phone glued to his ear. He talks fast, saying a whole lot of nothing in that way I've seen the guys do in Nigerian movies. He even says, in his "I was educated abroad" accent, that slight British twinge that so many famous Nigerians have adopted: "Yeah, uh, I just got off an international flight, you know…I'm in Canada right now." I nudge Tayo against my better judgment, but he doesn't even react.

"Ayo, you're late," Blessing says just as Ayo is hanging up his phone. He looks at her, smiles, and pulls off his shades to reveal tired eyes from a long flight. "I said you're late," she reiterates. Her voice is all business. I gotta hand it to her; she's really taking this wedding planner stuff seriously. "We keep to time here, you know."

"We don't," Chioma coughs out. Luckily, Genny doesn't hear.

Ayo grins and stares around at the entranceway, taking in the large decorative mirror beside him and a colorful chalk drawing of Auntie and Uncle, Chioma and Genny's parents, wearing their finest agbada and george. He steps closer to the drawing as if evaluating them before setting his eyes on Blessing and Genny. "Ah-beg, no vex. Genevieve, you are just looking...somehow. So beautiful," he says. His right hand stashes his sunglasses in his blazer pocket while his left hand clutches his phone. I can see the case a bit clearly now: It's Gucci, too.

Genny smiles genuinely, and it reminds me she can be sweet when she wants to be. She's been so on edge since wedding preparations amped up. "Ayo, Ayo," Genny croons. It's times like these where her accent becomes more prominent. I can hear that slight Igbo coloring that comes in and out when she talks to her parents or when she meets other Nigerian people. Other *Nigerian* Nigerian people, anyway. She doesn't always talk like this with us. "Please, I don't have your time today. Where is my list? Blessing said you would have it. Come meet my sister and our friends." She guides him into the house and he looks around, surveying like he's putting together a floor plan in his mind.

When Ayo finally sees us standing awkwardly in a row in the living room, he stops in his tracks. He first turns to Chioma as she tries her best to stand up taller. She's already taller than my 5'6". My dad would say she should "sofri to dey grow" otherwise boys won't want to date her, but he's mad old-school. Chioma doesn't care. She wears her height well and she's already had two secret boyfriends. I could never. "This is the sister?" he asks Genny, who nods right away. "Ah, okay, okay. And she is technically the maid of honor?"

"Yes," Genny replies while giving Chioma a quick once-over with her eyes. "She fits the height requirement."

"Height requirement?" I whisper.

"Yes, I see," Ayo hums, taking a step forward and extending his hand for her to shake. "Ayodele Michaels."

"Chioma," she answers.

"He-ey, pretty name, pretty girl," he chuckles. Chioma smiles pleasantly but the second he's turned away, she looks at me like we're breaking the fourth wall in a comedy. We both do our best not to laugh. "And who is this?"

Ayo saunters his way in front of me. He smiles, extending his hand in the same manner, and I take it. "This is our family friend, like our cousin here," Genny explains, following behind him. "Adanna Nkwachi."

"Ada-nna," Ayo repeats with that same hearty chuckle. "This is good. It's good."

He moves on to Tayo. Immediately, he reaches out for a full handshake, the kind that my dad does when him and my uncles get together, complete with a full backhand slap and middle finger snap. Tayo reciprocates and Ayo laughs, clasping Tayo's hand. "Ah-ah! This boy—you know, you resemble Femi well-well."

Tayo lights up at that. He forgets he's not talking to me

and nudges me in the arm, bouncing excitedly on the spot. "You hear? You hear?" he snickers. I fake choke and he says, "Jealousy dey worry you, o."

Ayo cackles at this, squeezing Tayo's hand tighter. "You sabi pidgin? It's good—God is good."

"And you know my girl, Blessing," Genny says, gesturing to Blessing, who is hanging by the entranceway. "She's the main one you've been talking to."

"Yes. How could I forget?" Ayo smirks.

Genny makes Chioma bring a beer from the fridge while we sit down in the living room. I check my phone: It's getting closer to when Justin said he would pick me up. I am as nervous for the Poetry Slam as I am for Justin showing up at Chioma's house. I can't think about it right now. Skeleboy's assistant is sitting across from me drinking beer. Oh my god.

Ayo leans forward, the beer bottle hanging lazily in one hand while the other holds tight to his phone. Genny says Skeleboy—Femi—specifically sent him to help Blessing with the wedding arrangements here since he's busy on tour. He wanted to make sure everything was planned without a hitch, and he also wanted to make sure that Genny and Blessing had as much help as possible.

"Okay, so," Ayo begins casually. "I need to see the venue so I can make suggestions on where . . . you know, the design, how the design is going to be, basically."

Blessing nods feverishly. "Of course. You'll like the venue. It's very spacious."

"I know," he chuckles. "I must like it. In fact, Femi is the one who said that I should just be here observing because the wedding is Genevieve's wedding. It's not my own." He laughs louder at that. Tayo and I join in, unsure if we sound a bit too amused. Chioma slouches further in her seat. Out of all of us, she's had to live with Genny during this whole process, so naturally the humor has been sucked dry for her. "So, okay, let me see the fabric for the aso ebi. And I need to see the menu. Mama Femi is very particular with what she likes in her moin-moin. No corned beef and whole eggs only."

Blessing is already taking notes in a worn-out notebook, but because Genny is Genny, she turns to Chioma, forcing a smile. "Can you write this down too? I don't want to offend Mama."

Without a word, Chioma gestures to Blessing as if to say, "What about her?" but I can tell she doesn't want to make a scene in front of Ayo. Reluctantly, she pulls out her phone and opens a notepad app. "No poor person's moin-moin. Whole eggs, not half," she mumbles as she types.

Ayo smirks. "Your sister is funny, o."

"Eh heh, she's too funny, sef," Genny says with a sneer. "It's not everyday jokes."

"No one is allowed to have any fun. Got it," Chioma

continues, typing. I bite down on my tongue to stop myself from showing any sort of reaction, else Genny's no-nonsense, viper glare will turn on me too.

Blessing raises her pen and doesn't wait to be called on before she speaks. "Can you confirm which relatives we'll have to video in? I don't want the speeches to be ten years long."

Ayo nods right away and brings out his phone. "Yes, yes, I wanted to talk to you about that. Let me write down that I should call, um, Richard. He knows the number."

Tayo raises his hand. "I have a question," he pipes up. Ayo nods at him before taking a gulp of his beer. "Will, uh, will the dancers from the 'Yanga' video be there?"

Genny quickly offers, "Tayo is the dancer boy I told you who knows the choreo," before Ayo begins to nod, heavy and deep. "Eh heh, so it's you I heard about?" he asks.

Tayo inhales sharply and purses his lips to suppress what I'm sure would be a wide, embarrassing grin. He whispers to me, "My moves are internationally known." I give a bit of a shrug, trying to play it cool. I'm getting whiplash from all this back and forth. So suddenly we're cool with each other?

"Right now," Ayo continues, "we're trying to choreograph the intermission performance for the wedding. We want it to be hot, you know, like, so when people see it, they say, 'yes, Skeleboy is getting married abroad.'"

"Good enough for a spot on Bella Naija blog?" Chioma snorts.

Blessing and Genny snap their attention to her, but it's Genny's glare that zones in on Chioma like a heat-seeking missile. If Ayo wasn't here, I'm sure she would've launched herself off the sofa and gone straight for her throat—or worse, her head, ripping out each twist one by one. I bet she's only keeping up appearances because she doesn't want Ayo to tell her future husband that she murdered her own sister. "Of course it will be good enough for Bella Naija, you. Bush. Child," Genny says, pressing into every syllable. "We're already planning the exclusives."

Chioma rolls her eyes. "Amazing." This girl really has no self-preservation skills at all.

Ayo takes another gulp. "Okay, so pictures? What is the fabric pattern?"

Blessing pulls out her phone to find them. I take the time to go through my messages and see if Justin texted me about being close by. So far, nothing. Chioma sends me a text and all it says is: *just make sure I'm cremated pls.*

I'm about to respond—*"save room in the jar"*—when a text notification from Justin cuts through the top half of my screen. He's outside, he says, and writes out Chioma's address asking if it's the right one. It is, so I text back a quick thumbs-up emoji and clasp my phone in my hands. This is it; this is really happening. The excitement of meeting Skeleboy's assistant hasn't taken away the sheer nerves and anxiety about meeting Sam. A tremble runs through my legs as I get to my feet—

"Where are you going?"

Genny saves her weapons for when she needs them and this, me trying to escape in the middle of a coveted wedding planning meeting, is one of those times. Her voice isn't sharp, but it still feels like a blunt smack in the face. She watches me with the full force of her ancestors, staring me down as if I called her a malicious she-goat in front of her husband. Everyone turns to look at me now: Blessing, holding her phone out in Ayo's direction; Ayo, his finger just about to touch the screen; Chioma, buried so far into the sofa that her neck meets her chest; and Tayo, leaned over into his phone with his eyes locked on mine. He doesn't look half as shocked as the others, and I figure it's because he still remembers what he overheard between me and Justin. Whatever that was, anyway.

"I, uh . . . ," I stutter, glancing around. "I have, uh, a thing I gotta go to. Sorry."

"What thing?" Genny asks. "Ah-beg, sit down. You can't go anywhere yet."

I sigh heavily and cast another weary glance to the doorway. "Genny, it's really important. I promised a friend that, uh, I have to study."

Ayo nods in approval. "Let her go, na," he tells Genny. "It's study the girl wants to study."

Tayo crows so loud, "Haaaaa!" that it takes everyone's eyes off me for a split second.

Genny scowls at him. "And what's wrong with you?"

He snickers before he pushes himself upright. "Nothing, nothing," he chuckles, waving away Genny's suspicion. I bolt before anyone changes their mind. My schoolbag is in the foyer under the chalk drawing and I grab for it while I quickly wrestle on my shoes. I see headlights outside. So close yet so far.

I reach for the doorknob and prepare to yell my goodbyes over my shoulder when I hear Tayo, his voice almost cracking at the awkward volume he's projecting. He's speaking loudly on purpose because he wants to get my attention. He wants to make sure I hear when he says, "She's going to study with this oyinbo boy—her boyfriend from school—but it's not just everyday study."

My hand fumbles the doorknob. Suddenly, it's so slippery and I can't get a hold on it. What is Tayo talking about? Justin isn't—he's not my boyfriend!

The damage is as good as done. First, I hear Blessing: "Wait, *another* boy?" Then, Genny's voice sounds out, incredulous and loud, "Excuse me, *what?*" Finally, I hear Ayo's gasp and soft, "Eh heh, oyinbo," as if this now explains a lot for him. But it's Chioma who comes racing into the foyer, mouth in a perfect O shape, as she practically tackles me, pinning me to the door. She's breathing heavy with—excitement? "Oh my god oh my god," she hisses, a manic look in her eyes. "Are you mad? Who is he who is he?"

"He's . . . no one," I stammer, wrestling my way out of her grasp. We get into a fake slap war, her hands trying to slap my hands over and over again, before I eventually shake her off. "He's my friend from school, literally *just* a friend from school."

"That's not what Tayo thinks."

"Well, Tayo is fucking jealous."

Just like magic, Tayo appears over Chioma's shoulder. He's had the worst timing lately. Besides, I'm only saying that because I'm mad at him. How would I know if he's actually jealous? I frown, shaking my head and expecting him to retaliate—call me a foolish goat, say there's nothing to be jealous of, anything—but the hurt and dismissal in his eyes roots me in place. For just a moment, I'm looking at him and he doesn't even bother looking back. He jams his hands into his pockets and turns away, looking like he's going to head back to the living room, but he doesn't. I want to take back what I said right away, and I could, if not for Genny thundering over, slipping between Tayo and Chioma to corner me by the door.

She is amused, a sly curve to her lips, as she watches me. "Adanna," she says, and that's it.

I suppress a groan. "Genny?"

"So," she goes on, folding her hands together. "You're leaving my house, where I asked you to come help me plan my wedding, to go and see a boy. An oyinbo boy," she says after a beat. "To do what? You know I can't let you just leave like this."

"Oh my god, Genny," I sigh. "He's just a friend from school, honestly, and we're for real going to study." I say it so many times that I start to believe the study part. "And you don't even need me here! You have Blessing, you have Ayo, you already picked all the aso ebi months ago."

"You think I don't need you here for emotional support?"

"Genny!"

"Just don't lie to me," she cuts in, her eyes dancing around my face. "I can't lie to your parents, either. You and this boy are just friends, and you're just going to study."

"Yes, yes."

"At his house?" Chioma cuts in, and Genny gasps because she hadn't thought of that.

"No," I tell them. "The, uh, this café. We always go to this café. He drives, so he came to pick me up—guys, I really gotta go."

Genny looks for a moment like she wants to say more, but she reaches around me for the door and unlocks it instead. "Don't have too much fun," she says, and shoos me outside. When I am safely on the other side, she shuts it, and presses her face against the glass so she can watch me get into the car. I skip down the stairs as fast as possible before she changes her mind or decides to play busybody auntie and come out to say hi. She's not even old enough to be my auntie, please!

Justin is in his car watching videos on his phone when I finally slip into the passenger seat. The Benz is always super clean and runs like it's new, even though it's his mom's old car. "Old" being the operative word, though; Justin's dad bought it around three years ago. He's a contractor and ever since middle school, Justin's dad has been going through cars like water through a sieve.

"Debate videos?" I ask, buckling up.

Justin shakes his head absently and after a moment or two, he says, "Spoken word videos. Wanna see?" He tilts the screen toward me but I still need to lean in to get a good look at what's going on. A girl is center stage speaking into a microphone, gesturing with her hands as she tells a story. There are highs and lows in the rhythm to her speech and at times she sounds like she's singing. It's so strange to my ears. I want to hate it because of Sam, but I really don't.

Justin hands me the phone and I bring it closer to my face while he backs out of the driveway and speeds down the road. I'm completely captivated by the inflections, her tone on certain words, and the bounce in her neck when she emphasizes a phrase. How she smiles after a line. How she growls after another. I've never seen anything like it; never heard anything like it.

"Sam is into this? Really?" I mumble to myself, my eyes skirting around the video. I try to imagine Sam up there, rhyming and bouncing from syllable to syllable like a verbal dance. This girl is good, but my breath hitches when I think of Sam, the Sam I knew, doing this, running away and leaving everything for this. There's nothing more I want than to see it for myself now.

CHAPTER NINE

THE STREET IN FRONT OF 2020 Brick Avenue is alive
with ticket holders and attendees looking for their friends
in line. So many eager voices chatter in the distance. People
are talking about who they're most excited to see, but it's
like every time they're about to say a name, I turn away and
focus on something else. I'm scared to hear them say "Obi"
or "Sam," even though I'm about to step foot into a venue
where he'll be performing. My brother, performing. I shuffle forward with the crowd, closer and closer to the main
doors, and take deep calming breaths as we wait.

Oh god, what if I cry or something?

"Are you nervous?"

Justin's voice is unwavering, so solid, and I realize it's

because he has no idea how much I'm panicking. He's so cool being so thoughtful, but the more I think about being nervous, the more nervous I become and not even my regularly scheduled high-profile lawyer fantasy can save me.

"No," I tell him quietly, glancing sideways at the people around us. One girl with hefty spacers looks at me twice like she's seen me before, as though she might see Sam's eyebrows or left dimple on my face and know immediately who I am and what I'm doing here. I look away before she does.

Justin's mouth twists in disbelief because he knows I'm lying. "Not even a little?"

"I don't know."

"Are you nervous because your brother is here, or is it because you're about to enter a room with a bunch of artists?"

The bubble shatters. All my self-importance crumbles as I frown, caught off guard at the question. It shakes me out of my nervousness and into familiar, comforting territory: me disagreeing with Justin on principle. "Um, and why would entering a room of artists bother me?"

"Are you kidding?" he snorts. "You hate illogical things. Like art, which you hate."

"No I don't."

"For sure you do."

"I don't *hate* art," I tell him, and he rolls his eyes. "I don't! I just don't see...the point."

"Same thing."

"Not the same thing," I press on. "It's, like ... not everyone can be Beyoncé, you know? Sometimes it's better to just focus on something legit to save you time. Something important."

"Something like ...," he goes on, thinking. "You wanting to be a baby lawyer."

I snort, pressing a hand to my mouth so I don't burst out laughing. "A *baby* lawyer?"

"We're, like, seventeen and I bet you already know where you want to intern," he teases, and I shut up quick because, okay, so what if I do? Is it a bad thing to be so prepared? I turn away because I know anything I say will just make me sound like the bigger nerd. We shuffle up a bit further in the line.

Suddenly, Justin asks, "Have you ever wanted to be anything other than a lawyer?"

"No," I reply almost immediately. "I mean, there's nothing else I'm good at ... a-and besides, all the things I'm good at kinda fit well with the law path. So I don't see it as a problem."

He shrugs, content with the answer, and glances over his shoulder at the growing crowd. "Sometimes," he utters, slowly, "I feel like I could be an artist. Like a photographer or someone who does weird installations at galleries or something. That'd be pretty sick."

"Well, you could probably get away with it."

He watches me curiously. "What does that mean?"

"Well...y-your mom didn't necessarily follow the most typical career path. Neither did your dad. You have a different example. Meanwhile, my parents basically told me there's only one way to have a good life," I tell him, trying to temper the irritation building in my voice. My parents immigrated here from Nigeria and decided there were only a few ways we could be successful in life. Number one: be a doctor. If you can't be a doctor, defer to number two: an engineer. If an engineer doesn't suit you, you may settle for number three: a lawyer. It's first-gen kid 101 and, as my parents call it, the key to successful living. A good life. There used to be a time when I could joke about it, but the older I get, I become more serious about doing right by my parents. Since Sam left, too, it feels like it's less of a choice and more of a requirement. I *have* to. It might be what my parents expect, but they're right. It's necessary. Too bad Sam couldn't see that.

"I guess so," he says. "That's cool. All I'm saying is maybe there are other ways to live a good life by societal standards. Or even not by societal standards. You don't have to be any one thing. That's so old-school. We're off that shit now."

"Well, of course you'd say that," I sigh. We inch forward a little just as Justin gives me a curious look, prodding me to continue. "I mean, come on," I say. "Your...your dad is a white Canadian. He didn't have to uproot his family and learn a whole new culture and . . . and put his hopes of survival on his kids. He didn't have, like, a whole . . ." I'm forgetting the word, so I gesture as if I'm creating a box in front of me. It's not helping. "Like, he didn't have—pressure. There was no pressure. There was no ancestral pressure to make up for this, this *huge* sacrifice."

Justin nods once, curt. "True. Understood." We don't speak for a second and I am antsy waiting for the time to pass. Maybe there are more reasons than one that we couldn't be together, even in my mind. Sometimes I feel like Justin gets me and I don't need to censor myself around him, but other times, I don't say what I feel because I'm afraid one day it'll just be too much. Words like "ancestral" and "survival" are still swarming in my head as we move up. We're getting closer to the door now. There are only a few people in front of us, only a few people between me and Sam.

"You know," Justin pipes up, glancing over my head a few times. He takes longer than usual to look me in the eye and it makes me feel bad. I didn't mean to make it sound like we're so drastically different that he could never understand me. But we *are* different, and I don't think it's a bad thing to point it out. Differences aren't a bad thing, after all. He says, "You know my mom immigrated here, right? From Hong Kong."

"I know." I watched a special documentary on her that

was filmed three years ago, but he doesn't need to know that.

"Obviously, I'm not saying we're the same. But she was studying to be a physicist at a point."

I gawk. "Are you joking? She's such a good interior designer, though. It's like she invented color theory with how she matches stuff."

He bites back a smile. "Well, she moved here and found her calling in university, interned for a big designer kinda by accident, built up her portfolio, was featured on that Home and Garden thing, got her own show, and long story short, I'm seventeen and I drive a Benz."

"Wow, o-kay, re-lax."

"The point is," he goes on, chuckling. "She got into something she *likes*. And it's paid off a lot for her." I hate that I can see where this is going. He's like a bad infomercial with deep brown eyes and very lush dark hair. "She's happy. That's why she's successful. Not just because she convinces people to put granite counters in the bathroom."

The words "not everyone is like that" are on the tip of my tongue, but I don't say them. I don't know Justin's mom's story, and I'm hesitant to relate it to my parents. She came here young for university and ended up marrying a local. My parents came over together and had to get recertification all over again just to continue their careers. Not every immigrant story is the same, I get that. But I can't listen to him talk about his mom and talk about her happiness as if that's the reality for everyone. It's such a weird divide.

We're one person away from the door when I say, "I can be happy after I get my first degree." In my heart, I want to believe I'm joking, but my voice sounds serious as ever. Honestly, I kinda don't like it.

Justin gives a dry chuckle before we shuffle up again. The fact that there's a bouncer for this event is kinda ridiculous. Who's trying to get into a poetry slam? Do these things get that hype? I think back to the video Justin showed me in the car and remember how the crowd would holler and snap and whistle when the girl said something they identified with. I highly doubt that kind of atmosphere could turn into a full-blown scrap, though.

The bouncer gives us black wristbands with a 2020 insignia on them and says, "The Ballroom is straight ahead that way," while he waves us in. There's a long hallway leading to what must be this event space, but we pass different doors as we go. As we step into The Ballroom, the sounds and the smells of the space assault my senses before I have a chance to see anything. If not for the string lights on the way into the main hall, it'd be pitch-black in here. The further we walk in, the more we can hear voices and see bodies hanging by the bar, by the entrance, by the standing tables. Old-school hip-hop music fills the air. A woman with a beer in her hand laughs loudly in the corner around a group of people. A man in a long pleather coat gestures wildly while he tells a story to another man. I feel so exposed in this space even though no one knows who I am. My steps slow, dragging more and more across the floor as we gravitate to an empty table. I wonder if Sam is somewhere in the crowd, lingering.

Justin looks over my shoulder, scanning the interior like he's never seen anything like it. I let my eyes rest firmly on the tabletop. I'm too scared to make eye contact with anyone. "You okay?" I hear him ask from beside me.

"Yeah," I lie and even fake a smile. "It's just so stuffy in here."

"I'll grab you a water," he says and before I can protest, he disappears through the crowd toward the bar.

I busy myself with my fingers—I can't stop toying with them, flexing them, cracking my knuckles, all of it. I let myself look around the room just once to take in the atmosphere. It's nice in here, really as artsy as I imagined with its black walls and framed mirrors, but it's hard for me to relax. My shoulders are permanently hunched. Not even deep breathing is helping. At any given time, I could run into someone I know. I could run into—Patricia.

Patricia?

Across the room, I see Patricia at another standing table. She's talking to a girl, leaning in and laughing, her signature array of bangles clanging against her wrist. Her laugh is super loud, so loud that her voice carries across the music playing in the background. When she cackles and throws her head back, the girl with her gestures toward my table none too enthusiastically, as if she's weirded out by my staring. And that's when Patricia sees me.

We haven't had a real conversation since I skipped school the other day. She sits in front of me turned all the way to the front and doesn't even say hi anymore. We've been like that for a couple of days, so seeing her now in the middle of this grungy club space is bizarre.

She purses her lips, clearly unimpressed that I'm here, while she marches over to my table with her friend in tow. For a second, I want to play dumb and look away, pretending I didn't see her, but when she comes up to me, she squints so hard into my face that there's no way I could get away with faking. "It *is* you," she gasps.

"It's me . . . ," I mumble, my lips pulling into a straight line.

We stand for a bit, not knowing what else to say to each other. Justin comes back and hands me a cold glass of water. I'm so thankful and so nervous that I start to chug it, hoping the ice-cold liquid will help calm my nerves and also take me the hell away from this awkward situation. All it does is give me a brain freeze at the most inopportune moment.

But when Justin nods to her, uttering a simple, "Patricia, hey, what are you doing here?", I realize the situation may only be awkward for me. They know each other?

"Justin!" Patricia says with a much more genuine smile than she's ever given me. "What are—oh." She glances away, shyly. "Sorry, I didn't know you guys were together."

Justin is quick to say, "Uh, not really." Damn, he couldn't let it sit for a second?

Patricia smirks, shutting her eyes a moment as she nods. "Yeah, yeah, okay," she says with a hint of sarcasm. "Cool." I want to believe she doesn't believe him, that maybe in a past conversation they had together, he mentioned something about me and it doesn't add up with what she's seeing. The thought takes hold in my mind and streams for much longer than it should.

When Patricia smiles, her septum ring peeks out. She sometimes hides it during school hours but it really does suit her. Suddenly, the amount of bangles she wears and her being at this event starts to make sense. She's one of them. She's just like Sam. Artsy, rebellious, maybe irresponsible. Just like him.

The girl who came with her looks at me with a stiff smile and clears her throat loudly to get Patricia's attention. "Oh!" Patricia links her arm with the girl's and says, "This is my girlfriend, Casey. She goes to ESA, the arts school."

Casey sticks out her hand for us to shake, a beautiful henna pattern adorned on her wrist, as if she'd been waiting to be introduced. "Nice to meet you guys. Do you all go to Tricia's school?"

"Yeah," Patricia cuts in, gesturing to us one at a time. "Justin and I took algebra together a year ago and I'm working on this media arts project with Sophie."

Justin turns to me. "Oh wait, you're working on the art project with Patricia?"

I can't remember if I talked smack about the project or Patricia with Justin, but I hope for the love of all things good and holy that he doesn't dredge that shit up. We lock eyes; I think we have an understanding. "Yeah," I say. "I think I told you, right?" He is staring at me and I am staring at him and I am not sure if my telepathy is working, but I'm starting to sweat.

"Not gonna lie," Patricia chimes in, glancing at Casey, "When I first heard I was getting paired with Sophie, I was kinda mad because she's *too* serious. Like, on another level. You are, girl, you are," she says the moment I look like I'm about to argue.

"What?" I gasp. "I'm not *too* serious."

"You are. She is, right?" she asks Justin. I purposefully shift so I can't see if he's nodding or shaking his head. "Sophie, everyone knows you as this super smart girl who—I can't lie—"

"I wish you would."

"—kinda seems like a bitch," she finishes bluntly. And then shrugs. Shrugs! "It's true. I couldn't even believe you skipped school the other day, like damn. Did you get in trouble? I bet a girl like you got in *mad* trouble."

"A girl like me, meaning what?"

"Wait, wait, what?" Justin interrupts, chuckling. Why is this boy laughing? "When'd you skip school? Are you allowed back in your house? Is that why I had to pick you up from your cousin's place?"

Patricia gasps. "Oh, so he drove you here?"

Too many questions! I brush a hand across my temple just as the lights dim further. God's timing is divine. "Damn, I think they're starting," I say, and whip around to face the stage. Patricia and Casey are whispering across the table behind me, but my mind is focused solely on that stage. My nerves are threatening to eat me alive and I don't blink, afraid I might miss something, or someone.

A brown-skinned girl with long, silky hair and a ruby-studded septum ring that matches Patricia's in size heads straight for the microphone in the center of the stage. She grins and I am fixated on her bright, clean smile. "How's everyone doing tonight?" she croons into the mic. Her voice is so smooth, like she belongs on a late-night radio show. It sets the mood perfectly. "Hope you didn't have a hard time getting in. I know RJ at the back did the most with these wristbands," she says, holding up her own wrist to show a set of four different-colored ones.

"It's my job!" the bouncer at the door hollers across the hall. A few people snicker and clap.

"It's his job, he's right," the girl goes on, chuckling. "Can't be mad at that, can't be mad." She pauses a minute and takes a deep breath just like Ms. Kay does at the start of homeroom. "Okay, y'all. I'm so happy you guys came out tonight. Some of you are looking fine as fuck, if I do say so myself." Patricia applauds extra loud at that. "You know me, Missy Dee, your host this evening. I'd like to welcome y'all to our monthly Poetry Slam featuring some of the dopest performers this side of the city, and beyond. I gotta intro them all for you, one sec." She clears her throat and brings out a cue card, eyes scanning quickly over the words. "All right, all right. So we got…Jace."

A wave of snaps erupts from our right. Missy grins while she continues to read. "Jace grew up west of Toronto and went from flipping burgers to flipping joints—on the radio." As she speaks, the snaps get louder and louder. "Yes, y'all, yes. You can catch him on 93.5 in the day, but tonight, he's here, ready to perform.

"And then we got Miss Stacey B," Missy continues. More snaps, more claps. "Hailing from Pakistan but always about that Scarborough life, Miss Stacey B speaks from her soul when it comes to culture and tradition. She's dope, if you don't know.

"And last, but definitely not least, it's my boy Obi."

My heart freezes. Just stops. When it picks up again, it beats louder and heavier and stronger. It booms in my chest, shaking my frame, echoing in my ears to the point I barely catch what she says about him.

"...a lyrical MC whose mind is just—off the fucking— he's amazing," Missy chuckles. "He's been around for a minute and if you're standing here tonight, you owe him more than you realize. Listen, I know you can show him more love than that." The audience snaps louder, claps harder, and I'm buried in the noise. What does she mean he's been around for a minute? And that we owe him?

Missy puts her cue cards away and grabs the microphone with her free hand. "I don't want to hear any silence in here, y'all. I'm serious. You're all in for a good-ass show tonight. Without any further ado, here is Jace." She blows a kiss to the audience, which some attendees fake grab, and exits the stage.

Then it's quiet.

A chubby boy approaches the microphone, adjusting the height of the stand while he stares out into the crowd. His hat is facing forward, but he flips it backward before he stands up tall. He doesn't have a book or anything, but when he opens his mouth, I know he knows what he's doing. He has everything memorized. His confidence is electrifying, even from where I'm sitting.

"It's Jace," he says. That's enough to warrant a sea of

snaps. "I wrote this the other day for you, all of you. Let me get into it right quick." He clears his throat.

Quiet.

He says, sings, rhymes:

I was night; something ethereal
and sublime.
So what if you didn't know me?
I could be whoever I wanted here.
I was new.

My teeth got in the way of my speech.
They weren't white—
okay, maybe they were.
Maybe that was the problem.
so if I twist my words like this and
push out my lips like that, can you
understand?
if I draw my words n cut em like dis,
u get it or nah?

My teeth got in the way of my words.
if I couldn't get u on a deeper level,
then we gots nothin to talk about.
there's no me and you—just this.
this stark change
this pretense

I was night; something ethereal
and sublime.
but y'all don't get it, tho
I had to be.

The snaps grow louder and my fingers join them, calmly at first and then enthusiastically as he finishes. I don't even remember when my brows begin to furrow listening to how he weaves the words, how he sings without a song. Patricia and Casey circle the table and join Justin and I on the other side facing the stage. Casey is bouncing excitedly on her heels—"The emotion!" she moans, clutching her chest dramatically. A nervous laugh bursts out of me, one I can't quite control. "It was *everything*. Online, he said he was working on a new piece, but I didn't think it was going to be on *this* level. I'm—my chest." She presses her hands to her chest again and groans through the longest sigh ever.

I can still hear Jace's voice and the rhythm of his words ringing in my ears. I just can't believe this complete stranger made me feel things I didn't know I could feel. It came gushing out of me like a wave. His teeth, his speech—native tongues, names that are hard to get around. I knew that all too well. White words. Sophie understands.

"He was really good," I whisper to Justin. My voice is shaky, excited, afraid. "Like, surprisingly."

"Surprisingly?" Justin smirks. "So not a complete waste of time?"

I chuckle, "Boy, shut up," and turn back to the stage. Jace launches into another poem with the same rhythm, the same subject. He speaks so authentically. In his voice, there's no room for lies. I wonder if he has two names too, and if he goes by one with some people and another with other people. I wonder if he shares his second name with anyone or if he keeps it hidden in case someone might ruin it for him. Make it ugly instead of honoring its meaning.

Jace rolls easily into his next piece and I stay as captivated through it as the last. Something about hearing all those ordinary words strung together is magical.

He gets a round of snaps and a lot of applause for his next piece. A grin so wide spreads across his face and he gives a bow amid the storm of applause. "Thanks, everyone," he says multiple times into the mic. His voice is quiet now, such a contrast to how dynamic and boisterous he was only seconds ago. It's weird to see the change so suddenly, but I can relate. Sophie and Ada need a switch too.

Missy takes the stage again, applauding and nodding. "Give it up one more time for Jace, y'all," she calls over the crowd. Another roar of snaps kicks up before the noise fades into her voice. "All right, all right. Grab a drink or something, guys. The bartender looks bored and we worked hard for this liquor license." A gentle rumble of laughter permeates the crowd and the smile on Missy's face grows. "We pay him. We pay him and not one of y'all are drunk."

I miss when Missy announces the next performer, but

soon, applause rolls through the crowd and I'm watching Miss Stacey B take the stage. Her and Missy share a hug before she takes her place behind the microphone stand. She's taller than Jace was, so she hikes up the mic until it's a comfortable height. Unlike Jace, she doesn't smile. She's very serious. I guess she reminds me of me—or, apparently, what people say about me.

"Good evening," she says.

I'm surprised to hear a lot of people echo "Good evening, Miss Stacey B" back to her. That must be her thing.

"Good evening," she says again. "My name is Miss Stacey B and this is from me to you."

I've never had crutches.
actually,
logistically,
the leaning face forward on a balance beam
the shifting weight
the hobbling left and right,
none of it is practical.

Instead of hobbling, I can
jump, or
skip, or
trudge, or
run, or
you know.

I can do so many things
without these crutches.

I've never had them.
to say they are practical
or to say they are not,
it doesn't make a difference to me.
because I can lean face forward
shift my weight
hobble left right
without them.

She is electric when she speaks, more reserved than Jace was when he was performing, but somehow her quiet confidence still strikes the same level of awe in me. She's so bold. Something about her is so brave.

"I think," Casey pipes up, folding her arms across her chest. It takes effort to pull my eyes away from the stage. "Hmm, I think that one was about juggling life's priorities. Sometimes you have help and sometimes you don't."

Patricia shakes her head right away. "I don't know, babe, it seemed more like crumbling under societal pressure. Because when she mentions the crutches, remember?"

Casey twists her mouth into a pout and hums as she thinks. "I guess so. I do see the societal pressure thing, though."

I stay quiet listening to their analysis, partially amused

that they're debating this so in-depth. I want to tell them, "*We're not in English class*," but I realize that's the exact sort of thing they'd expect me to say. Serious Sophie. Instead, I focus on the stage, on what Miss Stacey B is saying. Once she is done, she's going to step off the stage and Sam will step on. My mind is consumed with thoughts of that moment, what it will look like, what it will sound like. And the anger takes hold again. The abandonment.

Uneasiness creeps up on me fast and the urge to run kicks in. I lock eyes with Justin and blurt out, "I don't have to be here," like a mad person. "He left *me*. Why, why did I come?"

"Because *you* wanted to see him," he tells me calmly. He is so levelheaded while I am so frantic, and amid the chaos, I'm happy he agreed to come with me. "It'll be fine," he adds, and reaches for my hand. My head feels like it'll explode when he gives it a squeeze and lets it fall back to my side. I gawk at my hand; not at the subtlety of the gesture but the colossal mark it left. Is he kidding? He can't just ... he can't just do that and then ... and then—what?

The crowd erupts into a series of hollering and snaps, and my attention refocuses on the stage. I hold my hands together to stop from fidgeting, but also to graze my fingers over where Justin's fingertips were. I remember the hand squeeze, imagining maybe it'd be a precursor to something else if we weren't surrounded by so many people.

I watch the remainder of Miss Stacey B's set with short, bated breaths. She is good, each poem rawer than the last, but I'm distracted now. She does two, three more pieces.

And when she is done, the rousing applause fills my ears until I can't hear anything else but its ringing.

And Miss Stacey B bows, smiles, waves as she leaves. Missy takes her place and she's talking so loud into the mic. I can't understand any of it.

And.

And then Sam takes the stage.

Sam.

He is

He is taller than I remember, more defined, less gangly than he was six years ago. He holds the mic with such authority, pushing his dark hood away from his face to reveal the same close-shaved sides and high cheekbones I saw in the poster. Anger bubbles in the pit of my stomach. Then frustration. Then compliance. Then ease. I want to rush forward and slap him, I don't know, but I also want to disappear, die, never emerge from the earth's core. I don't know how much of the audience he can see, but I suddenly don't want him to see me. I want to hide.

I've seen it. I've seen it's really him. Now what?

"Yo," he says, the bass in his voice echoing into the room. It makes my chest tremble. I know this voice—I fucking *know* this voice. It's the same voice my dad uses when he calls me downstairs in the morning. It's the same voice my mom uses when she is on the phone after a long night's shift. It's our voice.

"It's Obi," he goes on, and he takes a moment to scan the crowd. His throaty chuckle fills the hall. He still laughs so much like Mom. "Some of y'all are new. I haven't seen some faces. I hope you can keep up with me tonight, but if not, I mean, tough shit." He shrugs. "I learned this language for you, so you need to learn mine now." A few vagrant claps ring out in the room at that.

eh heh, aha m bụ Obinna
na cry I wan cry oo
he-ey!
biko, na help I want.
more than anything,
no look me say i dey weak
look me say i dey strong well-well
because na with cry i dey talk so

and even if i am weak.
hear the sob of my voice,
feel more than that rattling through my chest
recognize
i want to cry out loud.
from my gut.

wetin you no understand for wey i dey speak?
what don't you get?

I want you to understand
that's really all.

the dark of the room,
the tic-tac-tap of the keyboard
this stress, anxiety in your jaw
locks you up
does any of this make sense?

ee dey pain me well-well
and na cry i wan cry oo
he-ey!
na help I want.

CHAPTER TEN

WHEN SAM'S SET ENDS, THE same wave of snaps and approval flutters through the room. My feet can't stay still. The second the lights fade from the stage, I turn to Justin and tell him quickly, "I'll be back, don't...don't leave," before I disappear into the crowd.

People have begun to shift now, crossing the room to talk with friends or moving toward the bar for another round of drinks. I can't see where Sam went, but every one of the other performers has exited stage left, so I head there in hopes of running into him. Oh god, and then what? What do I say when I am finally standing in front of him? Do I tell him how hard it's been for me since he peaced out? Do I slap him? Do I cry?

I get to the area where I swear he'll be but I don't see him. People move around me, smiling pleasantly as they pass with drinks in hand. I spot Missy talking to Jace in the corner, laughing just like how she was on stage. Miss Stacey B is having drinks with a small group of her supporters. The more I look and look into the dim corners, the less I see, and the more convinced I am that I may have missed him again and this was all a waste of time.

"A. Ada?"

A ripple of shock whips up my spine at the familiarity of the voice. *Our* voice. The same timbre, the same echo, and so close. I spin around so fast I almost lose balance. It's him. He is—it's Sam and he's, yes, he's taller than I remember and he chopped off his locs and he's here, he's here in front of me. My body is paralyzed. I berated myself so much about getting angry and crying, but my eyes have never been drier. My mouth, too.

"Holy...," I utter.

He takes a hesitant step forward and we face each other in the dim of the club. His eyes scan my face as if he's the one who doesn't know me. We blink the same way, twist our heads a little in intrigue at the person before us. We're so quiet.

And I don't know what to do.

"Shit...," he says with a small, tired smile. He's smiling? I don't know how to feel about that. He tries to pull me into a hug but my body seizes and I stiffen in his arms. "You're . . . here? You're really here? That's . . . a lot."

I falter before I say, "Wh-what does that mean?"

He steps back and we stare at each other again, him apprehensive, and me, awkward. I am so mad at him because of how he abandoned me, our parents, everyone. But in this moment now, I don't know how to talk to this ghost in front of me. He feels like a stranger.

"You came for the show?" he asks, his voice flat. "Did, uh, did you . . . like the other performers?"

I stand slack-jawed, unsure what words to say that can make this feel more real. Anger bubbles in my chest finally. I don't see him for six years—he doesn't contact me for six years and all he can say is "that's a lot"? "Did you like the other performers?" Is he kidding?

"Why did you leave?" I spit out.

He sighs heavily while he glances over his shoulder. When he shifts, leaning on his back foot, he feels farther away than he did a second ago. "Is this really the time?" he grunts.

"What other time is there?"

"You came here to tell me that?"

"I came here to—I don't know—see my brother." I am both taken aback by his brashness, ready to fight him so he can see what real anger looks like, but also aching with this particular brand of hurt. He doesn't know, does he, how I pictured this going? He has no idea that this is worse than my worst-case scenario. "And you're acting like you don't even know me. You fucking stormed out—" My voice hitches in my throat as the early onset of tears pokes through. I can't cry now, I can't cry now. "You stormed out and left me and Mom and Dad after everything they did for you, and not once did you think to reach out to us—to *me*. What did I ever do to you?"

He says, "I don't know, Ada, just..." and looks over my head, avoiding my eyes. When we finally look at each other, I can barely place the look he's giving me. It's sad, frustrated. More of that regret, but also resolve. It's my face reflected in a face I recognize but doesn't seem to recognize me. And we can't both be right.

Suddenly, he brings out his phone and opens his contacts. "Listen, I know this isn't... I don't know what they told you about me—"

"What they told me is you ran away, and that's all there is to know," I shoot back.

He purses his lips. Doesn't even try to dispute it. "Well, we're here now," he says tersely, rotating his phone in his hand. "What's your number?"

I barely hear a word he says. All I can see is that the phone he brought out is scuffed up, cracked at the corner, a little bit dingy—and the exact same one he had when he lived at home.

He has the same phone.

This was a choice.

Him choosing to run away, to not contact me or our family, to let me carry the weight of whatever he knew Mom and Dad would throw on me, was a fucking choice.

The tears breach my eyes as I take a step back. "F-forget it. I don't want to talk to you," I grumble before turning and pushing my way through the crowd and out the door.

I am mad, I'm *so* mad—like, if only he knew how many Sams I've seen in the years he's been gone. If only he knew how disappointing it is to get here and find out Mom and Dad were right: There was no point looking. *He* left *us*. He knew where to find me, exactly how to find me, and didn't do anything about it.

Justin drives me home. He only asks me what happened once and doesn't push it when I brush him off.

I tell him to pull up to the house beside mine just in case my parents are still up and watching from the window. I don't know if Tayo told them anything. God, I really hope not. I haven't thought about him all night, but I know tomorrow is about to be a shitfest if I don't straighten things out with him. I can't believe he told Genny—I can't believe he said Justin was my boyfriend in front of Skeleboy's assistant!

"Thanks, Justin," I say as I climb out of the car. He ruffles the fringe of his hair like it's bothering him and I do my best to not tell him to just cut it. "Like, really, thanks. I appreciate it."

He glances away and says quietly, "You don't have to thank me. I mean, it wasn't that bad. Poetry, and everything."

"Yeah, I guess. Don't tell anyone I said that."

"I don't have to," he says with a smirk. "You should've seen the way you were staring at those spoken word artists. Like you wanted to eat them. Even Patricia saw."

"Pleeeease," I groan, and he laughs. "Later. Thanks again." I shut the door and wave while he drives away.

The light in the living room is on, and from where I am at the entrance, I can hear loud sound effects and muffled yelling with way too much feedback through the speakers. That can only mean one thing: My parents are most definitely watching a Nigerian movie.

"Ada, bia," my mom calls from the corner of the living room.

I shuffle forward, dreading having to explain myself to my parents. As I walk, the words "*I just got back from studying at Williams*" cycle in my head over and over again. It's a perfect lie and a part of me wishes I had just gone to Williams to study instead of wasting my time with Sam.

Mom has her feet up on the ottoman while she leans back into the sofa, chewing on a handful of cashews. Dad is beside her with his feet decidedly on the ground. He can't tear his eyes away from the screen for more than two seconds. I'm guessing it's a scene in the village where the girl finds out she's a princess. I haven't even seen this movie, but I've *seen* it.

"Where are you coming from this night?" Mom asks me. My phone beeps in my bag but I ignore it.

I'm too tired to put up a fight, so I just sigh and say, "My friend and I were studying at Williams. It ran long. I'll go to bed now."

"Long ke." Mom tsks at me. "It's almost ten o'clock. You should have called."

"I know. I'm sorry."

"What were you studying?" Dad asks. His eyes settle on me, finally, and I am rooted to the floor. Something about the way he asks it has me paranoid that Tayo got to him. God, please, spare me.

"Debate," I say—and immediately regret it. Dad's eyebrows shoot up because he knows Justin is my debate partner. The last thing I need him to think is that I spent the last few hours with a boy. It's not wrong, but that doesn't mean I should let him think that. "I mean, then I was working on a project with a friend. She's a she."

It's Mom's turn to look away from the screen. "Where is she from?"

"Uh, I don't know." I shrug. "I didn't ask."

"Is she a Nigerian?" Dad pipes up. "What kind of project?"

"She's not, no," I tell them. "And it's this project for art class."

Dad's eyes wrinkle, his mouth scrunches into a distasteful pout, and he sits up a little bit straighter. "Art class?" he asks. The way he says it is, with such disgust and such bitterness, makes my skin crawl. I try to look away, but his gaze coaxes me back. "Since when are you taking that?"

Nothing I say will be good enough. It's required, I need it to graduate, I've been enrolled in it all semester, they made me take it, if I had a choice I would never take media arts—none of it matters. I'd get the exact same reaction. "Since the beginning of the semester. It's required," I tell him simply.

And just like clockwork, he snaps back, "So is that how you're wasting your time?"

Mom chews quickly on her cashews as she tugs on Dad's arm. She hisses, "Ah-beg-ee, must you shout?"

But Dad ignores her. He is sitting upright now, hands on his knees, as he glares at me. "So...so all your mates are excelling at maths and excelling at science, and you are here spending three, four hours on an *art* project," he says, his voice crisp. He snaps over his head twice and that's how I know he's really mad. "For three, four hours, you are just doing one subject. Nwa m, it cannot be so, o! I want you to think very, very well about this your art project, and ask yourself if it will be important for you next year when you're in the university."

I sigh. Even that seems to be the wrong thing to do. Dad blinks faster, waiting on my answer. "It's not like I'm not doing other work too. Plus, I'm pretty much getting As in everything. I got the second-highest mark on the philosophy midterm."

"And the person who got first, does he have two heads?"

Oh my god. "N-no."

"Eh? Go and sleep, jor." He kisses his teeth so loud it feels like a slap to the face. "I didn't come to this country for you to be useless."

"Eh-wo, that's enough, na," Mom says, waving a hand in front of my dad absently. "I'm trying to watch. Oya, rewind." She reaches for the remote and pokes the pause button before slowly, slowly pulsing rewind until the movie goes back a few minutes.

But Dad isn't done. He kisses his teeth again and says, "This girl is very mad! She wants to try me, abi? It will not happen in Jesus's name—my child will not come and kill me. Tufia-kwa!" like I'm not standing right here.

Mom says something to Dad in Igbo and he falls back onto the sofa, face frowning with the burden of having me as his major disappointment. Mom waves me off. "It's enough," she coos. "Don't mind this your... your old papa. See, it's because he's watching all these village movies, eh, that's when he knows he wants to come and fight. He's just finding your trouble. Biko, just go."

I turn away and make for the staircase before they change their minds and call me back for a second round of insults.

I race upstairs, kicking my room door shut and flinging my bag onto my bed. My jaw is set; my teeth clenched together as I collapse on my bed too. I'm already doing everything they ask of me and it's still not enough. As if I'm just wasting my time—as if I'm just wasting my *life*! Well, maybe I am. Thinking about a brother who didn't care to find me, spending my evening at a poetry event—maybe it's better for me to stick to what I know. Stick to what I'm good at. Forget everything else, just like Sam did.

Like, damn, he was supposed to be an engineer by now. Seeing him up on that stage tonight was so different. *He* was different. He gave off something I'd never seen before. He seemed happy and free, but even admitting that is too much right now. But how can he be happy when he left us behind?

My phone rings. I dive for it and scan the unknown number. It's Sam's number, the same one I deleted ages ago when I thought it stopped working. So he was just pretending he didn't have my number? Can't believe this. Scowling, I send the call to voice mail.

CHAPTER ELEVEN

WHEN I WAKE UP THE next morning, I have six missed calls from Sam. He doesn't leave a single voice mail, doesn't text. So then what does he want? There's no way I'm calling him back. For what? So we can have another bitter exchange and I can get my feelings hurt? He made it obvious that he could've contacted me and chose not to. Now, this is my choice.

Patricia has been sending me texts too. She's really into this music video idea and I can't be bothered to argue anymore. A music video about the school's fucked-up history with lobotomy sounds ridiculous, but whatever. If she likes it and we can do well with it, then that's all that matters at this point. I just wanna get this over with. It's not like I know much about the creative process. I'm not like her, I'm definitely not like Sam, and there's no way I'm anything like those spoken word artists. They were so unlike anything I've ever seen. So cool. So brave.

Forget Sam for a second; hearing those artists up there was on another level. I can't stop thinking about how passionate they were, the sort of passion where you can tell they're happy. Every time I catch myself in my feelings about how exhilarating it was, I have to check myself and shut it down. I don't have time to be thinking about poetry when I have university so clear in front of me. When I have things I'm good at to pursue.

"Who's trying to call you?"

Tayo's voice jolts me back and I remember where we are: in his car on the way to school. He's softened a bit since yesterday at Chioma's house, and I'm willing to bet it's because him and Ayo are friends on social media now. Man, this boy is so shallow. They even took a picture together: Tayo's vibrant smile and soft boy demeanor next to Ayo's dazzling shades and star-power-by-association. Even in that picture I can see the excitement, the endearment in Tayo's eyes and it makes me forget the way he behaved at Genny's house. It reminds me that it's easy to imagine him so entrenched in my future, and that maybe that's not such a bad thing after all. What's wrong with easy?

"You sound pressed no one's calling you," I say with a smirk, even though he looks the farthest thing from it.

He snorts. "Okay. Just tell me it's your oyinbo boyfriend and go."

"It's my mom," I lie. He gives a heavy sigh, looking like a weight has slipped off his shoulders. It's so obvious but I pretend not to notice for his sake. Instead, I flip my phone over in my hands, pushing Sam from the recesses of my mind. "She's chasing me about wedding stuff."

"Is she trying to tell you you're next?" he snickers. "Is she asking Genny's parents to fly in eligible bachelors?"

I cringe. "Don't even joke about that—"

"They'll bring in a lawyer, a doctor, and an engineer, and you'll have to pick," he goes on, chuckling. "The doctor will win, obviously."

"How is it obvious?" I bite back a smile, watching him blink a mile a minute, trying to come up with something clever. Tayo's parents want him to go to medical school, so in my mind, he's the doctor and he ends up being much more interesting, funny, and good-looking than anyone they can fly in from Nigeria. Well, anyone but Skeleboy, that is.

"Oh!" Tayo snaps his fingers like he remembered something. "So the doctor will win easily because he can just cure himself. The engineer is useless without technical drawings, and the lawyer is only good at theory but not human interaction. They both fail."

"What makes you think I wouldn't choose the lawyer instead?"

"Because you're the lawyer," he says plainly. "You'd want a polar opposite to some degree, right? That's what makes people compatible and happy and stuff. Or, I don't know, that's what I heard on TV."

An opposite to me wouldn't be a doctor, though, or at least wouldn't be one narrow idea of a doctor. I think I'm more complex than this, but I don't have the words to tell Tayo. I hate that I think of Sam and how he would string words together, letting them flow like water, and I'm jealous I can't be that way too. Not that I want to be a poet, but he just... he was so passionate. It's so annoying how deeply his words cut me and how loud I could feel them echo in my chest. Sam must've run away because he wanted to do poetry and Mom and Dad wanted him to do engineering instead. That's the only explanation. He wasn't high or strung out, a shadow of his former self. In fact, he was full, a concrete version to the memory Sam in my head.

He looked so happy.

God, why can't I just call him back?

"It definitely couldn't be the engineer, though. Too practical," Tayo goes on amid my silence. We lock eyes and he gives me a look like I've been drifting and he needs me to come back to our conversation. "Well, there's no engineers in your family, anyway, so I guess that doesn't matter. I mean, except for your dad."

And my brother.

Sam was training to be an engineer.

Say it, Ada, just say it.

"My...," I stutter. Tayo tries to look at me, but he's still driving. I clear my throat several times before I have the confidence to continue. The fear that he might say something to someone in his family knocks at my temples, making my head pound and tremble with unease. But still, I press on. "My brother... he was in school for engineering, remember? A-and he's not that practical."

Silence fills the car. Tayo eases toward a red light, but he doesn't look at me right away. I can see the confusion in his eyes while he measures his words. Finally, he asks, "Your brother?" I nod right away, almost afraid to let it sit too long. "The one who... left?"

My anger at Sam dissipates for a moment. It physically hurts to hear Tayo say that, but not because it's not true. It's because everyone knows and no one says anything about it. I don't know what my parents told everyone to make it seem like Sam never existed in the first place. "Yeah, my brother," I reply, trying to quell the shaking in my voice. It still sounds so foreign on my tongue: my brother, my brother.

Tayo's suspicion still isn't letting up. "I mean, I guess... he was in engineering."

"Yeah, he was."

He nods but stays quiet.

The light changes so he speeds ahead. I don't know what to do, so I flip my phone back over in my hands. Tayo's gaze holds fast to the road in front of us, as if he's purposefully trying not to look at me. I can't blame him; it's been so long since anyone has mentioned Sam, and I know what it's like to be overly cautious like this. Our parents say all sorts of things in hushed tones about family members here and there, and as kids, we feel responsible not to disrupt the flow of the community behind their backs. We don't always have to agree, but we can't be disrespectful. This, talking about Sam when he's so long been off the table as a topic of discussion? Disrespectful.

"Have you..." He clears his throat. The awkwardness is heavy in the air. "Uh, so, do you see him around?"

It's a trap. If I say yes—or, if I say no...? There's no easy way out of this. "Um, n-not...I mean, kinda," I tell him, and he gasps with shock. "Kinda," I repeat, as if my reassurance will take the edge off.

"Can I be honest?" Tayo whispers, and I nod. "I've seen him around too."

I gasp, nearly choking myself against the seat belt as I turn to him. "Legit?"

"Yeah, legit. Or, er, no," he utters. "I seen a guy at the mall and he looked *just* like him. I almost called out, but then he turned the corner and he was wearing glasses. Sam never wore glasses, right?"

"No, no way," I say. I can't believe I'm talking about Sam in public. Even if it's just Tayo's car, I mean, this is too much! "He used to have locs, remember? But he shaved them—"

"Yeah, I can imagine, especially if he went to jail like I heard," he says.

And I freeze. "What?"

Tayo nods again as he makes the turn into our school parking lot. "Uh…jail? Locs?" he repeats. "Where did I lose you?"

"Jail," I tell him, sternly. "Sam never went to jail. Who said that?"

"Who?" He sighs. "Man, everybody. It's what my parents heard from Auntie Edith and, uh, you remember Uncle Baffour? The Ghanaian uncle. Even he heard it from the Nigerian Network, and he's not even Nigerian! Everyone thinks Sam ain't shit for how he treated your parents, anyway."

I don't even know what to say to that besides: "He's not in jail." Can't believe I'm defending Sam right now after he's the one who abandoned me. I glower at Tayo like it's him who came up with the rumor. Jail, really? For what? Damn, what happened that everyone has this strong idea about him? Why won't anyone tell me?

The more I stew in my anger, the more unsettled I feel. Bitterness overtakes me. I'm angry at Sam and I'm angry that Tayo thinks this negatively of Sam—which, in turn, is making me angry at myself. "You can't just say whatever you want," I tell him finally. "You don't even know what happened."

"Well, do *you?*" he asks. He knows that's the final nail in the coffin. People used to look at me with pity immediately after he disappeared, but once they realized I was oblivious, they stopped looking at me altogether. Just expected me to fall in line, fill the void. "You were in the house, right? Shouldn't you know what happened? Why he left?"

It's not him I'm mad at; it's me for not knowing the one thing I should know and for letting this unease fester for so long. It's me I'm mad at for thinking I could tell someone, tell Tayo, and have everything be okay.

"Don't think about Sam anymore," he tells me, his voice quiet. He reaches out for my hand and the softness of his palm, the quick spark of his touch, brings me back down to earth. "It sucks losing a brother like that, so I'm sorry. And I didn't mean to offend you."

My eyebrows rise in shock. "*You're* apologizing to *me?* What happened?"

He hides a shy smile. "Sam is a touchy subject. I just didn't want you to feel worse."

"Worse?"

"I'm already up your ass about dating that Justin boy—"

"Justin is not my boyfriend!"

"—and it's really shitty of me to make fun of your

may-or-may-not-be-in-jail brother, so." He shrugs. "He's off-limits. I can respect that."

We sit in silence until he pulls into the closest parking spot. My mind is turning fast with memories of the night Sam left. Come on, Ada, try to remember. What were Dad and Sam fighting about? Did he ever mention the word "poetry" even once?

"You go ahead," I tell Tayo as I step out of the car. "I need to call my mom back before she comes here and smacks me."

He laughs. "Cool. But if that happens, though—"

"I won't tell you—"

"—tell me. Oh damn!" he howls. "Your mom looks like she'd have a fierce backhand. I just want to witness it once."

"If you stick around any longer, you can witness my backhand."

He pulls a face at me before throwing his bag over his shoulder. "Don't be late," he says and disappears toward the building.

I turn around and quickly dial Sam's number. He picks up on the third ring. He picks up. He's picked up. "Hey. Ada?" he says.

Now what?

"H-hi," I reply.

"So…" He clears his throat. The line is a bit staticky.

Maybe he's not home. "I been trying to call you. I wanted to apologize..."

After a moment, I say, "So apologize."

A warm chuckle comes through the line and I hate how quickly it pacifies me. He laughs the same, the exact same, as my memories. Maybe deep down, he's the same too. "I'm sorry. Let's go for lunch today. I think we should talk," he says. "I think we both have a lot of things to tell each other."

"You have no idea."

As soon as my second class is done, I try to rush out of the school's back doors, but Mr. Patel stops me. He even holds out a hand, his palm square in my face, as I approach. "Where are you going?" he asks. "Lunchtime practice session is happening upstairs. I've gotten no other tips from my adjudicator buddy, so I'm thinking our motion is set."

"Aw, really?" I frown. "I, um, I'm headed out for lunch, so I don't think I can come."

He purses his lips and crosses his arms, acting way too authoritarian. He's usually always so chill. "The competition is coming up fast, Sophie, and we need to make sure we've exhausted potential arguments."

"I'm on it, sir," I tell him as confidently as I can. "I'll spend some time brainstorming later, I promise. Besides, Justin probably will come up with everything I was gonna come up with, anyway."

Mr. Patel raises an eyebrow. "Are you kidding? You two never agree."

He's right. "N-no, we've gotten better at seeing eye to eye," I lie. "But, sir, I really need to go."

He stares at me a second longer before breaking into a slow nod. That's enough confirmation for me. I skip past him toward the back door.

I catch the closest bus to Fran's, this all-day breakfast spot. Sam was always a "breakfast anytime" person, so it doesn't surprise me when he says this is where we're going. The only way you could get him up early was to bribe him with breakfast food. It makes me smile a little because it's so like the Sam I knew, the Sam before he ran away. As the bus bumbles along, I have to keep reminding myself that I'm mad at him. Betrayal and abandonment. He had my number and he only thought to call me after I tracked him down. He might not even care about me, or Mom and Dad.

Sam is already seated when I enter and he waves me to a table by the window. He looks comfortable now, much more at ease than when I last saw him. As soon as I sit down, he says, "You ambushed me last time. I wasn't prepared, but don't think I wasn't happy to see you."

It's just like him to get his story straight first. "Sure," I utter and pull the menu close.

"I already ordered," he goes on. "Two classic breakfasts. I asked them to cut the crust off the bread for you and the lady gave me a funny look, so if you don't end up with crustless bread, just know I tried."

I'm alarmed at how easily he's able to speak. His words

sounded easy at the Poetry Slam too. It's like he's singing, stringing along words as he goes. Doesn't he know I'm angry? Can't he tell?

"So," he goes on, resting his head on his hand. "Here we are."

"Y-yeah," I say. My voice doesn't come out as strong as I'd liked. "You're here."

"I'm here."

"Where . . . do you live?"

"Like, five stops from here," he says, gesturing over his shoulder.

"Five stops?" I echo. Five stops on the subway isn't a million miles away. He's been so close this entire time and he never . . . "You live five stops from here and . . . you're a poet."

He nods with a stiff smile. "I am a poet, yes."

This is bizarre. What am I even doing here? Why did I come?

"Is that why you left?" I ask. "Because of . . . poetry?"

He lets out a tired, uneasy laugh as he leans back in his seat. The look of nonchalance in his eyes and that casual drawl in his voice tell me immediately that he's not going to give me an answer.

"What did you think of the event?" he asks suddenly. "I bet you'd never seen anything like it."

I frown. "Obviously I haven't."

"But you liked it?"

"Y-yeah," I concede. He grins at that, the smug kind that I remember from my childhood. He'd always get this way when we were kids and he won an argument. "Your set was good," I say, pushing the words out. "Your whole...like, the Nigerian thing was really cool."

"You think?"

I nod right away and I feel my temperament begin to change. The anger and vitriol that I came prepared with is mellowing the more I think of the spoken word artists. What is it about them that makes me get this way? "I liked the first poem you did, actually. Was it like..." It takes me a second, but I start reciting his verses, fumbling over words, stumbling into pidgin the same way he did during the show. He nods along, his grin growing wider and wider. He smiles the same way as Mom. "Also, you look different with no hair," I add, trying to smile too. It's more of a slight tug at the corner of my lips, but it's a start.

He chuckles and smooths a hand across his close-shaven head. "Yeah, eh? I got tired of the locs. They grew really long, but I couldn't keep up with maintenance. All that retwisting."

I nod.

His eyes fall on my schoolbag nestled in the seat beside me. "Tell me how school's going. Tell me about your life now. I want to hear all of it."

"*Why did you leave, then?*" is on the tip of my tongue. He

could've been here, watching me live out my day-to-day life like a normal brother. He wouldn't have to catch up if he was just there.

But instead of snapping at him, I reach into my bag and pull out my book where I keep all my debate notes. Sam looks at it curiously, flipping it open to examine the pages. "*This* is what I've been doing," I tell him plainly. "I joined debate. I'm the only girl in our team for regionals. The competition is coming up, so all I've been doing is practicing and coming up with arguments for the proposition and the opposition, just in case I…" He pauses at one of the pages where I've scribbled some notes about cross-cultural kids. I tilt my head to get a better look. In the corner, I wrote "*lobotomy music*," and suddenly, his confused expression makes sense. "Oh, uh…I have to do an art project," I go on. "It's stupid. My partner, this weird girl, wants to do a lobotomy music video or something."

Sam snorts and glances up at me. "What even is that?"

"No idea."

"You should do something that suits you a little bit more."

I scoff, rolling my eyes. "Like you know what suits me."

He winces under the weight of my words, letting them sit in the air between us. I almost want to take it back, but the seconds tick by and it becomes too late. "I just mean you could do better than this. Am I wrong?" he says.

Begrudgingly, I grunt, "No. But I don't care enough. I

just want a good grade. I'm not like you. I'm not an artist, or whatever."

His eyebrows twist, disbelief caressing the features on his face. "Not like me? Have you read this?" He turns the book around to face me and I stare down at my notes. "This is...it's verse. What made you write it like this?"

The page looks like any other page I've taken notes on. I scribble notes all over the place and put breaks in odd places, but only because it helps me understand the subject a bit better. When the words flow differently, my brain can wrap around them better. That doesn't mean it's poetry; that just means I'm adapting to the struggles of rote memorization. If he was still in school, he would know that.

"Verse ke? You're not serious," I scoff. "It's just regular notes."

"Which one na regular?" he chides in pidgin and I smile a little despite myself. Hearing it roll off his tongue is magic and steeps me in nostalgia. "It's free verse. Similar to the stuff I do. I can show you sometime, if you want. Actually, I can text you my address. We can, I don't know, h-hang out." He is nervous when he says it, but not as nervous as I am hearing it. Hanging out with Sam is the logical next step, but what would my parents do if they found out? After everything that happened, they'd be beyond pissed.

"I don't know," I mutter. "It'd have to be on a day when I don't have a lot of homework o-or debate practice."

"Of course. You can preview my next set, too." He brings out his phone and within seconds, he texts me his address. "And I can help you with whatever this art project thing is, since you 'don't think you're an artist.'" He air quotes it, chuckling. I want to laugh with him but I just can't bring myself to do it.

"I'm not," I mumble.

"But you liked the Poetry Slam, right? You must have been really into it—you memorized my poem," he says. "Lobotomy sounds cool and everything, but I think you and your pre-lawyer skills can come up with something better."

I snort. "But what if I don't care?"

"Start caring."

Start.

I really do know Sam's entire poem and I wasn't even trying to memorize it. I'm just good at memorizing. It's why I'm good at debate. I can memorize, I can project, and I can speak with a tempered voice. It's why I'll probably make a good lawyer.

But when I think of Sam on that stage, I think of someone who should've been an engineer by now. It's weird to say "should," but in our house, if he had stayed, he would have been an engineer, no question. And if he was, then he wouldn't know—or, *I* wouldn't know how good he is at this. At poetry. At getting up in front of people and speaking your mind. Telling people how you feel and what you think. Like debate—it's kinda like debate.

My eyes glaze over my debate notes written in verse while I'm on the bus back to school. There's a rhythm to them that I didn't notice before, but Sam noticed it right away. Maybe because he's more open than I am. Because he cares about things like this and I don't. Not really, anyway.

"Cross-cultural kids…" The breaks don't make sense on paper, but when I read them out loud, the picture comes together for me. The song comes together. It's…

from one to another,
different culture, usually like mother like child
or patriarchal?
who knows
it's more about assimilation, even if they say it's
not.
it's merging without merging two
that's why you have two names probably
does everyone have two names?
how they can call you one without
the other.

Damn.

I call Patricia and she picks up on the first ring. "Hello?"

"Heeeey," I sigh over the loud churning of the bus. "Don't kill me, but do you wanna try something?"

CHAPTER TWELVE

"POETRY?" BY THE TIME I get back to school, Patricia is waiting by the main doors before the next class starts, arms crossed with the most disbelieving expression on her face. To think, she thinks me suggesting poetry is strange, but we were all just gonna go along with her lobotomy music video shit? How is that not the stranger scenario? "*You?* You want to do poetry?" she asks again.

"I said we should *try* it," I tell her while trying to sound more confident than I am. When I met with Sam, I felt apprehensive, but the more I let the idea sit, the more I feel I can do a decent job of this. I wrote all my debate notes in verse, so how hard could it be to write a poem? Maybe I'm not a master-level poet like Sam, but isn't the whole point of art to try new things? Patricia and her million bangles should appreciate this. "But we could do it. Listen, a poetry reading could still count."

"We need two media components, though," she says, tapping her chin. "If we're scrapping the music video, then we should aim to do something bigger than lobotomy."

"Shouldn't be hard."

"Ooh, what about..." She gasps slowly, her eyes shining with a flood of ideas. It looks like she's struggling to decide on one. I can't lie; I'm kinda jealous. It took me forever to get one semi-formed idea and she seems to just have them ready and waiting. "Okay, you do a poem—do a poem like one of the ones we heard at the slam, you know? Like, real raw, real *real.* I can do, um, drums." She starts hitting imaginary bongos. "My dad used to be a percussionist in Jamaica and he taught me how to play, like, everything. I can drum the story of your life while you're speaking."

"And we can, um..." This brainstorming thing is hard. Patricia makes it seem so easy with her bongos, but I'm grasping at straws trying to figure out what else we can add to it. I bet Sam wouldn't struggle like this. God, can I really do this? I'm not creative like him.

Patricia waits and I hate that she does because it's building anxiety and pressure in my chest. "You were gonna say something...?" she prods.

"Um..." I take a deep breath. We look at each other for

a long time without speaking. I am thinking of—Ada. Ada doesn't have time for this. She is on track to win her debate competition as the final flourish on an already excellent résumé. She is going to study philosophy so she can study law so she can become a lawyer. She is doing this to make her parents, her family, everyone, proud.

But then she—*I* think of Sam.

I think of him, as he is now, existing. How he exists, speaking with one mind, and he's...He's not an engineer, but he's still...He bought me food and we talked a lot about what it was like for us growing up, how he once put bleach in the color cycle while doing laundry and ruined every-one's clothes, how I ate too much meat pie once and threw up on his floor—and I remembered that he's my brother. Mom and Dad don't want to talk about him like he commit-ted the worst betrayal, and maybe he did, but meeting him again after six years is different. It's different because it still feels the same.

What would Sam do if he were me?

What would I do if I were Sam?

"We should film it," I say all at once. Patricia raises her eyebrows in shock and I'm not even mad at her because I'm shocked too. I keep talking, keep throwing out ideas as fast as they come: "Yeah, we'll film it, just like how all my debate competitions are filmed. It'll be easier to send to Ms. Kay to grade. And, uh, we can perform it at the Poetry Slam. The next one at 2020 Brick Avenue. Will they even have a next one? I-it doesn't matter—I mean, obviously they will—but that's where we're performing."

Patricia's grin builds as she listens, like a flower blooming slowly in the sun. She teeters excitedly on her heels, rocking back and forth, which soon turns into dancing on the spot. "Yes! That'd be dope. Let me call them to see about securing a spot. *You* just focus on coming up with a fire poem first. And I mean *fi-re*. Who knows? Maybe we can even get a good grade with this."

She winks and nudges my arm when she says "good grade," and I can tell it's supposed to be a joke, but it just feels like a smack in the face. Yeah, that's right; that's all Sophie cares about. That's what makes her happy. I almost forgot.

After school, I lie and tell Tayo I need to do a practice run with Justin and Mr. Patel for the debate competition. In reality, I need to sit down and figure out this poetry business.

My lie doesn't even feel like a lie anymore because Tayo is too unbothered to ask questions. Instead, when we stand at the school doors as students shuffle by us on their way home, he turns his phone around to show me his screen. "Look at, look at this," he snickers, practically bouncing up and down on the spot. It's a perfectly grammatical text from Ayo that just says: "*Come with Blessing, Genevieve, and Chioma this weekend so we can figure out the entrance sequence.*" Tayo is grinning so wide. "I have *arrived*. I'm international now."

"Oh my god."

"FBI. Fine Boy International. FBNP. Fine Boy, No Pimple."

"Boy, shut up!" I say, cackling. Whatever mood I was in is completely overhauled with one stupid joke. Whether I can pull off this poetry thing isn't important anymore. Whether Tayo let the Justin thing go or not suddenly isn't important either. I like when we can just enjoy each other's company like this. When I stand a bit too close to him, he doesn't step back; instead, he continues scrolling, showing me the messages as if he doctored the whole thing himself. Him and Ayo have become fast friends, a budding duo affectionately called Ayo and Tayo, where every now and then Ayo will tell Tayo about something Skeleboy-related, and Tayo will feel like he's part of the club.

I leave him and disappear to room 114 because that's usually where the debate team hangs out. Today, it's empty. I flick the lights on and walk in, my backpack hitting the door as I slip by it. This room that's usually so loud with confrontation and conversation is now filled to the brim with silence. The emptiness forces all my intrusive thoughts to come flooding back: thoughts about who I am and who I want to be, and thoughts about who Sam is and who he turned himself into. It's enough to make me run away. Just go home, open a book, study. Go back.

Instead, my feet squeak against the floor as I make my way to the nearest desk and throw open my bag. Inside is my notebook for history class. I fold back a few of the pages and turn to a clean one while I plop down in my seat and fish for a pen.

I guess I should write something now.

"What do people write about?" I mumble to myself. Sam's set at the club was all about himself. Can I do that? Is that still considered poetry if I do it? Won't it just sound like a lecture, or worse, an argument in debate? *"The house believes that Ada and Sophie are the same person."* I don't know if it'd be easier to argue for or against that.

Whatever. I take a deep breath and start writing, but then I quickly scribble out the first word I write down. Damn, this is painful.

"Okay, what about law school?" Law school and my dreams to attend are the only things I can speak on. It feels so boring in comparison to what Sam or the other poets spoke about, but it's all I know.

I write "*LAW SCHOOL*" in capital letters at the top of the page. I squash the voice in my head that tells me this is all stupid.

It's been three years since I said I'd go
So I guess I have to
It's not too bad, because it's something I've always dreamed about
Thought about
Really wanted to become.

It feels like I'm pulling words like teeth from my brain. Everything looks so jangled and ugly on the page, but the one thing that sticks out to me, the one thing my mind hones in on, is: "*Wanted.*" I blink at the word, scrunching my nose at its appearance. My eyes even flicker to the pen in my hand like I can't believe it came from its ink. "Wanted?" I echo, and then cross it out to "*want.*" "Right?"

Really ~~wanted~~ want to become.
It's where I belong. It's where I need to go.

The words get heavier now, echoing in my chest. They don't feel real. None of this feels like it's me. It doesn't feel cool and effortless or cathartic like Sam's poem. It doesn't even sound like the voice I know when I talk. The thought that I might really actually suck at this burns my chest. I don't know what I was thinking. How am I supposed to write a poem and sell it to people? How can I get them to believe what I'm telling them, what I'm feeling, if I don't even know how to articulate my feelings half of the time?

Sam said one line, and I knew him. He said two lines, and I heard him speaking to me. I don't think I can connect with people like that.

I put my head down and take a deep breath. Come on, what else can I say about law school? It's where I belong, it's where I want to go, it's what I want to be. Nothing about those sentences excites me, but I still write them down, hoping seeing them on paper will make a difference. It doesn't. They still look as hollow as they feel, and they feel so subpar to me. So unlike ... so unlike who I want to be.

And who do I want to be?

Someone, I don't know, someone happy with my choices?

I don't have a choice
I don't want my parents to hate me
I don't know if I can do this
Actually.

I hate this.

I hate this. The only reason I chose law was because it was
easiest
couldn't be a doctor, too squeamish
couldn't be an engineer, can't math
this is my default
it doesn't feel real
it doesn't feel like a choice.
Why couldn't I be the one to run away?
this is not a fire poem
patricia will be p i s s e d.

CHAPTER THIRTEEN

I COULDN'T SLEEP, THINKING ABOUT the poem. Thoughts of law school and corporal punishment by way of my parents consumed me the whole night. My timing couldn't be worse. It's the morning of the debate competition and I can't even remember if I'm for or against because all I can hear in my head is: "*I don't know if I can do this, actually.*" Was I serious? Where did that even come from? If I don't go to law school, then where the hell will I go?

Mom has an early shift, so she's with me in the kitchen while I wait for Justin to pick me up. She is spooning boiled yam into one container and tomato stew into another smaller one, but she does it haphazardly while she watches me. When I take a bite of my breakfast cookie, she recoils with irritation.

"Biko, eat real food," she says firmly and with almost too much exasperation for a Wednesday morning. "This is why you're so skinny."

"I'm not skinny," I tell her with a mouth full of cookie. "Auntie Funmi doesn't think I'm skinny," I add, remembering the way she tugged on the measuring tape around my waist.

Mom frowns, jutting out her bottom lip. Her hands work quickly, putting her lunch in her bag and zipping it up. "What does Funmi know?" she tsks and gives me a look.

I try to shrug but buckle under her gaze. I might be imagining it, but her eyes are deeper, probing me as if I should have something to say about that. Should I? Or am I just on edge now that I've started talking to Sam again? I'm not stupid; if Mom and Dad find out, it'd be in the top two worst things that could happen to me, and it wouldn't be number two.

My mom snaps her container shut, startling me. She raises an eyebrow at my sudden jump. "Where is your friend?" she asks. "You said he'd be here by now."

"I thought so too," I mutter, glancing at my phone. It's just after nine thirty. I'm already so anxious about the competition and looking at the time isn't helping.

"You're missing school for this?"

"Yeah. My teachers okayed it, though."

"Hmm." With a wry smile, she says, "So then you must win."

"I will," I say, even though I'm not feeling very confident. I'm hoping that will change. I'm hoping when I get up on that stage and open my mouth, I will realize I belong there and I'll remember what's important to me, and to my family.

9:31 A.M.

I shove the rest of my cookie in my mouth and chew quickly. "Mom," I begin. She stares at me. "Mom, do you think it's weird I have two names?"

She chortles. "Ah-ah! Why is it weird, na? Some people have three, four, five names sef."

"No, but, like, they have all . . . similar names. Don't you feel a type of way that one of my names is so English and one is so Igbo?"

"A type of what?"

"Like a type of—I mean, don't you feel weird?"

"You people like to call everything *weird*," she snorts like she's spitting out the word. "Me, I don't know. Both your first and second names are very beautiful. So what is it?"

"Wouldn't you want people to call me Ada instead of Sophie?" I ask her.

"They can call you Ada . . ." She hums. "And Adanna, Adaoku, Adaeze—"

"Oh my god, Mom."

She laughs, her teeth bared with amusement on her tired face. "They can call you any of those names if they can pronounce it. But they cannot. So what is it?"

"I mean—"

"Ada, n'ezi-okwu, your own too much, o," she says, still chortling. She's acting like I just told her a joke. Me, her amusing daughter who's always saying such weird things. I'm not even trying to be funny right now! "I gave you two names that I like for a girl. I didn't think that one is better than the other. I didn't teach you that one is better, so what's the problem?" Man, the sharp way Nigerian parents ask "*what's the problem?*" really makes you feel like you're bottom of the barrel, in turmoil, just casually suffering.

I reach for another cookie, but Mom snaps, "My friend, go and eat food!" before my hand grazes it. She makes a point to stuff the cookie box back in the cupboard before she breezes past me to the door. It leaves me just enough space to think about what she said. There was no reason for me to bring it up now when I should be thinking about debate and cultural appropriation and cross-cultural kids. It's like I'm going through a quarter-life crisis at seventeen.

Maybe I'm just worried about debate. Cross-cultural kids is such a touchy subject. You're never wholly both, but also not one or the other. Having a first and middle name from two cultures feels like you're masking one side of yourself just to blend in with another. I never thought I had a problem with it, but maybe I do. Maybe I'm not okay with how I've been dealing with things. Maybe it just took the debate competition to see it.

Justin arrives a little after my mom leaves and we spend the ride to the competition school in near silence. The radio cranks out some soft rock song that sounds like it's way before our time. The beat is so irregular and awkward. It has no rhythm, no soul, no vibrant drumming. No poetry.

"Are you nervous?" Justin asks me.

It feels like this is all he asks me sometimes. "Not really."

"Mr. Patel said they're recording the whole thing to post online."

"Mmm."

"You fixed up the midsection of your argument, right?"

His anxiety is valid but horribly misdirected right now. We're a good team normally, so why's he freaking out the one time we illegally got the motion beforehand and had more time to prep? We should both be coasting right now.

"I got it," I tell him absently. "I had a whole section about different names, but I may not use it."

He gasps. "No way, why? The whole using-different-names-to-traverse-different-spaces thing . . . it's real. I don't think you should throw it away."

A nudge of pride swells in my chest. I'm happy to know at least one other person gets it, if only a little. "You have two names too, right?" I ask, shifting to face him. "Like you have your English name and your Chinese name...?"

"Are you asking me if I have a Chinese name?"

"Yes." Then I ask with a grimace, "Is that racist?"

"I mean..." He shrugs, trying to think of the best way to say *Yes, it is*, probably.

I shake my head right away. "Don't answer. I'm not trying to be one of 'those' people."

"Well, I can answer because it's you," he says. "I have one, but only my mom calls me by it, and only sometimes."

"What is it?"

"Wai Lun."

"That's dope."

He glances at me and I'm not sure why. "I guess," he says. "If not for Chinese school when I was younger, I probably wouldn't know what it is. My mom kinda insists on calling me Justin everywhere these days."

"Does she not like your name or something?"

"I don't think that's it," he goes on. "I mean, I don't really know. I thought about it a lot when I was a bit younger, like why she'd always just call me Justin. I wanted her to use my Chinese name a bit more because, you know... I don't look a lot like my mom, so I thought it'd be better if I could just tell people my Chinese name and they, you know, would realize I wasn't just white. I thought it'd be easier."

"Easier?" I repeat. I've been thinking about ease a lot

lately too, but something about the way Justin says it is different. There's sadness there where my ease was desperate. I slouch back in my seat, nodding slowly. "Yeah, well…I think you look like your mom."

He scoffs. "Yeah, okay. You're literally the only one who's ever said that."

"How?" I frown. "I look at your face all the time and I see way more of your mom than your dad."

Now it's his turn to frown, raising an eyebrow while he glances sideways at me. "Why are you looking at my face all the time?"

"Oh…uh." I clear my throat. My cheeks burn warmer the longer he watches me. "I just meant, like, it's me who has to look at you when you're speaking. Like, you don't have to…um…like, *you* don't look at yourself, so I just meant like…Anyway."

He turns back to the road, content with my non-answer. "Well, thanks," he says coolly. "That's a compliment."

"I know it is. Your mom is so pretty."

"Okay, listen, if you have a thing for my mom—"

"Please just take the compliment and go."

The debate competition is being held at Alderstone, a neighboring high school known more for its arts department than anything. The irony that I'm doing a debate competition at an arts school isn't lost on me.

We're shuttled into the auditorium, where a man is on

stage welcoming everyone. Mr. Patel is here already, seated at the back. Josh and Arjun are there too, looking just as nervous as they normally do. "How was the drive over?" Mr. Patel asks when we come to join them.

Justin and I both shrug and mumble, "Okay, I guess." "It was fine."

Mr. Patel frowns. "Now you're starting to sound like these two." He nods to Josh and Arjun.

"Well, I mean, the legality of it all…," Josh utters, casting a glance over his shoulder. "A-and then, what if, technically, we prepared for the wrong motion?"

"You haven't, trust me," Mr. Patel says, though his eyes are focused on the stage at the foot of the auditorium. When I tilt my head, he cuts in, "Don't look! It'll be fishy if we're all staring."

I snort. "Sir, it's fishy already."

"The motion is fine," he tells us. "And you guys are my best teams. Try and look a bit more lively, eh?" He gives a casual chuckle, staring around at us, but we're low on excitement. "Okay, come on. Let's go over the basics: clarity, clarity, clarity. No matter what, don't forget to articulate and make eye contact. Let people know how you feel."

How I feel.

Our team is facing a school called Northbridge from Scarborough. I recognize them immediately because they wear uniform blazers that say their school name and sit in the crowd near the back. Three girls and one boy, the opposite to our team. Every time the judges lean in and talk among themselves, the boy nudges the girl closest to him and points with his whole arm at their row. Not subtle at all.

I am calmer than I thought I would be, sipping water and watching each of the teams go up. The judges are unwavering and don't smile as they take notes on the papers in front of them. I spend more time watching the back of their heads than thinking about our motion. I guess that's okay because, technically, we aren't supposed to know what our motion is.

The seconds turn into minutes and by eleven, Justin, Josh, Arjun, and I are escorted backstage. "Are you nervous?" Justin asks me as we wait in the wings.

I shake my head. "You gotta stop asking me that."

"Habit," he mutters, and rubs his eyes.

"Hey, did you see the Northbridge kids?" Arjun whispers. "They're wearing school blazers. I think they're a Catholic school. Private school, too."

I cringe. "Worst combination."

Five minutes to our time, our team is introduced, taken on stage, and seated at our table. The auditorium is much larger and scarier from here. We can see the judges' faces now as they scribble and whisper with each other in the front row. They don't look anything like what we thought they would be: white, suburban, cold, unwavering. Instead,

I spy an older woman in a hijab at the end. There's a young black guy, too, who looks a lot like someone Tayo might be related to. I don't look at him, though, because I don't want him to sense my fear.

At this point, Justin and I and Josh and Arjun aren't one team anymore; we're two teams competing for the highest score. Justin and I take a seat at the first table and Josh and Arjun take a seat at the table beside us.

My ears gloss over the formalities but manage to pick up when the chief adjudicator says, "The motion is: 'The house believes all forms of cultural appropriation and appreciation are wrong.'" I give the biggest sigh of relief in my head. Thankfully Mr. Patel's sketchy connections came through. "Northbridge will argue the proposition. Clearwater for the opposition."

Right away, we begin scribbling on our notepads, coming up with arguments. Or, in our case, rehashing points we'd discussed already. All we have is fifteen minutes. I reproduce my notes in the same format as my notebook: in verse. Justin leans over, his brow furrowed at my sloppy writing. "Those are notes, right?" he hisses. "Like, I know you've been into poetry lately, but please."

"These are notes!" I hiss back. My mind goes back to the Poetry Slam, and Sam, and my notebook. Worst timing! "Stop distracting me. I need to concentrate."

"You're up first, you know that right?" he asks.

"Yeah, I got it."

I write faster and faster, scribbling out the argument points I remember, pushing poetry out of my mind. Still, it shows up on my page in verse, just like how Sam writes. Now, I can't unsee it, those similarities.

After fifteen minutes, the chief adjudicator says into his mic: "The proposition, Northbridge."

The Northbridge boy gets up first, thanking the judges before he takes his place on the podium. "My name is Kieran and I'm representing Northbridge Catholic Secondary School. Are we ready?" he begins, looking around for nods from his competition. Then, he takes a deep breath and says: "Is there even such a thing as cultural appropriation?"

I snicker against my better judgment and whisper, "We fucking won this." Justin flashes me a smile and nods.

The judge who looks like Tayo's cousin begins to write. Man, I wish I could see what's on his scorecard. If Kieran is trying to argue that cultural appropriation is wrong because it doesn't exist—that's not even worth a whole statement. That's just straight-up garbage.

Josh and Arjun are trying to be super professional at their table, but in my peripheral, I can see Arjun slowly lean forward. He glances at us, eyes wide for a moment, before he sinks back into his seat. It's so fast that I almost miss it, but that's Arjun's "*what the fuck?*" look. I'd know it anywhere.

A minute passes in Northbridge boy's speech, which

means he's open for attack—er, I mean, point of inquiry. I shoot up my hand.

"Yes?" Kieran pauses, gesturing that I should stand and speak.

So I do: "You said that cultural appropriation is rooted in power dynamics. What evidence do you have to support that cultural appropriation and appreciation affect white people and people of color the same way?"

Kieran nods while I speak. He pounces on my words, confidence ripping through his answer. "Yeah, of course—so, there's growing evidence to support that cultural appropriation negatively affects white people as well as people of color. Public perception of what is and isn't acceptable for white people can cause a different kind of stress, one that psychologists are currently looking into."

My eyebrow twitches. I can't help it. "So is that to say that the stress white people experience after the personal choice to appropriate is equal to the stress people of color face when it comes to having their cultures trivialized?"

Kieran's mouth twists as he contemplates. "I think the central takeaway here is that appropriation and appreciation is a thin line that negatively impacts *all* people, once again proving why any form of borrowing or supplementation should be strongly cautioned against."

I don't put up my hand again or else the judges will penalize me for heckling, so I sit and stew in my frustration.

Kieran is doing a good job with his argument. I know he is, because he's engaging and the judges love people like that, but I still can't help but bristle at what he says. Justin glances at me. I know what that look means. *Save it for opps.*

Kieran's five minutes end and he sits down, folding the flaps of his blazer inward. The head judge finishes writing down one last comment before he leans forward into his mic again. "The opposition, Clearwater," he says.

I shoot up and make my way over to the podium. My heart is racing, thumping louder and louder in my chest. I try to keep my mind on the argument. I try to stay calm.

The first thing I do is smile. "Good morning, I'm Sophie representing Clearwater Secondary School," I say. Suddenly, the apprehension and fears begin to dwindle, and as I speak, I realize I've said this speech so often that I could recite it in my sleep. "Does cultural appropriation exist? Yes. At the same time, are all depictions of cultural appropriation wrong? No." One of the male judges clears his throat in the front. I look at him, hoping that it comes off as a sign of confidence, but he is looking down, scribbling on the page in front of him. "When we talk about the white gaze, we can say expertly that the power dynamics inherent there have negatively affected people of color. However, there are other power structures intrinsic in discussions surrounding cultural appropriation, especially when it comes to cross-cultural kids. We're seeing it today. Our official definition states that these are kids who adopt culture from their parents, their environment, and oftentimes, a mixture of the two. Many of these cross-cultural kids are the children of immigrants, refugees, or international adoptees. Sometimes it isn't just a choice; it is survival, a necessity. These children have had to adopt ways to camouflage in order to be seen as worthy of their adopted culture, especially if this culture is a combination of their initial two. Especially if this culture is Western . . ."

Quickly, I gulp down my uncertainty and insecurity. I may have rehearsed this, but that doesn't stop me from feeling so seen, so vulnerable up here.

"Um, the adoption of Anglicized names to blend in with Western culture can oftentimes be a double-edged sword. In many instances, a child who is striving to be enough for both of their cultures is ostracized in public spaces for being 'too ethnic,'" I say with air quotes. "While other times, these same children are singled out in their communities for being, once again, 'too white.' White, in this situation, refers to Western cultures and ideals, and the construct of whiteness.

"There are many of us who move through life in two lanes. These lanes are often so different from one another that many of us—many of *you*, sorry—would be shocked to learn to what extent they differ. But still, both parts create the whole. If a child is born from two parents of a certain culture, but they happen to be living in another country, they are immediately immune from these preconceptions because there is no dominant adoption—and dominant adoption lies at the center of what cultural appropriation is. In this case, their belonging to a culture is steeped in their upbringing, not an adoption later in life, so these kids should be exempt from prior definitions and scrutiny when it comes to cultural appropriation. For cross-cultural kids, there is no appropriating what you really are."

CHAPTER FOURTEEN

WE RANK SECOND OVERALL IN the competition, which I'm okay with because at least we outranked Kieran's team. They placed fifth. Josh and Arjun were fourth. A team from St. Andrew's Catholic Secondary School edged ahead of us with their proposition on gun laws. Their stance was bold and clear: "Let it die before we do." Honestly, it's hard to argue with that.

"Good job, everyone, of course," Mr. Patel says with a grin, folding his arms across his chest. "You two were so nervous for nothing. Second place is really good in this situation, if you ask me. Those first-place kids? Incredible. You just can't argue against better gun laws, can you?"

Justin shakes his head. "Yeah, no."

And I agree. "No way."

I am tempted to call Sam and tell him how the competition went, or at least promise to show him the video when it's posted online. A long time ago, he used to be that person for me, someone I could always talk to. My hand hesitates around my phone and I hate that it does. I hate that my first instinct isn't to call him up immediately and scream, "Guess what!" as loud as I can.

"He might not even answer...," I mutter to myself as I dial his number. The phone rings three times and I brace for the worst. It connects on the fourth ring. "Oh, um," I say at the same time as Sam says, "Hey!"

"Hey," I repeat, relieved at how happy he is to hear from me. "How's it, uh, going?"

"Good, good," he replies with a sigh. The conversation fizzles out as soon as it begins. I panic and fight the urge to just hang up when he says, "How's your poem going?"

"Oh, the poem..." Not even debate is enough to make me forget the words I wrote about law, all that uncertainty, everything. In my core, I'm still shaken by my disloyalty. "My team ranked second in debate," I blurt out.

"Uh...oh, legit?" he gasps. "He-ey, congrats, o! That's dope, but expected, of course. You no know say Naija no dey carry last!"

I giggle at what's become an unofficial Nigerian proverb

these days. "I know, o... I know," I say, and then nothing more.

If Sam feels the awkwardness, he doesn't bring it up. Instead, he prods again, "So how's the poem?"

After a beat of silence, I tell him, "I think I might need help. I need your expertise. You're the creative one, remember?"

He chuckles, "Don't make me call you out for those notes again. You have my address already. Come through whenever this week. Yo, I can cook jollof rice. That bomb-ass kind Mom used to make."

I gasp, nearly staggering back from excitement. Jollof rice is the great equalizer among West African people, even though we all like to fight about whose is the best. Mom makes the best jollof rice: tinged with a smoky flavor, the right amount of pepper and tomatoes, and the right softness so the grains almost bounce in your mouth while you chew. It's my weakness. If I'm being honest, it's all our weaknesses. So when I say "Deal" and Sam bursts out laughing, I can't even be mad. This feels like our real first step back to being cool with each other again.

I spend the next day thinking more seriously about the type of poem I want to write for this assignment—and trying to shelve that horrendous first attempt at the back of my mind. My uncertainty about law school creeps up every time I think of poetry. The words: "*I don't think I can do this...*"

Something about them is so haunting, like a cloud hanging over my head. Makes me scared someone will find out.

Patricia texts me some videos of spoken word artists performing and it does nothing to make me feel any better. I tell her thanks even though I don't intend to watch any of them. Plus, I don't have time. Not only am I struggling with my supposed creativity but I need to help decide on table placements for arguably the biggest Nigerian wedding to ever land on this side of the Atlantic. I don't think I'm ready.

By the time Saturday rolls around, I know I'm not. The entrance and main hall of the venue looks way more different than it did two months ago. Large swaths of royal blue fabric drape over the windows outlined by light cream-colored chiffon. Countless naked tables fill the hall, but they're thrown all over the place like no one had a chance to arrange them yet. Boxes of decorations and centerpieces are stacked in the far corner. Brand-new chafing dishes in boxes are sitting under a long table by the kitchen door. Staring at all the small things lying around is making me dizzy. There's even someone with a measuring tape and a small clipboard running around, but I have no idea what he's meant to be doing. He just measures a doorway, jots down the reading, tsks at the open air, and shuffles off to another corner.

"Wow," I remark, looking around. "I don't remember any of this."

Blessing barely pays me any attention when I walk in. Her glasses are askew, hanging off her nose, and she still has to squint to get a good look at me. In her hand, she has a small notepad and pen. She's also balancing her cell on her ear while she speaks rapidly into it.

I spot Chioma and wave as I approach. She has her arms crossed, her mouth in a permanent frown. That's how I know I left her alone with Genny and Blessing too long. Chioma doesn't have the same effortless cool and cranky thing Genny has going on. Instead, she's just cranky. "Oh, you don't remember?" she barks. "Na wa for you. So you missed *one* meeting and we're supposed to just wait for you to catch up?"

"Wow, okay, calm down," I tease, pinching her in the arm. It loosens her up a little. "What does Blessing need help with?"

Chioma rolls her eyes. "Many, many things." I follow as she heads over to a stack of chairs and pulls the top one down before sitting on it. Chioma pushes her long twists over her shoulder as she leans back. "I'm losing my mind. Genny is public enemy number one, but it looks like Blessing is trying to come for that spot. She's trying to get tables for the press, you know, like local press. Nigerian press is one thing, but I doubt some Toronto blog is gonna care that the girl in the Jesus meme is getting married."

I snort. "Won't they, though?"

"No!" she hisses. Blessing turns to us from across the hall, throwing a finger to her mouth, signaling that we should be quiet. Chioma grumbles and shifts away from Blessing's gaze. "Tayo is so annoying too, you know?" she goes on with a grimace. "He's so far up Ayo's ass about the assistant-ing. Like, Ayo isn't even really helping—he'll say something like, 'oh, oya, Chi-chi'—who even said he could call me that?— 'Chi-chi, come stand here so I can see how far we should position the main stage.' I'm just standing there like, 'main stage?' We're going to have room for a main stage after we section off the high table, the dance floor, the reserved tables, the gifting table, the livestream—they want a livestream! Can you imagine?"

Livestream is the last straw and I burst out laughing despite myself. She frowns at me, her mouth and nose scrunching so hard they nearly touch. "Did I laugh?" she says. "Or I'm funny, abi? God will punish you—"

"I'm sorry," I say, even though I can't stop laughing. "You're really surprised? As if you don't know your own sister."

"Sister, ugh," she groans, rushing her hands through her hair. "I'd rather not have a sibling, like..." She looks at me. It's coincidental, but the moment our eyes lock, I can see the panic behind them. "*You*," she was going to say. She'd rather not have a sibling like how I don't.

She glances away, guilt taking up space where there was exasperation. Maybe it's confidence from ranking second in debate, or maybe it's foolishness from not learning my lesson with Tayo, but I pipe up immediately, "I *have* a sibling," as if that will help the situation.

Chioma's eyes twitch with knowing. "Oh, y-yeah. Yeah." That's it.

Just like Tayo fidgeted with uncertainty when I brought up Sam, Chioma shifts in her seat and lets her eyes wander. She looks at the floor, at the wall, at the ceiling, before she even tries to make eye contact with me. I can't blame her, but I really wish she'd talk to me. She and Sam used to be close too. When the adults would share cake at parties, he would go up and ask for another slice just to give it to her. He didn't even like cake! But whenever Chioma stumbled up and asked if he would grab her an extra, he didn't even think twice. Sam looked out for all of us, so why is it that I'm the only one who can say his name out loud?

"So ...," Chioma starts. "Do you ... like, do your parents talk to him? My dad heard after he got locked up, they completely cut all ties. Harsh, but not surprising."

Again with this? "He's not in jail," I grumble. "He was never in jail. And why is that not surprising?"

She sighs. "Come on, really? Your parents are so strict with the weirdest things. I'd be shocked if they didn't cut all contact. Plus—"

We hear a crash and immediately look over our shoulders to the kitchen entrance where the man who was measuring things has run into a stack of boxes. He bends and restacks them together, muttering and cursing under his breath, while Blessing marches over and begins to yell at him.

The moment is gone. I want to say again, "*Sam was never in jail*," but it's overcompensating at this point. The fact that people are lying about Sam isn't the problem; it's why they had to lie to begin with. Was him being into poetry so bad that Mom and Dad had to lie like this? The rumor mill is out of control.

"That guy is really..." Chioma sighs and flashes me a tired smile, like she's happy to be changing the subject and she thinks I am too. "Genny told Blessing that she wants a masquerade thing, like from a real Igbo village or whatever, and that guy's supposed to make sure the doorways are wide enough for the costume."

"Wild."

"I know."

Silence.

"Different dancers?" I offer.

"Yeah," she says. "They're bringing in the dancers from the 'Yanga' video, and they'll do two sets and then the masquerade will come in and do their performance, but only after Genny and Skeleboy change into their Igbo traditional blue."

"Damn."

"Yeah. She has four outfit changes. Did you know?"

I roll my eyes. "No, but look at my face and find the surprise."

She laughs at that. "She's got white wedding, Igbo traditional blue, Yoruba traditional red, and then the regular ankara print aso ebi that we're wearing."

"Jeeez!"

"That's what I'm saying, ugh," she groans, tossing her head back. "I'm sick of Genny. The second that front door opens, I'm telling you right now that I'm running."

"And you're just going to leave me here?" I gasp. "This is the worst betrayal."

"Excuse me, *I* have been here," she teases. "Besides, you're not the only one in school."

"Oh, so you're going to that still?"

She pulls a face that screams "of course I am!" but we both know she feels classes are more of a suggestion than a requirement. I was there when she was making her university schedule, so excited by the process, but she picked a bunch of classes haphazardly and called it a day. She's not into school the way I am.

"Just because I don't read the dictionary, doesn't mean I don't still go to class," she chuckles. "You're acting like I, too, should be a debate championship winner and have multiple boyfriends or something."

I cringe at the mention of boyfriend-plural, but I know Chioma, and I know she's just saying that so I can take the bait. Lucky for her, the only thing I'm really nervous about right now has everything to do with poetry and nothing to do with which Justin or Tayo fantasy currently makes the most sense in my head. "Yeah, true. School is mad these days. And we ranked second in that competition, by the way. Are my parents really telling people we won first? Also, hey." I cringe as I say, "Did I tell you I have to write a poem for my media arts class? It's this project I'm working on."

Her eyebrows wrinkle with confusion. "Why a poem?"

"It's, uh, what my partner chose," I lie. "I'm trying to write something unique, but I don't know what it should be about."

"What do you mean?" she scoffs. "This is a school project, right? Casually excelling at everything shouldn't even be a problem for someone like you, first-class over-sabi."

I laugh. "What?"

"Just write about, I don't know, life," she says. "How hard it is being seventeen and already knowing you want to go into law. Acing debate competitions so you can have the buffest résumé ever. Keeping so firmly on track that even my own parents are like, 'you should be more like Ada.'" She snorts at that, a hint of bitterness poking through. I pretend not to hear it. "There must be something there, right?"

Another laugh gets caught in my throat and I cough over it like it doesn't belong to me. That cloud, that uncertainty about law school, comes back and circles overhead. I swallow, hard, knowing full well Chioma can't see it, but still afraid she can sense it like I can.

Chioma chuckles nervously while she watches me. "What's wrong with you?" she asks.

"Nothing," I say, though my mind is still somewhere in poetry land.

"Having second thoughts about law school?" she prods, leaning in closer and lowering her voice.

Every now and then, I feel the cloud get closer and closer. It's hovering mere inches from my head now and it's boring down on me. I'm so uncomfortable. "N-no way. I'm just—my mind is just all about this art project thing. I want to get a good grade, you know. Yeah. How shitty would it be if an art class brought down my average?"

Chioma straightens back up, unconvinced. "You know," she says. "We clown you a lot about this pre-lawyer stuff, but it's okay to change your mind. You're so damn serious. When I finished high school, I thought I would go into engineering too, but now? Don't tell my parents but I switched most my courses to psychology. They'll find out when I get my degree, anyway."

"What?"

"No one knows what they want when they first start high school," she goes on. "And if they do, they definitely don't follow through."

"Yeah, but what else...?" What else do I do? What else do I become?

The front door clicks open in the distance but Chioma doesn't move. She knows it's Genny, anyway.

"It's so cold in here," Genny calls out. "Someone turn on the heating, please." Neither Chioma nor I move. She claps her hands loudly twice. "Hello? Are you people asleep?" she calls again, stalking over in her heeled boots. I turn just in time to see Ayo tailing behind her, one hand with his phone glued to his ear and the other hand holding a Louis Vuitton bag. They're both wearing sleek sunglasses, but only Genny takes hers off. "Am I interrupting something or what?" she asks.

"Do you want me to answer truthfully, or?"

"Chioma, if I sound you this night, you will never know peace."

"I thought Blessing was the one who was planning your wedding. Shouldn't you be talking to her?"

Genny inhales sharply, a hiss that's as good as a slap.

Chioma holds up her hands in surrender. "We were just talking about school." Genny looks at me and I nod quickly. We *were* talking about school, but the way Genny looks at me makes me feel like I'm lying. God, how does she do that? "Ada has this art project at school and she's thinking she might do a poem or something."

Genny's eyes bulge for a moment while she steels her

gaze on me. I've never seen her so still. She's mechanical in the way she moves, eyes clocking me before I even have a chance to register what's going on. For a moment, I see a hint of a softer Genny, one who isn't buried in wedding planning, one who I'm much more used to. She says, "Poetry?" and it's not even an attack. She's being sincere.

I give a noncommittal shrug. "Yeah, but, it's just for this school thing. It's not that...it's not that deep."

Genny keeps watching me and it's making me mad uncomfortable. I don't know where to look or put my hands. Even Chioma is weirded out. "That sounds cool," Genny tells me plainly. "Do you like...poetry?"

Chioma and I exchange uncertain looks. "It's not something that I've..." My mouth is moving without a clear direction. "It's, uh, it's just for school. It's really not..."

"Are you gonna tell her parents or something?" Chioma cuts in, confused. "Look, you're making the girl nervous."

"For what?" Genny asks, genuinely shocked. She looks at me and I try to put on my most confident, not-confused, not-intimidated face. "Am I making you nervous?"

"N-no," I stutter. Genny doesn't buy it for a second. "It's fine."

"I'm just saying if you like poetry, that's cool," she tells me before glaring at Chioma. "Maybe it's you who I'm making nervous."

Chioma cringes. "That's a direct insult, ah-beg."

Genny doesn't spare another word for us. She breezes past us into the hall, Ayo trotting behind her. She might as well have had a cape with the way she crosses the room with purpose. I envy her, truly. She's tall and beautiful with perfect eyebrows and matching foundation, always. A real Nigerian girl, poised and elegant. And sure of herself, too.

Genny sets down her shades and purse on a table near the dance floor and looks around. "Blessing? This room is... it's so cluttered," she says just as Blessing waltzes over.

"We're doing measurements," she tells her. "Today's the final day for us to confirm with the performers so I want to make sure we have space."

Ayo looks around too. How he can see anything with those dark-ass shades is beyond me. "Okay, but some of these tables should still be moved. Oya," he calls to us, waving a hand. Chioma groans loudly as she rises and trudges over. I follow much quieter. "You two move these tables, but leave space enough to walk behind. Like this." He shifts left and right between two close tables, showing the distance necessary. Ayo isn't a large man and I think he's forgetting there will be aunties upon aunties wearing three layers of fabric trying to navigate this space. Blessing raises an eyebrow as she watches him. She knows.

Genny points to the dance floor. "But I want you guys to also leave some space to the left and right of the dance floor," she tells us, then turns to Blessing. "Right? The dancers need to spread out and we also need the room for the traditional portion."

"And the livestream deck," Blessing adds, tapping her pen on her lip. "I'll show you where I'm thinking we'll set up the computer. I want him by the DJ, but I'll see what you think."

Suddenly, Ayo's phone rings. He brings it to his ear and says, pretty loudly, "Hello? Yeah, yeah, yeah, I'm here right now. I'm just, you know, doing some wedding things, you know..."

"Ada," Genny says, fanning her arms out around the room. "I want your opinion too, you know."

"I know."

"Be honest: Do you think this is big enough for the traditional wedding *and* the dancers?"

"I think so," I say, looking around. The walls feel ages away from where I'm standing. Soon, the hall will be decked out in gold and royal blue everything from top to bottom. It'll smell like wine and rice and assorted fried meats. It will be smoky with the scent of perfume and cologne from each auntie and uncle who bought the latest offerings at the border. It will be witness to the grandest wedding celebration probably ever. "'Yanga' only has two rows of dancers and they don't need much more space than this," I tell her.

"Um!" Blessing cuts in. "But to be safe, should we add another row of space?"

"Ada has watched that video a million times, so let's go with her on this one."

Wow, exposed.

Blessing jots something down but not before flashing me a disgruntled look.

Genny nods slowly as she looks from wall to wall. I wonder if it's all coming together for her now. Her eyes twinkle and I find myself thinking, wow, she's *really* getting married to Skeleboy. Like, actually. It's exactly the sort of thing that would happen to her.

She catches me watching her and hides a smile. "You would like something like this," she says to me.

"A traditional wedding?"

She nods. "Listen, you can modernize whatever you want, but that doesn't make it special. It took me a long time to understand that. At the end of the day, this is your tradition. It's who you are, and that means something."

CHAPTER FIFTEEN

I TAKE TWO BUSES: THE first picks me and my heavy schoolbag up around the corner from my house after I convince my parents to let me bus to the library. Mom insists she can just drop me, but I tell her I want to use the time on the bus to study more—to pre-study. Neither her nor Dad watch as I get scooped up and driven twenty minutes away to a busy junction. My next stop is on one of the diagonals, but it takes me too long to figure out which and by the time I do, the bus I need rushes by me. The next one takes me ten minutes into a suburb I haven't been to before. Forest Hill area, I think. I imagine everyone here has a career job and drives nice cars, but maybe not.

The bus curves down a street with rows of apartment

complexes that are all the same copper brick save for different colored doors. I step off the bus in front of one of the buildings, this one with a green door. A group of guys stands outside laughing and talking loudly with backpacks hiked up their shoulders. None of them pay me any attention as I slip past.

The seventh floor is the top floor but it isn't labeled as penthouse like it would be in other buildings. When the elevator doors stagger open, I see why. It's less of a penthouse and more like a pre-rooftop; a hazy hallway with musty windows that used to shine light through them. At the very end of the hall, there's a door that leads outside onto the real roof, but I stop my feet just short of it. I head straight to number 706.

Sam opens the door without me having to knock.

He grins and pulls the door open wider. I'm immediately assaulted by the smell of jollof rice, always a staple in our house, and it hits me with a deep nostalgia. It's like nostalgia for a simpler time, hunger, and relief all at once. "You're late," he says plainly. No greeting, nothing. And I don't even feel mad about it.

I grin widely, my first in a long time with Sam. "Pleeeeease. Instead of you to greet me—"

"Ah-ah, greet wetin? I'm your elder," he jokes.

"Elder for where? Common mumu like you."

He snorts. "Okay, get in."

My eyes take in every inch of his place as if I'll never be back here again. I memorize every corner, every scuffed-up wall, every desk stacked high with books. So many books. Engineering books, too. With one step closer, it's easy to see the layer of dust on top of them. It must have been ages since he was actually in school.

Sam pops his head out from around the corner. "Sit, sit," he says, gesturing to the worn-in leather sofa by the wall. "Give me one second. How's the poetry going?"

I sit and sink into the sofa immediately. "Sorry?"

He calls again, "The poetry," and emerges from past the kitchen wall. "Have you written anything yet or are we starting from scratch?"

"I'll let you decide...," I utter sheepishly. When he's done cooking and I'm well fed with way too much jollof rice, I'll tell him that I have nothing. Absolutely nothing. I became scared of my newly dubbed poetry book after I wrote that sacrilege about law school, and I've been terrified to try again. What if I say something else I don't mean? Or, worse, what if I say something horrible and mean it?

Sam returns my smile albeit sadder. I wonder if he can see right through me. He always could. "You like extra spicy rice, right?" he asks.

"Of course!" I say right away.

He laughs. "Okay, but I only got maybe three water bottles in the fridge. You know I don't trust tap water."

Sam learned to cook rice just like Mom's with that rich, smoky flavor I love. I remember when he asked Mom to teach him a long time ago. Maybe I was seven or eight. Dad laughed but Mom agreed to teach him because, yes, times were changing, it's good for her son to know how to feed himself. "So you want him to just go useless some girl's life?" Mom had said. Dad stayed quiet after that.

Sam brings out two bowls of rice, placing them at different seats at his makeshift dining table. I take up an empty chair and curl in as the steam from the rice wafts into my nostrils. Heaven, pure heaven. I shovel forkfuls of rice into my mouth like I haven't ever seen food before. I'm so into this rice that I don't notice Sam go into my bag by the sofa at first until he circles back around to join me at the table. I don't even protest as he flips my book open, and flips, and flips. I watch him without watching, glancing away when I catch him wanting to make eye contact with me. "Ada," he speaks up. "This book is pretty much empty."

"It's not … it's not empty," I tell him, covering my mouth so rice doesn't fly out all over the place. "There's a few pages where you can see I *kinda* tried it."

"You barely tried it," he chortles and then lets the book fall to the table. "You gotta give me something to work with here."

"I know. It's just harder than I thought. A-and when I thought I was getting somewhere, well … weird stuff kept coming up."

He raises an eyebrow. "Weird how?"

I swallow, uneasy. "I don't know... Stuff about law school." Sam's eyebrow is still raised, confused, as he prods me to go on. "Law school... and the whole lawyer thing. I was writing about that for a second but I stopped."

"What about it?"

I shrug, unable to say the words, but he takes one look at me and he knows. Maybe it's the pout I'm fighting to hold back; maybe it's the way my eyes hyper-focus. He *knows*. He says, "You don't wanna do it."

"I do!" I say, hurriedly. "I'm already good at everything I need to be in order to be a good lawyer, so—"

"You do realize you can be good at more than one thing, right?" he chuckles.

My eyes steel on him as I reply, "Not everyone has that luxury."

He wants to roll his eyes, I know he does, because he doesn't get it yet. I can see the pull behind them, the beginning of a lazy swing, but instead, he snaps my book shut. "Okay, stop eating. Stop. Give me that." He reaches forward for my plate. I inch it away from him but he snatches it in the end, setting it beside him on the table. "Get up. Let's try something."

"Get *up*? Like stand up?"

"Uh, yes?" he snorts, replicating my tone. "What else?"

I begrudgingly get to my feet and he gestures for me to

join him in the middle of the room. I shuffle over, slouched and still hungry. My eyes fly over to my unfinished plate, but Sam snaps his fingers in front of my face to bring me back to where we are: standing in the middle of his mismatched, cramped living room.

"Roll your shoulders back. Like this," he tells me while he demonstrates. "You're too damn stiff. If you want to spark your creativity, sometimes it helps to move around a bit. Find the words you want to say through movement."

"I—"

"Hold your hands up."

"What?"

"Over your head. Fast fast."

I do as I'm told and I feel stupid. "You're not going to join me?" I ask.

He follows suit, laughing. "How's school going?"

I frown. "Why you wanna know about school?"

"I don't," he says. "I'm trying to get you talking and thinking and moving at the same time. Arms in front." He holds his arms out at chest level and I do the same. "How's school? Tell me about everything."

"Um…uh." I clear my throat, trying to steady my arms. "Things are calmer now that we did the debate competition."

"Can't believe you placed second."

"I wanted to be first, though."

"You always want to be first," he says with a small smile. A sad one, too. "Tell me more about this art project you have to do. It's what the poem is for, right?"

"Uh . . . I don't know what else to say. It's different, it's too brand-new, it's harder than I thought it would be."

"Why?"

I roll my eyes. "Because I'm not an artist."

"We went over this," he chides. "Everyone's an artist."

"Not everyone."

"Yes, everyone. Arms out to the side."

I hold my arms out before he can. "You guys made it seem so effortless out there on the stage. Like, you just opened your mouth and started speaking—and you speak Igbo? Since when?"

He laughs. "Bro, you know I only know how to say one damn thing. Mom and Dad never taught us."

"Yeah . . ." I sigh. Sam grins at my obvious discouragement. "What?"

"You're sad about this," he says very matter-of-factly. "You're sad about not being able to speak it."

"I mean, yeah," I say with a shrug. My arms are starting to feel heavier and heavier. "When can we change positions?"

"Yeah, uh. Turn around," he tells me and spins so his back is facing me. I move to face the far window overlooking the street below. We're too high up for me to see any of it. "Would you learn now if you could?" he calls over his shoulder.

I nod, and then say, "Yeah, maybe," once I remember he can't see me.

"Why maybe?"

"I don't know. A part of me feels like it's too late." A crass chuckle escapes my lips. I'm shocked by how bitter it sounds.

Sam says, "Why do you feel like it's too late? You're only seventeen. You have approximately a million years to learn it. Plus, there are textbooks or classes and places where you can pick it up easy."

"Well, a part of me also feels like my parents should teach me," I spit out, that same bitterness still on my tongue. There is silence between us, the kind that is hard to break. Still, I utter, my anger relentless, "*They* should have taught me." My ears are hot, my chest is tight, and my breathing hitches with tension. All of these physical reactions to just one thought. Thank God Sam can't see my face right now.

The silence doesn't let up. Anxiety creeps up my fingers, into my hands, and I start clenching and unclenching my fists. Why isn't he saying anything? I stutter out a "Why did you..." before my throat dries. What's the problem? I've asked this before, but it feels different now that we're back-to-back. I try again: "Why..." but I can't get the words out. I'm frustrated because the question wants to come out, but it's me, I'm the one who keeps stopping it. I'm enraged with the thought that it's me who's standing in my own way. So I take a deep breath, and I say, "Why did you leave?"

There's no relief after the question hits the open air. Instead, that bubbling frustration and rage and unrest hits its peak, and I can't calm down anymore.

"What?" His voice cracks without warning and I can hear his uneasiness, almost feel it, behind me. "Me?"

"Who else? Why did you leave?"

"This exercise is supposed to be for you—"

"Yeah, well *I* want to know why *you* left." My chest is still tight with more words I can't say, words I thought I was over and done with: "*You betrayed me, you betrayed Mom and Dad and everything they did for us, you didn't even try to look for me, you pretended like we didn't exist for six years.*"

"I didn't *leave*," Sam tells me softly. "I was kicked out."

"Wait... what?"

Kicked out... that's...

That's not what could've happened, right? I'm trying to remember.

God, wasn't it... It was the night before my first day of middle school, Sam came into my room, pushed a stack of books aside and sat on my desk, locs tied messily atop his head. "Middle school is a different beast," he had snickered, and I was too young and too naive to believe otherwise. He leaned forward, steepling his fingers like some second-rate mad scientist, and said, "You have to know advanced algebra by October or you'll never get above an 80, and Mom and Dad will send you to Nigeria."

I had wanted to go to Nigeria, but not as a form of punishment. "You liar," I laughed, throwing a pillow at him.

He had caught it easily because his reflexes were better than mine. At nineteen, his limbs were longer too. "I'm deadass serious," he had snickered again. I tried not to let it get me worked up, but like a true older brother, Sam knew exactly what to say to get me thinking about the worst-case scenario. I was nervous as hell starting my first day, wondering if seating would be assigned or if I'd have to figure it out on my own. My favorite dress hung by the wayside. I wasn't sure if its sleek fabric or stripes were too try-hard. But then Sam took my mind off it all. He was always doing that and he was so good at it too.

And then the next day, he was gone. The image of him sitting on my desk with steepled fingers as he threatened me with familial expulsion was replaced with an empty space. All I remember was a lot of yelling downstairs, slammed doors, and curses from my parents. Then, just like that, he was gone. And the worst part is I don't know why.

I didn't even have time to be sad about it. The next morning, Mom opened my door and said, "Get up, get ready for school," and that was that. Nothing about Sam or where he disappeared to or how. The void Sam left was immediate, following me while I did my hair, circling me while I brushed my teeth. It trailed me to the door where Chioma was waiting to drive me on my first day, and it hasn't let go since. It is with me in libraries, classrooms, while I study, whispering to me that Sam is gone and I'm all my parents have left, so I better not rock the boat. I can't disappear the way he did.

Except now he's saying he didn't disappear at all.

"Sam?"

He doesn't answer, so I finally turn back around to face him. He does the same. I search his eyes for more of an answer, something else to make sense of what he told me. But his expression is as blank as if he told me about the weather or how many tomatoes he blended for stew. "What?" I repeat. "You were kicked out? By . . . by who?"

"Who else?" he scoffs. When I don't respond, he says, "Mom and Dad, obviously."

"They wouldn't," I snap, shaking my head. "There's no way they'd kick you out. You're . . . you're their only son. My only brother."

"How would there be no way?" he speaks over me.

My lips pull into a tight line. "Was it because of poetry?"

He presses on as if he didn't hear me, but the way his eyes shift shows that he's choosing not to answer. "Even if I wanted to go back, Mom and Dad are just . . . they're so—"

"Was it because of poetry?"

"Why's that so important to you? You keep asking that

question like it means anything, but you don't know the whole story."

"So then *tell* me the whole story!" I bite back. "No one likes to talk about what happened, but all I know is the day after you peaced out, I had to be twice as good, twice as smart, twice as this, twice as that, more like a girl, less like a child—because you weren't good enough anymore. You were gone. I'm the only daughter, I'm the only son."

Sam's demeanor shifts. He can't look me in the eye, but even from the lazy way he stands, I know he doesn't share my rage. He doesn't understand what it's been like for me. I don't know the full story, I don't know what happened— but those are all excuses. If he doesn't care about me, I mean, if he never cared about me, then he should just tell me so I can stop wasting my time. All of this—the poetry, the thinking I'm good for anything other than law school or that I deserve any sort of—anything—happiness, whatever, it's all a waste of time. I don't have his options.

I spin on my heel and make my way back to the table. My unfinished rice stares back at me, but honestly, I don't even want to eat. Just wanna go home.

Sam joins me at the table. He's holding my notebook, pressing it open to a new page. "I don't, uh … I don't have a pen," he mumbles, looking around.

Is he serious? I furrow my brows so hard my face begins

to hurt. "I'm not going to write a poem just because I'm mad."

"I'm not saying you should write a poem," he corrects, fishing out a pen from the desk behind us. He slides both the notebook and the pen over to me. "I'm saying you should write. Something, anything."

I glance down at the empty page like it's taunting me. "This is dumb," I remark. Still, my fingers are itching to write something down but I don't know what. I'm back in my head, thinking too much. "What do I even write about? How my brother was kicked out, consequently abandoned the family, and started writing poetry to spite everyone?"

His eyebrow twitches at that. Good. "I'm thinking like this," he begins. "I'm thinking . . . it's not every day . . .

"It's not every day all the words I want to say are
stuck, like
damn, they're
stuck.
And I know the way to dig them out, I know the way to coax
them, like damn,
they're stuck.
Papa said, 'If na you this be, ah-beg leave
me, because my eyes only see work
na labor they dey count.

No be all this foolishness you dey sprout.

Biko, I don't have your time.'

Like

damn, they're stuck.

But I gotta catch up with my mind out there

I gotta catch up with my mind.

I can't let it die in this house, in here

I can't let it die in this house.

At some point, my sister's gotta get

out, like

damn, she's gotta get

out."

We look at each other, him with that same calmness and cool, and me with my tears. They trickle hot down my face. I wipe them away quickly, smudging them to the corners of my chin, burying them in my pores.

Sam nudges the notebook back toward me. "Okay, your turn," he says.

I take the book and stare down at the blank page. It's scary. It's so open and empty and daunting. "I'm not as good as you," I mumble.

"Well, good," he snorts. "So you can be better."

But I don't want to be better.

I'm so tired of being better. I'm better already. I'm so better it hurts. I'm better at everything I've ever tried, at any academic subject, at any English paper, at any debate topic. I'm done being better. I want to be happy, too.

The pen feels weightier in my grasp and I let it teeter left and right between my fingers. My hand writes the word "*happy*." Sam looks but says nothing. I ask him, "A-are you happy?"

"Me?" he chuckles out nervously. He is hesitant to say so, but he is happier; I can tell. He has his own space, his own mind, his own heart. But he's sadder too, maybe sadder than he's ever been, and I think he knows it. Eventually, he says, "Yeah . . . kinda."

"Kinda?"

"Yeah."

"I want to be happy too," I tell him shyly. The words sound almost childish coming from my mouth but I force myself not to cringe.

He smiles, warm, as he leans toward me at the table. "What kinds of things make you happy right now?"

I pause, racking my brain for a quick answer. "School," is the first thing I say and it makes me want to laugh and cry. "Eww, n-no, not school . . ." But there's nothing else to replace the thought. My mind is completely and utterly blank.

"Okay, try it this way," Sam goes on. "What *would* make you happy?"

"Everything. Nothing," I sigh. Suddenly, my mind is a

mixture of every thought I've ever had come back to haunt me. What if this and what if that all swarm together like a million little voices shouting at me. I sift through them as best as I can. "If I...didn't have to hide so many parts of myself from other people," I say.

Sam nods. "Okay, okay. And what else?"

"If my family...if Chioma or Tayo or our other cousins wouldn't be so weird when I remind them I have a brother." He doesn't blink. Sam understands why they do it, why they are hesitant to engage, but he knows as well as I do that it's wrong.

"What else?" he whispers.

"If you..." I clear my throat. "If you and Mom and Dad could talk." He looks away, groaning awkwardly at that. "I don't know why it bothers me so much. If it's just because you're a poet, I mean...did you kill someone? You know? Is it that deep?"

"Apparently," he sighs, scratching his head. "Ada, I don't know if that's the best idea."

"Why not? You're back for good, aren't you?"

He grimaces, and I brace myself for opposition. "I don't know what that means, but I'm here," he utters.

"Then come to Genny's wedding."

"What?" he gasps. "Uh, wait, that's—Genny's getting married? To who?"

I return his gasp of shock, nearly slamming down my pen in the process. "I didn't tell you?"

"To *who*, Ada?"

A rush of excitement comes over me like the very first time I was told the news, but I play it cool just to watch Sam freak out when I say, "Skeleboy." I'm even impressed with how calm and collected I sound.

Sam's eyes bulge out of his head. "Are you playing with me right now? Skeleboy? *The* Skeleboy? 'Oga I go give your wife one million,' that same Skeleboy?"

"Eww, that's not even his best song!"

"That. Same. Skeleboy?" He gawks. "Jesus...how in the *fuck*?"

"It's Genny, though, like are you even surprised? You know she was a meme last year, right?"

"Damn, yeah, I saw that!"

"She met him in a club, Sam," I say. "An ordinary club, just casually, while she was probably being messy drunk with her friends. And now she's engaged!"

"Jesu..."

"Come to the wedding," I press on. My eyes are pleading while he stares back, dumbfounded that I'm telling the truth. "Prove that you're staying for good, prove that you being here isn't a sham, and come to the wedding. We used to have so much fun, r-remember? You and me and Genny and Chioma and Tayo. We used to...oh my god." I grin, memories rushing back like a wave. "Remember how Auntie Beauty used to cater all the events and her jollof rice was *so* bad? And so we used to go get different meats and different sides and stuff, and tried to figure out what we could pair with the rice to actually make the food tolerable?" The memory warms me and lifts my spirits. I think our final decision was if we took vegetable stew and ate it with the rice, it made the rice taste better, but only if Auntie Beauty didn't also cook the vegetable stew. If that was the case, then we just used to chug malt with the rice to wash out the taste.

Sam has regained focus, but I can still see the small cogs behind his eyes working, thinking about Skeleboy being part of our extended family. He nods quickly. "Y-yeah. Yeah, malt was the answer."

"Malt is *always* the answer."

"Skeleboy, wow."

I chuckle. "Come to the wedding. Listen, don't even worry about it, okay? I got you. I'll ask Blessing. I'll ask Genny. She's gotta say yes. Don't even worry about it, I said!" I put in just as it looks like he's going to protest. "If I ask them and they say yes, which they most definitely maybe potentially will . . . will you come?"

Sam sighs, leaning back in his chair while he thinks. I'm hopeful, twisting the pen back and forth in my hands. He asks, "Would that make you happy?"

I smile. "I think it actually would."

CHAPTER SIXTEEN

I AM AT WILLIAMS WAITING for Patricia. It's weird to see her walk past the double doors into the café and look around for me, because this is usually where Justin and I meet to talk about debate. Instead of him asking me to watch some new debate video or talking about an online video game I've never heard of, Patricia walks toward my table. I barely notice because I'm fully focused on this poem that's almost on fire in my notebook. It is the rawest thing I've ever written. I didn't even know I was capable of writing something like this, but it exists and it's on paper and it's real and I'm terrified of letting anyone see it.

So of course, the first thing Patricia does as she drops down in the opposite seat is squeal and reach for my book, her bangles clanging as they knock against the table. "Let me see, let me see!" I slam my hand down to pin it to the table, but she's faster than I am and slips it out from underneath my grasp. I cry "no!" just as she gasps "yes!" and the entire café is staring at us like we have a problem. "Is this it? It's this one, right?" She doesn't even turn the book around for me to verify; she just reads from the latest page. The page with the least amount of scratches.

"Don't make fun of me, okay?" I blurt out.

Patricia waves a hand and shushes me. She's dead silent when she reads. The sounds of the café are amplified in the absence of her voice. And then she raises her eyebrow— does that mean she's shocked? Does that subtle sniffle mean she's offended? Does she need me to translate some lines?

"Is this…"

"What?" I ask.

"Is this about you?" she goes on, tearing her eyes away from the page. Her eyebrows are still raised and I'm pretty sure that means she hates it.

I hold my breath. "It's… about a girl."

"It's about you." Her eyes sink back into the page where they sit and sway with the words. "This is intense. I can't lie—this is—it's… it's…"

"It's too much, isn't it?"

She sets down the book and shakes her head quickly. "No. It's *good*. It's straight fire," she tells me, her smile creeping back. "I knew you were this good. Like, I just *knew* it. You know what I mean?"

"N-no."

"I could just sense it," Patricia goes on, grinning. "I have a cousin just like you: all brains, no fun. But when he gets in front of a guitar every now and then, whoo! You should hear him."

I nod slowly. My heart rate picks up, tempered and then fast, ringing in my ears. To think I could be anything like her cousin, someone who comes alive with an instrument. A guitar, or a pen.

"And hey, for what it's worth, this right here? It's enough to get us a good grade."

I frown instinctively and push out the words: "But do *you* like it?"

Patricia is taken aback, her eyebrows perfect arches on her face. "Uh, obviously. It's dope."

"That's all that matters, then." My voice is as shaky as my hands as I pull the book back to me. For the first time in a while, I was thinking only about what she thought of it. If she thought it was good enough. If she could identify with it too somehow.

"So I'll need to hear you do the poem before we pick the drum pattern, but I got some ideas already..." She brings out her phone and pulls up a video off YouTube. I lean in while the video loads and jump a little when the electric drumming starts up at full volume. Patricia scrambles to turn down the audio, its loud and chaotic drum pattern piercing the air. She bobs her head and shakes her shoulders in time with the beat. When she notices I'm not dancing along with her, she pauses the video. "Too much?"

"Yeah, this ain't it."

"Okay, are you imagining more this style?" She switches to another video. This beat is much less aggressive than the first and parts of it are soft and mellow. It's more like a river than a violent storm. I can see it fitting with the softer parts of my poem. I can almost hear the words coming out of my mouth to this.

Patricia watches me to gauge my reaction and begins to smile when she sees it. "This one, huh?" she asks.

I nod right away, grinning. "Yeah, this one."

"Cool. I need you to send me a recording of you doing the poem so I can work on the drums."

I shiver at the idea of me recording somewhere in my house and my parents listening in. Patricia must notice the shift in my demeanor. She says, "Unless you wanna just perform it now and I'll record it?"

"N-no," I pipe up. "I'll record it later and send it to you."

"Good, because I called 2020, right," she goes on, setting her phone down. "And I was able to finesse us a spot. Lots of begging, lots of pretending to be interested in the guy's conversation. You know the type. But we got it."

My heart thuds in my chest. "A spot?"

"Yeah," she continues, "to perform. We got the last spot in their monthly Poetry Slam. Yo, we get two hundred dollars for performing, did you know that? We can split it even, obviously. But we don't have to tell Ms. Kay. I don't know if we'd get suspended if she found out we're getting paid to do a project, so this is about to be a prime case of 'see none, won't be none.'"

"We really got it?" I ask. Small jolts of excitement run through me, causing a rumbling uneasiness in my fingers until I start to fidget, clasping and unclasping my hands together. I don't know what I'm feeling. We get to perform, the project is finally coming together—we get to *perform*? In front of *people* who are going to listen to me? "Oh, shit, no," I utter.

Patricia is bouncing up and down in her seat, beaming and laughing and gushing about the performance but I can barely register what she's saying. People are going to be listening to my words. They're going to judge me no matter what, whether they agree or disagree—they're going to be listening to me. Am I happy about this? Is the numbing in my fingers and the dryness in my throat happiness or, I don't know, existential dread?

Patricia knocks the table in front of me and I come back to attention, still as uneasy as before. "Hey, don't worry," she says as if she can see the wheels turning in my head.

"We'll be fine. That poem? Fire. Plus, you're good at debate, so I have faith."

Faith.

Faith does nothing for me as Patricia shows me the poster for the next Poetry Slam. It's the Tuesday following Genny's wedding. Genny and Skeleboy on Saturday, poetry on Tuesday. Faith can suck it.

When I get home, I crawl into my closet and record the poem in hushed tones. I do three versions before I get one that's perfectly audible, and I email it to Patricia. It's so strange hearing my voice like this, with this kind of rhythm strung into the words. Quietly, I listen to the recording a few more times, letting myself be impressed. *I* wrote this. I mean, I had help, but this voice, these words, this is *me*. Patricia definitely seems to think so too. She sends a slew of brown-skinned thumbs-up emojis back.

Justin calls me in the evening. I haven't been thinking about him lately since the idea of him and I as overachieving lawyers seems really trite amid the reality that I may not want to actually be a lawyer. Even my fantasy world is out of whack. Suddenly I'm thinking more about my family and reconciliation, whatever that means. If I can get Sam to come to Genny's wedding, then maybe Mom and Dad would be willing to talk to him, and once they see he's stable and cool and not a nameless bard on the street, they'll see it's not that deep and they won't be so mad.

At me.

Because I don't want to do law.

Not...entirely.

"Hello?" I answer just as the crushing weight of inadequacy presses down on me. I swear I can feel myself sinking further into my bed. This may as well be my final resting place if my parents—*once* my parents find out about my shunted law school ambitions. Jesus, be a shield.

"Are you okay?" he asks. "Your... you sound dead."

"I am."

"Your parents are still mad we only placed second, huh? Because, same," he says.

"They are..." I roll onto my stomach, letting my face sink into the thick cotton of my duvet. It's harder to breathe and speak this way, but it soothes my nerves. "I have something I want to tell you," I mumble, mouth full of comforter.

"O-oh?" he chokes out. It's then I realize my statement is a little suggestive. How it could mean something else. A confession. The love kind. "What's up?"

I push myself up from the bed quickly and shake my head. "Or, I mean, like I want your opinion on something that's been bothering me—"

"Oh... shit... yeah, of course."

"Of course—"

"Biko, what is bothering you?"

I was so deeply buried in my duvet that I didn't hear the

footsteps come up the stairs and lumber toward my door. When I turn around, my dad is standing in the doorway, a jacket looped on his arm as he peers through his glasses at me. He looks tired from work, but even more than that, he looks troubled that something is bothering me. It's a ruse: If I tell him what it really is, I don't think he'd be as nice. What am I supposed to say? "*I don't want to do law and also I've been talking to Sam—remember, your son?—and he's a poet . . . yeah, a poet . . . and not that* I'm *a poet, but he exists as a not-engineer so maybe I can exist as a not-lawyer*"? Please.

I cover the phone and say "Good evening" to him.

He nods back. "How are you?"

"Fine."

"What are you doing?"

I gesture to the device in my hand. "On the phone."

"With who?"

"Justin from school and debate. The one who was here. We're talking about how debate went." I explain quickly so he doesn't have a moment to criticize or jump to conclusions. His face goes through the most hectic emotional journey: outrage that I'm talking to a boy, relief that it's for school, annoyance that it's the same boy he met, pride that I did well in the debate competition.

In the end, he smiles a little. "Nwa m, you're working very hard."

"I try," I say.

"I keep watching your video, the one of you at the competition," he goes on. "I sent it to your uncles too. They are all saying, 'That's the child I raised.'"

He seems so content, so proud to have me as a daughter. I wonder if that will change.

"It will all pay off," he tells me, tapping the doorframe. "In Jesus's name, it will be well. When you enter the university, then you will already be prepared to enter law school—and *gbam*, just like that, you will become a lawyer."

I force a tight smile, unsure what to say to that. My heart sinks further and further into my chest and it takes all the energy I have to stutter out, "Y-yes." There's no way I can tell him now. Maybe a time will come but that time isn't today. Who am I kidding? I'm still plagued by that need to do well, that need to finish this race as it is. Can't deviate too much. Whether or not I've been talking to Sam, whether or not he's been helping me with this poem, I can't abandon my parents the same way he did. I hate so much that this, having another idea that isn't part of the plan, feels like abandonment. My stomach twists with all the contradictions.

"Anyway," he sighs, and then turns to leave. His footsteps slug down the hall toward his room.

I press the phone back to my ear. "Sorry, that was my dad," I tell Justin.

There's a beat of silence where I swear he hung up,

but after a breath or two, he says, "All good. I'm playing *Division*."

I snort. "Am I interrupting?"

"No," he tells me. Another pause. "What did you want to tell me? Or, uh, what did you want my opinion on?"

Dad is safely in his room behind a closed door. He can't hear me; no one can hear me. Still, I get to my feet and slowly nudge my door until it's barely touching the frame. My ears strain to hear if there's someone else who may interrupt, but there's no one. I'm alone, and even still, it's hard for me to say it in the safety of my room. This room has heard all of my hopes and my desires. It's not the place dreams go to die. It's almost like a betrayal when I inch out the words: "I don't think . . . I want to go into law."

Nothing.

There's no bolt of lightning or thundering footsteps from another room crashing into my door. No ancestral curse has been activated from voicing the words. My bones are still intact. It's just my chest, my heart is beating so slowly like it's waiting for the repercussions too. I will it to beat slower and slower because I'm still straining to hear someone, any-one, tell me this is a big mistake; tell me that even though Sam did it, it doesn't mean I can run off like this too.

Justin says, "Oh damn," and I think for a second that he gets it. But then he says, "That's cool," and I realize that no, he doesn't, he really doesn't.

"It's not cool," I hiss, plopping back down on my bed. "I don't know what to do. I've had this plan for so long and now to just toss it? That doesn't make any sense. Who does that?"

He chuckles softly, and I want to be mad, but the low, throaty, almost taunting sound sends a very enticing shiver down my spine. "We're, like, seventeen. Consider the fact that it's not that deep."

I frown. "We are *exactly* seventeen. It is *exactly* that deep."

"You're funny."

"I'm serious," I go on. "I don't know..." If he doesn't get it, he doesn't get it. My chest is tight with all these emotions stuck inside and the pressure refuses to let up because I know, no matter what I say, I won't hear the answer I want to hear. I don't even know what that is. "*Yeah, you need to have your entire future decided right now*"? "*Yes, you're right, we're off to university next year so you need to get your shit in order*"? "*There's no time to be indecisive; just do what you're supposed to and live with it somehow*"? Those are all the things I think I should hear, but I don't know if that's what I need.

"It's okay not to know," Justin says, breaking me out of my trance. "And it's cool if you change your mind. Maybe you should focus on what you like instead."

What I like *ke*? What does he think this is? "I guess," I grunt. I don't have anything to add; I really want to change the topic. I don't want to think about pursuing something I like right now, especially when there's a giant law school–size hole where my future used to be. What's the point?

"Have you talked to your brother lately?"

The crushing emptiness of my indecision fades at the mention of Sam. I sit up straighter.

"Can I even ask that?" he goes on. "I know it was a touchy subject before, so ..."

"No, it's fine," I say. My voice sounds perkier to my ears when my mind wanders back to Sam and the poem. And this final project. Why is it the faintest bright spot on a pretty uncertain future right now? "We're cool. Didn't I tell you? He's even helping me with that poem I have to perform for art class at 2020."

"What? Performing?" he gasps. "Am I invited?"

I snort. "No. I don't need an audience."

"Uh, these things *require* an audience, otherwise they wouldn't be a performance."

"Nerd."

"Plus," he goes on, "I went with you the first time, remember? Don't I get loyalty points for that?"

What I want to say is: "*Definitely not, especially after Patricia's girlfriend asked if we were dating and you boldly said no before we could let the idea breathe.*"

Instead, I say, "I don't give out loyalty points. I'm not a hardware store." It makes me laugh because it sounds exactly like something my dad would say.

Justin snickers. "What? Is the only reason you're saying no because you're afraid it's not gonna go well?"

The small pull in my chest makes me believe that's partially the reason. I've done debate a million times over. I know how to win over a crowd, how to talk to them, how to make them see what I see. But I've never done poetry. That's something else completely.

When I don't respond, Justin cuts in, "I'm joking. Obviously. You'll be good."

"How do you know?"

"Because you're good at everything," he says so coolly, so matter-of-factly.

I let out a dry laugh. "That's just because I'm Nigerian."

"Am I supposed to understand what that means?"

I laugh harder, thinking of Tayo and Chioma and even Genny who would immediately understand what I meant by that. There'd be another round of laughing, a raucous kind of abrasive laughter, where we'd hiss and smack each other's arms uncontrollably. Tayo would probably start dancing because he's a fool. He's the definition of foolish goat, truly. It's hard to picture Sam in a scenario like that, but I want to. I put him into my daydream and place him beside Genny, since they're closer in age. Maybe he's laughing as much as Tayo, but he doesn't start dancing with him. Maybe he slaps his hands together like Chioma would, but he doesn't have the same high-pitched laugh as her. Or maybe he doesn't care; maybe he sits like Genny, smiling smugly at the rightness of it all, but otherwise unbothered. Sam isn't in any of these memories I have with Tayo, Chioma, and Genny after I started middle school, but imagining him there doesn't seem weird at all. It feels normal.

"Hey," I say to Justin. "I invited my brother," I whisper the word, "to my cousin's wedding. Bad idea? Yes, no, maybe?"

"Maybe," he tells me. "Shouldn't your cousin be the one to invite him?"

"I guess," I reply, even though I don't really think so. Nigerian parties don't always work that way. I'm technically a family member, so if I said I wanted to invite someone, it wouldn't be as big of a deal as he's thinking. Granted, this is Wedding Genny, not regular Genny. "That's not the problem, though. The problem is that I really need my parents to talk to my—to him, and I don't know what else would work except inviting him to this."

"So you're ambushing your parents?"

"Your bluntness is not appreciated."

"I'm just calling it what it is."

"It's not an ambush; it's an open forum," I go on, believing my own lie. "They won't reach out to each other, so I'm bringing them together. If my parents can see that he's living a good life doing what he wants and what he likes, then maybe..." Maybe.

Justin reads my mind immediately. "Maybe they won't be so hard on you when you tell them ... you're quitting?"

I nod and mumble, "Maybe," with my eyes skirting to the closed door. "It's worth a shot, right? All our family will be there. Why shouldn't he be too, you know?"

"Got it," he utters, and I feel like, unlike before, he understands. There is a moment of silence between us where I'm imagining Sam at the wedding, imagining him in the same ankara pattern as all of us. It makes me smile despite the unease I'm feeling. It's fine. I can wade through the uneasiness if it means there's some solid ground on the other side.

CHAPTER SEVENTEEN

SUNDAY AFTERNOON IS RESERVED FOR Genny and our final fitting for the aso ebi. Blessing even sent out a calendar invite we had to RSVP to. The closer and closer we get to the wedding, the more my time seems to be commandeered by Genny's world. Debate is done so I don't even have that excuse anymore, and if I tell her I need to practice for my art project, it won't make a difference. "Adanna," she would say, staring at me without blinking once. "It is my *wed-ding*." That's all the justification she needs.

Tayo already has his clothes for the wedding. Auntie Funmi doesn't sew men's clothing, so his was done by another auntie. He already took a million pictures for his daily #OutfitOfTheDay social posts, the crisp blue and gold of the fabric popping off his dark skin. The colors suit him much better than they suit me. They make him look regal and sophisticated, which is so different from the joking farm animal he usually is.

He doesn't need to come to Genny's with me, but he does anyway. He wants to show off the new watch Ayo gave him, and he does it in a very unsubtle way. It's positioned almost comically on his arm, the clasp barely hanging on as he drives with both hands stuck at the ten and two positions. If he's waiting for me to notice it, he can keep waiting.

Tayo takes a sharp turn and the watch jangles. My eyes bore into the road ahead. His lips twist into a frown as he says, "Do you think the styles Genny picked will look good on you guys?"

"We'll have to see," I say. "Honestly, I'm not even thinking about it. My mind is so set on this art project."

"Oh, right, your juju lobotomy music video."

I laugh. "It's not that anymore. It's the live poetry thing, remember?"

"Like a rap song."

"Not a rap song, really."

"But it's like rap."

"Hip-hop is poetry, so it has the potential to be, yes."

"Potential *nko*," he chortles. "See new oyinbo."

"Ah-beg," I laugh again. "'Potential' isn't even a big word, abi you no go school again?" As I say it, I smack his arm.

Huge mistake. The watch jingles and my eyes are drawn to the sound right away. He sees me looking at the watch and cackles so loud and so ugly that I almost want to launch myself out of the car out of both disgust and shame.

"You've been sitting here this entire time like you haven't seen the watch Ayo gave me," he goes on, taunting me with his wrist in my face. "Well, just so you know, this watch isn't *just* from Ayo—the original Ske-le-boy sent it in from Dubai to give to me because he wanted to say thanks for helping with the wedding planning. So you can shove it—"

"Ayo just gave it to you because you're Yoruba and all you Yoruba boys must stick together—"

"He-ey, jealousy, jea-lous-y!"

"And why would he send a watch from Dubai? So there's no good watches from Aba?"

"Ch-ai! Who asked you?"

We both laugh, boisterous and loud. Tayo almost swerves into the next lane and my laugh morphs into a scream before he quickly steadies the wheel and pulls over safely. A car honks as it breezes by us. "Oh snap," Tayo breathes out, looking through his window. "I'm half on the shoulder."

I snort. "Can you even drive at all?"

Genny and Chioma's house is filled with the heady scent of palm fruit and fresh banga soup when we get there. Tayo takes the deepest inhale, trying to breathe it in until it fills his stomach. His face breaks into a handsome grin and he shakes his shoulders as he kicks off his shoes and parades through the doorway. "Auntie, where is the soup?" he calls unceremoniously.

Auntie Suzanna laughs when she sees him. He begins to prostrate, but she grabs him into a hug before he can touch the floor. Her stiff curls almost envelope Tayo's face completely. I wait my turn to greet Auntie. "Ada, how are you?" she says, the warmth of her accent ringing me in for another kind of hug. "How is your mom?"

"She's good," I tell her. "Where's Genny?"

"Hmph," she huffs. Her demeanor changes, and a sneer so fierce and so wretched crosses her face. She kisses her teeth, a loud *mtchew* pressing from her lips, and she says, "Just follow the *ti-ti-ti* upstairs and you'll find her and her companion. Yes. My own daughter wants to kill me with *wed-ding*! Because nobody go marry again after am."

Auntie Funmi, who has been sitting at the dining table with her bowl of soup and eba, just laughs. Her laugh is wily and laden with the effects of banga soup. "Is it only you who Genny will kill? See how much cloth I had to sew." She waves her hand around suitcases and suitcases of matching clothes. I'm used to seeing Auntie Funmi show up with a suitcase or two of clothes she's dropping off for a family event, but I've never seen anything like this. The suitcases are propped open with gold and blue folded outfits practically bursting out of them. Geez, how many people are wearing the same aso ebi?

"Adanna, come," she says and I walk over, tiptoeing through the suitcases. "This is your own." She nods to a nicely folded dress and a paper with my name on it. "Go upstairs and change. Let me see how it fits. Where is your mom?"

"She's working," I tell her as I scoop up the clothes. "I'll show her later."

"Tell me where it's tight so I can loose it."

"Okay, Auntie." Tayo makes himself at home with his food and waves, almost salutes, from the kitchen table while I head to the staircase. Auntie Suzanna was right; all I have to do is follow Genny's voice for me to find her and Blessing buried among boxes and dresses and fabric in her room. Genny usually keeps a tidy space, but there's no room for anything in this chaos. Chioma is there too, already donning her gold and blue outfit. Two other girls I recognize but don't know are seated on the far corner of Genny's bed, large eyes fixed on me as I enter. Genny is sitting at her desk talking quickly, but quietly, on the phone. Blessing is beside her, talking away on her phone too. She won't stop rolling her eyes at whatever she's hearing.

Chioma approaches the second I'm past the doorway. She tugs on the folded dress in my arms. "Let me see yours. Your style will probably look better than mine."

"I'm not so sure about that. Aren't they all pretty similar?"

"Apparently..." Chioma glances over her shoulder at Genny and, once she feels she can't hear us, pulls me into a corner and speaks in a hushed tone. "Okay, so apparently Genny went back to Auntie Funmi and told her to do three different styles. So no three girls will have the same dress. I want to see what yours looks like. I hope it's better than this." At that, she waves a hand from her head to her toes at her long-sleeved but short-skirted one-piece outfit. She spins and I notice it's backless.

"Yours is nice, though," I say. "There's no back—"

"How'm I supposed to wear a bra?" she hisses and I suck my lips in to stop from laughing. She looks dead serious, though. "My chest can't be out here flopping all over the place in the Lord's house. Please."

"Get one of those backless ones."

"A-and it's kinda short," she says, tugging at the hemline.

I raise an eyebrow. "Excuse? You're complaining because it's too—" Before I can finish my sentence, she quickly flips up the skirt and flashes an inch more of thigh. I can see what looks like a patch covered in some kind of plastic wrap. The kind people usually put over a... "Oh my god!"

"Shut up!" She quickly steers me out through the door-way. "Go try yours on. If it's longer, I'm taking it."

She shuts me into the washroom and all I can hear are her footsteps stalking away. Damn, I can't believe she got a tattoo! They're gonna kill her, like she's actually gonna die.

I make quick work of unfurling the dress and putting it on. It looks fun and playful with its short sleeves and flared short skirt. I don't think it's longer than Chioma's, though, so she better hope her skirt doesn't fly up while she's dancing.

I emerge from the washroom and shuffle my way to Genny's room with a grin on my face. I feel so regal in this pattern. I'm reminded of Tayo and how his clothes suit him so well. In my mind, we're a power couple, dressed in matching fabrics like other Nigerian couples. Maybe I'm wearing gold gele to match my clothes, and all the aunties say how beautiful I am in the color. Maybe they compliment me on finally, *finally*, settling down with Tayo now that he just got promoted at the hospital he works in. He's in oncology. And I am

Um.

I don't know. He's always been the doctor and I'm the lawyer, but if I'm not the lawyer, then ...?

"Woooow, sister."

My eyes refocus just as the shorter girl who was sitting on the bed approaches me, grinning. She sizes me up, circling me like I'm on display, and claps briefly like she approves of what she sees. "It just matches you so well, like, so good." Her Yoruba accent is fresh, her words rounded and light, while she speaks.

I smile sheepishly. "Thanks ... Sorry, I don't know your names." I look at her and over her shoulder at the other slender girl who looks as if she didn't hear me. "I'm Adanna," I say.

A tight smile pulls across the girl's lips. It's the kind I'm used to getting when I introduce myself with my native name to Nigerian people. In the past, people used to correct me like I couldn't say my name properly. I don't like to admit it, but it always sounded better coming from them. "Lolade, or Lola," she says. "And that is Folasade. She's Femi's sister."

The girl called Folasade barely acknowledges when her name is called. Instead, she crosses her legs, uncrosses them, and tosses her long hair over her shoulder. She sure looks like she'd be the sister of an artist-producer like Skeleboy. Something about her is so glamorous, even here among all of Genny's scattered things. She's like Genny-Lite.

Chioma saunters over to investigate my skirt length, but Blessing wanders up and nudges her aside. "While you're all here," she begins, tinkering on her phone. "I'm sending you the photo poses that we're going to do for the bridesmaids, so study them." Around the room, I hear phones pinging with Blessing's email. "And please, girls, know yourselves. If your legs are short, please take a center-right or center-left position. If your legs are long, then stay at the ends only for pose one, or crouch for pose two. No one should be taller than Genny in the center."

"So we *have* to do these poses?" Chioma grunts.

Blessing looks at her, a flicker of exhaustion showing in her eyes before it tempers out. "The blogs are asking for these specific shots, so we will do what the blog says. Chioma, when you get married to a billionaire, please, just be posing however you want." She kisses her teeth and falls back to Genny's computer.

Folasade gets to her feet and walks over to join us. Her presence commands attention. I'm invested in the way her eyes flick over both Chioma and I before she pouts, reaching out to touch the shoulder of my dress. I stand perfectly still. "My dress is strapless, but if it had sleeves, it would be good, sha," she says. "Strapless is kind of tacky these days."

Blessing looks over for a moment, and when she sees it's just Folasade talking smack, she pretends she didn't hear us. I guess no one would say anything bad to her else it gets back to Femi.

"Come," Folasade says in her layered British-Yoruba accent, and gestures for us to join her on Genny's bed in the corner. She sits elegantly, crossing her legs like this is her room and we're all lucky to be here. "I don't know what to expect with this wedding of a thing. Femi asked me to come here and hang out with Genny, but I'm going back to Lagos next week before I fly in with my brother. In the time I've been here … I'll be honest with you." She takes a deep breath and we all wait, almost holding our breath in the process. Then, she says: "I haven't seen *one* fine boy since."

Chioma starts cackling, but quickly presses her hand to

her mouth before Genny hears and snaps at her. Lola just nods solemnly at her side. "Are you kidding?" I ask, chuckling. "Where have you been so far?"

"Ayo took us to this restaurant," she says. "And then we've been shopping at that big mall, the Eaton Center, but that's it."

Chioma stops her laughing for a split second, smoothing out her skirt as she says, "Well, you're in luck. I happen to know a guy you may like." She's going to say Tayo, I know she is. "He's Yoruba too." It's Tayo.

"But does he speak it?" she asks, exchanging a bemused look with Lola. "If he doesn't speak Yoruba, then I don't know."

None of us kids here really speak the language through no fault of our own, but how am I going to explain how common that is to someone who didn't grow up here? I frown and hesitate, but Chioma has less of a filter than I do, so she has no shame cutting in with ease. She shrugs and says, "He doesn't, but none of us do. I mean, I'm Igbo, so I definitely don't."

Folasade gasps. "Really? Ah-ah, so you're really all oyinbo kids."

"That's not fair," I say, casting a nervous look at Chioma. She looks like she's ready to fight. "Growing up here is different. Our parents didn't really teach us because they thought being good at English would mean better opportunities, so that's how we were raised." Unfortunately.

"Yeah, plus," Chioma cuts in, "I said one thing in Igbo once and Auntie Funmi has been making fun of me ever since. One thing! And she's not even Igbo. The fuck?"

Lola laughs. Her laugh is much less menacing, but I can't tell if she's making fun of us or not. "It's all right. Honestly. As long as you want to learn, then it's fine."

I nod at the same moment Chioma shakes her head. "I'm good," she says with a sideways glance toward me, and Lola and Folasade look like they've lost all understanding of her. "I tried and it didn't really stick. Plus, I can't get the accent."

Folasade blinks twice, her large eyes and decorated lashes fluttering. "But it's your language," she says bluntly. She expects that to be enough, but Chioma doesn't concede. She just shrugs. Folasade bites her lip like she's tasted something sour. "If you don't speak it, then who will? And what will you teach your children?"

Chioma shrugs again. She's really digging herself into a very large grave here. I step in, happy to deflect with a carefully rehearsed answer. "I think it'd be good to learn. It's important, too. Language is part of culture, after all."

But Folasade is so fixated on Chioma's stubbornness that she barely hears me. Instead, she leans forward, eyebrows furrowed at the perplexity that is this Igbo girl who has all the luxuries in the world except her mother tongue. "So, what if you're marrying a Nigerian...," Folasade goes on.

"What if you're about to marry and he expects you to speak the same language? What about that?"

"First of all, he should've known I didn't speak it from the jump, so that's on him. Secondly, there are tons of inter-tribal marriages," Chioma rattles on. "We know an auntie and an uncle who are Ika and Isoko, and they're fine. Their kids are good too. One's a psychotherapist."

"Okay, but do they speak Isoko or Ika?"

"No—"

"Ha-ba!" she snickers. "So it's a waste! Everybody is speaking oyinbo, but that's not special."

"Language isn't everything to a culture, you know," Chioma says, a tinge of bitterness in her voice. "So you're saying I'm less Igbo because I can't speak it?"

Folasade is still snickering, but she doesn't say anything. The last thing I need is for her to say yes and let all hell break loose at Genny's wedding. Eventually, she shakes her head and some of the tension is diffused. Chioma is still on edge. "Anyway, as for me," Folasade continues casually. "My husband has to speak Yoruba if he's Yoruba. And if he's not, then let him speak what he speaks. But it cannot just be common oyinbo. If I want someone who can speak just oyinbo, then I will marry oyinbo. But I don't even know if I can do that, sha."

Genny puts her phone down and it's like we all know to be on our best behavior. The mood shift is tangible. Even

Folasade fixes her hair and glances away like she wasn't just talking smack to us a second ago. Lola smiles at Genny, that same tight-lipped smile from before, as Genny approaches. "Sister, how far?" she asks.

Genny sighs and touches her temples, massaging them rigidly. "The woman making the cake told Blessing she may not have enough custard filling. Can you imagine?" Lola is the only one who smiles and nods back while the rest of us divert our eyes. I'd be lying if I said I wasn't thinking about what Folasade said, how important it is to speak our native language, and how I feel about not understanding. She's right in a way. But Chioma is right too. I know I'm not any less of what I am just because I don't have that knowledge, but knowing it and understanding it are two different things. I know I am enough, but I don't always feel that way.

Genny claps her hands together loudly and we all jump. "Oya, what is it? What's wrong with you people?" She frowns, staring around at us. "You all got so quiet. What were you talking about?"

Folasade sighs and gets to her feet. "Let's go and eat. I've been smelling banga soup from here and the smell just dey sweet me one kind," she says, and hoists Lola up with her. "Will you come?" she asks Chioma and I pointedly.

"Yeah," I butt in before Chioma opens her mouth. She's done enough damage. I don't want Skeleboy's only sister to hate us. "We'll just change back into our old clothes first. I don't want to accidentally spill anything."

"Plus, these are so tight. There's no room to grow," Chioma says, massaging her stomach in the most exaggerated way.

Folasade laughs as she loops arms with Lola. "Jester. I love it." The two of them float out of the room and all at once, it gets mad quiet. It even feels like there's more breathing room. Less pretense, too.

Blessing rises from Genny's computer and circles back to us. "The livestream tech will show up early on the day of," she tells Genny. "I got him to agree to a larger screen too. Let me call the cake lady again."

Genny nods tiredly. "Tell her if she can't add enough custard, she should drop the price."

"Of course."

My phone pings and I struggle a bit in my dress to dig it out from where I stashed it in my bra. It's a text from Sam. I hide the screen immediately in case the notification catches Chioma's eye. I wouldn't dare open it here, but I really want to text him back. I want to tell him I just met Skeleboy's little sister and she's exactly how I imagined she'd be. I want to tell him that Chioma tried to set her up with Tayo. I want to tell him that I actually think she's not Tayo's type.

I want to tell him he better make it to the wedding.

Clutching my phone to my chest, I nudge Chioma and she almost falls off the bed. "Chioma, go change first," I say.

"You go first."

"You go first," I say again and hope that'll be enough to persuade her. It isn't. The look of apathy on her face says enough. "You probably need extra time getting that skirt off." And my eyes zone in on her hidden tattoo.

Apathy turns to panic as she springs up immediately, saying "You're right" as she disappears.

As soon as she's gone, I jump to my feet and make a beeline for Genny. She's crouched over her desk, trying to pull a paper out from under a stack. "Genny," I say, waiting for her to turn around. "Gen—"

"Look at this," she interrupts, gesturing to the paper. "It's the order invoice for the cake. See? 'Custard filling double,'" she reads aloud, showing it to both myself and Blessing. Then, she asks me, "What do you think of Folasade?"

Blessing gets this smug look on her face while she waits for me to answer. Probably ready to add more gossip to her repertoire. "She's exactly how I thought she'd be. She reminds me a bit of you," I add.

Genny bites back a smile and shakes her head regretfully. "She is, both of them," she says with a dry laugh. "Her and Femi are close, so I have to be careful what I say around her. Can you believe it? *Me?*"

I snort. "Yeah, that sounds fake. Does she know you were a meme?"

"Of course she knows," Blessing puts in, glancing at Genny. "They wanted to get T-shirts made, but Genny said no."

Genny lets out another dry laugh, and then nothing. She looks at me with an expression I can't read, and says, "Don't mind her."

I stare back, confused. "Sorry?"

"What she said, what Lola was saying, about speaking Igbo," she explains.

"Oh, you heard all that?" I wave away her concern. "It's all good. I don't—I mean, I'm not even sure if I disagree with her."

Genny frowns. "It's not your fault you can't speak it, so get that out of your head. Femi's mom is worried because I can't speak Igbo and I can barely understand it anymore. When she first met me, she was prepared to house-girl me into oblivion." I grimace at the idea of Femi's mom treating Genny like a house-girl, ordering her around, snapping at her for no reason. It's only funny because Genny is so immovable. There's no way she'd take it. "But I stuck it out, honestly. I made the decision that I was good enough, no matter how Nigerian she thinks I am. And now, I'm marrying her son." She lays out her hands like "there you go," and I have to laugh. "Plus, maybe your boyfriend can just teach your children whatever language he knows." And I'm done, I'm done laughing.

Blessing narrows her eyes while she thinks, trying to figure out what boyfriend Genny is talking about. And Genny is chuckling because she's evil. I cross my arms and look at the ground, resisting the urge to say for the umpteenth time that I'm not dating Justin. Instead, I sigh and say, "My life is in shambles." It isn't, but I feel like I'm being pulled in a million different directions and all I want to do is lie down.

Genny laughs, "Shut up, please," as she touches her forehead. She takes me by the arm and, after an apologetic glance to Blessing, steers me to the corner of the room. "Okay, what is it? What do you want to ask me?"

"What?"

"That's why you sent Chioma away, obviously." Yikes, not even Genny knows about the tattoo, huh? "What is it? Is it if you should date a white boy? Will Auntie rage? Will Uncle prepare his own last rites? Maybe. But you'll be fine. Next question."

I laugh a little, thrown off by her frankness. "Can I invite someone to the wedding?"

She purses her lips, thinking, and I am prepared for her to say no or, even worse, ask Blessing. But then she asks me, "Who?"

"Just a friend." This is as persuasive as I can get, and the thought embarrasses me that I, a debate championship runner-up, can't put together a good argument.

We look at each other. She doesn't believe me and I can see it in the way she narrows her eyes, letting them wash over my fidgeting figure. "Fine. I'll tell Blessing to add another person at your table. But I don't want any trouble, okay?" she says quietly. Something in her voice hushes me. I'm lulled by this false sense of security where it feels like she and I have an understanding. In reality, she has no idea what I'm planning. "Be smart."

I grin. "I am always."

"Too smart sometimes," she says.

CHAPTER EIGHTEEN

TEXTING DOESN'T DO THIS JUSTICE. I need to tell Sam ASAP that I secured him an invite to the biggest wedding of all time. I race to his apartment, rehearsing the ways I'll break the news. I bet he'll be so excited that he'll pack his bags and come back home right away. He'll have to buy his ankara fabric last minute, though. Oh, and he'll need to get in contact with Tayo's tailor. How fast can she sew clothes for him? One day? Two?

By the time Sam finally opens the door, I am stumbling over myself, babbling words all out of order. "You—it worked—you're coming, you're coming to the wedding!" I sing, dancing my way in past him.

He starts to dance too and I'm immediately reminded

that he's always been the better dancer of the two of us. He's not as good as Tayo, but not a lot of people are. "Ayyy," he choruses to an imaginary beat we can both hear. He pulls me into a hug, sloppy and quick. It's the first hug he's given me since…forever. It feels so homey, so comforting. I'm doing the right thing; I know it now.

"So you're coming, right?" I ask, beaming and nearly breathless. "You gotta! Sam, you *gotta*."

"Ha." Sam gives a sharp, hollow laugh that sounds more like a cough.

"It'll be like old times…remember?" I go on. "Come on, you promised." I need this to happen. I need him to reconcile with Mom and Dad so we'll all be okay—so *I'll* be okay.

"I promised…," he sighs, taking a step back. He heads further into the living room and I follow on his heels, plopping down on the sofa. "I mean, Ada, that's…you get these people kicked me out, right?" The bluntness in his voice slaps me in the face and I am frozen, suddenly immobilized with the reality of the situation. It's so final. It is harsh and dull at the same time. "Genny knows it's me? She knows that *I'm* the one you invited?"

"Of course," I lie. Anything to get him to agree. "Just say you'll be there." Please, just say so.

He doesn't look convinced, but I pretend he is. His eyebrows pull together in concern, but in my mind, he is smiling and nodding, and asking about the fabric patterns. I curl my legs underneath me on the sofa and fold my hands together. "Let me brief you on what's been going down," I tell him, and immediately wait for the protest. It doesn't come, so I take that as my cue. "Nice. So, Skeleboy's actual sister came down early to hang out with Genny and she brought a friend. The sister's name is Folasade, and I knew another Folasade before, so I was waiting for her to tell us we could call her Sade, but it never happened. Her friend's name is Lolade, or Lola, and she's much nicer. Honestly, Folasade was a bit intense. She really snapped too! She was like, 'Why don't you speak Igbo? You foolish goat.' Okay, she didn't call me a goat, but she might as well have. And honestly, she was nice, but I can't help but feel like if I say something to her the wrong way, she'd slap me." I pause for effect, waiting for a snicker or chuckle from Sam. Nothing. "Anyway—"

"Have you been practicing?" he asks suddenly and I cock my head to the side, confused. "Your poem. Have you been practicing? Your performance is coming up fast, you know."

"Yeah, but the wedding is coming up sooner."

He purses his lips. "Yeah, but when it's done, though."

"I know," I say. "I've been up in front of people before. I've done debate. I just did a competition, like, yesterday."

"Poetry is different, though." He stresses "different" like I seriously don't know that. Why is he being so patronizing? I just want to talk about the wedding, our family, and everything finally coming back together. "If you're being fake for a second, people can tell and you won't be able to connect with them anymore. You gotta be willing to be real."

"I am real. You saw what the poem looks like. If I wanted to fake anything, why would I even bother saying that stuff?"

He shakes his head, frowning. "It's not just about what you say, though. It's about how you say it."

"Okay, once again, I *know* all of this," I groan. "Why are you being so difficult? I just want to talk about the wedding."

"Well, I want to hear about the poem," he shoots back and then points to the center of his living room. "Get up and show me the whole thing."

I cringe. "Eww, no, why? Right now?"

"Yeah, right now."

"Oh my god," I grumble. "You don't think I can actually do a good job of this—"

"I know you can do a good job. That's why—"

"You think I'm, I don't know, not taking it seriously or whatever. That I don't know what it's like to have a group of people stare at me and judge me based on what I'm saying," I snap. "I *just* did a debate competition where my entire argument was based on the existence and validity of people just like me—coasting somewhere between two different cultures—and I ranked second. How d'you think that makes me feel?"

"But you lost out to the gun law debate, which we agreed was more pertinent."

"I know what we agreed, damn!"

We are quiet. I can hear nothing but my own breathing echoing in my ears as I make my way to the center of the room. Sam stands too, facing me. Our eyes lock in an instant where I am irritated at him and he's fed up with me and our emotions are clashing with each other, causing sparks all over the living room. And then, we laugh. Both of us. Full mouth, bending over, choking and laughing.

"Yo, you're so dumb," Sam snickers, knocking me in the shoulder. I dance away from him and he laughs even more. "I see now how you lied your way into debate."

"Lied where?"

"That's why your ass placed second."

"Damn, wow, your jealousy right now!"

"Ah-beg, mind yourself, o," he teases. "Do the poem, bro. I want to hear it from the top. I want to hear emotion, crying, rage, all of that. I want you to shaku-shaku while you're reading." And he does the dance move like someone's uncle hanging by the bar waiting for his third Guinness.

"You know I don't know how to do that."

"I know. You disgrace us every time you start dancing."

I snort. "Whatever. I'll do the poem, but then you have to promise me you'll come to the wedding."

He wrinkles his nose and, despite his smile, sighs so loud it shakes his frame. Still, I feel like I've won. He has to say yes. "Do the poem first," he tells me. "You have to kill it, though. Fucking murder it."

That's the intention. I want to prove to Sam I can do this, but more than anything, I want to prove to myself I can say these things out loud and not second-guess myself. So I take a deep, deep breath before I get into it. And when I open my mouth, all the words come out.

Sam nods to the rhythm in my words. He taps my hands when he thinks I need to gesture wider, talk louder with my fingers. He holds his breath when I hold my breath, snaps his fingers when my words hit a crescendo. He shows me how to hold space, honoring silence. There's a hint of a smile when I pull off a really cool rhythm sequence, and it's the kind of smile that says, "*I taught you that.*" He didn't, but I'll let him have it. Besides, for the past while, I didn't have an older brother to help me with homework or life decisions or anything. I got used to doing it on my own, but when Sam snaps and says, "Yes!" after I get through a verse, I realize being on my own isn't something I need to get used to. This is cool. Having him teach me another way to be is cool.

The room empties out as I speak my last word. I didn't realize how loud my voice was, how it carried to each corner, each window, each wall. Sam lets out a resounding "woo!" in excitement. "That's fucking dope," he says, rushing forward and pulling me into a tight hug. I laugh but I let myself be taken in, tense and exhausted as I am. The longer I'm in his embrace, the harder it is for me to relax. But I want to, so badly. I want to relax and hug him back and maybe cry. I just want to *be*.

"I-I don't want..." I take a shallow breath against his shoulder. He shifts slightly but I latch onto him, afraid to let him see my face as I force the words out: "You were right. I don't want to go to law school and I don't want to be a lawyer. I-I don't... I'm not..." I swallow and wait. "My... I have to tell them. I have to tell Mom and Dad, but I can't. I don't know how. That's why I need you to be there." My stomach feels unstable as if I've just given away the biggest secret of my life. I unearthed it from the pit of my stomach and now that it's out there, I don't know what to do with it.

Sam pulls away, keeping his hands gripped firmly on my shoulders. He smiles, searching for my eyes even though I avoid his. "Hey..." He nudges softly before I finally look him square in the eyes. He can see the sadness there and we bond over the nothingness that's left. He knows the kind really well, the nothingness that surfaces after an expectation washes up unfulfilled. That kind of guilt.

"Ada, Ada," he sings. I bite my lips right away, fighting the urge to cry. "There is no one way to do anything. You get me? There's never just one way. This..." He gestures to the room around him—and me. He points at me. "This is *your* way, and it's good enough."

My lips curl in and I press down, trying to quell the quivering feeling. "Okay," I manage to whisper. "Okay."

He smiles, real easy. "You're ready, I think."

"Yeah?"

"Yeah."

Sam's words give me courage. He might not have been here when I was starting middle school, but he's here now. I spent a lot of time trying to compensate for the fact that I didn't have a brother anymore, but now that he's back, it's like all those years with a ghost following me around are gone. I have my brother back and that's all that matters.

I have my family back.

I try not to think about the poetry reading, especially when the wedding is right around the corner.

Once the following Sunday hits, Blessing sends a calendar invite to all the bridesmaids. "GENNY WEDDING WEEK" flashes on my screen at every waking moment. It's finally happening.

But first: dinner.

The reports are that Skeleboy flew in this morning and was held up at the airport. We saw it on Bella Naija and other Nigerian pop culture sites before we heard it from Genny. She was mad pissed about that. "We'll need security at the dinner, then," Blessing told her with a groan. "And more at the wedding. I'll tell Ayo."

Well, no one could tell Ayo because he went to pick

Skeleboy up from the airport, meaning he rented a car, made Tayo drive, and rode shotgun. I bet Tayo is losing his mind at the idea of picking Skeleboy up at the airport. Just two months ago, he was hounding me for an invite to the wedding and now he's his driver? As my parents would say: "Na God." Although I don't think Tayo's been dreaming about being Skeleboy's driver. Or maybe he has. Who knows! People can change. People can change their minds.

And I don't want to do law.

Chioma and I run things back and forth to the aunties setting up the buffet line at the hall—the hall we rented out for Skeleboy's arrival dinner. It's homier than the wedding hall with smaller doorways and more muted, green decor. Plus, it holds less people so it'll be way more intimate than the wedding. Last I checked the dinner is at two hundred, give or take.

Blessing is busy counting tables and scribbling into her notepad while she raps into her Bluetooth headset. Every now and then, she crosses the hall, her heeled boots clicking behind her, and says something like, "Pressure is nothing. I've coordinated a video shoutout from Tiwa Savage for fuck's sake!"

Genny is wearing her curlers, robe, and slippers, rushing around and asking borderline useless questions to relatives while they get everything in order. Auntie Suzanna is trying to get her to calm down, but nothing is working. Every so often, Auntie Suzanna snaps and says, "Chine-ke, see me see trouble, o! If they have sent you to kill me today, Isioma, you will not succeed!" and Chioma and I have to run away to stop from laughing.

Mom is supervising the aunties setting up food at the buffet table. Auntie Pat is doing the most, putting way too much rice in the chafing dish. Mom scolds her, "Wetin, na? Make una put small-small." I pretend I don't see when Auntie Pat rolls her eyes. "Ah-Adanna? Adanna!"

"Yes, Mom?" I call, skipping over. "What happened?"

"Don't ask me what happened," she tsks at me. "Go and get the moin-moin from the cooler."

I do as I'm told, heading back into the kitchen and passing Chioma on her way out. She crosses her eyes and makes a face like she's dead. "Shut up. You haven't even begun to suffer," I tease, which maybe is the wrong thing to say because she's been arguably suffering the most.

"Please!" Chioma scoffs. "Every day and night, it's 'Chioma, if I *slap* you' or 'Chioma, if I *sound* you'—"

"'Chioma, I can't believe you got a tattoo on *your* body when it's *my* wedding!'"

"Shush!" she gasps, rushing forward to cover my mouth. "Yo, I swear, I don't want them to see it until I graduate."

I snort. "Yeah, okay. 'Mom, Dad, here's my tattoo, and also I have a completely different degree than what you thought I'd have.' That'll work."

Chioma grunts just as we hear our names called out around us.

"Adanna!"

"Yes?"

"Chioma, bia!"

We both split in different directions: me to the kitchen and Chioma to the main hall. I find the cooler Mom was talking about and carry it back to the buffet table. The second I'm within an inch of the hall's entrance, Mom points frantically to the end of the row, signaling where I should drop it. Another auntie, Auntie Celine, takes the cooler from me without a word and props it up on the table. I—

"Ada!"

"Yes?" I turn around to see Auntie Suzanna waving me over. I approach. "Yes?"

"Where is Chioma?"

"I don't know."

"Okay, go and find me a bottle opener."

"Okay."

There are literally no bottle openers in the kitchen. I march in and pull open all the drawers only to slam them shut again when they come up empty. Where could they all be?

Luckily, my dad always keeps one on his key chain. I skip out of the kitchen, rushing to the main doors to beg for his. Dad is unloading large speakers from the back of a van into the entranceway. He nods when he sees me. "Ada, where is your mom?" he asks.

"Inside. Dad, can I borrow your bottle opener?"

"Which one?"

"The one on your key chain."

"For who?"

"Auntie Suzanna is asking."

"What does Suzanna need a bottle opener for?" he asks, kissing his teeth. He hesitates like he's not going to do it. "Call Tayo to buy one on his way here."

"Oh my god, Dad, Tayo is driving Skeleboy," I groan, throwing up my arms in exasperation. "He can't just pop into the dollar store on the way here."

He unloads another speaker, a slightly smaller one. "Okay. Okay, take this one inside," he tells me, gesturing to it.

I begrudgingly bend and lift the speaker, letting myself adjust to its weight. It's much lighter than it looks. I turn and hobble my way back into the hall just as Chioma dashes out with a full garbage bag. We exchange another look: when will this end, we're so tired, shoot me, I never want to hear my name being called again. The usual.

I don't know where to drop the speaker, so I make my way to the front of the hall. Usually, the speakers are set up in all corners, but the technician isn't here yet, so I can't be sure. Blessing spots me and makes as if she's going to wave me over, but it looks like she's getting a call. She freezes, hand to her headset, and waits. Suddenly, Auntie Pat rushes over to me, crying, "Ha-ba! What is it?" The way she yells makes it seem like something catastrophic is going on and it startles me so much that I almost fall over. "Isn't this heavy? Where is your brother to help you come and carry this thing, na?"

I drop the speaker.

"My—my what?" I blurt out. My heart is beating so fast. So fast. She's ... this is ... no one ever acknowledges Sam. Hearing Auntie Pat say "my brother" is so weird, so foreign, but so liberating. I want to hear her say it again, to prove that she knows he exists. "Sorry, my what?"

But then: "I meant, my son," she snaps back. There's a hint of nervousness in her eyes and all at once, I know she said something she wasn't meant to. Our eyes break and she looks over her shoulder around the hall. "Ewo-nem, where is this boy, na?"

Her son. Not my brother.

"Ikechukwu!" she yells up and down the hall. "I-ke-chu-kwu!"

"Yes, Mom?" the boy named Ikechukwu grumbles as he trudges up to us. He's been taking orders from Blessing, moving tables all day. I think I saw him sitting down earlier, which is a huge no-no. There's no such thing as rest for Nigerian children, and definitely not when an Afrobeats superstar is about to be here.

"Don't 'yes, Mom' me," she hisses. "Come on, pick up this thing right now."

Ikechukwu slumps down and snatches the speaker. He stands back up and immediately takes off with it as if he knows where it will go. My guess is he just wants to get away from Auntie Pat. She gives me one final look as she steps away, as if she's begging me not to say anything about her slipup.

"Adanna!" Damn, how is Mom's voice so loud? I make my way back to the buffet table where she's beckoning me like the building is on fire. "Where is Chioma?" she asks right away.

"Not here," I mumble—and immediately regret it. "I mean, I don't know."

"Okay, go and change, then," she says hurriedly. "Tayo called Bola and said they will be here soon."

Oh my god.

I gasp so hard it stings my throat and burns my chest. All the fatigue I've been feeling washes away—I'm about to meet Skeleboy! My aching feet, my sore hands, this mental drain of hearing "Ada! Ada!" for the past hour and a half straight will all be worth it in T minus 20 minutes.

I rush away from the table to find Chioma. All I can manage is, "Skeleboy is here, he's coming, go change, go change!" before she starts freaking out. We both rush to grab our dinner clothes, squabbling over each other on our way to the washrooms. These clothes are different from our wedding clothes—ankara we've worn at other parties and events—but still very chic and good enough to make a killer first impression. Mom doesn't want Skeleboy's family to think we're all bush people, so we have to look really nice. That means nails, hair, clothes, everything. Genny even goes to change and, after taking down her curlers and putting on her lashes, she looks like she might have mistaken today for the wedding. She looks glamorous as she waltzes in and sits at the main table.

Tayo enters the hall first. He looks really sharp in his new suit. I can see he's been initiated into the I-wear-sunglasses-indoors club. Oh, and it looks like he and Folasade seem to be getting along real well, too. Too well. Miss he-has-to-speak-Yoruba doesn't have her arm around Tayo, obviously because she doesn't want to be crucified here, but the way she follows close behind him as he heads to his parents' table says it all.

For a second I freeze, shocked at the churning feeling creeping into my stomach. The unease. I feel as if everyone can see how uncomfortable I am, how confused, how defeated. Unsurprisingly, Blessing, who has since changed and donned her finest ankara jumpsuit, cranes her neck toward me when they enter. I avoid her gaze completely. She should know Tayo and I aren't a pair. Just because he's my plus one, just because he's my friend, just because we … Whatever. He can do whatever he wants. Not like I care.

I swallow down bitterness and nudge Chioma. When she finally rips her eyes from the scene, I point with my lips at the display. Chioma snickers. "Me, I cannot date oyinbo," she says, putting on a high voice like Folasade's. "I can only date Yoruba if he sabi Yoruba. If not, ah-beg just comot, jor." We both laugh.

Mom and Dad sit across from us with their vibrant, matching traditional clothes. Mom leans forward, her bold eyeshadow and red lips staring back at us. "So you want to be laughing ke-ke like that, instead of you to shine your eye and be looking for your own husband."

Chioma cringes. "Auntie, Jesus Christ—"

"—is Lord," Mom finishes, eyes narrowed.

The hall grows quieter after Tayo and Folasade take their seats. With one look at the entrance, I understand why. It's him. Skeleboy. He looks just like the pictures and just like the videos. That's the same face that sang "do me yanga" and "you know say I get money." That's the same face that, for the longest time, only existed on my computer or my TV. Now he's in the same room as me, and he's about to marry my cousin.

He is dressed in a sleek custom black and ankara fabric suit, his hair and facial hair trimmed precisely. I almost can't stop gawking at how polished and put together he looks. He's a king fit for a very particular kind of queen.

A queen like Genny. She stands up from her spot at the high table when he enters the room and smiles so wide that she nearly gives off the impression of being pleasant. Skeleboy stops in his tracks and staggers back, pretending to be so completely taken with Genny's beauty that he can't deal. His entourage holds his shades and his wallet as he makes a huge show of bending on his knees and bowing several times at her. The hall laughs. I hear one uncle say, "Oga, na only you?" Genny giggles as she approaches, holding out her hands to help him back up. And when they stand together, they really do look perfect. They fit.

Genny kneels when she greets his mom and dad, both dressed in shimmering fabrics. They smile and embrace her like their own. And then she points at our table. Wait.

"Wait..." I grip Chioma's arm. "What's happening? Why is she bringing them here?"

"She's—let go—we have to greet them, obviously. Stop being weird. Do not screw this up for me!"

Genny waltzes over with Skeleboy and his parents and the only thing I can think of is how Skeleboy is standing one foot away from me. Oh god oh god. He radiates wealth. He smells like bourbon. "This is my family," she says, gesturing around the table to us. "My mom, my dad, my sister Chioma. My auntie Jackie, my uncle Gabriel, and my cousin Adanna." We only have a split second to wave and say hello before Genny, grinning, places a hand on Skeleboy's chest and says, "And this is Femi."

I am gawking without meaning to as he smiles at us. The charm in his smile alone is enough to render me speechless. Chioma pipes up, "Can we call him Femi?"

Genny's eyebrow twitches. "No. You have to pay."

Skeleboy, or Femi, laughs heartily. His voice is so smooth and easy, just like it sounds on his songs! Oh god. "Isioma, it's all right," he tells her, clutching her hand in his. Swoon! "Aren't these soon to be my in-laws? It's all right. You can call me Femi, you can call me Obafemi, you can call me Obafemi-chukwu." My parents laugh extra hard at that cross-tribal joke.

"My sister here," Genny says, gesturing to Chioma, "is a big fan of yours. She knows all the words to 'Yanga.'"

Chioma instantly hides her face and groans, "Oh my god, Genny."

"He-ey, that's all right," Femi chuckles. "I already told Tayo he can put all the songs he wants on the playlist for the wedding. You know the 'Yanga' dancers are coming, right?"

I nod right away. "Oh, we know."

Femi looks at me—he's looking at me! Skeleboy is looking into my face! I'm sweating and I've lost the ability to think. "Okay, so I expect you two will come dance with them," he teases.

"Oh, what? No," Chioma says, glancing at me nervously.

"We're not Tayo. He's about that dance life. We'll just be by the buffet eating." I will kill this girl this night. Why is she embarrassing me in front of Skeleboy?

"Not just eating, I hope," Femi says. "I'm bringing all my boys with me, you know, so maybe you can find one you like."

"Eh heh!" Auntie Suzanna calls out to us across from the table. It's amazing she's heard nothing else until now. "Tell her, o!"

The embarrassment won't stop mounting. I'm praying for Genny to move on at the precise moment her eyes suddenly fall on me, a quaint smile on her lips. I don't know how to take that, so I just smile back, uneasy. She tugs at Femi's shirt a little and says, "If you only know Yoruba boys, this one may be out of luck," as she juts her lips at me. "Nigerian, sef."

Oooooh myyyyy goddddd.

Femi looks at me, eyebrows pulled together in confusion. "What do you mean?"

Genny has always been a bit up and down, hit or miss, growing up. She's not mean; she's tricky. Sometimes she just says things the way she wants to. I admire her for it. Other times, there's nothing worse than being on that receiving end. This—*this*, when I'm sitting in front of Skeleboy, the one and only Obafemi Balogun, the original FBI, Fine Boy International—is one of the latter times.

But then: "Nothing," she hums, and leads him around the table to talk more with our parents.

Chioma's mouth hangs open as she watches Genny leave. "Can you imagine?" she hisses, nudging me. "My own sister, a real enemy of progress."

I groan. "Genny is Genny."

"She's a monster. She's happy, so she won't let anyone else be happy," she grumbles. "So what if your boyfriend isn't Nigerian? That's none of her business. People date outside of their culture all the time."

"I don't have a boyfriend," I hiss back. "Just because I have a friend who happens to be a boy doesn't mean we're dating."

"Don't lie to me," she snorts. "You like him, though, right?"

I hesitate, feeling the warmth of uncertainty bubble beneath my cheeks. I can't answer. I do like Justin, but that's just in my head. We had all of high school to become a real thing and I never pushed it, so it never happened. It is what it is.

Chioma chuckles, getting ready to launch into a string of taunts, but a serious expression wipes away any glee she showed a second ago. She looks over my head long enough that I follow her gaze, just in time to see Tayo and Folasade hanging around behind me. Tayo's lips are pursed uncomfortably as he shifts his weight from one foot to the next. Folasade is smiling sweetly at us. "Hello, dears," she coos.

Dears? Is she joking? "Hi," I mumble, glancing away.

"Tayo said I should come and meet his family, but I said I met them already," she tells me.

I look at Tayo, who is pointedly avoiding my gaze. He must have been around long enough to hear my hesitation. Why is the question always about Justin? If someone asked me about Tayo, who's to say I wouldn't hesitate the same way? This isn't fair. "Yeah, we met already," I say, more so to him than anyone. "It was at Chioma's place. You were downstairs drinking banga soup."

He nods like, yeah, true, but he doesn't chuckle, not even a little bit. His nervousness is making me nervous. Immediately, I turn in my seat until I'm facing the opposite side where Genny and Femi are talking to my parents. Tayo swings around to where Chioma is sitting and I shift even more so I don't have to look at him, so he doesn't have to see the shame in my face.

Curiously, Folasade comes around to my side, that same sweet smile on her face. "Listen, no vex, ah-beg," she whispers, rubbing her hands together. "I know you and Tayo are very good friends."

"W-what? What do you mean?"

"It's not like we're dating. We're just seeing each other during the wedding. He can't come back to Lagos with me, anyway."

My face grows hot. "I don't care. Why are you telling me this?"

"Because it looked like you were thinking something else," she tells me bluntly. "There's nothing to think. He's very nice but—"

"But he doesn't speak Yoruba, right?"

Her lips tighten further and I know I've annoyed her. She stands straighter, placing her hand on her hip and shrugging her long hair away from her shoulder. "No. Because I think he may be more interested in someone else."

Folasade turns on her heel and joins Tayo where he is crouched by Chioma. She taps his shoulder, but it's me he looks up at before he looks at her.

CHAPTER NINETEEN

FEMI BRINGS GIFTS FOR EVERYONE, even my parents and I. He gives Mom and Dad shining Gucci watches, not much unlike the one that Tayo is sporting. Dad loves it and thinks it gives him even more status as an engineer.

"And for you. Genny tells me you're very serious about school," Femi tells me, holding out a small box. Inside is a leather-bound notebook with rustic unlined pages. It's an unusual gift because it looks so inexpensive compared to everyone else's. But Genny must have told him something different about me, because the more I look at this note-book, the less it looks like it's just for school. It begins to look a lot like a book for journaling.

Like writing poems.

I'm anxious having this book. My old notebook had a spiral binder and ragged pages that scream rushed notes and last-minute revision. This new one is asking for a different style of writing, I can tell.

The day after the dinner, I take my time transcribing my poem from my old notebook to this new one. It feels fresher as I write out each line, whispering it to myself over and over again. For a split second, with Femi's gift in my hands, I feel like a new person. Someone who is creative, or something like it.

Femi shows up with his parents to Genny's house the night before the wedding. It's still so surreal seeing him here in my world, interacting with people I know. He is suave as he introduces his parents again with a flourish of his arm, cracking witty but age-appropriate jokes with each elder. First he gists with Genny's mom—"Ah-ah, Mama, wetin, na? See how Gucci just dey match you!"—before he gets to Tayo's dad—"Now I see where our young oga gets all his style from!"—until he finally makes his way to my dad, whose gold-rimmed glasses have been polished to the max—"Papa Ada, this your glass na wa, o, make I just clean my own!"

He navigates the room coolly, bowing and shaking hands and hugging everyone like he was a part of this family all along. His parents settle in beside Genny's parents and they laugh together, clapping and raising drinks like longtime friends, even though I heard a few months ago, Femi's mom almost fought Auntie about the type of gele Genny should wear for the wedding.

Femi and his family brought kola nuts, bags of rice, bottles of wine, and a Bible. This part of the traditional ceremony is my favorite. It's meant to be a dowry but has since been modernized to a show of pageantry, a toast between two families who will soon become one.

The magic of the evening is electric, and for a hot second I almost forget my apprehension about the future. Today is about family, even though it's glaringly obvious that someone is missing.

But he'll be at the wedding. I *know* he will.

I am lingering by the doorway when Genny enters the room, her hair elegantly coiffed and her eyelashes expertly applied. She does a double take when she realizes it's me. "Ada, why are you hiding by the door?"

"I'm not hiding," I say, and gesture into the overcrowded living room. Between Femi, his family, his entourage, my family, Tayo's family, and Genny's family, there's barely anywhere to sit.

Genny frowns as she scans the living room. In true Genny fashion, she enters, snapping her fingers and clapping her hands, beckoning everyone who looks like they've never done a day of hard labor in their life. "We're running out of chairs. All the young people should go sit downstairs," she says.

Tayo's mom starts to cackle. "Miss Madam, soffri o, so you and your husband should join them?"

The room laughs at that but they still don't hesitate to bump their children from the sofas and chairs so more of Femi's entourage can sit. I'm used to being relegated to an upstairs or downstairs room during adult gatherings, so I immediately make a break for the basement where at least there's TV and a stronger Wi-Fi connection.

I want to call Sam, but that would be stupid of me to try with so much family around. Instead, I text: "*see you at the wedding!! you're coming for real, right?*" Two, three minutes pass, and nothing. I can give it a bit more time. Maybe he's busy editing a poem or he's out with friends or napping. He said he'd come, didn't he? He has to.

"Ada?"

I stop by the wall separating the kitchen and the door to the basement when I hear Tayo call me. He waves me over to the kitchen entrance so Chioma and an instantly suspicious Lola can make their way down the stairs.

A slight smile flashes across his face and I can't help but think how much he looks like Femi, how his handsomeness is so consistent. He fiddles with his fingers as I approach but he doesn't say anything until we're snug as close as possible to the wall, out of earshot of visitors in the living room.

"H-how's it going?" Tayo stutters out.

"How's it going?" I echo, crossing my arms. "That's all you pulled me aside for? Just a common greeting?"

"Jeez, okay, wow," he says, throwing his arms up in surrender. "I just wanted to, I don't know, say hi or whatever. It feels like we haven't seen each other in a minute."

"This is true."

He takes a deep breath before saying, "Me and Folasade are just hanging out. Like, just that. It's not... I mean, we're not... anyway. Yeah, that's—yeah."

I'm taken aback at his confession and unsure why he's telling me this, especially here where there are so many prying ears. He hides his face when I try to get a good look at his eyes. Tayo never behaves like this. His confidence is shattered in the presence of what I may think of him and Folasade being a thing.

And what *do* I think?

That same unease and bitterness from the time I saw them together rises in my throat, but I swallow it down as fast as I can.

"Oh, okay," I utter, suddenly as shy as he is. We're both not looking at each other in the corner of the kitchen, pretending we're in two different conversations when we're really not. "That's cool."

"Yeah, s-so," he stutters, clearing his throat. "Don't be mad, okay?"

"I'm not mad."

"Well, now that I told you me and Folasade are chill, maybe, um…" He clears his throat once, twice. I've never seen him so nervous. But when he says, "Maybe you should, uh, tell me about how you and your friend are just hanging out…right?" I realize this isn't about him and Folasade at all. It's about Justin.

"W-what?" I cough out. "Are you serious?"

"I'm just curious," he says, defensive. "You never seem to give a straight answer when you talk about him, so…I mean…I'm your friend, too. Why shouldn't I be concerned?"

"Concerned?"

"You know what I mean."

"Do I?"

"See, you can't even answer the question," he scoffs, pushing himself away from the cabinets and standing up straighter. "Are you and him, like, together?"

My heart skips a beat and I'm reminded of how deep in my feelings I get when I think about the theoretics. Theoretically and in my mind, we are, we can still be together. But feelings are not theoretical, and I can't lie to Tayo and say I don't feel differently about Justin.

But that's not fair, because I feel differently about him, too. Equally differently.

Tayo sees my hesitance to continue and mistakes it for a confession. He frowns. "This entire time I've been trying to figure it out," he tells me. "You guys always hang out together, and you never talk about him like he's just an ordinary friend. It's like you were trying to keep it a secret—like you didn't want anyone to know."

I'm so mad I almost blurt out: "*And why wouldn't I keep it a secret?*" but he has it all wrong. Justin is not my big secret. I like him, but that pales in comparison to the heavy spark in my chest when I think about the future. About what my future could look like, about what it's allowed to look like. If I'm a writer or a poet or a photographer or a salesperson, if there will be a Justin or a Tayo or a nobody, and what I'll be doing, and if I'll be happy, like *really* happy. This heavy spark in my chest, it's happiness. And it's burning like a motherfucker.

"That's not it," I hiss at him. For the first time in my life, I feel brave. My palms are sweating and my voice trembles when I speak, but I say it, finally, with my full chest: "I'm not doing law school anymore." He gawks instantly, taking a step back, but I keep going. "That's the real secret. I hate it. I don't... I mean, I never wanted to do it, I don't think. I chose it because it was easiest—I'm always choosing the easiest thing, for my personality, for my life, everything. But I don't wanna do it anymore. I can be good at *so* many things—like, next week, I'm performing at a poetry slam, Tayo, a fucking poetry slam, and it's making me nervous as hell but I'm *so* excited to just *be* there. I want to be happy, like really happy, and my happiness doesn't look like pre-law."

For a moment, the weight on my shoulders crumbles and I can stand straighter, more confident. The adrenaline rush of saying this out loud has me wanting to laugh and smile as wide as I can. Tayo looks at me like I'm losing my mind. "What?" he hisses, taking a cautious step toward me. "Ada . . . w-what?"

But before I can say anything, a large hand appears over Tayo's right shoulder and hoists him backward before the owner steps in front of me.

Dad. It's my dad.

CHAPTER TWENTY

I'VE NEVER NOTICED HOW TALL my dad is. He lumbers over like his feet are too heavy for his legs and when he's standing in front of me, it's like I've never known a deeper fear in my life. My bravery? Gone. I am a coward who's been allowed to think I have a choice.

There's no emotion behind his dark brown eyes. The way he scans me, back and forth, up and down like a printer, makes me feel like I've never been more insignificant.

"Adanna," he speaks firmly. My name sounds so chilling in his mouth. "What... what did I just hear you talking about?"

It would be so stupid of me to say it twice, so I keep quiet.

A roar of laughter erupts from the living room but my dad doesn't budge. Instead, he raises a hand—points his finger square at me as he says, "So your cousin is getting married tomorrow and this is the kind of nonsense you're talking about? You better just mind yourself, o. Mind yourself." I know that tone well from the day after Sam left and I know exactly what it means: Change your mind, be quiet, never speak of this again.

"Where is Papa Adanna?" someone calls laughing from the other room. "Where is he?"

Dad looks over his shoulder and I take the opportunity to breathe for a moment. My breath hitches in my throat the second he looks at me and I have to swallow the fear again. I don't even know what I'm afraid of anymore. The fear is so strong and so impenetrable that all I can do is tremble and wait.

Dad tsks. "Rubbish," he hisses and it stings like a slap. "If Genny wasn't getting married, would you be talking this kind of nonsense? If this was your house, will you say it?" He says something in Igbo that I don't understand, but the sneer of his mouth and the twist of his nose tells me all I need to know. The same voice calls him again and he takes a step back before turning toward the living room.

And I stop holding my breath.

Tayo steps forward in his absence, mouth pulled into a tight line. He reaches out and I let him hug me because I don't know what else to do. I don't feel like crying; instead, I'm just angry at my reaction. I was so sure of myself, at how I wanted to change, and now I'm just...

"He'll, um..." Tayo clears his throat. "*You don't have to say anything if you don't want to,*" is what I want to tell him, but I can't form the words. "Your dad has always been so strict, but, you know... Nigerian parents."

I pull away and stare at him, unable to think straight. Fatigue sets into my eyes and all I can do is shrug like, yeah, Nigerian parents. My parents. This is how they are, so I guess it's fine, and things like that. We gaze at each other like we both got smacked for saying something we shouldn't have and have been left to cry it out.

Then he says, "You're smart, Ada. You'll figure it out," and I want nothing more than to cry because I really don't think I can figure it out this time. And I don't want to. Other people get to relax, feel support effortlessly from the people around them, so why can't I?

I don't have any words left for Tayo. Instead, I turn and make my way to the staircase. My bag is tucked away in the corner and I throw it over my shoulder.

"Wait, where are you going?" Tayo asks.

"I don't know. Out?" I utter, useless as it is. I am scared for my dad to find me again, corner me, and make me repeat those words until he burns them from my mouth.

Tayo raises a confused eyebrow while he follows me

from the staircase through the kitchen to the back door. The backyard is pitch-black, but I know my way around the house to the road with my eyes closed. "Where are you going? Come on, your dad says that shit all the time—"

I stop dead in my tracks, causing Tayo to walk into me. He stumbles back, steadying himself on the ceramic tile, before I whip around to face him. "So I should just wait for him to come back so he can make me feel worse?" I snap. "Make me feel like what I'm saying isn't important?"

He frowns. "No, I don't mean it that way."

"What other way is there?" I hiss.

"Ada—"

"It's like I always need to be good, but I'm not good enough—"

"You *are* good—listen to me." He swerves in my way, blocking my path to the back door. "Don't let what your dad said get to you. Maybe he doesn't understand, but just… I don't know. I'm blanking here. I just…can you…stay? Please?"

His words root me in place. The softness of them, the plead in his voice, all of it holds me until I'm perfectly still. He is looking at me with such conviction. It makes me want to say yes so badly. "N-no. I can't," I mutter. "I don't want to stay here anymore."

"But—"

"Cover for me?" I cut in, reaching out for his hand.

Something about his touch feels so safe, but my feet are still itching to run. "Tell them I'm sick or I'm lying down or something. Tell them I'll be back. I don't know."

He huffs out a stubborn sigh, glancing at his feet. "You know I will," he tells me.

"I'll see you tomorrow," I say, "at the wedding."

"Yeah."

"It'll be fine," I tell him, more for myself than anything. Sam still hasn't responded and I'm panicking, trying to trust that he'll be there. He sold me this dream on choice and happiness, and I can't accept that he'd flake on me now. He can't. He has to help me see this through.

The door barely clicks as I swing it open and duck outside. My eyes take a moment to adjust to the darkness, but my feet already know the uneven path. I trail the building, cutting around the rusted shed that Uncle hasn't opened in years, and follow the streetlight to the road. Out front, I see my parents' car, Tayo's parents' car, and a slew of sleek black Mercedes-Benzes lined up and down the block. There's a man dressed in a black suit who walks up and down the sidewalk beside the cars. He's hired security, most likely.

Away from the judgment of my family, I dial Sam's number. It goes straight to voice mail. My heart skips when I hear the beginning of the message: "Hey, you've reached Sam, I'm not here right now..."

"Then where are you?" I grumble, ending the call. Why isn't he answering?

I hop on the bus, telling myself I don't know where I'm headed when I clearly do. Another bus takes me down Royal York, where I watch the houses that line the side streets get bigger and bigger. The streetlights look brighter too. Bungalows and town houses are replaced by sprawling lots, two-story properties, and gated mansions with pools.

I get off at Royal York and North and start walking. I walk past two houses large enough to house three families each, and eventually make the long trip up the driveway to 42 North Drive. I have never been to Justin's house before, but I know where it is because he showed me once on a map app in middle school. When his mom used to guest on other syndicated design shows, she did a makeover episode on their kitchen and he told everyone who would listen that his mom was famous. That was back when he felt comfortable doing so. Now, it's like every time I point out what I feel is an obvious resemblance, he gets quiet and clammy and weird.

Kinda how I get when I ring the doorbell and Celia Lam John answers it. Even though I should be used to seeing celebrities in real life by now, I'm still shell-shocked. Her eyes are dark and inviting, and her black pixie cut makes her look cool, edgy, artsy, even. Her resemblance to Justin is plain as day: same cheekbones, similar nose. I gawk but I don't mean to. She scans me up and down before eventually stumbling through: "So ... phie? Right?"

Celia Lam John remembers my name.

"Y-yes," I answer, timid. "Sorry to bother you. Is Justin home?"

She smiles, stiffly. "Yes. He's probably on his computer. Come in," she says, and pulls open the door for me. I can't believe Celia Lam John is inviting me into her house. "I apologize if you tried to call him. These days it's like if a small, animated caricature isn't talking to him, he won't answer." She forces a laugh, but even though Celia Lam John is cooler than the average parent, she's still a parent, and I know that laugh means she's pissed. I've heard it from Chioma's parents so often.

I take off my shoes and slip my feet into a pair of house slippers she nudges toward me. She leads me down the massive marble-floored hall to a wide-set polished staircase leading to the basement. As we descend, she begins calling things in Cantonese. It's only when I hear Justin's voice call back from the basement do I realize she's talking to him. He replies in Cantonese before he eventually grumbles out, "Of *course* I'm wearing pants," to which I blank.

Celia glances over her shoulder and waves at me to follow. I stick close behind her, letting my feet savor the cushy carpet on the way down. The basement is large and cool in temperature. There's a projector on one side surrounded by the most comfortable arrangement of couches I've ever seen, and a mini gym takes up the majority of the opposite side. In between, there are office spaces, one of which must belong to Celia or her husband, and the other which is being taken over by Justin and his multiscreen desktop. "This place is huge," I whisper to no one as I follow her toward Justin.

"Sophie came to visit," Celia says pointedly before giving the computer one last glare. "Turn that thing off. Tell me if you want snacks. I can bring fruit." Then, she turns to me and grabs my hand, squeezing it softly in hers as she says, "Don't be shy, okay? You can ask him for anything."

I nod, biting back a grin. "Thank you."

She says one more thing to Justin in Cantonese before she disappears back up the stairs. He watches her leave, none too impressed that she was down here to begin with. Why the hostility? If Celia Lam John was my mom, life would be so dope. Just look at this house!

"Did you call me or something?" Justin asks, fishing around his crowded desk for his phone. "My phone is probably on silent..."

"No," I say. "I was at a family thing, but it got a bit much... My dad overheard me telling Tayo that I don't wanna do law anymore, and he kinda snapped, so I left."

"Snapped?" Justin repeats, pushing himself up into a seated position.

"Yeah. He was just like 'if I hear pim,'" I say, putting on

my best impression of Dad. "It's a threat," I add when Justin stares back, confused. "Like, if I hear anything from you, then...use your imagination."

"Harsh. Does he think it's because of that art project you're doing with Patricia?"

"He doesn't even know about the art project." I grimace. "A-and I'd prefer to keep it that way for now."

"Fair."

"Are you beefing with your mom or something?"

He frowns. "How? Why would I be?"

"You seemed kinda mad at her."

"No, she's just been, like..." He groans. "She's leaving for Houston soon to shoot another renovation, so she's just been hovering. She won't stop cooking, and every five seconds she's calling me about something useless. That's all."

"Normally, I would sympathize," I say, glancing over my shoulder at the lushness of my surroundings. "But she's Celia Lam John, so on principle, I can't feel sorry for you."

"She's literally just my mom," he says with a roll of his eyes. "Wanna watch a movie?" His voice triggers the projector, which buzzes to life on the far wall. Immediately, it loads up a streaming app. I can't stop gawking at how the other half lives.

"Not really, but sure," I say, my eyes glazing over the screen.

A part of me feels as though I came to Justin's house for

a reason, like I want him to talk me out of something or into something, but another part of me feels I need this time to relax. I don't know how to relax; it bothers me that every conversation has to be layered and nuanced. My mind needs a break too. Thoughts of the wedding tomorrow, the Poetry Slam next week—all of it takes a back seat for a moment as I kick off my house slippers and curl into the sofa. It is so lush in here. I don't blame Justin for hiding out in the basement.

But then the bubble bursts and I remember Genny's wedding is tomorrow and I haven't heard from Sam.

And my dad just found out I don't want to do law.

And I am running away.

I have to keep believing Sam will come tomorrow. Sam, who promised me he'd be there. Sam, who showed me a way out just by existing. I know if Mom and Dad can meet him again and really understand where he's coming from, then they'll understand. We could be a family again, all four of us.

Dad asked me if I was serious with what I said about law school and I backed down, but I can't do that this time. I have to be brave. Sophie isn't a coward.

CHAPTER TWENTY-ONE

IT'S TODAY.

Everything is behind schedule, just like we all secretly thought but didn't want to say out loud. I've never heard of a Nigerian event starting on time, anyway. According to Blessing, the caterers aren't getting to the hall for another hour, which would be okay if not for the fact that they're also bringing the cake. Auntie Suzanna specifically said that the cake should be in the background of Genny and Femi's entrance to the chapel and then, once they officially enter the party hall, it will be moved to the foot of the high table so it can resume its place as official photo-bomber.

So there's no cake yet. Perfect. And then there's the whole issue that the DJ doesn't think Tayo's mix is as good as the one he came up with, even though they both sound like they were inspired from the same Spotify African Heat playlist. The only difference? Tayo's has a sicker fade between tracks. He's young and he knows what young people expect at a party. The DJ, maybe falsely named DJ Hip, is being way too stingy about sharing the spotlight, so Tayo had to call Ayo to come talk to him. Even though they don't know each other, Ayo has status with Femi, so DJ Hip will listen to him over Tayo, which I know makes Tayo a bit mad because he's spent the morning without the watch Femi supposedly flew in from Dubai.

But none of this matters to me because Sam has not called. He has not texted.

And it's *today*.

He needs to be here. He needs to talk to Mom and Dad, he needs to tell them he's okay, so that they'll understand that maybe I'll be okay too. Not everything has to go according to their plan to be a success; I know that now. If they see Sam, understand how happy and stable he is, they'll get it.

Justin drove me home after a Sicilian pizza and two episodes of *Forensic Files* last night. He didn't make eye contact with his mom on the way out, but I made sure to thank her. She smiled at me and told me to come back any time, and

I died a little inside. In my mind, she's definitely okay with me being her daughter-in-law.

This morning, I grabbed my stuff and fled to Chioma's place before Mom or Dad could bring up what I told Tayo about law school. If I see them at the wedding, it's whatever. They won't cuss me in front of everyone. Plus, by the time the wedding is over, they'll have spoken to Sam and cooled off a little. Easy.

My face is flawless thanks to Genny's hired makeup artists, my official wedding aso ebi looks amazing, and I'm about to see Genny get married to a Nigerian superstar. Focus on that, Ada. Be brave. Sam will come for sure and this will all be over.

Chioma tiptoes everywhere so that her skirt won't shift too much and no one will see her tattoo. "When we start dancing, everyone will be too drunk to notice," she tells me, tapping her temple with bravado.

We're both wearing gold gele on our heads to match our coordinated outfits. A woman in the lobby is charging fifteen dollars per girl to tie the gele in a new style from Nigeria. She snaps pictures of everyone for her business's social page after. "Look at us. Like real madams," Chioma laughs, fixing her headdress. It keeps tipping off because of the waxiness of her twists. Man, she should've used Marley hair, not kanekalon. Mistake number one!

"Mind yourself," I tell her. "You know your mom is

looking for a husband for you too. Don't waste time. Just marry Ayo."

"He-ey!" she cries, slapping me in the arm before tossing her head back in a full body laugh. "Shut up, don't even joke about that! If Mom hears you, na go be that."

I laugh too, a hollow sound, as my mind wanders back to Sam. I wonder more and more if I should tell her that Sam should be coming. I mean, no matter what she says, it doesn't make a difference because he's probably on his way. She wasn't so enthusiastic the last time I tried to bring him up, but she'll change her mind once she sees him. I know she will.

"Oh my god!" Chioma gasps, whipping around in excitement. She holds her breath and strains to listen, leaning away from me and toward the door. I don't hear anything, but by the grin on her face, she definitely does. "Someone's here!"

That someone could be anyone at this point. We've been awake for so long already, but the Genny x Femi festivities are only at stage one: photos and socializing with close family and about fifty local and prominent Nigerian journalists and photographers at the chapel. After this, Pastor Festus will do his yearlong sermon and marriage rites followed by more pictures in the atrium before we all head over to the main hall for food, food, food, and of course, dance, dance, dance. A Nigerian party wouldn't be complete without it.

Chioma was right that she heard something: Folasade and Lola show up with another bridesmaid in a regal silver Rolls-Royce. I thought it would be Genny, who I haven't even caught a glimpse of all morning, despite being one of her actual bridesmaids.

Folasade practically glides in her heels. She makes the rest of us look like barn animals clunking around in shoes we're not used to. She only spares one look for us before she and Lola step away, continuing what I assume is their conversation from the car.

Auntie Suzanna flies in holding a pristine iPhone and gathers us in the main hall for pictures. "Oya, you people stand together. We're late," she announces. We all huddle together, including Blessing who is doing double time as a bridesmaid and wedding planner. She laughs with a few of Genny's friends I don't know, but her eyes are watchful to make sure we're all doing the poses like she wants us to. After two poses, Chioma and I crouch and do ridiculous mixtape cover shot poses. Auntie snaps, "Stop doing yanga!"

At the same time, Chioma and I look at each other and sing, "Do me, do me, do me yanga o!" Auntie Suzanna is not impressed. Neither are Genny's friends. Lola bursts out laughing, but when Folasade looks at her, she immediately curls up and pushes a hand through her hair, looking away.

We barely hear when the front doors open again, a suave Tayo stepping through them. He looks so grown-up and mature in his crisp, tailored black suit. My chest flutters, panic and excitement coming to the surface. He is looking at his phone, but when he looks up, he catches me staring. That's when he dances his way over to us.

"That's enough," Chioma scoffs as he's mid zanku. "Who asked you to start dancing? Is it your wedding?"

"Wow, damn," he exclaims, laughing. I snort too, a bit too loudly, because it gets the attention of Folasade and Lola in the corner. Lola gasps and nudges Folasade, who shows little to no emotion as she stares us down. I can feel her eyes on the back of my head as Tayo chuckles and pockets his shades. Is she mad? She knows she can come hang with us too, right? If she's cool with us only speaking English, anyway.

Tayo's smile fades once he sees Folasade in the corner, and suddenly, he's tense like a soldier. "Um, I gotta go," he says, nodding. "I'll see you guys later, though, right?"

"Of course," Chioma says, and casts one look over her shoulder to Folasade and Lola. "Honestly, I'm surprised she didn't dump you yet. She probably doesn't realize that all the Yoruba you know you picked up from WizKid songs."

Tayo snorts. "Oh, now you're funny?"

"I've been funny."

"It's . . . a-anyway," he stutters, looking away shyly. "See you." I may be imagining it, but he looks at me a second longer than usual before he takes off. Now that things are in full wedding mode, there's no time to think about anything that isn't Genny- or Femi-related.

The front doors burst open again. Can no one enter peacefully? Ayo flies in in a panic, his shiny gator shoes click-clacking along the tiled floor. He's holding a set of car keys, waving them around like he doesn't know what they're for. Once he sees Tayo, he tsks and waves him over. "Come, come here," he says. "They're here already. Bridesmaids," he calls to us. "Get ready, o! You know your formation."

"Wasted opportunity," Chioma whispers.

We quickly line up around the chapel doors and wait. The boys walk in first, including Tayo who joins them quickly at the end as if he'd walked in at the same time. I had no idea he scammed his way into joining the grooms-men! Honestly, what an accomplishment.

Chioma is at the head of the line for the bridesmaids, and she walks in first with us tailing behind her. The music is louder from inside the chapel. Instead of a classic tune, "Here Comes the Bride" or something, DJ Hip is playing some highlife song. Who okayed this?

The groomsmen stand on the left and the bridesmaids occupy the right. The front rows are filled with journal-ists waiting to snap their first shot of Genny, and the row directly behind them has our immediate family, followed by other family or close friends filling up the remaining rows. A few people are standing in the back. I don't recognize a lot of people. I assume they're more of Femi's family, or friends that have latched onto Genny at the eleventh hour.

Suddenly, Femi makes his entrance in a pristine custom black suit that looks like it was crafted on his body. DJ Hip changes the song to a Skeleboy song and Femi shamelessly begins to dance his way down the aisle, laughing as he goes. His boys join in from opposite us. Chioma looks like she might start dancing too, but we both hear a hiss so loud and so sharp that it has to be coming from Auntie Suzanna. Chioma freezes in place.

Femi gets to the altar and gives all his groomsmen that coveted handshake: slap and snap as you pull away. The music cuts—cuts!—and awkwardly stumbles into a Tiwa Savage song. Blessing's idea, no doubt. Genny is steps away from making her entrance. Everyone rises as she appears in the doorway. Her strapless silk and lace gown flows down her back and swirls at her feet as she takes measured steps forward. Her hair is perfectly wavy, draped over her left shoulder and held together by elaborate silver pins. She looks just like a classy Nollywood diva. Judging by her wide eyes, even Chioma is taken aback by how beautiful Genny looks.

Femi holds a hand to his chest and says, "Ololufe mi... iyawo mi, o."

Genny grins. Does she even know what that means?

Pastor Festus steps forward, clutching his Bible. His small

waxy forehead glints under the chapel lights, giving off the impression of someone who's already spent time sweating through a sermon this morning. "Welcome, everybody, today…" He smiles wider and wider, gazing out onto the crowd. "Today we are here to see these two young people join in…marriage. We are blessed here to have…Mr. FBI, Mr. Fine Boy International, Skeleboy…Mr. Obafemi Oluwadurotimi Balogun," he says, resting a thick hand on Femi's shoulder. "And the beautiful Miss…Genevieve Isioma Ezejiofor…here."

Chioma groans, and leans in to whisper to me, "If this man goes *any* slower, we're all going to die here."

"Marriage is…," Pastor Festus continues, staring around at us. He pauses so the cameras can get a good shot. I swear I'm imagining it, but he even shifts so he's poised and posing as he speaks. "A sacred bond between two people that proves God's love is everlasting. He will never put two people together whose paths are not meant to cross…He will never!" he shouts. "In fact, as you are all sitting here, He is listening and watching. He knows those of you who are not married and are waiting for marriage—*gbam!*—you will get it." The applause and amens trickle in. "He knows those of you who are married and are having problems with your husband or your wife—*gbek!*—you will prosper. He knows the enemies who are blocking your path will not succeed. I say what? I say they will not succeed in Jesus's mighty name…"

My phone begins to buzz in my chest. I managed to suction it to the corner of my bra. It's currently being held up by adhesive tape and a lot of hope, but if my phone buzzes again, I can't guarantee it won't drop all the way down my leg to the ground. Please let whoever is texting me just relax for the next few minutes. I can't reach into my bra in front of God.

Pastor Festus launches into a well-known Nigerian praise song, clapping his hand against the Bible to keep time. "We are saying thank you, Jesus…" he sings, coaxing the crowd to join him. Almost everyone gets up and croons back, "Thank you, Lord…"

Femi and Genny have started singing and two-stepping, clapping along with Pastor Festus. He stares around at the groomsmen and bridesmaids before we all join in on the impromptu song.

Eventually, Pastor Festus settles into his final "Thank you, Lord!" and the chorus ends. Some patrons sit down but most guests stay up, awaiting that fateful moment when Genny and Femi become husband and wife. Auntie Suzanna slips out of the row to hover over the videographer and make sure he's getting a good angle. Pastor Festus, with a smug look on his face, points into the crowd and says, "I know what all you people are waiting for. Yes. Let's call in our Heavenly Father…" and launches into another prayer. I suppress a groan.

The second prayer is on par with the first and lasts twice as long. My left foot begins to lose feeling in these heels. A tremble runs through Pastor Festus that I know he'll play off as the Holy Spirit, before he lifts his hands over Genny and Femi. He says, "It is well. Yes. The Lord has told me … it is well. So now … I now pronounce … in the mighty name of Jesus, Mr. and Mrs. Obafemi Oluwadurotimi Balogun. You may kiss the bride."

Femi and Genny lean toward each other for the most chaste kiss I've ever seen. Mom leaps up first and cries, "Praise!"—so embarrassing! DJ Hip cranks the music from 0 to 100, startling half the crowd with the loud bass while Femi and Genny, smiling and dancing, make their way out of the chapel. Each groomsman and each bridesmaid link up as we exit the space. My partner just so happens to be Tayo. He grins and starts azonto-ing like we're in middle school. Normally I'd be embarrassed, but I like that we ended up together.

"Hey," he whispers as we leave the chapel. His voice is hoarse over the loudness of the music. "Can we talk later?"

"Sure," I say, even though I'm worried it's about the law school thing. There's nothing more to say, but the thought of having to explain myself a second time, and potentially be caught by another family member, is making me anxious. Speaking of other family members: Where's Sam? I can't believe he missed the ceremony. He better get here in time for the reception. "Give me one second..."

I slip away from Tayo and reach for my phone. Everyone is too enamored with Genny and Femi posing for pictures in the atrium with different groups: family, friends, politicians, gossip bloggers.

It was Justin who was texting me. I'm a little sad it's not Sam asking for directions or telling me he's five, six, seven minutes away. Please let him show up.

I swipe open to Justin's message. "*wanna hang out later?*" it says.

I reply: "*Not today! cousin's wedding, remember?*" I quickly switch to my camera and take a somewhat blurry selfie where he can at least see the neckline of my dress.

A few seconds pass before he texts back: "*oh yeah that's today.*" What? He knew it was today. I just saw him yesterday! "*you look nice btw.*"

I'm pathetic for grabbing at the smallest compliment, but I smile anyway. He's been so nice to me lately. I hate that I read into things like this so much. He said I looked "nice" and I panic. He could've said I looked pretty, but he said "nice." Maybe I don't know what to think of that after all. "*thanks bro,*" I say.

"*lol bro??*"

"*fam**"

"*l o l. okok, text me later if you can.*"

"*ok!*" I reply, and wait. I don't know what I'm waiting for.

I quickly bring up my chat with Sam and type fast: "*where are you?? you missed the ceremony and the reception is happening soon!*"

I am spoiled by Justin's fast replies, because Sam doesn't respond. He doesn't respond when Blessing coordinates pictures with Genny and Femi, and the bridesmaids and groomsmen. He doesn't respond when the caterer finally loads in all the food, when the extended relatives and friends and family eventually show up two hours late toting faux designer bags and concealed Tupperware. He doesn't respond when Pastor Festus does another five-year prayer mid-reception for no discernable reason. Not even when Femi and Genny dance their way in and invite close family to join them. Close family. Chioma and I link arms as we trail behind them, but Sam is close family too. Where *is* he?

Our table has an extra seat, just like I requested. It sits vacant, waiting for Sam.

Suddenly, Blessing takes hold of the mic at the front of the hall. And it really is a beautiful hall. The decorations, the crystal centerpieces, the floor lamps that light the way to the dance floor. She smiles as she says, "Hello everyone, it's Blessing Chukwudi. I'm a wedding planner and my card is on your tables, if you're interested." The hustle never stops, I guess. "I just wanted to let you know that the livestream is up and running." She gestures to the projector and the screen glowing large to the right of the DJ booth. It streams a video of the dance floor before switching to a video of the high table. Each camera must be on rotation. "We've been fortunate enough to have huge social media partners, and our media partner in Nigeria came through for sponsorship, so a big thank-you to them. If you are watching from the stream..." She turns until she finds a camera and speaks into it. "Yes, hello, if you're watching from a stream, welcome. The feed is subscription-based, so you'll have access for twenty-four hours upon the conclusion of the wedding. Please feel free to use the online portal to take pictures. And don't forget our hashtag! #SkeleboyWedsGenny.

"And now, before we start the dancing..." She takes a deep breath and breaks into a grin. "Everyone please take a look at this screen here for a special shoutout!"

Chioma and I hold our breath, fixing our eyes on a second screen against the wall that's directly across from the high table. Suddenly, Yemi Alade appears, smiling and waving. She manages to say, "Hello," before the room erupts in screams and excited giggles. One of Femi's groomsmen rips off his shades and gawks at the screen in delight. Chioma and I clutch hands, clawing and talking over each other while we watch the shoutout. How does Blessing get these celebs? She's definitely earned whatever fee she charged for all this.

My heart is still racing after the video fades and DJ Hip starts spinning music. Femi's mom gets up slowly and begins to dance her way to the main floor. She's holding a stack of American one-dollar bills, ready to spray both Genny and Femi with them. She approaches, pressing a bill into each of their foreheads and reciting prayers for good luck, wealth, and a happy marriage. Her careful allocation of money becomes a free-for-all as she tosses it over their heads, letting the bills cascade around them until the ground is covered with all the ones she brought. Femi's father comes up and does the same. Then, Genny's parents, my parents, a group of extended relatives, and Genny's squad begin to spray them. A cascade of chiefs follow suit, shouting, "Igbo kwenu!" and throwing twenty-dollar bills in the air like it's nothing. Soon, many guests have danced up with their stacks of money, inching closer and closer so they can spray the new couple.

Tayo comes to our table. He boldly extends a hand to me, saying, "Come dance with me."

"Teach me how to shoki," I say.

He gasps, "Man, you can't even do that?" and extends his hand again. Our hands touch and that safe feeling, that comfort, comes back again, flooding my senses as he leads me onto the dance floor. My phone remains at the table, turned upside down so the screen isn't visible. Sam hasn't texted me back yet, but I really hope he shows up. He has to. He promised me.

Tayo is so serious about dancing but he's so much fun to be around because of it. Some of the other groomsmen come over to dance near him and watch. The second a new dance craze hits Nigerian media, Tayo already knows about it and has mastered it.

The song transitions into a mid-tempo one, a quintessential Nigerian love song we all love to sing and act out. Tayo inches closer and says as cleanly as he can over the music, "Hey, do you wanna talk?"

My eyebrows knot in confusion. "About what? Are you good?"

"Oh, uh, yeah." He clears his throat, suddenly backing up. Why's he being so weird? "Or, uh, I know you like this song. We can talk after."

On impulse, I reach for his hand again. His eyes float to our entwined fingers as I say, "It doesn't matter to me. You know they're gonna play this song, like, three times."

"Yeah, true," he chuckles, nervously, and gives my hand a squeeze. A part of me hopes Folasade is watching. "I was just thinking if, like, after this, you wanted to hang out or something?"

I nod right away. "Yeah, sure. I—"

One of my mom's friends, an auntie I know by face but

not by name, waltzes up and takes my other hand while she dances around us. Tayo and I exchange a confused look. Auntie steps a bit closer to me and says loudly over the music, "Ada, Ada! How are you? Your parents have been showing us your debate video."

"O-oh." I bite back a shy smile.

"You've done very well, o," she goes on, grinning. "They're very lucky to have you. A lawyer!"

I cringe, letting my hand grow slack in her grasp. "Thanks."

Tayo senses my unease immediately. He's so good at that, so attentive. "Auntie," he cuts in, that teasing tone singing in his voice. "I no dey find your trouble, o, but this one wey you come enter my front . . . e get as e be."

Auntie cackles and drops my hand for Tayo's. "Ah! Tayo ba-by," she choruses. "You too dey make mouth. Okay, o, I dey go."

When she finally dances away, I do my best to hold in a laugh, but it doesn't work. "Thank you, oh my god," I giggle. "I don't even know who that lady was."

"Same," he snorts, glancing away.

"So what did you wanna tell me?" When he gives me a blank stare, I prod, "You were gonna say something just now. About hanging out?"

"Oh, yeah, uh." He clears his throat. I'm so taken with the song, so excited to be here with Tayo, that I barely notice his apprehension. Still, I can see it growing in his eyes. It's stuck there. I know the kind because I've experienced the same thing, when there's just something you need to say.

And he does. "Do you...wanna go out sometime? Like, just the two of us. On a d-date, or something like that."

I stop dancing. It immediately makes him nervous and I feel guilty that it does, because I'm nervous too but I'm afraid to show it. "Oh, Tayo...," I cough out. I don't know what else to say past that. My heart thumps in my chest once, twice. I try to reach for his hand again, for that sense of safety.

And that's when I see him.

Him.

Over Tayo's shoulder, Sam weaves through the crowd with a plate of food, slow and cautious, but with the ease of someone who has been here all along. He is in a slim-fit navy suit that looks like it still needs to be hemmed at the leg. He's quick to make eye contact with people but looks away when they stare too hard. Some people who don't know him assume he's with Femi's family. But those that recognize the same cheekbones, the same chin, the same eyes...they're wondering who this phantom is.

I am grinning. He's here, he's really here! I wave frantically from the middle of the dance floor before I nudge Tayo. "It's him, it's him," I breathe out.

Tayo frowns. "Who?"

"Look," I say, and spin him around to face my table. "Sam. It's…it's Sam."

Tayo gawks at once as if he's really just seen a ghost. I barely register my feet moving across the floor toward my table; I barely feel myself pull up a chair beside him.

He smiles hesitantly. I throw my arms around him in a sloppy hug. "Wow, please," Sam chuckles. Hearing his voice, seeing him in this room. It's real.

When I pull away, he gestures to his plate: rice, plantain, fish, hard chicken, and stewed goat. "Who cooked the rice?" he asks. "It's really good."

"Blessing had some of it catered, but you know our family…Everyone wanted to cook," I say. I'm grinning so much that my face is starting to hurt.

Tayo wanders up to the table in shock. Sam has to do a double take, and nearly screams, jumping to his feet when he recognizes him. "What? Tayo, bro, is that *you*?" He pulls him in for a hug, which Tayo accepts, dazed as he is. "Yo, you're looking fresh! This line-up, though!"

A nervous smile breaks on Tayo's face. "Th-thanks, man," he replies. He's so stunned that he doesn't know what else to say, and I don't blame him.

I jump to my feet. "When you're done eating, we gotta find Mom and Dad. Oh! And we gotta introduce you to Femi. He's *so* cool, like honestly. He'll love you!"

"I…" Sam's gaze breaks from mine and rests someplace

behind me, behind Tayo. Coldness seeps into his eyes and his jaw tenses at the object of his attention. I'm almost too scared to turn around. I don't need to. I feel the presence of someone else's gaze behind me. I feel footsteps approaching.

Sam stands and pushes back from the table just as Dad stumbles into view. Out on the dance floor, people are still having a good time, completely oblivious to the intensity between Sam and my dad. Dad's fists are clenched and when he speaks, his voice is sharp like a knife. "What are you doing here?" He doesn't even give Sam a second to answer before he yells again, "Biko, I said what. Are. You. Doing. Here?"

DJ Hip notices the scuffle and turns the music down slowly until Dad's voice carries across the hall.

Sam's lips are pursed tightly. He is unwavering, but I see the way he clenches his fists too, and I know part of it is out of fear. Dad is as tall as he is. He is heavier, too. "I was invited," Sam tells him sternly.

"Chine-ke! God!" Dad cries and slaps his hands together. The sound echoes eerily in the hall. "And who would invite such . . . such rubbish like this?" As he says it, his hand gestures from Sam's head to his feet, sneering all the while at the boy in front of him. At his own son. "How dare you come here and disgrace this place with your presence?"

"Dad . . . ," I utter. Tayo's hand on my arm grows firmer and he tries to lead me away, but I won't go. "Dad—"

"You be quiet!" Dad snaps at me. I flinch from the reverb in his voice. "It's you who invited this...this *thing*, abi? It's because of him that you're talking about not going to, to... to study law again? Eh?"

Now, murmurs spread across the room and for the first time all evening, I can feel all eyes on me, poking around like they're trying to pick apart my skin. My hands fly to my arms and I pull them in close, letting my eyes fall to the floor as Dad thunders on, "See the kind of example this foolish somebody has given you. Eh? Is this how you want to useless your life? Chasing after an example set by this useless—do you even know what this, this rotten boy did to your mother and I? Do you?"

Sam lets out a short sigh, pressing a hand to his mouth, but all I can do is shake my head. "It...wasn't that bad, what-whatever it was," I stutter out. Dad just gawks, stunned that I would say anything. "Nothing can be as bad as to kick out your own son. A-and look—he's okay. He's fine. So what if he didn't become an engineer like you wanted? He's still—"

"Don't let your mother come hear his nonsense. Can you imagine? Eh? Somebody who doesn't even know what they're talking about," Dad snaps. "So you don't even know, and you invited this rat to come to this place?"

My bottom lip is quivering now. It's too quiet and I don't know what else to say except: "He's my brother."

"Brother *ke?*" Dad grimaces. "Make I speak oyinbo so

you fit understand. This your brother is a thief! Yes! Or you didn't know? This boy is a thief!" He calls it out loud, turning so everyone in the hall can hear him. He claps his hands and stomps his feet and makes a spectacle of both of them. We are all captive to his story. And Sam looks so damn uncomfortable. He fidgets with his fingers though he steels his eyes on Dad. I'm scared he will run away again.

"This boy," Dad goes on, pointing an accusatory finger at him. "This boy stole twenty thousand dollars from me and your mama! Everything, one by one, all the money we gave him for school. The money from years of working, he just took it, *gbam*, like that—it was gone! Given away to, to . . . to drugs or whatever. Just stolen! Yes!"

I feel numb and for the first time since Dad started talking, my voice starts shaking. "W-what?" I ask. Even Sam can hear the quiver in my voice now, and the remorse that fills his eyes is monumental. I can't believe it. He never brought it up when I texted him or when we hung out at his house. He never brought it up in his poetry. "It's not true," I say.

Dad turns on me again, stammering through his anger. "Will . . . will . . . will you just be quiet? Do you know what's true and what's not true? Who sent you?"

"It's not true," I say again, this time louder. I'm looking right at Sam this time, but he's not looking at me. "Right? Sam?"

Sam doesn't say anything. God, why won't he say anything?

"Uncle, that's enough, na." A brave voice cuts through the silence. Our eyes follow the sound until we see Genny gliding through the crowd. People part for her, careful not to step on her dress, and Blessing follows, her footsteps quick and her eyes eager to know what's going on. She frowns, a small twitch in her eyebrows as she stares down my dad. "Please," she says. "That's enough. You can talk to him later. But do you have to do this now?"

The hall has quieted down. Dad looks as if he's calmed too. With regret in his eyes, he turns to Genny and says, "Genevieve, nwa m, ndo. I didn't know this boy would come here today."

Sam sighs out again. "Fucking knew this was a mistake," he says, and in that moment, I know he's talking to me. This, us meeting again, me going against our parents, all of it—a mistake. Before I can say anything, he turns and storms out of the hall. He's running again.

"Sam—" Dad gets in my way just before I take off after him. He scowls, staring down at me with the same anger and disillusionment he showed Sam. It frightens me. Dad has never looked at me this way before.

"Adanna, you," he hisses. "If you follow that boy, then go, follow him, o. If you want to be useless like him, then you get out of my house too."

CHAPTER
TWENTY-TWO

MY FEET ARE HEAVY AND awkward in these shoes. I can't run properly and I'm mad at myself for even wearing them—they're not that nice, their golden heels don't even really match, they're so clunky! By the time I dodge my dad and get out of the hall to the parking lot, Sam is gone. He's gone—no matter where I turn, I can't see his fleeing figure or a speeding car anywhere. Fuck. Fuck fuck. My hands fumble my phone and they shake while I dial his number. Nothing. Another time. Nothing. Again. Fucking nothing—

"Ada! A-da!"

Chioma races over to me. She was smart and took her

shoes off first. One hand clutches them by the heels while the other grabs my forearm, nails digging into my skin like she's trying to cut me. There's something so chaotic about her energy, like she might deck me in the face with her shoes. I flinch preemptively, my phone slipping out of my shaking hands. Chioma snatches it just before it hits the ground. "Give it back," I say.

She sneers and I really think she might hit me this time, so I wriggle and pull myself away from her grasp. "Are you actually joking? You really invited Sam to my sister's wedding? My own sister——?"

"Okay, you shut up——"

"Who are you telling to shut up?"

"You didn't even give a shit about this wedding until literally right now," I shoot back. She narrows her eyes at me with nothing short of disgust. As if what I did was really that bad! What's so wrong about wanting my brother to be with his family? "Give me my phone!"

"So you can text him and tell him to come back?" Chioma mocks, looking at the device in her hands. She moves like she's going to throw it but I grab her forearm before she does. "Disgrace. Not everything is about you, you know. Why, on today of all days, would you decide to invite Sam after you know he's been beefing with your family since time? Why would you wanna ruin Genny's wedding?"

"Ruin what?" I go on. "Genny said it was okay for me to invite someone else."

"Yeah, but someone else like your white boyfriend—"

"He's not my—he's not—he's biracial!"

"Not *Sam*! Not especially after he did that shit to your parents."

I frown. "It can't…it wasn't—"

"You heard what happened!" she cries, pointing behind us toward the hall. My eyes follow her gesture and I notice a few people one by one begin to pop out, curious at our raised voices. Some of Femi's boys are there. Blessing hangs by the door, watching cautiously, as if she's wondering if she should come and interfere. And Tayo is there. His hands are jammed into his pockets and he slouches, uneasy, but he doesn't approach. He seems hesitant to get in the middle of Chioma's antics and I don't blame him. I don't even want to be here right now. "No offense, I get he's your brother, but you heard what happened and you're still trying to cape for him? He stole all that money from your parents and who knows what he did with it. He probably didn't even graduate. Such a shame, the golden son."

"Shut up, don't talk about him like tha—"

"You keep defending him! What's wrong with you? Do you not realize this isn't just about you?" She points behind her again, and it's not lost on me just what this small disturbance may have cost her. "My sister has been looking forward to this forever—a day she wanted to spend with her family."

Anger is bubbling so high up my throat that I feel like I'm going to explode. "Fuck you, you don't know anything!" I say, shoving her in her chest. She stumbles back, nearly dropping her shoes. Why doesn't she just put the shoes down, damn! "He's *my* family too."

"*We're* your family," she says, slapping her chest and gesturing at the small crowd near the entrance. "And family doesn't pull shit like this. I don't know what's worse: the fact that you actually invited him to Genny's wedding without really knowing what went down or the fact you ... you didn't even tell me." The hurt in her voice seeps out. Maybe this isn't even about Sam; maybe it's about Chioma and me. How she's been like the best sister to me after Sam left and I couldn't even work up the courage to be real with her. Her bottom lip quivers against her better judgment. She is angry, but she doesn't want me to see how sad she is too.

I can't think anymore. So many words, so many things I want to say to her, but none of them are forming right. I'm angry at her, but I'm angry at myself too. Angry at her, Sam, myself, Dad, everyone. Maybe I don't really believe Sam is capable of what they're saying. But then, if Dad wasn't telling the truth, why did Sam run? If he's innocent, why didn't he stay?

"Forget this. I have to go," I mumble and disappear through the parking lot.

Chioma calls, "You can't just *leave*!" But I'm already through the first two rows of cars and I'm not turning back. I slip past a van of women, most likely a group of dancers, carrying bags and suitcases filled with costumes into the venue. There's so much I'll be missing, and even as I walk by them, the thought occurs to me that I could just . . . stay. But my mind is already made up and my feet shuffle on their own farther and farther away from the hall.

I try dialing Sam's number again, but there's still nothing. He has to pick up at some point, and when he does, my first question is going to be: Why? Why didn't he tell me that's why he was kicked out? Didn't he think it was important enough to tell me? Am I not important to him?

I am that exotically dressed stranger on the bus. I pretend not to notice when people ogle the fabric I'm wearing or the gele on my head. I can't do anything about the clothes, but I take off the headwrap and rest it on my lap. Feeling self-conscious is nothing. Right now, my mind is doing a mile a minute and it can't slow down. What do I do? Dad hates that I don't want to do law. He's so commandeering, so overbearing, so patriarchal and fretful it hurts. I wonder if this is what he did to Sam, just up and kicked him out without even asking why. What was Sam doing with all that money? (What am I going to do if not law?) Was it really for something illegal? (What else am I good at?) Where did all of it go? (What makes me happy?)

I can't go home.

I am unhappy.

Happiness, *ke*. To think I'm thinking of happiness at a time like this.

I need to go home.

I don't know what I'm expecting when I walk into the house. No one is there and they won't be for a while. The wedding is barely into its second act right now. I'm missing the real traditional marriage ceremony, the first outfit swap, and the "Yanga" dancers. I hope Tayo films it. I wish I could talk to him right now.

I change out of my wedding clothes, scrub down, and settle into comfy pants and an oversize sweater. I'm so lost, not even my arms know what to do with themselves. I settle on the sofa, still feeling awkward and uncomfortable, waiting for the sound of the front door clicking open. I don't even know how I'll face my parents. *"You could've just stayed, Ada,"* I tell myself again. *"Played the good girl, kept in line. You could've just stayed."*

I call Sam again. No answer. I try him again and again until I fall asleep, my head against the armrest.

When I wake up:

"If na suffer e wan suffer, ah-beg, let am go, sha!"

When I wake up, there's something soft and cold on my neck. Fabric.

"Wetin, na? Where she go go, sef?"

When I wake up, there's something soft and cold on my neck. It's fabric, it's my fabric, it's my clothes.

I bolt up just in time for another shirt to get thrown at my feet. "What…?" I croak, my voice still groggy with sleep. My eyes take a moment to focus. It's dark outside but all the lights are on in here. My mom is still dressed in her elaborate wedding clothes, poised by the breakfast bar as she yells around the corner to the staircase. My dad yells back from the top of the stairs, and when he comes thundering down in his agbada, he's carrying—he's carrying my clothes. All of my things.

He pauses when he sees me. "Eh heh, so shame no let you sleep well, abi?"

"What's going on?" I mumble, looking around. There are so many of my things on the floor. Clothes, books, accessories, bags. "What's all this?"

"Is it not your own?"

"W-well, yeah—"

"So why are you asking me such questions?" he grunts and drops his latest armful on the floor by my feet. I bend down to scoop up my things, gathering them frantically like they're going to disappear. "Didn't I tell you to go and follow that useless boy?" he snaps.

"Dad—"

"Don't 'dad' me. I said, didn't I tell you to go and follow

him?" he asks again, tugging at his ear as he leans toward me. "Didn't I?"

I swallow. "Yes."

"But you still came back to this house. And for what? Ah-beg, pack all these things and get out."

He can't be serious. We're reaching true Nollywood-level dramatics here, except this time I'm not watching a Nigerian movie; I'm in it. I turn to Mom who is whispering to herself in the kitchen. "Mom," I call. She glances at me and just shakes her head. What? "Mom, honestly? This isn't fair!"

"Fair, *ke*? Did I ask for fair?" Dad cuts in. "I'm going to change. If I come back and still meet you here…" He trails off into Igbo, snapping his fingers above his head. I know it's a threat by the way he points and snaps and speaks deep and slow. I just can't believe he's saying this to me. Me, nwa m, his daughter.

He storms upstairs and it is silent for a moment. Mom comes over just as I'm peeling clothes off the sofa and putting them into a pile. She picks one up and helps fold it gently, that motherly look of disappointment on her face. I can't stand it. Why is she disappointed in me? I didn't fucking do anything wrong.

"Ada," she says, quietly, setting a shirt aside. Her voice almost sings my name. "Adanna. Why can't you just leave it alone, na? Why not?"

Tears trickle down my face. I don't realize they're there

until I feel a drop hit my hand as I'm folding a skirt. Damn, I don't know how many more times I can say "he's my brother" before it starts to lose its meaning. He's my brother, he's my brother. Why doesn't that mean anything to Mom and Dad, or anyone?

"I didn't know what happened," I utter through a sniffle. "I didn't know he took your money—"

"Just took our money?" she gasps. "A-da-nna! It's not just took our money, o. That boy has robbed us! All the money we gave him for school, all the time we invested in him, it is gone. Eve-ry-thing." As she says it, she claps her hands together and throws them in the air like she's letting something free, something she's been holding a long time. "When we came to this country, we said just go to school. That's it. Did we complain when he wanted to, eh, do his hair like dada?"

Sam's famous locs pop into my head.

When I don't respond right away, she kisses her teeth and says again, "Eh? Sheh-bi, I am talking to myself?"

I shake my head quickly. "No."

"Did we complain when you wanted to do piano or some other such instrument?"

"No."

"All we said is that you people must go to school," she goes on, the plead in her voice growing stronger. There is depth that I've never heard before, the cry of a person who has suffered and endured and adapted more than I can understand. "Just go to school. Become something. And so that your brother took the money your father and I worked hard for and just *dashed* it to some, some ashawo. Somebody." She snaps her fingers over her head twice. "And did we see the money again? Mba! Did we see the first degree? Mba mba!"

"B-but maybe if you talked to Sam," I put in timidly. Foolishly, at this point. "Maybe if you talked to him, you could hear what ha—"

"*Tah!*" My mom hisses. She pinches her fingers together before continuing to help me fold my clothes. She slides a folded shirt and two folded jeans over to me before saying something in Igbo—a proverb, or something like it. She translates, "'There is a kind of pain only a child can give you.' I don't want to talk about Obinna. Take these things back to your room and go to sleep."

I get to my feet, unsteadily, arms full of as much stuff as I can carry. "You heard Dad," I say. "He told me to get out."

"And I'm telling you to go to your room," she reiterates firmly. "It's not your dad that carried you. Bush girl."

I frown. "So I go back to my room and then what? I go to school and eventually end up at law school?"

"Yes," she answers like I'm the one who isn't making any sense. "What's the problem?"

"And Sam, we just never speak about Sam again?"

She snaps at me, something in Igbo, and I just wait

because there's nothing else I can do. Nothing will change if I stay here. They don't care about what I want to do, they don't care about Sam, they don't care about me being happy. And I so badly want to be happy.

Mom is staring at me curiously like I should answer her, but she knows I don't know what she said because she never taught me. I don't speak Igbo; all I speak is English and uncoordinated pidgin, so I turn up my nose and purse my lips as I say, "It's okay. I can go. I don't want you telling Auntie Suzanna that I don't listen to my parents." And I bend quickly to throw as much as I can into my duffel bag.

Mom gasps. "What are you talking about?"

I'm too frustrated to answer. She keeps asking me what's happening, where am I going, what am I doing, but I don't have it in me to reply. I clench my jaw hearing Dad's footsteps pace across the top floor. He expects me to be gone by the time he comes back and I keep feeling more and more that I shouldn't be here anymore. I throw the bag over my shoulder and Mom shrieks—"Where are you going to?"—as I march to the doorway, my feet eager to both run and stay rooted in place. I can hear Mom's voice call after me, her legs chase after me, but I'm out the door and down the driveway before she can stop me.

I'm ten paces away before I call Sam again. No answer. How dare he.

I want to call Tayo, but I don't know what I would say to

him. I didn't give him a real answer when he asked me out, and things have escalated so much at home that I don't even feel like my answer is important right now. He'd tell me to talk to my parents or he'll offer to talk to his parents, but in the end, it will all be a lot of circling and posturing.

I want to call Justin too. I want him to ask where I am and what I'm doing in that voice I so like. I miss his basement and the remote-less projector and being so close to him on the sofa that it feels like we are touching.

Chioma is a definite no. We'd kill each other in the night.

I'm running out of options, which is why I call *her*. All I have to say is "I need a favor" before she's asking me to come over. I'm lucky she only lives a bus away, a long bus ride, and the last one of the night, but thankfully, it's just the one. The path to her house comes alive with motion-sensor lights and by the time I reach the top step, she pulls open the door to greet me. "Come in," Patricia says, nudging the door open wider. It's so warm in here. I've never been in a warmer house.

CHAPTER TWENTY-THREE

PATRICIA GIVES ME A TOUR of her house, which is how I know we're different right away. No one who wasn't a family member or family friend has ever been in my whole house, but I know exactly what her room, her dining room, her kitchen, and her basement hangout space look like within ten minutes of me stepping foot in there. Her house smells like sage and five-spice mix and cinnamon and brown sugar. It's so different from the smells of my kitchen and my house, but it's still comforting.

Patricia's mom looks just like her: the same wide eyes and wide grin, except she has long, long braids that reach her knees. They're tied up messily while she stirs a pot of thick stew on the stove. "You're Tricia's friend?" she asks, grinning, before Patricia can even introduce me. Her voice is light but laden with her Jamaican accent.

"Mom, this is Sophie," Patricia tells her and I offer a small, feeble wave. I'm still lugging around this duffel bag and it's weighing on my shoulder.

Patricia's mom eyes my bag. "Will you be staying for dinner, Sophie?" She asks it like she knows I will be, and possibly for longer than that too.

"I hope so," I say, eyeing the pot.

"Well, welcome," she tells me. "Tricia tells me you're a very good poet."

I turn to Patricia, who simply shrugs. "I, uh, I think she was just being too nice to me," I reply.

"No way I wasn't," Patricia chortles. "Mom knows we're performing next week. I told her all about it."

"Sounds like you've got a talent." Her mom winks at me over her shoulder.

"Thanks." Does being talented even mean anything? I'm talented, so now what?

Patricia tugs the duffel bag off my shoulder. I don't feel any lighter, but I force a smile so she knows I appreciate it. "Let me show you our spare room," she says.

"Yes," Patricia's mom says. "You'll love it. Very spacious and you get to look out at the garden. You'll tell me if my flowers start blooming overnight, won't you?"

I nod right away. "O-of course." It makes her laugh that I'm so serious because she's clearly joking. I bet she thinks I'm weird. I bet she's thinking, "*Where did Patricia find this girl who doesn't know how to lighten up?*" I bet she's hoping I'll leave.

"Come on." Patricia traipses past me to the staircase and I follow silently.

The spare room is beside Patricia's room at the top of the stairs. It's a large space with a done-up bed, a mildly dusty wooden dresser, and a plush loveseat that looks as if it used to be a charming family room staple. I step through the room and immediately crash on the bed, wanting to feel some sort of warmth aside from the burning in my chest. I'm still shaken up from leaving home and from not being able to get ahold of Sam. This entire day is just spiraling and it feels like nothing can save it.

Patricia watches me from the doorway while she sets down my duffel bag. "You good?"

"Yeah, yep," I lie immediately.

"What's all that, then?" She nods to the bag. I shift and look at it, remembering how it felt to wake up to all my things strewn across the living room floor. Patricia instantly sees the discomfort and annoyance building in my eyes when they graze the bag. "Did you have a fight with your parents?" she asks.

I scoff. She should know "*a fight with my parents*" sounds like something white people get up to. I don't fight with my parents; we just had a classic one-sided disagreement.

That's all. "No," I tell her, and sit up. "A lot's just been going on, but it's not that... It's nothing."

She nods. "Hold on a second. I'll grab you a drink."

Patricia makes her way out of the room and for a moment, I'm left with nothing but this storm of thoughts racing through my head. I can hear her footsteps descend to the kitchen, every thump vibrating in the emptiness of the room.

Without thinking, I grab my phone and redial Sam's number. It rings and rings.

And rings.

And I hang up before it connects.

Fuck. I really am a coward.

Patricia comes back with two ginger ales and hands me one. She settles into the loveseat and chugs her drink, watching me while I sip mine. After a moment, she pulls the cup away from her lips and says, "So. Wanna tell me why you ran away from home?"

"I didn't run away... I was kicked out," I mumble nervously. Patricia sits up straighter, worry forming between her eyebrows. "My brother showed up at the wedding because I invited him, right, but it didn't go so well. My parents got kinda mad..." My jaw clenches on its own and not even taking another sip of ginger ale helps. I do it anyway.

"*Kinda* mad?" Patricia echoes. Tact is not her strong suit. "Are you serious? They kicked you *out*."

"Thanks, wow."

"Just because your brother showed up?" she asks.

I nod right away. "I also told them about law school."

She frowns. "Wait, I missed this. What about law school? You got . . . early admission or something?"

I shake my head, equally amused that she thinks that sort of thing could happen to me. When I say, "I don't want to do it anymore," her eyes pop out of her head.

"Oh my god?" she gasps.

"It's fine," I say, even though we both know it currently isn't. "I'm thinking about what I want to do and what makes me happy, you know? Or . . . you know." I sigh. Nothing I'm saying is making any sense. None of this sounds credible anymore. "I don't know. I tried so hard to chase this . . . this *happiness*, but maybe it's just not for me. What good has it got me? My parents hate me. They think I'm going to turn out just like my brother, but, ugh, they don't know how *good* he is."

A smile comes to Patricia's face. "*I* remember how good he is. Obi from the Poetry Slam, right?" When I nod, her smile deepens. "I knew it, I could tell from his face. He was dope. Real talented."

I nod, smiling too. I can't help but feel lighter when I talk about Sam. He's passionate about something that means a lot to him, but just because he isn't an engineer, he's considered a failure? This can't be right.

Then she asks, "So you're just not gonna go back home?"

and any fleeting joy I felt from thinking about Sam and how cool he is disappears. "Don't take it the wrong way, because you're cool to stay as long as you want. I just mean you can't really resolve anything like this."

"I know that."

"Listen, I don't know what it's like to live in your house," she says carefully. "But your parents care about you, right? They wouldn't force you to do something you really didn't want to do."

"It doesn't matter," I say. "There's nothing I can say that will change that."

"Do they know you're doing the Poetry Slam?"

"What? Look at me. No."

"If they knew," she goes on, "don't you think they'd maybe change their mind? They could come and watch for themselves. Girl, you're talented and they don't know that about you. They only know you ranked second in debate."

"Should've been first."

She chuckles. "You're petty as hell. Your parents proba-bly think that's the kind of thing you care about most."

"They keep sharing my debate video," I grunt with a roll of my eyes. "Showing it to all my aunts and uncles, like, 'this is her, this is what Sophie does best.'"

Patricia raises an eyebrow. "Can you blame them? They don't know what you like or how many things you're good at or the kinds of things you think about. You should tell them. Give them another kind of video to share around," she adds with a smile.

I burrow my fingers in the duvet, my mind wandering to the upcoming performance. Patricia and I barely got along at first, but in this moment, I feel she understands me the most. Her, Justin, even Sam—all of them believe I can do this. The only person who's still unsure is me.

I have to say something. I can't let this become my reality.

"I should ...," I tell her, my voice shaky. Patricia applauds with her fingertips from across the room and I purse my lips to keep from smiling because that's such a Patricia thing to do. She is exactly how she was the first day we spoke to each other in media arts class. Nothing about her has changed. She doesn't need to pretend.

I sit up straighter and reach for my phone. Dad is probably still mad, but I text him the details for the Poetry Slam anyway: "Tuesday at 7 P.M.," it says. "Please come." When I hit send, it feels like a million butterflies descend on my stomach and start to eat away its lining. I feel exhilarated and terrified at the same time. Might pass out.

"Holy shit," I breathe out. My dad may take one look and decide wiping me from the family tree is the best course of action. My mom may see the invite and decide it's time for me to go live with my grandma in her village. But until then, I wait.

Patricia is watching me intently. I don't look at her when I say, "I, uh, invited my dad to the event."

She gasps. "What do you think he's going to say?"

"Chine-ke, what is wrong with you?"

"What is this nonsense?"

"So instead of studying, this is what you've been doing?"

"If na that your useless he-goat brother you want to be, well, you have succeeded!"

"Is this better than reading law in school?"

"I don't know," I tell her.

CHAPTER TWENTY-FOUR

PATRICIA BRINGS ME ANOTHER GINGER ale before disappearing to her room. "FaceTime with Casey," she says, waving her phone enticingly, as if I should want to be included. "Do you mind if I step out for a second? I don't wanna leave you if you're still feeling bad."

I shake my head right away. "No way, it's fine. I don't want to interrupt your life."

She snickers, "Life. You're funny," before disappearing around the corner.

My phone starts to ring. Hesitantly, I flip it around to see who's calling and am shocked to see "MOM" flashing across the screen. "Oh no…," I utter. My palms are sweaty as I try once, twice, three times to decline the call. Maybe she's calling to ask about the Poetry Slam. Maybe Dad asked her to call because he was so angry and couldn't keep it together. Maybe they're both trying to figure out where I am right now. I wonder how long it'll be before they start calling aunties and uncles, Chioma's parents, or Tayo's parents, asking if they've seen me. Or I wonder if they'll cover it all up like they did with Sam.

"My life is in shambles," I whisper to no one. The solitary voice in my head says yes, yes it is, and you may have just made it worse.

I call Justin once my phone stops ringing. He answers on the third ring. "Hey."

"Hi," I say. I didn't call him just to hear the sound of his voice, or to hear him breathe over the line while I stare at the wall, but it soothes me in a way I didn't expect. There's something so calming about his raspy undertone and casual drawl. This is the only sense of normalcy I have right now. It makes me wish I had called him sooner.

"You okay?" I can hear a keyboard clicking in the background.

"I'm at Patricia's," I blurt out.

"How come?"

My dad kicked me out. He threw all my belongings on

the ground and told me to leave. "Visiting," I say. "For a while."

"How long is 'a while'?" he asks.

"I don't know."

"D'you guys have food?"

I snort, momentarily shaken out of my downward spiral. All it takes is one word, one mention of food, and my home life takes a back seat to the rumble in my stomach. "Her mom is cooking," I tell him. "I can't lie, though, I really want a burger."

"From The Burger Joint?"

My mouth begins to water at the thought of a suicide burger with extra suicide sauce. Patricia's mom's stew thing looks cool, but a suicide burger would probably fix my problems. It'll make me forget how messed up this entire situation is. "Are you going?" I ask. "Can you get me something? I'll pay you back."

He laughs. "That burger is, like, five dollars. Don't insult me."

Going to The Burger Joint was always a thing I did with Tayo. Thinking about him now is so strange because I want to call him so badly, but we're too close for him to be impartial. He'll for sure come get me and tell me to go back home. But how can I? I don't want to do law school and Mom and Dad will never accept that. They don't care that I chose it as a last-ditch effort or that the thought of it makes me feel like I'm running in place. They only care that I fall in line and become what they want me to be. The joke is I can be anything and everything, and the thought scares me, but the alternative, become just one, solitary thing, scares me even more.

I creep downstairs past Patricia's room and sit on the front step as Justin pulls into the driveway. I barely say hi before he hands me the bag and I pull out my truest love, a suicide burger. I peel back the wrapper while he sits beside me, and for a second I forget where I am while I take the first of many unseemly bites.

He laughs softly. "I was worried for nothing. You don't look like you're suffering at all."

"What?" I say, nervous. "Why were you worried about me?"

He shrugs. "I don't know," he says, and I don't know how I feel about that. It's immature of me to think he was especially worried about me as anything more than a friend. I take another bite and chew aggressively, so much so that my jaw hurts. I hate this. I hate everything.

As I finish up my burger, feeling the wrapper scrunch against my palms, I say, "My life is in shambles," because it is, and maybe vocalizing it will fix that.

But Justin is laughing in that handsome way he always does. He looks at me in the dim of the streetlights. "No way," he says. "Your life isn't in shambles. You have everything."

I frown. "Me? No, *you* have everything. I have the least amount of everything by comparison."

He purses his lips, nodding slowly while his eyes drift to the ground. "Are we always gonna be in competition?"

"*Are* we in competition?" I frown again.

He shakes his head, brushing his hair out of his face a little. "I hope not. I think you're really smart, and...you know."

"No I don't know," I say after a beat.

He doesn't say anything. The street is so quiet except for the distant pots clanging and the laughing from Patricia's house behind us, and my chest is swelling with that kind of anxiety that won't let go. He doesn't look at me and I am nervous not looking at him. This is as quiet as we have ever been around each other. This is as confused as I have ever been too.

"I like you a lot," I say, blunt but timid. My voice doesn't carry as loud as I think it will, and hearing the words "I like you" bounce around my ears makes me feel really shier than I am. "Like a friend, but also not like a friend...so much not like a friend, a-actually. And I wasn't gonna tell you but, like I said, my life is in shambles, so." I shrug to take the edge off but it's still there, heavy and sharp, making my heart pound like a drum.

Justin is trying not to smile. I think this is what makes him so endearing to me, but deep down inside, I hate that

I can't tell what this smile means. Then he looks away and says, "I don't know what to say to that," and I nearly die. Nearly, almost completely, die.

I'm blindsided. He doesn't like me back. It's just that I always thought... I mean, even just a little...

"It's cool," I utter, eyes falling back to my lap. "You don't have to say anything." My feet want to run. This is the worst, most embarrassing thing I have ever willingly walked into. What good is bravery? This is an insult on top of injury.

"Wait—oh, uh." He gasps and shakes his head real quick, a jolt of panic in his eyes. "I didn't mean it that way. I meant, like... because you said your life is in shambles, right, so I meant I didn't know what to say to that because, uh, I don't really know if it's true. I wasn't saying that about..." By the time I work up the courage to look at him again, he is disheveled, running his hands through his hair like this misunderstanding will be the end of him. I know him and how meticulous about everything he is. He won't be able to live with himself if he lets me walk out of here not knowing the truth: that he probably doesn't have any feelings for me at all.

It's not like I wanted anything to happen. Did I?

Just hearing the words come out of my mouth, the idea of me telling him something I thought I'd keep to myself forever, is so surreal. This, like many other things, isn't a secret anymore. It's free; it's open, just like me. Free, but displaced.

My nerves calm. My breathing slows. I still can't look at him, and at any moment, I feel the tension may return. I shudder through a deep sigh and say again, "It's cool. You really don't have to say anything. I was just, I don't know…" I shrug. "Feeling brave or whatever."

"Feeling brave, huh…," he echoes, nodding slowly.

"Yeah…Actually, what—" I say at the same time he says, "That's—" and we both look at each other, nearly startled that the other spoke first. I turn away, easily embarrassed. "You go first."

"No, wait, what were you gonna say?"

"It's—no, honestly, you go first. Bravery is a scam."

He bites back a chuckle. "I was gonna say that's actually what I like about you, that you're a lot bolder than I am, like, by a lot."

I nod, feeling my heart pound in my chest, almost knocking me back to that place of panic. "Me?" I laugh out. "Bold? How?"

"You want me to give you multiple reasons or just one?"

"There are multiple…reasons?"

"There's at least one important one," he tells me. "You're really honest. I think that's pretty underrated."

To think he admires me for being honest is almost funny. I spent so long trying to keep two sides of myself from meeting because I was afraid of being too different, too this for some people, or too that for others. That pressure amounted to nothing because, at the end of the day, that separation didn't matter. I have always been the same person.

"Thanks," I say with a smile. "That means a lot."

"It's—yeah. You're welcome." He returns my smile but looks away shyly. Without a word, he holds out his hand to me and I take it. My hand fits surprisingly well in his. He gives me a squeeze and intertwines my fingers with his. My god, this feels easy too. I am trying not to think of how balmy my palms are. I am trying to focus on this, whatever this is.

The idea of us doesn't seem so difficult, even though I'm not sure what that would even look like anymore. If I'm being honest, I have spent too much time chasing ideals and fantasies about everyone else but myself. I should know that isn't the only thing that makes me happy. I should know maybe now isn't the time to hyper focus on something new.

This is fine. It's enough.

CHAPTER TWENTY-FIVE

WHEN I WAKE UP, IT'S to the sound of drums being smacked in the distance. I sit up, panicked, as my eyes strain to focus in the bright guest room. The house smells like sage now and the constant drumming fills the upper floor with a distinct rhythm that's both electrifying and intimidating. I don't even remember when I fell asleep or when I got back into the house. Justin gave me a hug, the more-than-a-friend kind, and I still remember the feel of his arms wrapped tight around my back. I must be dead. I must still be dreaming.

I crawl out of bed to the doorway and poke my head into

the hall. The drumming is coming from the lower floors. I look haggard and ridiculous, but I brush my hair aside before I follow the sound downstairs. Patricia is sitting on the only sofa in their well-decorated living room while she claps in time with her father's drumming. Masks and instruments line the walls of the cramped room, along with small wooden stools of various sizes. Patricia's dad is perched on one of them. He is short and stocky with thick, curly hair that vibrates and sings with every turn of his head. He smiles when he sees me. Patricia jumps to her feet and pulls me into a hug—a hug I didn't ask for but need very much. I hug her back.

"You're up," she says, smiling, as she squeezes my shoulders. "I hope it's not because of the drumming."

"It's fine," I tell her. My eyes wander back to her dad, who plays through his song without stopping. He nods his head as a hello and I nod back. "Your dad is a musician?"

"Sometimes," she says. "He teaches djembe drumming in 'Sauga, but during the day, he's a stockbroker."

My eyebrows shoot up. "Oh, legit?"

"Yeah. He's all about that math life," she whispers with a grimace. "I can't lie, I'm not even sure we're related. Not even Mom understands."

Patricia's dad does another round before tapering off and slowing his pace. When the reverb from the drums disappears, we're left with nothing but the sound of his heavy breathing. He chuckles. "I felt that one in here, Tricia," he sighs out, touching his fingers to his chest. He then turns his attention to me and I stiffen under his watchful eye. He is not intimidating in the least but his gaze makes me feel vulnerable. "So you're Tricia's friend? The runaway," he adds, a hint of snark in his voice.

"I—"

"She didn't run away," Patricia pipes up. "She was kicked out."

"Kicked out, now?" he gasps, looking at me for confirmation. "That must have been some fight you had with your parents."

"It wasn't, really," I tell him. "It was, um, one-sided. A lot."

He nods, sagely. "I get it," he says before setting aside his drum and getting to his feet. "Sometimes relations are difficult, but the most important thing is always to go into them open, you know? Wide open." He taps his right temple twice. "Need to be conscious up here. That way, you can never be fooled. That way, at least you're showing up authentically."

It's hard to say if an authentic mind or whatever would've helped. I can't visualize anything other than what happened the exact way it went down. Still, I say, "Thanks, sir," as earnestly as I can.

"Leroy, please," he offers with a chuckle. "My dad's name is 'sir.'"

Patricia's eyes pop with embarrassment as she turns to me. "He's been making that joke since I was born, you know, and it still hurts me the same way."

My ringtone goes off from upstairs, echoing into the living room. "Sorry, I should check that . . . ," I tell both Patricia and her dad, who only waves away my apology. He is about to start up another round on the drums as I dash upstairs and head to my phone buried under the pillow upstairs. "Sam?" I mumble before I look at the screen.

It's not him.

Clear as day, the word "PAPA" flashes on the call screen. I hesitate, my thumb hovering over the green call symbol. I can't answer—it's too soon, it's only been a day. If he wants to cuss me about doing the performance, please, he should at least wait until after he inevitably doesn't show up. I let it ring out. In place of the call screen, I see another missed call from him, and another, and another, and one from Mom. There's two from Chioma, five from Tayo, and two from an unknown number. Text messages saying *"where are you?"* and *"why won't you call me back?"* litter my inbox. I reply to Chioma and Tayo—*"I'm fine"*—and mark the others as being read. I should tell my parents I'm okay. They deserve to know, but I'm so . . . I don't know.

And Sam hasn't called me once.

Sam, who hasn't said a word to me since the wedding fiasco.

Sam, who I spent time defending and defending, just because he's my brother.

Why do I even bother? If he wanted to talk to me, he would've reached out himself. He would've come back home or found me at school, said that he missed his sister and even though he got into a fight with Mom and Dad, he still wanted to be in my life. Would've said he was sorry for abandoning me like that, because he knew what his leaving would mean, that I would have to be everything to everyone all at once. There was no room for growth. He took that away from me. And if he cared about me at all, the very least he could do is tell me the truth.

Fuck this. He owes me.

I shower quickly and tie my hair up, trying my best to look presentable even though my insides are raging. I slip out of Patricia's place with my bag and poetry notebook, and begin the long, arduous journey to Sam's apartment. He better be home. I'm so tired of this shit.

I run the familiar route toward the front doors, speed my way up to his floor, and knock once, twice, three times as loud as I can on the door. "Sam!" I call.

Nothing.

I knock again. "Sam! Obinna!"

Another apartment down the hall bangs on their wall. Seriously?

I press my ear to Sam's door. The creak of floorboards tells me he's close to the door if not circling it. So it's me he's hiding from all of a sudden? No way. I bang on the door again. "O-bi-nna! What are you, dodging me?" I call as loud as I can. "Am I your parents? You foolish goat, I'm your sister, you can't do me like this!"

Like clockwork, my hand slams one more time on the door and it pushes wide open. I stagger forward with the force of my swing, and I nearly stumble into Sam. He looks tired, grumpy, different. Stubble decorates his chin where there usually is none and his hairline is a damn mess. He says, "A goat? A foolish goat and not a regular one?" and I can't tell if he's trying to be funny or not. How dare he try and joke with me right now!

I sneer and toss my book at him. He lets it ricochet off his chest and slide to the floor. "What's wrong with you?"

"What's wrong with *you*?"

"What?" I grunt. "Be serious. I was worried about you after the wedding." I inch forward and nudge the door closed behind me, trying to seem braver than I am. Trying to not be a coward.

Sam sighs and disappears into the apartment. He circles his way toward the table and as he passes the sofa, I notice the clothes he wore to the wedding still strewn across the back. They bring a quiet sadness to the room. I'm tempted to go over and fold them or straighten them out or something, but I leave them, awkwardly staring as if he left them there for me to see.

Sam pulls the table chair out and its scratch against the floor brings me back to reality. He sits down. I settle into the chair opposite him, trying to be as put together as I can be. My phone starts buzzing but I don't let it distract me. I finally have Sam's undivided attention.

So I take a deep breath and I ask, "What happened to the money?"

He scoffs, slouching further in his seat. "Is that all you came here to ask me?"

"Yes. N-no," I say, crossing my arms. "I wanted to see if you were good. You left after the wedding and I've been trying to call you, if you didn't notice."

"I noticed."

"Well, what the hell?"

He shrugs and I groan at his indignation. Why's he being so difficult? He folds his hands together and leans toward me across the table. "Listen, what's your issue? I showed up like I said I would, and it didn't go the way you wanted. I don't know what else to say past that."

"But why didn't you tell me?" I go on. "You never thought to tell me what happened to make you and Mom and Dad fall out like that? I thought they were pissed about the poetry thing, so I thought if they could see you were good, they'd squash it. But you *stole* from them—"

"I didn't steal anything!" he shoots back.

"Was it for drugs?"

"What? No—"

"For some girl?"

"Listen to yourself: You sound like our parents," he says through gritted teeth. "You think whatever they want you to think. I don't blame you, but damn, can't you see it doesn't make a difference? Whether it was for this or that, or for the collective, they still consider it stealing."

I raise an eyebrow. "What collective?"

"Does it even matter?" he scoffs, waving away my question. "Fuck that. Please, Ada, I didn't send you to defend me, so don't die over this."

"Don't die?" I narrow my eyes at him. "I. Got. Kicked. Out. Because. Of. You." The words are icy in my mouth, and I spit them out, hoping one of them lands in his eye.

He recoils instantly. A wave of satisfaction washes over me, but as he grows more and more concerned at what I said, I grow weary and sick. The reality hits me in the face that this, the reason I stood up to my parents and dared to dream a different dream, *this* is what I get. No home, no loyalty.

"Ada, what do you mean 'kicked out'?" he asks, his frown deepening.

I can't open my mouth without crying, so I bury my head in my hands and frantically wipe away tears before they can see the light of day. My voice wavers as I mumble, "Mom said I should stay, but Dad told me to go, so I left. Simple."

Sam's hand reaches forward and pulls my hands from my face. I try to hide my face again, but he pins my hands down on the table in front of me. It's all I can do to drop my head, turn away, so he doesn't see me full-on sobbing. He is frowning and glaring so hard, he starts to look more like Mom when she is angry. He's emanating such heat, such anger, that it's stifling. "What the *fuck*?" he shouts. "Since when?"

I shake my head again.

"Ada, since when?" he presses. "Why—"

"Don't ask why I didn't call you," I snap, narrowing my eyes at him. "Because I've *been* calling you and you're the one who decided you were too good to answer."

He winces. "Y-yeah. I mean—"

"Just drop it," I tell him, and his grip on my wrists loosens until he's slid back to his chair.

"This isn't how I wanted it to be," he tells me quietly. "Why would they do this to you? You're all they have."

"They have *two* of us!" I cry. "Stop saying that like you don't count too. It's hard enough trying to be two different people, trying to be the one good example, when I really don't have to be."

"Yeah, but what can I do?" he groans, throwing up his hands. "I'm pissed, Ada, I'm pissed for you. But what, like, you saw how everything went down at the wedding. Mom and Dad don't even want to look at me. I can't do anything for you and I'm pissed about it. Am I not allowed to be angry?"

I don't say anything. This isn't about his anger right now.

He gives a heavy sigh, his eyes narrowed on the table between us. Neither of us speak for a moment, each of us steeped in our own thoughts. Sam glances at me as if his eyes are trying to tell me something, debating whether or not he should say what he feels he needs to. Eventually, he finds his answer. "So I took the money." His voice is plain, his tone muted, as he says it. I push out a breath through my nose, waiting for him to continue. "I took it. It was for school, but I ... used it for something else."

"What else?"

"The collective," he tells me. I open my mouth to ask what that even means, but he barrels on, taken by the memory. "But, I mean, Mom and Dad obviously weren't trying to hear that. The day they found out, I think it was the night before the first day back at class ..." He shuts his eyes briefly and lets his words paint the scene. "Dad found out because my school contacted him about a payment. Like, it's so stupid now because I can't even remember ... a-and I was so good at covering my tracks, but this *one* time I didn't, and he found out. Just started *yelling* at me. Mom joined in, you know, crying and praying and kneeling, all of it. It was so loud and dramatic. They wouldn't even listen to me. I was like, 'I don't even care about this program, I wanna do something different,' and I may as well have said, like, 'I have a meth problem' or something, because they didn't care at all. 'Oya, get out, get out,'" he goes on, mimicking Dad's angry voice. "And maybe I was young and dumb too, because I fucking left, Ada, just like they told me. Took what I could. Didn't look back." We lock eyes: his, somber with regret, and mine, still wet with tears. "And now the same thing is happening to you, and all because of what? Saying what's on your mind? Is what other people think of us so important? What kind of life is that?"

I hang my head as Sam reaches forward to squeeze my hand. He whispers, "This isn't fair. I'll talk to Dad. I'll talk to them."

The urge to say *"I don't need you to look out for me"* is strong, but I stay quiet. Sam always used to look out for me, and I miss it, having someone watch my back.

"I invited them to the Poetry Slam, you know," I tell him quietly. He perks up at the mention of the event. "It's in two days. I'm not going to beg you, not like with the wedding, but I want you to be there."

He nods right away, a sober look in his eyes. "I will be," he says. "And I'll call you tomorrow morning. I'll fix this."

It's hard to imagine what that even looks like.

Still, he keeps his word and his phone number lights up

my screen the very next morning before school. He is the only phone call I answer.

Chioma texts me a classic *"Sorry o, who knew you could vex like this."* It makes me smile despite myself as I round the corner to the washroom after lunch. I can hear it in Chioma's voice, that unapologetic twinge. Dad keeps calling. Mom, too. Tayo calls, and I feel guilty every time I ignore him. I owe him too.

CHAPTER
TWENTY-SIX

AT SCHOOL, THE FINAL BELL rings and Tayo ambushes me before I leave class. He stands directly outside my class-room door, seemingly anxious at what I will do when I see him. Wondering if I'll run too. I haven't spoken to him face-to-face since the wedding and I am as anxious as he is. We stand in front of each other, staring, waiting.

Suddenly, he says, "What's up with you?" The ice is shat-tered. The uneasiness, curbed, if only a little. "Do you have time to hang out?"

I glance away. "I guess, yeah."

He sighs, and I can tell a huge weight falls off his

shoulders when he hears my response. "Cool. I'm happy you're okay, by the way," he says earnestly. "You haven't really texted anyone and we've been worried. I know you may not think we have been, but we are. Your parents keep asking my parents . . . a-and they keep asking me. They want to know where you are . . ."

I don't have anything to say about that. Tayo means well, but I bet he'll just convince me to come home and I don't think I'm ready yet.

He must sense my apprehension, watching the curve of my mouth soften, and quickly speaks up, "A-anyway. Let's go. I'll drive you wherever you want."

"Wherever I want?"

"Okay, within reason. I'm watching my mileage," he mumbles shyly. "Where did you say you were staying?"

"Don't worry about it."

"I bet they don't have eba and egusi soup there," he says with a smirk.

"I don't even like egusi soup that much."

"I bet they don't have eba and banga soup there."

I have to laugh. He's really trying it. "What about your parents?" I ask through a fit of giggles. "Listen, I really don't want them to see me."

"That's cool," he says with a nod. "We have that basement apartment, remember? It has a kitchen and a separate entrance and all that. We can chill there and I can drive you home after…" My phone buzzes again. I ignore it and urge Tayo on with my eyes. "Or wherever you're staying. Uh, aren't you going to get that?"

"Nope. What were you saying again? Your place?"

Tayo doesn't bump Skeleboy in the car on the drive to his house. I'd like to think it's because he matured, but it takes six songs before I realize he's just found a different favorite artist. A female voice croons in heavy auto-tune: "Oga, you and me, this one na destiny…" He's so stiff beside me. It's weird being in a car where Tayo isn't dancing. Oddly enough, this is the safest he's ever driven.

He parks on the street and we walk quickly around the side of his house to the basement entrance. Tayo's basement is always cold, and because of that, his parents never come down here. The kitchenette and kitchen table are barely used and the sofa is practically brand-new. I settle in like it's my house, and in a way, it feels like it is. I know all the smells so well.

"I'll go grab soup and stuff," he says. "Don't go anywhere."

"Where will I go?" I say. The moment it's out of my mouth, I know it's in bad taste.

He gives a shy chuckle before heading for the staircase. When he returns, it's with a small bowl of banga soup and a plate of freshly made eba. "I forgot the water," he tells me before he races back upstairs.

He brought way too much food for just one person, but

when he returns with two glasses of water, I realize we're supposed to eat together. "You know...," he begins, sitting down at the table with me. His fingers dip into the eba, forming a perfectly small piece in his hand, before he dips it in the soup and dashes it quickly in his mouth. "I find that certain families will cook certain things more. Like, you guys are a banga soup family. My family? Tomato stew all the time. Chioma and them? If there's one day their house doesn't smell like egusi, then I'm dead."

I smile as I dig into the eba and soup. "Yeah, that's true. I like your mom's stew, though."

"Her shaki stew is out of control," he groans. "Like, do you know how much meat I have stuck between my teeth on a given day?"

"Wow, please!"

"I'm serious," he says. If he tries to show me his teeth, I'll dash soup in his eye, I swear.

We eat in silence for a bit longer. I feel like he's watching me every time I put another ball of eba in my mouth, or every time I eye the meat and stake claim on which piece I want to eat. He's being so cautious of me and I really wish he wouldn't.

"How was the rest of the wedding?" I ask. He is visibly shocked, his back straighter and his eyes stiffer after I ask. "I mean, do you have any pictures?"

"Oh, uh..." He licks his fingers several times before

wiping them on a nearby napkin and reaching for his phone. "Yeah, I got mad pictures. I'll show you. Here, look at this one."

He flips through a picture of him and all the groomsmen posing in front of the stage. Then, a picture of him with all the bridesmaids. Chioma's face looks so stiff. I can see anger written all over it. I can't help but notice Folasade is standing closest to Tayo. That same heat and unease rises in the pit of my stomach, but I don't say anything about it.

Instead I say, "No pictures of you and Femi? Is the bromance dead?" and I snicker.

He rolls his eyes and swipes three more pictures. There it is: the coveted selfie with him and Skeleboy. Man, Skeleboy marrying into our family will never get old. "This is so cool," I say. "Put it as your display picture."

"You no know me again?" he laughs, and then swipes over to his social profile. He already set it as the picture. "My DMs are blowing up. Everyone wants to know how I know Skeleboy. Well, the Nigerian people, anyway. Everyone else is like, 'heh heh, is that your brother?'" He rolls his eyes. "I wish he was my brother, damn."

"Yeah, you two look like you could be."

"Speaking of brothers..." He sets down his phone and I wish he didn't, because now it feels like we're about to have a Very Important Talk. "How is he? Sam," Tayo asks, his voice softer than usual. "Your dad—I mean everyone looked pretty mad, but him and your dad, especially."

Memories of Sam at the wedding come bursting through and I chew faster to try and suppress them. There's no point getting sad about it all over again. "He's good," I tell Tayo. It feels a bit like a lie. "Did you know he's a poet? He's actually so talented."

"Oh, legit?" he says. "Poetry? Man, that's different. But Sam was always the best. He was good at everything. My parents wanted me to be just like him."

I snort. "Same."

We both dig back into the food. I squint at the one piece of beef in the soup and glance at Tayo. I don't know what kind of bush boy brings one piece of beef for two people to share, honestly. "Can I have this?" I ask boldly.

"Yeah."

"We can split if you want, though."

"How will we split it?" he snickers. "Will you bite half and then give it to me?"

"I could," I tease. "We're already sitting here eating like—" Married people. We're sharing a meal like my parents would do, except they are married, and Tayo and I? So very not. "—uh, some common goats."

That wasn't a good save and Tayo knows it. He bursts out laughing, throwing his head back at what I said. "Okay, and?" he cackles. "You're right; you bite first. The oldest goat must taste for the youngest."

"Shut up, that's not even a real thing!" I laugh so hard my throat hurts. If I choke on this soup, that's it for me. Sam choked on banga soup once and the sting of pepper and palm oil gave him a sore throat for a week.

Tayo makes a big show of taking the piece of beef and biting it in half, chewing on his piece before setting the other one back in the soup. I swirl it around in the soup for a bit before I pop it in my mouth to get the full effect of the flavor.

Oh god, we really are married.

"Hey, do you remember at the wedding?" Tayo isn't looking at me while he speaks. He eyes the bowl of soup as if it will produce another piece of beef, but I know him and I know he's nervous. I can guess what he's going to bring up. "Remember when we were dancing, and uh..." He swallows, and then immediately reaches for his glass of water. When he sets down the glass, he stares at me dead in the eyes, takes a deep breath, and says, "Would you go out with me? Like, on a date. N-not just to my basement for fufu."

I'm so aware of how little space there is between us. In any other situation, maybe we would kiss and taste the remnants of banga soup on each other's lips. Maybe we would shift closer to each other, like married couples do. Like a couple.

But we're not that.

Still, I can't pretend this means nothing.

"I like you a lot, you know," I tell him. Hearing the words in my ears is deafening. I said it so starkly, so self-assured. It almost doesn't sound like me, but at the same time, it does. So I say, "I really like you," just to hear myself again. I sound good.

Tayo's eyes light up, a broad smile coming to his lips. "Really?"

I nod.

After a moment, he asks, "S-so is that a yes...?"

My face is warm as I glance away and say, "I don't know if dating is such a good idea."

His energy shifts, closing off to me while he reaches again for his glass of water. I know him well enough to know he's not mad, just thinking. "Because you're seeing someone, right?" he says.

I sincerely shake my head no. A week ago, I would've relished the idea of Tayo and I together, or even Justin and I together, but I can see now that it was just me wanting a different kind of freedom. I don't have to imagine it anymore; it can be real for me now. I think.

"I gotta figure out my life," I tell him easily. "Plus, my parents would murder me if that were the case."

He smiles a little. "Yeah, well, if we dated—just saying— they probably wouldn't kill you. Even if you don't tell them, they'd be happy because it'd be easier to integrate me into the culture. Yoruba people, Igbo people…" He takes each hand and brings them together, intertwining his fingers.

I shift away now so I can face him properly. "What about me being happy, though?"

"W-well, I just meant that they'd be happy, but you'd obviously also be happy because you, uh, you like me."

We let the words hang in the silence of the basement for a moment longer.

I want to reach out for his arm, but my fingers are sticky with soup. Instead, my gaze softens; my voice tempers. "You're cool. I think I want to figure out what it's like to be *really* good, like, on my own."

He frowns. "But you've been on your own. You've never dated anybody."

"Yeah, but I thought I wanted to be a lawyer up until a month ago. I don't know what I want. I don't know how to choose."

"Choose?" He tilts his head, scanning me quickly. I know at once he must be thinking of Justin. Whether he is or isn't, now I'm thinking about Justin and how easily we fit together too. Tayo gives an exaggerated shrug and says, "Honestly, sometimes the easier choice may be the better one."

I frown. "There is no easy choice here."

He doesn't say anything. Instead, he digs back into his food, taking way too much soup for the amount of eba he has in his fingers. He smacks his lips like my dad does sometimes when he's really enjoying food, and it makes me think of home.

"You're always talking about happiness," Tayo says abruptly. "But you've had a real good life. I always thought you were happy."

"Me too."

He shakes his head. "Man...so what changed?"

I smile without meaning to. Just the thought of talking about something that matters to me has me feeling so good about everything. It's hard for me to explain to Tayo. "I think I found other things I'm good at, and that makes me happy. It makes me feel like there are so many other things I'm good at that I didn't even think of before."

"Like what?"

"Like..." I take a deep breath and turn to him. "Okay, so remember that media arts project I'm working on? Well, my partner and I are performing it live. Tomorrow, actually. I'm doing the spoken word portion."

His eyebrows bunch together. "So you're the rapper?"

"For the last time, *not* a rapper!"

"And you're performing tomorrow?"

"Yes," I tell him, and after a beat, I say, "Come. Tell Chioma to come too. I'll text you both the address. Well, actually, it's at 2020 Brick Avenue. That's conveniently the name of the venue and the address, so."

"That was easy."

"Yeah."

"And it's... rapping?"

"It's spoken word, I said!"

"Spoken word is just a subsect of rap."

I snort. "And you know? You who haven't even finished school, how do you know anything?"

"I know a lot of stuff and things," Tayo boasts, a smug look on his face. He polishes off the rest of the soup until the bowl is nearly spotless. He finishes off his water too, and I want to laugh so hard because he really reminds me of my dad, the way he stretches back in the chair like he's eaten way too much.

And then he says, "I don't want to be a doctor."

I gasp like a Nollywood vixen. "What? What are—"

"Yo, don't tell my parents."

"I don't... I won't say anything, but *what?*"

"I want to be a choreographer," he says shyly. He can't even look at me when he says it, as if I'm going to judge him. As if I have a right to judge anybody. "Femi says I could definitely make it work, a-and he offered to help me get started, you know, introduce me to some people. I want to do music videos first and then, hopefully, concerts."

I grin. "That's so dope."

"It's a big leap, I know. Like, who's gonna hire *one*

Nigerian kid who can dance well out of a *sea* of Nigerian kids who can dance well, right?"

"I think you'll be good at it."

"Do *not* tell my parents, though."

"Done."

"We can't all be ostracized like you and survive," he snickers.

I gasp again and smack him in the arm. "Ah-ah!"

"I said what I said."

CHAPTER
TWENTY-SEVEN

DAD LEAVES ME A VOICE mail early in the morning. I know his schedule and I know he's supposed to be at work, so I'm shocked when I see the voice mail notification at a time he should be commuting. I imagine him trying to work his Bluetooth connection to his car audio dashboard and barely succeeding. The voice mail would have his obvious frustrations captured in audio format. I'd listen to them and feel nostalgic for home.

The voice mail sits idle until curiosity gets the better of me during last period. Two minutes before the bell rings, I lower my head, shifting so my teacher won't see, and listen to his long message:

"Adanna, where are you? Okay, o, maybe it's time for you to be coming home. We have not heard from you for a whole week and we are very worried. When I called, you didn't pick it. Your mama and I are very worried. So because I told you to run, that's why you should run, abi? So I should call the police? Eh? . . . I saw that your invitation. To the art performance. We will be there. But please, nwa m, it's enough, na. Start coming home now. Okay. Bye."

His voice is so somber, lacking its usual zest and indignation. For him, this is as heavy as it gets, but I still chuckle a little at his grand exaggeration—it's been, like, four days! To Dad, maybe it feels like a month. The house must be empty with just him and Mom. I wonder if they talk to each other often, or if they're like passing ships in the night. I can't remember if Mom is on nights this week or if she's doing day shifts. There was so much rice in the fridge too, and I doubt she and Dad would be able to eat it all before it goes bad.

But they're coming to the show.

They're coming to the show and Dad tried to call me, but I didn't pick up because I was scared. Scared of what he might say and scared of what my options may become. When he watches the performance, will he be able to tell it's me? Will I sound different to him? Will he still be as proud as he is when he watches my debate video?

I want to go home so badly. This ache to be with my family is only outweighed by the fear that conformity is probably the only thing that's waiting for me there. Tonight is the Poetry Slam and I have to be brave, because that is who Sophie is. That's who Ada is, too.

Justin says he'll drive me back to Patricia's so we can all go together, so I wait for him outside by the curb of the senior parking lot. I'm minding my business when a car rushes into the school compound, going fast, and then slows down on the speed-bumped road. It stops directly in front of me, nearly clipping my feet at the curb. "Who..." I bend a little to look into the car and gasp when I see Genny. "Uh..."

She opens her door and pops out, turning toward me over the car roof with a glare in her eyes and a pucker in her lips. "Didn't I tell you to call me?" she says. Man, suddenly, the bark of her voice is so soothing.

"I don't know," I say, pretending to look at my phone for the message. Genny was one of my missed calls, but I didn't think it was this serious for her to show up at my school.

She bends to press the unlock button and then points at the passenger's side door. "Get in."

My heart thumps in my chest, the fear building that she's going to drive me right to my parents' house. "Where are we going?"

"Don't ask me. Just get in."

"Genny, I'm s-sorry." The apology spills from my mouth and it hangs between us like an unwelcome friend. Genny doesn't falter; the poise of her lips and tilt of her head tells me at once that she doesn't want to accept something she didn't ask for. It's so Genny of her. I press on anyway. "I'm sorry about the wedding. I didn't... it was never my intention to ruin it."

"Shush, hush," she says, waving away my apology. "Did I ask for you to apologize? You didn't ruin anything. Just get in."

I do as I'm told. "Where are we going?" I ask again.

She sits and belts up. Soon, we're driving out of the school parking lot, coasting slow down the road. Genny doesn't answer me; instead, she turns on the radio. Soft news highlights stream out. I focus on them to feel less awkward, less stuck in this weird container where I may or may not have been willingly kidnapped by my cousin whose wedding I definitely ruined. The urge to apologize again hits hard, but I know if I do, Genny may hit harder.

We circle the block once. I clutch my phone in my lap, expecting it to vibrate. I should text Justin and tell him he shouldn't bother waiting for me. "Can I text my friend?" I ask.

Genny glances at me. "You can text whoever you want. It's not like I have your phone."

I craft a quick message to Justin—"*hey, cousin kidnapped*

me, details pending. see you at the poetry thing later?"—and stash my phone. When I look around me again, Genny has driven into the parking lot of the convenience store beside the school. We drove a long way to go absolutely nowhere.

She turns off the car and looks at me. Just looks at me.

I say, "I'm sorry" again, like I have a death wish.

But instead of snapping or narrowing her eyes at me, she just sighs. It's a heavy sigh and one that I know too well these days. Something has been bothering her for a very long time. "It's me who should be apologizing," she says quietly.

"What?"

She pushes her hair over her shoulder, shrugging a little so it can fall the way she wants it. "I'm going to Mykonos on Saturday morning and then from there, I'll be in Bali for a week and Tokyo for another week. It's for my honeymoon. Femi and I are going."

I frown. "Okay?"

"I wanted to talk to you before I left," she tells me. "If I went without saying anything, I don't think I would've enjoyed myself."

"So you're doing this for you?"

She snorts. "I'm doing this for both of us."

For both of us?

"What's this about?" I ask. I steady my breathing so I can prepare for whatever she's going to tell me. Whatever it is, it can't be that bad. *I'm* the one who ruined her wedding. Genny is always so dramatic, so this is probably nothing.

It's all nothing, I reassure myself, so when she says, "I've been in contact with Sam for the past six years," I am not prepared. I am not prepared at all.

"Sorry, *what?*" I say. All my thoughts about school and how lonely I was and how badly I wished he could've been here, all of them are tainted by the fact that Genny knew what was going on with Sam and she never told me. She never thought I was important enough to know. She didn't think it was my business. "What?" I ask again. Even my voice sounds hollow and distant to my ears. It's echoing in my mind. She's been echoing—"*I've been in contact with Sam . . . for the past six years.*"

"Genny. What?" My voice is shaking. Why can't I be stern?

She swallows slowly and takes a deep breath.

I am losing my patience. Leaning toward her, I say, "You and Sam?" I start hyperventilating before I can stop myself. Heavy breathing, Nollywood-level pettiness, the works. "All these years? Genny?"

"You can't blame me, o. You don't know—"

"So then tell me!" I cry. "What sense does any of this make? For years—for *years*—I've been looking for Sam and you knew where he was this entire time?"

She frowns, that same sad sigh resurfacing. "Ada . . ."

"My parents told me he was gone, he abandoned the family, he was useless, all sorts of stuff," I say. My shoulders are shaking. I can't stop trembling. "And I had to listen to them say it to everyone. I thought he left me—and you *knew* this whole time he was still around?" Hysterics turn to anger and a violent shake rips through my back. I press my hands into my face and feel my skin slick and sweaty under my fingertips. Holy shit, I can't even look at her. She reaches forward to touch my arm but I slap her hand away. "Don't touch me," I grumble from behind my hands.

I feel her weight shift on the driver's seat. "Okay, are you finished or what?" she asks. "Can I explain now?"

Typical Genny. As if *I'm* the bad one here. "Explain *please*," I groan, and finally wipe my hands down and away from my face. She is staring at me, unwavering.

I glower at her but she doesn't return my anger or bitterness. Not even a little. She is calm when she speaks. "I know what Sam was doing when he left, and no matter what your parents say, it wasn't drugs or…or prostitutes," she says and then rolls her eyes. "You know Nigerian parents: Everyone is a prostitute."

I can't even commiserate with her even though, yeah, that's exactly what they think. "Okay, so?"

"Yeah, well," she goes on. "You know Sam is younger than me, so of course…he came to ask me if it was a good idea, what he wanted to do."

"And what was that?"

"Help his collective build an arts center."

I don't bother hiding my confusion. Sam had said the word "collective" before, but this is the first time I'm hearing about an arts center. "What? That's what he used the money for?"

"Bush girl," she says. "You don't know your brother? Even from when he was young, he'd always look out for other people and want to connect with them. And now he does poetry. Honestly, who is surprised?"

"You know all this?" I utter.

Genny nods. "Yeah. He told me. He said he didn't care about engineering anymore. Didn't want his degree. I said, 'Ah-ah, you dey craze? It's not a good idea, o!' A dropout? Does he want to disgrace his parents, my parents, me, everyone? They work so hard for him. Stuff like that. He didn't listen. He cared so much about this art thing. He said they were fundraising for a new performance space and that it'd be good to help give kids something to do. You may have heard of the place, 2020 Brick Avenue?"

"What?" I choke out. "*Sam* . . . helped build it?"

"Yeah, him and some of his friends," she goes on, ignoring my obvious shock. "They noticed these kids just hanging around street corners and they'd ask where their parents were, why weren't they in school, whatever else. These kids didn't have anything, so he and some people in his program brought it to a local art collective, and well…" She watches my face, trying to figure out if my wide eyes and slightly ajar mouth mean what she thinks they mean. "It sounds stupid, right? Like, who sent him?"

"No." I shake my head right away. "It sounds like something he would do." The same Sam who helped me with my homework all through elementary school, who made me feel like I was smart and capable and already successful. The Sam who hasn't spoken to our parents in so long, but still offered to call them and beg for me to come back home. It sounds just like the Sam I remember.

Genny offers a small smile. "Yeah, well, it cost him a lot. He was helping them fundraise. I even donated a bit too. Whatever money he asked for from your parents, he put into the center. They were on the eve of the opening, I guess, but… well, you know the rest. His school sent a letter to your house, I think, about Sam being de-enrolled, and then it was over for him."

I nod slowly, remembering what Sam told me. It's all coming together differently now. The idea of Sam being that selfless is changing the story Mom and Dad told about him being a thief. Those words were so harsh. If they had known their son helped build a center that was meant to help neighborhood kids, would they still hold a grudge?

Genny clasps her hands together, fiddling with her

shellac nails. "I'm only telling you what I know. If there's anything else, you have to talk to him."

"I know. I believe you, too," I say.

She smiles now, much more genuine than before. "He was talking to me about you," she tells me. "He said your poem is really good."

I gasp and swallow away the burgeoning urge to cry. "You talked to him recently?"

She nods.

"How come he didn't know you were getting married?"

"If I told him, then what?" She sighs. "He wouldn't have been able to come. And then Blessing took over the invitations, and I was too busy trying to nail down the aesthetic I wanted... By that point, it felt stupid to bring it up."

We are silent for a moment longer before she says, "He said you're performing. Tonight, actually. Why didn't you tell me?"

"I was afraid to talk to you," I tell her. "I thought I ruined your wedding."

She pouts. "You didn't ruin anything, I said. Your parents' pride ruined it. Classic stubbornness."

"Jeeez!"

"Don't... Shut up, don't tell anyone I said that," she cuts in, pointing a finger at me. She tries not to laugh as she says, "This no be my mata. Nkwachi palava too much. I no go die for am, ah-beg. You hear?"

"Yes, yes, o," I chuckle.

We are quiet for a moment, stifled laughter bouncing off the interior of the car. I glance at Genny and to my surprise, she is smiling back at me like we are sisters sharing secrets. This is the Genny I remember: free from wedding constraints and responsibilities, funny, warm, but always sharp.

"So will you come to the Poetry Slam?" I ask, hopeful. "I was going to head there super early to practice. Everyone else will be there. My friends, too."

"Of course," she says with a twinkle in her eye. "Maybe Femi will be interested in seeing it. I'll call him when we get there."

My heart skips and I clutch my chest. Genny snorts, rolling her eyes at my dramatics, even though she should know by now that we all get it from her. "Skeleboy is going to watch my spoken word performance?"

"*Femi.* You can call him by name now. We're family."

"Oh my goodness."

"He'll love it. What is it, like rapping?" she goes on.

"Not really, but yeah."

"Cool," she says, and reaches forward to pinch my cheek.

She is still smiling when she pulls out of the parking lot. We drive with her humming as the perfect background music all the way to 2020 Brick Avenue.

CHAPTER TWENTY-EIGHT

GENNY PARKS A STREET AWAY from the venue and we walk in near silence to its massive opaque doors. I am filled with anxiety, nearly trembling with the thought that my parents are coming to this. Sam may come. I may not do a good job. For a moment, I'm scared that this, angering everyone and throwing everything off balance, could all be for nothing. But the fear dissipates when I enter the hall. This place is familiar to me, in some weird way. This is the place Sam helped build, and being in its walls is the perfect comfort.

Genny calls Femi while I frantically text Justin and

Patricia to come early if they can. *"My cousin who married a Nigerian superstar is here and she's bringing HIM,"* I say. I can't remember if I'd ever told either of them much about what goes on in the good parts of my family life, but today is as good a day as any to start.

About an hour later, Patricia rushes through the doors of The Ballroom, arms wide open as if she's going to hug me. I hug her first and it doesn't feel awkward. "Are we ready or are we ready?" she asks, scanning the empty hall. "We're early, eh? Won't this make your nerves worse?"

"Nope," I lie. "It'll be good to relax. See everyone."

"Everyone?"

"My family is coming," I tell her. That same anxiety that tells me this may be a disaster threatens to bubble to the surface, but I swallow it down quick. "I'm nervous but I think it'll be good."

Patricia grasps my hands. "If you get disowned, my parents can maybe adopt you."

"Good to have a plan, I guess."

"Always."

Patricia and I chill by the bar, even though it's not open yet. An organizer comes by and gives us water but makes a point to ask if we want juice instead. Just how young do we look?

A bit later, Justin arrives, waving before he reaches me. I wave back, nervous. But when he reaches over and gives my hand a quick squeeze, the grin I was trying so hard to hide shows out in full force. "How's it going? Better?" he asks me.

I don't have the bandwidth to lie at this point. "No, not really," I say, and I laugh so hard. The bursts of nervous laughter quell the shaking in my chest.

Justin snickers. "You need to have this breakdown after the performance, like a professional."

"You're absolutely right."

"Don't forget to breathe," he says and I can't tell if he's making fun of me or not.

"Obviously I'm going to remember," I mumble, but I make a mental note of it anyway. Breathe, look at the audience, speak clearly. It's like debate. It's *just* like debate. I spent so much time on arguments and this and that, and... "We should've gotten first." Justin raises an eyebrow, confused at my sudden admission, so I clarify. "We should've gotten first. At the competition, remember?"

"Ooooh." He nods slowly while he takes in my words.

"I was just thinking out loud."

"We had a really layered argument, but I think..." He sighs. "At the end of the day, everything is relative and people can only vibe with what they understand."

I frown. "Yeah, but what is it about cross-cultural kids that people don't understand?"

He shrugs. "I don't know, Ada."

I pause, blinking into my disbelief. "W-what did you call

me?" He said Ada, with less emphasis on the "ah," with the same weight and heaviness that I'm used to hearing. My lips purse with the urge to smile. God, does it sound normal and freeing and exciting coming from him. It sounds easier than I thought.

He laughs at my shock, but there's a nervousness as he pushes his hair back that I can't overlook. "What? Did I say it wrong?"

"No. Surprisingly," I tease. "Have you been practicing or what?"

"It would be uncool for me to say 'yes,' so."

I'm grinning so hard that it's all I can do to hum, "Mmhmm."

Suddenly, Patricia smacks her hands together in front of us, and says, "Get it together. You." She points to Justin. "Stop distracting her with your cultural fluidity. She needs to focus."

He nods right away. "Yes, sir."

"And you," she says, turning to me. "Practice."

"I will, I am." My cheeks hurt from smiling, which is such a weird adjustment after everything that's happened. For a second, I forget all about everything: Mom and Dad being mad, the fact that they won't talk to Sam, the fact that I told them I don't want to do law school in the future, the fact that they may show up to the Poetry Slam tonight and murder me, the fact that I have no idea what I want to do, but it's all okay, because I'm in an arts center my parents' money built. It is the best kind of irony.

I settle by a corner booth and go over my poem in my mind over and over again. Time passes in fragments. The Ballroom fills slowly with early comers and staff. Other performers hang by the corners, frantically going over their lines too. Casey shows up sporting a small tattoo on the inside of her right arm and shows it to Justin. I think of Chioma and her tattoo, and how I still haven't really seen it.

Slowly but surely, there's a shift in the air. I look up at the exact moment I see a tall figure strut through the front doors. He's almost shrouded in the shadows until he emerges. It's Femi. I should've known. Only someone with such star power could shift the natural balance of the room like this.

I bolt to my feet when his eyes fall on me. His business casual attire is more casual than business, and his shoes shine so brightly it almost looks like he's dancing toward me. "Adanna," he says, embracing me in a hug. My ghost takes a deep breath. When Femi takes a step back, he is grinning. "I'm happy Isioma called me. You know I love this kind of thing."

"Spoken word?" I ask.

"Kinda," he replies with a shrug. A cool shrug. "Like, we Nigerians can excel at anything we want, so I like to see when we choose new things. My cousin, he's a genius with maths, right, but as for me, I cannot." He chuckles at that like I know his cousin. "But it's okay, because God didn't put us here to only be maths geniuses. You get me?"

I nod right away. Femi is so assured in his speech and I can't help but feel like it comes from the mastery he's achieved in his career. I'm in awe of him. I want that mastery too. "I agree," I say.

"It's the disease of our people," he tsks. "Sameness. Good for you for not listening to that rubbish. I'm ready to see my in-law rapping."

I have to laugh. "Okay, not *rapping*—"

"Ada, you goat!"

That voice, that insult. I turn just in time to get pounced by Chioma and pinched by Tayo. A laugh so unholy grips my throat and I struggle for air as I pull my way out from under them.

Before I can say anything, Tayo brings out a small gift bag and hands it to me. My heart leaps as I take it and peer inside. "You got me something?"

"It's from both of us," he says. I can see Chioma shaking her head behind him.

I reach into the bag and pull out a candle in a glass container. The scent is "Success." I break into the widest grin. "I love this!"

"Just so you can get used to it," he tells me, glancing away shyly. "The smell of success. You know?"

I take a deep breath. "Thank you. *So* much. That's . . . that's—"

"Corny. You can say it," Chioma cuts in.

"I was gonna say 'sweet.'"

Chioma giggles, "Sure." She smiles and pulls me into a deep hug. I let my head rest by her shoulder while she squeezes tighter. When she pulls away, she says, "I'm happy you texted me." The simplicity and sincerity in her voice has me feeling weepy, and I hug her again to avoid shedding tears.

"You missed a really good party, you know. The, uh. The dancers showed up and did the full 'Yanga' routine. Then Tayo joined them. Did he tell you? He was so good. A-and then the masquerade came and I'd only seen that kinda stuff in movies, so I was just staring the whole time. It was so colorful but honestly, a bit scary. And, uh, and—and you know you should've stayed, right?" Her lips pull into a thin line, a muted, apologetic smile. "You should've been there."

I nod solemnly but stay quiet. Her hands are intertwined so tightly that I'm afraid some of her fingers are losing circulation. I didn't realize how much my being there meant to her. It didn't occur to me that there are missing spaces in her memory where I should have been.

It makes me think of Sam. I can't help it.

"I'm sorry," I say. "I spoke to Genny and I apologized too. I should've said something to someone about Sam coming—"

"You could've told me," she says. "I was so shocked and all I could do was rage. I didn't realize you were serious about Sam. If you told me, I would've helped you."

"I know. I know that now, anyway."

Chioma says, "I remember once when we were young, Auntie Bola got on my case about eating boiled plantain with margarine," and has to pause while her small chuckles evolve into a full laugh.

I can't contain myself either and soon, the fatigue in my chest is being beaten away by the most earnest laugh. Auntie Bola was so annoying when we were young! All she did was harass us about everything and then she had the audacity to buy us towels for Christmas. "Yeah, I remember," I say. "That's real village living."

"It's a delicacy, you rat," she jokes. "Auntie Bola was like, 'ah-ah, who taught you this?' She was so mad, even though she was technically at *our* house for Christmas. Like, how bold, honestly. And then, um…Sam came in." She hums as the memory grows in her mind. "He didn't say anything. He just sat down and started eating with me. Actually, I was pissed because I didn't want to share my food. But then Auntie Bola disappeared. She didn't say anything to him because, you know how it was, Sam was so smart. He was such a good role model for all of us. No one could touch Uncle Gabriel's son, you know." And she rolls her eyes, playfully. "When I tell you…when I tell you that no one was more shocked to hear he had disappeared, that he had robbed your parents... all of that." She cringes, a shiver running down her spine. "But I mean, he's your brother. You must have felt it the most."

"Yeah," I say, "I really have." Then, without warning, I reach forward and smack her thigh. "Show me what your tattoo looks like later."

Chioma smirks. "I forgot you hadn't seen it!"

"I don't even know what it is, either!"

"My bad," Chioma snickers, then touches her thigh as if I can see through her clothes. "It's this—don't laugh—it's a rose, and then on the stem, it says, 'highly favored' in cursive. I love it."

I grin. "Sounds cool."

"Yo, at the wedding, after I came back inside, I was running so my mom saw my skirt go up and she screamed because she thought someone had drawn on my leg. I had to tell her after that."

"One secret at a time, or they'd kill you," Tayo cuts in, snickering. "Tell them about the tattoo. Save telling them you changed your major for later."

Chioma touches her nose, tapping it knowingly. "You right, you right."

Tayo looks around, making an exaggerated show of swinging his head from corner to corner. "So, uh... Where's Sam?"

"Not here yet," I answer, none too confidently. "Oh, but hey, d'you know what I found out? Sam helped build this place. That's what he used the money for."

"No way," Tayo gasps.

I nod. "So you guys better spread the correct version this time."

"There was no ashawo. Got it," Chioma says, nodding as if pretending to check off an imaginary checklist. "That's dope. I bet your parents think it's cool too."

"They probably don't know," I say.

"Well, they will now," Tayo says, and nods over my head. I follow his gaze to the entrance where Mom and Dad tread carefully through the dim of the room toward me.

CHAPTER
TWENTY-NINE

DAD HAS ALWAYS WALKED WITH a bravado I admire. His head is high, his shoulders back, and his mouth in a stern line as he goes. It's only when you talk to him do the lines of his face soften enough for dialogue, for a smile. Mom isn't quite like that. She enjoys talking but she is careful with her words. Today, she looks almost fretful. Their eyes bounce around the unfamiliar interior until they finally land on me. Mom all but pushes Femi aside to crash into me. In true Igbo mother fashion, she drops to her knees and begins to cry prayers. I hear, "I said they cannot come and kill my children," before I bend to try and help her up.

"Adanna," she cries, standing and pulling me into a tight hug. "Oh my God, thank you Jesus, thank you," she recites over and over again as she binds me in her arms.

When she finally pulls away, the only words left on my tongue are: "I'm so sorry."

She frowns. "I told you to stay here." There is sadness behind her accusation. When she repeats it, I can only nod because I don't want to explain to her how much I needed to go away to come back. "Did I say you should come and kill yourself for law? Did I?"

I dot the tears from my eyes. "N-no, Mom."

"Did I?" she harps again. Her voice is so loud that other patrons begin to stare. Dad places a hand on her back, rubbing softly, trying to soothe her. "So then who told you that? Who told you it concerned me? Mba mba mba," she sings, shaking her head fervently. "I want you to go to school. I want you to be successful in school. I didn't say you should come and kill yourself for law, o! I didn't say that!" She breaks down, sobbing uncontrollably, and now it is my turn to hold her together. She cries deep into my shoulder, squeezing me as if she's afraid I will disappear. As if I will run away again.

"Okay, o, that's enough," Dad whispers, trying to gently pry Mom off me.

She says nothing. As she loosens her hold, she pulls a container from her bag and shoves it into my hands. When I look down at the warm Tupperware filled with jollof rice and chicken, I want to both laugh and immediately die. "Oh my god?"

"Wetin do your God?" she tsks. "What have you been eating? All this yama-yama."

"I can't hold this now, I gotta perform soon!"

"I'll hold it," Tayo pipes up. Mom smacks him in the arm. "Ah-ah, Auntie, why na? I no wan make the rice spoil."

Even she can't resist Tayo's charm. She bites back a smile, sheltering the container under her arm.

"Adanna," Dad says, and gestures for me to follow him a few paces away. His face is so solemn and stoic while I follow. But when we're safely away from the group, the lines of his jaw soften and, all at once, he is transformed, smiling and reaching forward to touch my face. He hugs me. "Have you been eating?" he asks, which means: *We've missed you.*

I can't help but cry. A shaky smile forms on my lips as I say, "I have. I'm sorry."

"No." Dad shakes his head, sternly. He is silent for a moment before he says, "You came home," and in those three words, I can hear the weight with which he sent off Sam and what it's taking for him to welcome me back.

The one thing I was most afraid of, talking to my parents and finding they hate me even more because of this poetry thing, doesn't exist anymore. I can see in his eyes that his greatest fear doesn't exist anymore either. He can see I'm okay.

"I spoke to your brother," he tells me carefully.

I give a slow nod. "He said he'd try and talk to you."

"Eh heh. He said we should let you come back home," he continues. "I told him I had been trying to call you since when you left. I said I always wanted you to come back. It was my mistake, sha."

The words "I'm sorry" sit on my tongue, but this isn't the time or place for them. I give Dad room to speak, swallowing the need to apologize and explain away my feelings.

"At first, when I picked the phone and heard his voice, I said, '*Ah ah!* Is this you?' He sounds like a man now." Dad nods, content. "He talked and talked and I said, 'Okay, let me think.' So when he hung up, I sat down and I said, 'Ah, Gabe...ee be like say you don dey do shakara for here. Where are these your children? Where are they?'" He pauses a moment to clear his throat. I can hear the crack in his voice as he goes on. "I...we...We are always talking about your future, and we only know one way to become a success. That is because where we are from, these are the rules. You understand?"

I nod.

"But, in this place here, the rules are not always the same," he says. "Sometimes, it's important to understand how to play checkers when you are playing chess, because if somebody calls you now to come play checkers, you will at least know. You see? And I don't know how to play checkers. But I think you and Obinna know very well. You understand?"

"Yes, Dad."

"Eh heh," he says. "So... when I was thinking about it, I said, 'Your children are already very good, very special, and you just let them waka-waka like this because of... eh, because of *pride*.'" The word is harsh on his tongue and he spits it out with disgust, his nose scrunching at the thought of it. Pride. "We have tried for you. Your mama and I have tried so much."

I nod right away. "I know, Dad."

"So. When I see you here..." He gestures around the venue as it gets more and more packed with attendees. "I can see how you are brave like your mama, how you are sharp like me. But also, I can see how you are Sophie."

I nod again. I can't stop nodding. "Yes."

"Ada-nna, that is you."

A smile breaks forth and I can't push it away even if I tried. "Thanks, Dad."

"Nwa m, ada m, you will be fine," he says.

His words are so soothing in my ears: "*My child, my daughter, you will be fine.*"

"I'm going to figure out something else to do," I tell him quickly. His eyebrow raises at my sudden admission, but when I clarify, "About school," he nods like he understands. "I know you and Mom are mad I don't want to do law school, but I'll figure something else out. I have a lot of other options. I'm good at other things, too."

"I know you will," he replies. "You're very smart, so I'm not worried about you. I don't worry about any of my children."

I didn't realize I needed this reassurance until now. He really thinks I'm capable, and that alone gives me a sense of pride and happiness I've never felt before. I'll carry this acknowledgment with me forever.

I hear my mom gasp in the center of the room and I don't need to crane my neck too hard to see Sam. He is taller than her, and she hugs him so deeply that I'm afraid the container of rice in her bag will jiggle loose. As I approach, he shakes Femi's hand and gives both Chioma and Tayo cautious hugs. A grin the literal size of my head fixes itself on my face and won't let go. I gasp, "Sam, you're here!"

"Of course," he says coolly. He reaches his hand out and we touch knuckles like that's a thing we've been doing our whole lives. "I said I would be, remember?"

I nod at once, brimming with happiness. "You did. You're right."

"Can't miss your first-ever show."

"Only show."

"Ehhh," he sighs, tipping his head in disbelief. "We'll see."

"You didn't say before that this was the center the collective built," I tell him hurriedly. "I had no idea. No one did."

Sam chuckles, fanning out his arms at the room. "Does it feel cooler to you now that you know my degree helped pay for this?"

"Very."

"*Tah!*" Dad's voice cuts in at the mention of the degree. He had been standing here watching us talk for minutes uninterrupted. But suddenly, he cuts in front of me and pulls Sam into a hug. The two of them embrace for a long time, Sam's head buried in Dad's shoulder as Dad pats him on the back once, twice.

He says: "Nwa m, kedu?"

My child, how are you?

Sam says, "I'm okay."

When Dad pulls away, chuckling softly, he looks at the both of us standing side by side and I know he feels the same fullness I do. This is how things were supposed to be all along.

I don't even notice Sam is holding something in his other hand until he swings it around for me to see. "You forgot this," he says, handing me my poetry notebook. Its uneven edges feel so good under my fingertips now. "Didn't want you to forget your lines."

"I don't need it," I tell him. "I've memorized the whole thing."

CHAPTER THIRTY

I wanted to be adaptable and change with the times
I wanted to be liked.
I wanted to be cool.
Cool held such
cool,
and I wanted to be
I wanted to be—
I don't know
—something like that.

When I was young, I prayed to god
said, well, if you're there, show me something

real. Something
real.
Stared up at the sky, waited
thought rings would encompass me
Jupiter
instead, all I got was rain.

and a name.
Adanna nne gave me o
"Oya, make una stand straight."
I had this slouch, you know
but after year one, two, and three, it's gone,
you know
After year you, you, and me, it's gone,
you know.
And you can call me Sophie
because she is reformed.

I am not too good for what you named me.
and na only one time I been wan change am, so
-phie is pale, ivory, baseless.
You look me say that one be my own?
Okay, show me where the difficulty is
Show me where.
I have two different parts of me that I wish
I could share

But not one is greater than the other than the other is
great
and I don't know who can relate.

Because I am the only one of my kind.
the first and the second: the whole.
You can't mispronounce these two
anymore.

ACKNOWLEDGMENTS

There's a lot of stress associated with telling a story from a non-Western cultural perspective, and I constantly worried I was doing too much for a Western audience and not enough for my fellow Nigerian diaspora kids. Thankfully, I've come to a place now where I feel like I told the story as best I could have, and there's really nothing else I could've done differently, or else it would've been inauthentic for me. I'm grateful I got to share this story with you all in this way. Thank you for reading.

Thank you to my family. You have made my life so much richer and for that, I'm grateful. An extra thank you to the cousinfolk Lola and Shade Waheed, whose names I unceremoniously stole when I realized I couldn't think of any other female Yoruba names. I used the names as a placeholder first, and I laughed about it for a day before I realized I was dead serious. So there it is! You may roast me for this when it's most convenient for you, thanks.

I have to say thanks to my amazing agent, Claire, my wonderful editors, Suzanne and Foyinsi, and the entire editorial and design teams at HarperCollins Canada and Feiwel & Friends. It was my decision not to overexplain or water down a lot of cultural elements, but I'm so happy I didn't have to or wasn't asked to. Throughout this entire process, I felt empowered in my decisions and I thank you so much for that. Couldn't have asked for a better team!

Thank you to Sarah Rana for your help fine-tuning the debate team elements, and Emily Lam and Jessica Jade for your help with the Cantonese elements of the story. Your direction was necessary and so very appreciated. Extra thanks to Emily for letting me use both her last name (unintentional, I swear!) and her cousin's name (completely intentional).

Thank you to Rimma, Jane, and Debbie who read early versions and snippets and helped me realize that I'm Nigerian enough to tell this story. Your feedback helped form the foundation of this book and I'm so, so thankful.

Also thank you to everyone African who really showed out for me when I told them I was writing a book about a Nigerian girl. You know I love your enthusiasm. I love us!

A bold thank you to contemporary Nigerian writers who

showed me that I don't have to be old or a man to write stories about my culture; that people will care; and, most important, that I should care about what culture means to me.

Also thank you to me for sticking through this one. We out here!!

THANK YOU FOR READING THIS FEIWEL & FRIENDS BOOK.

The friends who made

Twice as Perfect

possible are:

JEAN FEIWEL, Publisher

LIZ SZABLA, Associate Publisher

RICH DEAS, Senior Creative Director

HOLLY WEST, Senior Editor

ANNA ROBERTO, Senior Editor

KAT BRZOZOWSKI, Senior Editor

DAWN RYAN, Executive Managing Editor

KIM WAYMER, Senior Production Manager

ERIN SIU, Associate Editor

EMILY SETTLE, Associate Editor

FOYINSI ADEGBONMIRE, Associate Editor

RACHEL DIEBEL, Assistant Editor

ANGELA JUN, Designer

LELIA MANDER, Production Editor

FOLLOW US ON FACEBOOK OR VISIT US ONLINE AT MACKIDS.COM.
OUR BOOKS ARE FRIENDS FOR LIFE.